THE
Scandalous
LADIES *of* LONDON

The Countess

ALSO BY SOPHIE JORDAN

The Duke Hunt Series

The Scoundrel Falls Hard • The Rake Gets Ravished
The Duke Goes Down

The Rogue Files Series

The Duke Effect
The Virgin and the Rogue
The Duke's Stolen Bride
This Scot of Mine
The Duke Buys a Bride
The Scandal of It All
While the Duke Was Sleeping

The Devil's Rock Series

Beautiful Sinner
Beautiful Lawman
Fury on Fire
Hell Breaks Loose
All Chained Up

Historical Romances

All the Ways to Ruin a Rogue
A Good Debutante's Guide to Ruin
How to Lose a Bride in One Night
Lessons from a Scandalous Bride
Wicked in Your Arms
Wicked Nights with a Lover
In Scandal They Wed
Sins of a Wicked Duke
Surrender to Me
One Night with You
Too Wicked to Tame
Once Upon a Wedding Night

THE *Scandalous* LADIES *of* LONDON

The Countess

SOPHIE JORDAN

AVON

An Imprint of HarperCollins*Publishers*

HarperCollins books may be purchased for educational, business, or sales promotional use. For information, please email the Special Markets Department at SPsales@harpercollins.com.

FIRST EDITION

Designed by Diahann Sturge
Chapter opener art © m2art; Alena Ohneva / Shutterstock

Library of Congress Cataloging-in-Publication Data has been applied for.

ISBN 978-0-06-327070-1

23 24 25 26 27 LBC 5 4 3 2 1

For Katie Horton . . . my refuge in the wilderness.
I'm so glad you came into my life.

THE

Scandalous

LADIES *of* LONDON

The Countess

THE LONDON TITTLE TATTLE

14 April 1821

It is official. The Lady Cordelia Chatham is out, and Society is agog! She is all that is beauty and grace. Surely her impeccable pedigree will be enough to outweigh any scarcity of dowry that might attend the daughter of an earl known to spend more than a passing amount of time in the gaming hells. Fortune hunters need not apply, but those wishing for a titled and well-positioned bride need look no further than this striking, if not costly, adornment to grace the arm of any gentleman lucky enough to win her. The belle of the season has arrived . . .

Chapter 1

A lady rarely chooses her husband, but she may choose her friends. Is it any wonder she prefers her friends' company?
—Gertrude, the Countess of Chatham

Grosvenor Square
London, England

Gertrude set the scandal rag down with a contented little sigh, fully aware that this might have been the first time she had ever touched the wretched paper with anything other than contempt in her heart. As much as she loathed scandal rags for all the damage they could do—*and did*—this one was positively delightful. None of its usual swill, to be sure.

Good things were happening for Delia, and this signaled it. She would have choices. Her pick of suitors. A fate of her own design. All things Tru had vowed her daughter would have. It was all coming together quite nicely.

She reached for her nearby cup of tea.

"You look very pleased with yourself," Hilda said as she fluttered about the bedchamber, tidying the space and gathering things to ready Tru for the day.

"Oh, I am."

"And it has to do with that?" Hilda pointed a discarded slipper at the newspaper in dubious fashion.

"Indeed. Delia has found herself a subject of high praise in the *Tittle Tattle* today." Chatham himself might have been delivered a subtle slap, but no insult had been done to Delia. There was that. And *that* was everything.

"Oh." Her maid's eyebrows winged high. "Has she now?" Hilda gently draped Tru's freshly pressed day dress upon the chaise. "Then Lady Delia should be pleased."

"Indeed." Tru nodded, her smile less than certain. She hoped so. This portended great things. Things her daughter was too young and inexperienced to appreciate, but Tru did.

Tru wholly understood.

Hilda angled her head thoughtfully. "What do you think, my lady? Your pearls? Or perhaps the sapphire brooch is best?"

Tru considered the sunny yellow frock she was to wear that day. "Sapphires feel more suitable for spring, I think."

Nodding agreeably, her maid helped her dress for the day, cinching her tightly into her corset.

"Not too tight," Tru instructed. Gone were the days of a minuscule waist. She cared for Cook's crumpets far too much. "I'd like to breathe."

"Yes, my lady."

Tru studied her wild-haired reflection in her cheval mirror. She'd suffered a restless night fretting over Delia's first season, and her hair bore testament to that. It would take Hilda some time to tame the riotous tumble into something presentable.

She sighed. People always said life was short, but it was interminably long when miserable—when unhappily matched. The days dragged then, plodding unhurriedly along like the slow, gentle drip of water from an eave.

Days turned to weeks, turned to months, turned to years with no reprieve. Delia would be spared that.

And yet, even as Tru entertained that comforting thought, there was a niggling worry. A dark little suspicion worming through her mind that could have been prescience if she was one to believe in such foolishness, which she most definitely was not.

There was only the happiness (or unhappiness) one made and claimed in this life.

She would see to it that her daughter was given every chance to claim that happiness for herself.

JASPER THORNE READ the paper and then read it again before lowering it to his chest. He had yet to rise from his bed. Steam wafted from the cup of coffee his valet had poured for him and left on a tray on his night table, welcoming him to the day. In the distance, he could hear the servants stirring in the bowels of the building.

The scandal rags weren't his usual proclivity, but life had a way of changing, surprising even him, and that meant he found himself not only waited upon by a valet but reading the Society pages and gossip columns as though he were a blue-blooded gentleman who cared for such things. How else was he to learn about the world he wished to infiltrate?

The belle of the season has arrived . . .

"Lady Cordelia Chatham," he murmured, testing out the sound of her name on his tongue.

Lady Cordelia.

She sounded precisely like what he was looking for—*whom* he was looking for. He flicked the back of his fingers against the paper in satisfaction. *Those wishing for a titled and well-positioned bride need look no further.* Indeed.

THE EARL OF Chatham shot straight up in bed, fisting the paper in his hand in astonishment, a curse bursting from his lips. He read again, distrusting his eyes.

Lady Cordelia Chatham. His daughter. How old was the girl? His mind raced, quickly doing the math. The chit . . . was *out*.

He could not recall the last time he had seen her. He certainly had not thought of her in . . . well, perhaps ever. Not beyond the day of her birth when the midwife had emerged to inform him he had a daughter. A girl. A useless girl. Not a son.

He looked again at the paper. Perhaps not so useless after all.

In his mind she still wore plaits and spent her days in the nursery doing whatever it was female children did. Somehow she had moved past that though. She was grown and his wife had missed apprising him of that fact. *Of course.* Gertie was a priggish cow, not wont to do anything to satisfy him.

The woman sleeping next to him stirred, but she did not move from the warm nest of his bed. With her eyes still closed, she reached for the bedding and pulled it up over the naked curve of her enticing hip.

Since the moment he had married Gertie she had been an acute disappointment, a yoke about his neck, his one great regret, but there was no undoing it. Unfortunately, his wife was hale and hearty and would likely outlive him. He was stuck with her. "Stupid woman," he muttered.

The sound of his voice startled his bedmate. She lifted her head with an inarticulate mutter, followed by "What is happening?"

"Nothing to concern yourself with. Go back to sleep," he commanded.

"Then stop talking, would you?"

He glared down at the prime piece curled up beside him. She was a saucy bit of baggage, but he had spent substantial time and money wooing and winning her, so he would not begrudge her the impudence. He would endure her saucy mouth if it meant he got to have that mouth whenever and wherever he wanted it.

"It's my daughter," he grumbled.

Fatima opened a bleary eye. "Your daughter? Didn't know you had one."

"Apparently she's taken her curtsey and I missed it."

"How's that?" Fatima propped herself up on her elbow, looking delicious in her sleep-mussed state as she squinted at the paper in his hand.

"My wife failed to mention it."

"Your wife? You have one of those, too?"

"Of course I do," he sneered.

"And you don't live together."

"Good God, no." He'd gotten his own place shortly after their wedding. A lifetime ago.

"Then how would she inform you?"

He scowled at her reasoning. "Are you siding with her? The Countess of Chatham might be admired by the *ton*, but I know her to be a—"

"Oh. The Countess of Chatham? I spotted a letter from her on your desk in your study. Quite pretty penmanship, I remember thinking."

"There is? When did it arrive?"

She shrugged one delectable shoulder. "I don't know. Weeks ago."

"Weeks ago? Why did you not tell me, you daft woman?"

Her expression clouded. "I am not your secretary. It is on *your* desk. It is not my fault you chose to ignore it. It has been there with all the rest of the correspondence you've been neglecting for some time."

He compressed his lips. It was on his desk. Unopened alongside countless unattended bills from the finest merchants in London. The draper. The haberdasher. His club. They were all a pesky lot. Bloody impertinent nuisances daring to beleaguer him as though he were of no account and not an earl of the realm.

In truth, he had probably seen the letter and ignored it. A letter from his wife would have been viewed as something bothersome, equal to that of a bill. He would have pushed it to the side and forgotten it—much as he had done with her.

No matter now.

Now he knew. Now he could take control.

His daughter was of marriageable age. Suddenly she was of use. And he intended to use her to full advantage.

THE DUCHESS OF Dedham let out a whoop of triumph over her eggs and kippers and surged to her feet.

The footman dozing near the door to the dining room jolted awake, blinking wildly. "Is anything amiss, Your Grace?"

Valencia crushed the paper in her hand and waved it aloft. "Nothing is wrong at all! Indeed, everything is quite right."

At least for dear Delia. She had just become the toast of the season. Tru must be thrilled. Navigating her sweet daughter through the choppy waters of the Marriage Mart had just become a less challenging prospect.

Still grinning, Valencia sank back into her seat at the table. Her smile slipped. She stared around her at the empty chairs surrounding the length and blew out a breath. It was a lonely sight. As it was every morning. She had thought her husband and children would occupy these seats by now. Except there were no children, and her husband was not the husband she had married. When she'd married Dedham she had envisioned a great many things.

She had not, however, imagined her mornings spent in such

lonely solitude, but here she was. This was her life. Her lot. If not for her friends, it would be an abject misery.

At least Delia would have the chance for something different. Something better.

"WHAT HAS YOU so engrossed, wife?"

The Marchioness of Sutton looked up from the paper she was reading, snug in her favorite chair before the fire.

Her husband stood in the threshold, leaning heavily on his gold-knobbed and gem-studded cane. Hazel was, as he said, quite engrossed. For no other reason could she not have heard him as he made his way toward the drawing room doors. His thudding cane always alerted of his advance.

"Oh, the *Tittle Tattle* is full of delicious material this morning."

"As long as it is not about us. We've spent enough time featured in those pages."

The marquess was correct on that score. Fortunately things had been quiet lately. Peaceful. Her name had not been mentioned in the scandal sheets in quite some time. It was almost as though Society had accepted Hazel's presence.

"No, this is about Lady Cordelia, Chatham's daughter. Apparently she is favored as this season's darling."

"Indeed? Well, her mother was always a handsome woman."

"Yes, Tru is quite pretty."

Her husband advanced the rest of the way into the room and sank down on a settee near the fire with a slow groan and popping joints. They had been married five years now and his mobility had diminished greatly in that time. She suspected he would soon be entirely immobile and bedridden. That was what came of marrying a man well into his twilight years.

With good fortune and strategy and her mother's careful guidance, such would not become Lady Cordelia's fate. The Countess of Chatham was a wise woman. She would do right by her daughter and see her well matched. Perhaps even entrenched in a love match.

Not living the life of a young woman bound to an old man. Never that.

That was only Hazel's fate.

LADY CORDELIA FLUNG the paper across the room.

"Something amiss, my lady?"

"That . . . that infernal rag!"

Her maid's gaze followed the paper as it dropped and landed in a crumpled pile on the floor. "I thought you would be pleased?"

"Pleased? Pleased?" She recognized that her voice had reached shrill proportions, but she could not help herself.

"Your mother is pleased."

"Mama?" Delia scowled. "How do you know that?"

Stella smiled enigmatically. "The staff knows everything."

Delia nodded distractedly. Yes. Of course. Mama had instilled that truth into her . . . along with countless other dogmas. *Always mind your words.* Servants might blend into the background, but they were always there. Watching. Listening.

"Quarry," she growled. "I've been reduced to quarry. I am merely prey."

Stella's eyes widened. "Would you rather not be remarked upon at all? Or worse—remarked upon and found lacking somehow."

"Please do not try to be reasonable with me, Stella. I am upset and I wish to remain so."

Her maid nodded good-naturedly and moved to pick up the paper from where Delia had tossed it. "How long do you plan to be, ah, er . . . upset?"

"I don't know," Delia grumbled, falling back on her bed and glaring reproachfully up at the canopy.

"The rest of the day?" Stella gently inquired.

"Perhaps." She reached for a pillow and hugged it to her chest. "Well, for twenty minutes, at least."

"You take your twenty minutes, my lady." Stella patted her arm with a chuckle. "Gather your mettle. I am certain you will have callers after your resounding success." She gave the crumpled paper a shake for verification. "You shall want to rest and be refreshed."

The wash of white canopy fabric swam above her until she felt dizzy. "So I can be my charming and beautiful self," she muttered.

"Indeed," Stella agreed.

"And if I can't?"

"Can't . . . what?"

"What happens if . . ." She paused, moistening her lips. "What happens when I can't be? When they all find out that I'm merely a girl and not that very special?" Not special *at all*? What happened then?

What happened when they found her to be a fraud?

Chapter 2

It is a strange fate that a lady should be valued only for her looks and ability to produce offspring—two qualities that are quite beyond her ability to control.

—Gertrude, the Countess of Chatham

It was a rare occasion when the Countess of Chatham's husband visited.

Tru was alerted immediately of his presence when Mrs. Fitzgibbon met her at the door of the house upon her return home. Her stomach sank, immediately understanding the implication of her housekeeper's grim expression as she crossed the threshold in a whisper of starched skirts. There was only one reason for such a dark countenance. She did not need to say the words. Tru knew.

The earl was here.

She moistened her lips and swallowed. "When did he arrive, Mrs. Fitzgibbon?"

"Over an hour ago, my lady," she answered as she efficiently untied the ribbons of Tru's cloak and lifted it from her shoulders.

Over an hour ago.

Chatham would not be happy to be kept waiting that long. Nothing extraordinary in that regard though. She could not recall a time when the earl was happy. At least not in her company.

Mrs. Fitzgibbon anxiously motioned for a maid to come forward and fetch the parcels the footmen carried in behind Tru and her companions.

"Fret not," Mrs. Fitzgibbon assured her, no doubt reading the dread in her expression. "I've been plying him with food and that French brandy he is so fond of. He is content."

"Thank you, Mrs. Fitzgibbon." She released a relieved breath, even if she did not fully believe the words herself.

Her husband content? Such a thing was impossible. He was always full of complaints. The food, the drink, the very temperature of a room, the company—*her*—could always be better. Especially her. Nothing was ever good enough for the man.

In all the years of their marriage, Tru doubted she had ever spent a full uninterrupted month in her husband's company. Known simply in her mind as "The Earl" or "Chatham" (he had never invited her to call him anything else), the gentleman had been in her presence just enough to sire their two children.

Procreation, she had learned, did not require an extended period of time together. In fact, Tru knew firsthand that the begetting of offspring took only a few moments. If not for the arrival of babies several months later, she would scarcely know Chatham had been in her bedchamber—*or bed*—at all.

"He awaits you in the drawing room." Mrs. Fitzgibbon motioned to the double doors. They were closed, but Tru imagined him on the other side, eating and drinking what the housekeeper had generously supplied.

Tru had spotted him a fortnight past at the Marsten ball. It had been a cursory glimpse as he made his way to the card room, where the gentlemen indulged in cigars, whist, and hazard. Of course, he had not greeted her. The card room was his destination. She and Cordelia were not his reason for attending. He was there for only himself.

She slipped off her gloves and dropped them into Mrs. Fitzgibbon's waiting hands. "Then I won't keep him any longer." She turned back around to where her companions of the day watched with wide eyes. Rosalind and Valencia were equally aware that the earl's visit was quite the singular event.

"My apologies, but I must rescind the invitation for refreshments."

They had spent the afternoon shopping and Tru had suggested they adjourn to her house for tea.

"We can stay with you," Valencia suggested, her dark eyes kind with concern.

"Yes. Let us join you." Rosalind nodded emphatically. "I would be happy to say hello to my brother-in-law."

Tru grimaced, imagining that scenario.

Her sister had never pretended to like Chatham, and the sentiment was mutual between them, to be sure. Whenever they were thrust together, their conversation quickly escalated into barbs and thinly veiled insults. That did not help matters. In those moments it made Chatham even more difficult to manage, and managing her feckless husband had never been Tru's strong suit.

"I do not think so, Ros. Go home. I will apprise you tomorrow."

"If you are certain?" Valencia still looked unconvinced. Her distrust was understandable. She knew something of profligate husbands.

"Thank you for your concern, but I am certain."

Her sister and friend stepped forward to press a kiss to her cheek. "We shall see you tomorrow."

She murmured in agreement, but she had already moved ahead in her thoughts to the man waiting for her on the other side of those doors.

At her stoic nod, a liveried footman standing nearby opened the drawing room doors for her. Tru stepped inside. The soft snick of the door shutting behind her rang as resoundingly as a bell.

She found her husband much as she expected: boots kicked off, stocking-clad feet propped on a footstool as he heartily drank and ate from the full service spread before him. Mrs. Fitzgibbon had supplied him a veritable feast.

Even though he did not call often, he was the Earl of Chatham and the kitchen staff was acquainted with all his preferences. They knew better than to leave him less than satisfied. He might not reside at their Grosvenor Square address, but he was lord and master. He was in control of their livelihoods. Unfortunate but true . . . and that was never forgotten.

Tru had married at eighteen, which had not felt so very young at the time. Not when all her friends were also marrying. It was the thing to do—the *thing* being *done*. Thinking back to who she was then, she had been absolutely puerile in her naive hopes and unrealistic expectations.

She had thought she was living a fairy tale, and Chatham the prince of that story. It was an easy mistake for a young girl to make—a mistake for which she was still paying. Some mistakes were like that . . . with far-reaching consequences that still stung.

Only six years older, Chatham had been remarkably handsome in those days—the catch of the season with his boyish good looks. She had been the envy of all her friends. Not that he was hideous now. He was passably attractive for a man of his years, even if his once-lush hair was gone. Sparse, pale brown strands stretched across the crown of his head. He bore a slight paunch, which he presently seemed intent on feeding, based on the manner in which he voraciously consumed a rack of lamb.

She wished she could go back and warn herself not to be lulled by appearances or superficial charm. She wished she had learned the manner of man he was on the inside before she spoke those iron-clad vows. She wished she had resisted her parents' insistence that she accept his proposal.

She wished . . .

She wished for a great many things, but she did not permit regret to consume her. It would be for naught as there was no undoing the past. If the past could be rewritten, then she would not have Delia and Charles.

"Chatham," she greeted as he had yet to look up and note her arrival in the room.

His gaze slid to her. He continued to chew as he surveyed her indolently. "Hallo there, wife. Nice of you to finally join me."

"I did not know you would be paying a call today or I would have been here to greet you." She knew her duty.

He ignored the excuse. "Out shopping?"

"Bond Street, yes."

He dropped a bone, picked clean of meat. "You are ever talented at spending my money."

My money.

The gall of the man. Everything within her ignited at the unfairness of that remark. She inhaled thinly, resisting the hot rejoinders that burned on her tongue. It was in these moments that she could scarcely reconcile him to the man she had first met, the man she had wed.

Chatham did not have two coins to rub together when she had married him. He had been penniless and on the hunt for an heiress, and she had been every inch of that. One of the shining heiresses of the season, pursued by Chatham and a score of others.

Tru had been the answer to Chatham's prayers. Assuming he prayed, and that was unlikely. Her husband was not the devout sort. He prayed at the altar of loose women, gaming hells, and his current favorite horse at Tattersalls.

And yet he'd had something to offer. Something that made her parents overlook his insolvency. He possessed an old and venerable title, and two homes—one in Town and a sprawling, ancient mausoleum in the Lake District with bones that creaked louder than old King George in winter. Both houses were falling down around his ears, but they were still impressive and valuable commodities. It had been more than enough to dazzle her parents, so she had become the Countess of Chatham.

For years they had lived off her very generous bridal portion. When those funds dwindled low Chatham returned to her parents for more. Her mother made her painfully aware of that—each and every time. Not that it stopped Mama from handing over money. Appearances mattered. They were everything to Mama. She could not have her daughter, the Countess of Chatham, going about impoverished.

His accusation that *she* carelessly spent Chatham's money irked considering her parents supported them and *he* brazenly outspent her.

Chatham treated himself to only the finest things. After their wedding, he renovated his country seat and bought a third house for himself to live in—away from her and the children. A lavish house in Gresham Square where he was free to entertain and keep whatever women he chose to warm his bed.

He knew nothing of restraint. Whilst he maintained multiple homes, dressed in the height of fashion, spent copious time (and money) in gambling dens, took lavish trips (with lavish women), she lived a demure and unremarked-upon existence with the children.

"To what do I owe this visit, my lord?"

"Hm. Yes." He reached for a wedge of cheese and took a hearty bite. "Our daughter."

She tensed. Never in eighteen years had he approached her about their daughter. It was not a subject he broached. He had been uninterested in her upbringing. Tru had made all the decisions pertaining to Cordelia and she felt a stab of unwelcome fear at his sudden interest.

"What about her?"

"She is eighteen now."

"I am wholly aware." If her tone possessed an edge, he did not seem alert to the fact. He dipped another rib into the mint jelly and swirled it around the dish. "It's time she weds."

Breathe.

So that was it. The reason for his visit.

She knew this day would come. It was inevitable. Obviously he would take an interest in their daughter's marital prospects. Delia had become quite the darling of the *ton* this season. Especially since the publication of the *Tittle Tattle* column a week ago. He must have heard that she was well favored and decided to do something about it.

Tru had been navigating Delia about Society prudently, mindful that her daughter always knew she had choices, that she needn't rush into matrimony, that she could—*should*—take her time and become well acquainted with her future husband. Tru would not have Delia repeat her mistakes. She would not have her feel pressured the way Tru had felt at the age of eighteen.

"Delia has been honored with a great many prospects," she said carefully. "You should be proud. I am certain in time she will make a fine choice that pleases you."

"Oh, I am quite pleased and ready to reap the rewards." He finished sucking a rib lengthways into his mouth and then tossed it back down onto the pile accumulating on his plate. "I have already chosen for her."

A long beat of silence fell in which Tru replayed her husband's words. *I have already chosen for her.*

The words resonated like a death knell—each word a long, clangorous peal vibrating inside her. She felt ill.

He continued. "I've a fine match for her that will be of great benefit. So long as our daughter pleases him, that is."

An invisible noose tightened around her throat that her hands longed to claw free. His words sent a bitter wash of fear to her mouth. She swallowed against the terrible taste as she fought for her composure. She knew better than to show fear. Fear was vulnerability. Animals attacked the vulnerable, and yes, in this respect, when it came to her husband, the analogy was apt.

When she had first married him, she had been naive enough to think he might care for her feelings. She had bared her heart to him, revealed her vulnerabilities.

But he had not cared.

She moved further into the room, her skirts a whisper on the air. She seated herself across from her husband, holding herself poised, and carefully asked, "I beg your pardon?"

She had a solid notion of his meaning, but she could not yet bring herself to give voice to it—as though doing so would make her worst suspicions come true.

He paused chewing and glared at her. "Has your hearing begun to fail you in your advanced years?"

Her smile tightened, but she did not rise to the bait. Advanced years, indeed. She was several years younger than Chatham, but he treated her as though she had one foot in the grave. She supposed that made sense to him though. He preferred his women young. Purportedly, his paramours were not a day over thirty.

"I have chosen a husband for Cordelia," he repeated with a heavy dose of exasperation, clearly annoyed at what he perceived as her denseness.

Suspicions confirmed then. She inhaled a shuddering breath.

It was inconceivable and yet so very unsurprising. Her husband had scarcely seen their daughter over the course of her life, but now he had found a husband for her.

"A husband," she mumbled. "What do you mean?"

His eyes snapped knives. "What do you think I mean, Gertie? Bloody hell, have you always been so witless?"

She flinched. Not at his waspish tone, although there was that. No, she flinched at that dreaded name. *Gertie.*

The earl was the only one who called her *Gertie*, and she despised it. She had politely corrected him when they first began courting, but he had continued to use the moniker, and she had convinced herself that she could like it, that she *should* . . . that it was endearing. After their wedding, she soon accepted that she hated it. She had always hated it. She had accepted that truth as she accepted others about her new husband.

"Delia has a great many prospects," she repeated. "It is much too soon for her to narrow her choices this early in the season."

"I will be the one to say when it is time to narrow her choices."

A maid entered the room then, carrying a tray of fresh hors d'oeuvres. Abigail smiled and nodded to Tru as she passed her and stopped before the earl. She executed a quick curtsey and proffered the tray. "My lord."

"Ah." He sat up and leaned forward, hovering a hand over the tray. "These look delectable." Even as he said the words, his gaze roamed the young maid, particularly the generous curves of her body tucked beneath her demure apron.

Tru expelled a heavy sigh, hoping the sound would put a halt to his lewd perusal. Of course it did not. He lacked all shame.

The maid was not unaware of the attention either. Her cheeks pinkened as she waited, her arms shaking as she held the tray extended toward him.

Chatham selected a tiny crepe laden with honey-drizzled duck and popped it into his mouth. "Mmm. Delicious. Your cook is a marvel. I really should visit more often if this is the fare I can expect."

Tru's stomach twisted and dipped. *Good heavens. No.*

Perhaps plying him with excellent food and parading pretty servant girls before him was not the best decision. Not if it kept him around.

"You can leave the tray, Abigail. Thank you," Tru said by way of dismissal.

The girl made space for the tray on the table in front of Chatham, and then sent a relieved look Tru's way before hastily fleeing the room.

Chatham watched her with a decided look of appreciation, angling his head to better view her as she departed. "I do not recall her. Is she new?"

Tru deliberately ignored the question, not interested in fueling her husband's inappropriate interest in the young females on her staff. She had thus far spared the women in this house from his . . . appetites. She hoped to continue that custom.

Moistening her lips, she flexed her fingers over the knees of her gown. "Might I have the name of the gentleman you have chosen?" It was with great difficulty she conveyed those words. There was an inherent acceptance in them . . . and the last thing she felt was acceptance. She simply knew how to manage her husband. Direct opposition was never the way. She had to be more skillful than that. Subtlety and cunning were in order.

He dragged his gaze back to her, blinking as though confused. The pretty maid and fresh canapés had clearly distracted him. He'd already forgotten the thread of their conversation.

"The name of this man you have . . . er, chosen?" she prompted.

"Oh. He is Jasper Thorne."

She searched her memory. "I am not familiar with the gentleman." She thought she knew the names of all the eligible men in

Town. She had a daughter of marriageable age, after all. What manner of mama would she be if she did not?

"You would not be acquainted with him. He does not travel in our circles."

"Then why would you recommend him?" If this Thorne fellow did not move in their social strata, why would he even be a candidate in the earl's mind?

Her husband was acutely conscious of his place among the hierarchy of the *ton*—of his very elevated place. In fact, he had time for no one who did not further his social ambitions and serve him in some manner. She would hazard to guess that Jasper Thorne was someone who could advance him socially. There could be no other explanation. The man was either rich or the next king of England.

At Chatham's silence, she went on. "The young Lord Ruthford is quite enamored of Delia, and she has known him all her life."

His lip curled. "Ruthford? That little lordling is not what I had in mind."

"There's not a mean streak in the lad's body, and he has always possessed a soft spot for Delia."

There was great comfort in that. Tru knew he would never mistreat her. It was in his kind eyes. They softened when they looked at Delia. He worshipped her and would be grateful to call her wife.

He shook his head. "Ruthford's family possesses only moderate fortune. We can do much better than that. Thorne is a man of great fortune. Quite enough to go around." Chatham's eyes gleamed much in the manner they had when he had admired young Abigail.

"Delia would be quite comfortable as the future Viscountess Ruthford—"

"Delia's comfort is of no concern."

Of course it was not. She was merely a daughter. A female. Little better than chattel. No matter the class, no matter the rank, women were pawns to be maneuvered on the chessboard of life. The players, as always, were men.

Chatham went on. "I've only one daughter, thanks to you, and I intend to get the most I can out of her. With only one son, what choice do I have?"

Tru ignored the pointed jab. She was well aware he blamed her for what he considered too few offspring. "Please, Chatham. I have never even met this Thorne fellow. More importantly, Delia has never met him."

The earl shrugged. "A matter soon to be rectified."

Her mind desperately sought something, grasping for anything that might affect Chatham and sway him from this course. "I thought for certain you would want someone titled for Delia."

He gave yet another shrug. "A title means naught if a man lacks the funds to support it."

This, she knew, he had learned firsthand. It was what led him to marrying her . . . for her fortune. And now it led him to this—to selecting a suitor for his daughter based not on pedigree, or character, or love, but solely on how deep a prospective suitor's pockets ran.

She watched him as he continued to eat, helplessness welling up within her. "Ruthford can comfortably support her. He's not a spendthrift. He spends no time at the hells or on women. He is very sensible." *Unlike you.*

His gaze sharpened on her as though he heard her inner thoughts. "Put Ruthford from your mind. He's not good enough."

Not good enough for Chatham. Because he can't—or won't—support his father-in-law in addition to his wife. Indeed not. Ruthford's parents would not permit that.

"And this Mr. Thorne is?"

"Fret not. You will meet him soon. I've made the arrangements."

Soon? How soon? She stared at him expectantly, her chest tightening with dismay as she waited for him to elaborate. He continued to eat idly, prompting her to demand, "Arrangements?"

"The Lindley ball is tomorrow night. He will be there. I've made certain of that myself, securing him an invitation. I expect Cordelia to be most accommodating. Be certain to school her on her manners and what is expected of her. She should be most pleasing to him. She will not be the only young lady there intent on landing him." He frowned in silent contemplation of that. "Do you think you are capable of handling this matter to my satisfaction, wife?"

Clearly he had his doubts. She had her doubts, too.

Her thoughts whirled. Of course they had planned to attend the Lindley ball. They never missed one of Lady Lindley's fetes.

Now the earl stared at her expectantly, awaiting her response.

"She will be polite," she promised because no other answer would be accepted. "I will make certain."

Not that Tru need do anything particularly special to fulfill that promise. Delia was exceedingly well mannered. A gentle soul. Almost too kind for this world, and that worried Tru as she knew just how unkind this world could be to the gentle ones.

Debutantes could be cutthroat creatures and Delia had a target on her back as one of the loveliest debutantes of the season.

"I expect her to be *more* than polite." The earl's gaze fixed on Tru again, and there was a decided amount of threat in the look. "See that it is so, wife. Perhaps have someone else school her as this may not be your particular expertise. I can recommend a few ladies. Your friend, the Duchess of Dedham . . . oh"—he snapped his fingers—"or the delectable Marchioness of Sutton." A faraway, lustful expression came over his face as he clearly envisioned Hazel—more than likely without her clothes. "Now *that* is a woman who knows how to effectively use her wiles. I regret not having her when I could have."

He was a pig.

Tru could only sit in her chair, feeling impossibly small and helpless and full of impotent rage as her husband waxed on about another lady's charms—one of her friends, no less.

And yet even as she sat so very still, a fiery ball of determination burned in the pit of her stomach. Her daughter would have better than this. Her husband would not win.

Tru might forever be stuck, a prisoner of her husband's will, subject to his whims, but she would not sentence Delia to such a fate.

She would fight. She would fight for Delia. She would fight for her as she had never fought for herself.

Perhaps for the first time in her life Tru would fight, and she would bloody well win.

Chapter 3

Séances are awfully common and low, full of disgraceful frauds and tricksters. I cannot wait to attend.

—The Right Honorable Lady Rosalind Shawley

Solitude was not to be found.

Valencia and Rosalind had ignored her instructions to leave. Tru found them waiting for her in her bedchamber—a pair of cats ready to pounce the moment she walked into the room.

Sighing, she collapsed back against the length of her bedchamber door, appreciating the solid support after her encounter with Chatham but not necessarily wanting to face either Ros or Valencia just yet. She preferred punching her pillow in privacy. She could not do that in front of them, of course.

She only ever presented herself as composed and calm. It did not matter that these were her friends. She was the eldest of their set. The one who kept a cool head and held them all together. Her facade could not give way and crack.

She released a shuddering breath.

Tru had never quite appreciated the fact that her husband left her to her own devices until he put in an appearance. And today's appearance had been perhaps the worst, one of the most dreadful, and there had been plenty of dreadful moments in the course of her marriage.

Soon after she uttered her vows, casting them into the air, Tru realized she had made a grave mistake. They lived together in the beginning. Chatham had not yet acquired his own private residence. The relief of that came later. Thus, their first year as husband and wife had entailed copious amounts of dreadful *and* unbearable moments.

But this? This was different altogether, as it involved Delia. That kicked the dreadful up a notch.

She should have known the day would arrive when he would do this, when he would use his daughter as a commodity to further himself. She supposed she *did* know that. She had merely avoided thinking about it as she fixated on helping Delia find her way through Society, fervently hoping she might secure a match of her own choosing before the earl caught wind that his daughter was out and about and collecting hearts as easily as one captured an ague.

Apparently they had not moved quickly enough.

Rosalind bounded from the bed with the same energy she had possessed as a child. No one would look at her and think she was a spinster of thirty years. She was ever youthful. Lovely, animated, and quite content to be firmly on the shelf whilst still residing with Mama and Papa. "Is that wretch still here?"

"No. He is gone." He never stayed long. He would rather be anywhere than in her company. There was that at least.

"Good riddance." Rosalind nodded. "What did he say? What did he want?"

What did he want? Rosalind knew the earl well enough to know there always had to be a reason for him to call. He was only ever motivated by his own needs.

These days Charles was the only reason he even visited. He never made any effort to see his daughter. When Charles returned home on holidays from school Chatham called to see him. The earl had a vested interest in his son. Charles was his heir, after all.

It had been difficult explaining Chatham's lack of interest to a little girl who saw only that her father favored his son over her. Tru had tried until, eventually, she did not have to try anymore. Delia became old enough to draw her own conclusions about what manner of man her father was. Sooner or later, reality, just like truth, surfaced.

As a result, Delia harbored no tender sentiment for her sire, and Charles was already like-minded at the age of sixteen. It did not matter that his father visited *him*. He observed his father's lack of interest in his mother and his sister and it had left a lasting impression on him. He was a sweet and loyal lad. Both her children were good and kind people . . . nothing like their father.

It was Tru's responsibility to protect them. Even if that meant protecting them from Chatham. Now more than ever, she was determined to do that.

Tru took a bracing breath and said much more casually and unaffectedly than she felt, "He was here to inform me that he has found a husband for Delia." That was her nature—or how she had learned to be, how the world had fashioned her. She never revealed the turmoil of her heart. Never the crushing disappointments she felt. What good would it do? Her life's story was written. It could not be changed. She presented herself only as controlled and austere. A woman of unflappable composure.

"He found her a husband?" Rosalind propped her hands on her hips and looked ready to stalk from the chamber and go after Chatham herself. That was quite the possibility with Rosalind. Her sister was fearless, water to Tru's land. To have withstood the pressure from Mama and Papa and not accepted one of the several offers she had received over the years took true courage . . . and doggedness. "The wretched man!"

"Who has he chosen for her?" Valencia asked, ever pragmatic. Of course she would understand. She, too, had married her first season out at the behest of her father. At the behest of their family, friends . . . all of Society. That was how it was done.

She, like Tru, knew all about the expectations young ladies faced . . . expectations Rosalind had somehow ignored. Ros, it seemed, had that luxury. She was the youngest. Her brother and sisters had married ahead of her. She was allowed her act of rebellion without reprisal, and Tru was glad for her. Truly. There was no resentment.

"A Mr. Thorne." Tru shook her head and released another sigh. "Have you heard of him? He's rich as Croesus, according to Chatham, but I've not heard a murmur of him."

"Nor have I, but he has money, of course. He must." Rosalind snorted. "What other requirement would Chatham have?"

Tru looked to Valencia. Her friend shrugged to indicate she had not heard of him either. It dismayed her. She was well acquainted with members of the *ton*. What rock had Chatham found this man beneath?

"I shall investigate and learn everything I can about him," Tru vowed.

"Yes." Valencia nodded. "We will help. We will set Maeve to the task also. She has many connections."

"She has many connections in government. What government official or diplomat is rich as Croesus?" Rosalind questioned. "If he were anyone in Society, we would know him. Which begs the question . . . what manner of man has Chatham unearthed?"

They fell silent, mulling that over in mute worry.

"What of Hazel?" Rosalind suggested.

"Hazel." Valencia's features instantly twisted at the mention of her father's wife.

"Come now. I know you dislike the woman, but she is your family—"

"She is no kin of mine. Do not call her that," Valencia interrupted in familiar protest.

Rosalind continued. "She knows a great many people. People who do not move about Society. Men we do not know. Men of capital. We should not overlook her as a resource. Perhaps she knows of this Mr. Thorne."

"Of course she *knows* men." The color rode high in Valencia's cheeks.

"She is privy to a world about which we know nothing. Should we not ask her if she knows him?" Rosalind lifted an eyebrow inquiringly. "For Delia's sake?"

Tru nodded. "'Tis sound logic."

Valencia compressed her lips into an unhappy line but did not object further, even as much as she wanted to. For Delia, it seemed, she would suffer her stepmother.

"Oh!" Rosalind snapped her fingers in sudden recall. "Let us not forget. We are going to Madame Klara's tonight. Hazel will be there."

Valencia sent Tru a quick inquiring glance. Valencia might have outranked Tru as a duchess, but she deferred to Tru in most matters.

Perhaps it was because Tru was six years older. Or perhaps it was because of her vaunted reputation among the *ton*. She was greatly esteemed as one of the reigning dames of the beau monde. It was a reputation she had cultivated for nearly two decades.

"Tru said such an outing was the height of foolishness." Valencia looked at Tru, clearly waiting for her confirmation on that matter.

"It will give us an opportunity to talk to Hazel," Rosalind countered.

Valencia shot her a sour look. "You could call on Hazel at any time. Why do you not simply admit you wish to attend this séance?"

It was true. Rosalind had been in raptures over securing the invitation.

"I am curious," Rosalind admitted. "I do not deny it. Madame Klara is quite the center of *on dit* about Town."

"Valencia is correct. We could simply call on Hazel." Tru wondered if she sounded as tired as she felt. The last thing she wanted to do was socialize at some silly séance tonight.

"You promised we could go, Tru." Rosalind reminded her of the little girl she had once been just then, begging for Tru to abandon her lessons and come play with her. "I cannot attend without you." Hope hummed in her voice. She desperately wanted this. There were a scarcity of adventures to be had for an unwed spinster, and her sister viewed this as one of them.

Tru would rather not attend the séance of the notorious Madame Klara. It was rubbish and she could not be persuaded to believe otherwise.

But the invitations were a coveted commodity . . . and Hazel would be there. It would be a prime opportunity to ask her what, if anything, she knew of Jasper Thorne. And her sister spoke the truth. She had promised.

It was a small thing to do to make Rosalind happy. Her sister was always good to her. Tru could do this for her.

"Very well. To Madame Klara's we go."

Chapter 4

I fail to see how a séance could offer any thrills, but perhaps I am jaded. After all, I did survive the Marriage Mart and nineteen years (thus far) of wedded gloom. There could be nothing else quite so adventurous as that.

—Gertrude, the Countess of Chatham

It might come as a surprise to her fellow members of the *ton*, but Tru, known to the world as the Cold Countess of Chatham, was not a lover of people. Oh, in small doses they were fine and tolerable. She enjoyed her friends. Her sister. Her children. Her lady's maid, Hilda, was a particular delight. Crowds, however, were another thing altogether.

The masses of Good Society could be quite nightmarish to one's senses—to *her* senses—but it was not permissible to live year-round in the countryside. Not with a daughter that must be brought up in the *ton*. Tru could not afford the luxury of solitude or country living. Like everyone else, she was permitted to spend only a few months a year away from Town. When the season landed, she had no choice but to land on London alongside it.

She might be a consummate hostess and know everyone who was anyone in London, but most people were dreadful. Especially the Society mavens . . . and yes, she was included in their ranks—at the forefront of their ranks, in fact. Even so, compatriots or not, they were not so easy to absorb in large doses.

And yet Tru knew how to wear a properly perfect smile and play her part amid a sea of soirées and receptions and drawing room teas, amid the mamas currying favor whilst simultaneously tossing elbows to earn the best position for their darling offspring.

Tru wore one such smile now as she prepared to descend from her carriage and face the world this evening.

Light blazed from the windows and the outside lamps. There was a festive air to the night, reminiscent of Vauxhall Gardens. Conveyances lined the street for several blocks, coachmen calling out to one another and horses alike as they attempted to maneuver closer to the front doors of the house. Attendants attired in resplendent livery stood at the ready to open doors and assist individuals down.

Rosalind leaned across her lap to peer out the window at the busy street, heedless of the fact that she was digging her elbow into Tru's hip. "The neighbors cannot relish living next to such a constant spectacle."

"Perhaps Madame Klara offers them complimentary readings," Tru suggested drolly, attempting to dislodge her sister's bony elbow.

Rosalind lifted off Tru's lap and flopped back against her seat. "Would that not be a boon?"

"I am sure it would be for you." Tru, on the other hand, could not fathom a more regrettable neighbor. The allure of a spiritualist next door would be too great a distraction for her staff. Not to mention the whole of Society. Her home would no longer be a sanctuary for herself. Rosalind would be over all the time—not that she was not already.

A liveried, bewigged footman appeared at the window bearing a list. He called up to their coachman, verifying the occupants on the parchment in his hands. Nodding as though satisfied, he motioned that the three of them could emerge.

"Very expedient," Valencia murmured, stepping down beside her.

"Rather uncivil." Tru rarely had to introduce herself. People simply knew.

"Oh, do not be such a stick-in-the-mud. How would you be known to Madame Klara? You've never called on her before, and she is relatively new to Town." Rosalind shook her head and sent her a reproving look. "You remind me of Mama. We are here. Be glad of it." Rosalind breathed, staring at the house with a rapturous expression as though she were a monk paying homage to a holy site.

Standing before the house, Tru sniffed and looked about, surveying the still busy street and the carriages yet coming. The footmen continued to quiz the coachmen moving forward. Some carriages were being waved on with no one stepping down. Apparently no one gained entry without approval.

She knew Madame Klara was popular, but she had not expected this. Nor had she expected the number of people being turned away, barred from even stepping foot down from their carriages.

Their small party stepped ahead, passing through the doors with no difficulty, but there they were politely stopped.

This evening's séance was not open to simply anyone, and that was again emphasized in the foyer, where donations were collected. Clearly Madame Klara was not motivated by an altruistic nature. Only those with pocketbooks ripe enough to be plucked qualified.

A well-dressed lady held an ornately lacquered chest, the lid open like a great devouring maw. She smiled as she accepted thick envelopes proffered from each guest, depositing the "donations" within. Beside her stood a man. His fine attire did not disguise the fact that he weighed close to twenty stone and possessed ham-sized fists that looked capable of crushing bricks.

Tru felt certain he was there to enforce the requisite donations with his intimidating presence. The *sine qua non* was implied. Although no one appeared to have any difficulty producing the benefaction. Rosalind fished it out of her reticule and dropped it in the box.

A liveried footman led them into the salon. Hazel was already inside, sipping champagne and looking splendid in a red silk gown trimmed with white ermine. Tru spotted her as soon as she entered the room. She glowed, her features flushed with excitement. Apparently Rosalind was not the only one thrilled to find herself in this most unusual setting.

Hazel lifted her glass in welcoming salute to her. Tru offered a small wave in return. Hazel's gaze slid from her to Valencia, and her smile notably faded, growing brittle as years-old parchment on her face. She would not approach them. Tru knew that.

For five years Hazel had been married to the Marquess of Sutton. Tru was well versed in Valencia's and Hazel's conduct toward each other by now. They either sparred or coldly ignored each other. When they were invited to large enough gatherings—and yes, this one qualified—they did not usually interact. Thus had been the pattern of behavior for years. Tru did not count herself influential enough to change that. She did not imagine herself to be a grand arbiter. She might be a mother of two young adults, but she was not *their* mother.

Even as much as Tru disapproved of their shared hostility, she left them to their war. A war that was, for the most part, silent and waged in snubs and glares and sneers. Except when it was not and they erupted into outright combat and attacked each other. She counted both of them her friends and did her best to treat them well. How they treated each other was between them. They would have to sort it out. She could not resolve matters for them.

It was with some challenge that Tru maneuvered through the mad crush of bodies. Far too many bodies. The room was not fashioned to hold more than thirty persons, but no one had informed Madame Klara or her staff of that. God willing, someone did not knock over a candelabra. Someone's skirts would ignite and the whole house would go up like a tinderbox.

Tru waved her fan vigorously, desperately craving air free of stinging perfume and body odor. Everyone crowded the table, vying for a seat. Eagerness seeped from pores in the most pungent manner. She took several careful breaths, struggling for composure. This was her life, her world. Even all these years later, she had to fight her way to survive it.

It was quite the largest table Tru had ever seen. A gleaming round mahogany monstrosity that seated over twenty. The guests well outnumbered that, filling the space between the table and walls well beyond capacity, the ladies' silk and brocade skirts being crushed in the process.

It was indeed a packed house.

Breathe. Just breathe.

"Lady Chatham!" Tru turned at the sound of her name, her stomach sinking as Mrs. Lawrence approached, splendid in a gown of two-toned purple silk. "My, oh my, how unexpected!" The lady leaned in to press a kiss to each of Tru's cheeks, the annoying sound smacking in her ears. "Who could have imagined you here, mingling with so many of us philistines?"

Rosalind sent Mrs. Lawrence a contemptuous look that the

lady, thankfully, did not notice. Tru's sister was never very good at artifice.

"I do not know what you mean," Tru responded vaguely.

"Och. The grand Lady Chatham at a séance?" She chuckled and shook her head. "One would think this is much too vulgar a scene for you."

"Of course it is not, elsewise I would not be here, would I?" she countered with a tight smile. "Nor, I am sure, would you."

"Of course, of course." Mrs. Lawrence returned a disingenuous smile of her own. "And what of Lord Chatham? Is he accompanying you?" She looked beyond Tru's shoulder, searching in clear exaggeration, as though she expected to see the earl. It was all for show. A decided jab. There was no such expectation.

It was in these moments Tru was reminded that long ago she had not been the only one to set her cap for the Earl of Chatham. She and Betsy Lawrence had both come out the same year, taking their curtsies together at Almack's. Only Betsy had been Betsy Childs-Rutgers then and in possession of a vicious tongue, which she would use to flay other debutantes in the absence of provocation.

She had been quite open in her admiration for Chatham, and rather fierce in her pursuit of him. There had been rumors that Betsy stepped out into the dark walks of Vauxhall Gardens with him. Rumors only. Nothing substantiated. Nothing ruinous. Although Tru would not put it past Chatham. He was even more of a rake then.

In the end, however, Chatham chose Tru. Or rather, he chose Tru's more sizable dowry. Would that Betsy's papa had been in possession of a fatter purse, she could have been Lady Chatham instead of Tru.

"No. He is engaged otherwise." As Mrs. Lawrence well knew. As everyone knew. He never accompanied Tru anywhere and he had not done so in years.

"Of course." Again with that tight, condescending smile.

Mrs. Lawrence worked her ornate jade fan, stirring the air over the glistening skin of her face. The room was rather warm. "Oy, it is a mad crush in here! If you'll excuse me. I see my dear Mr. Lawrence has secured a seat for me." She leaned forward with a conspiring air. "What am I to do? That man dotes on me so."

"What a trial," Tru said drolly.

Mrs. Lawrence's smile slipped.

"Indeed," Rosalind echoed. "Cannot abide a gentleman who sticks to you like glue. My condolences, Mrs. Lawrence."

Splotches of red broke out over Mrs. Lawrence's face, as though she suddenly had a reaction to something disagreeable. Rosalind often had that effect on people. "Well, we cannot *all* be unwed and averse to gentlemen, can we? What would come of humanity?"

This time Rosalind's smile slipped.

Mrs. Lawrence blinked innocently, as though she were not taking a jab at Rosalind's unwed status.

"He looks quite lost without you, Mrs. Lawrence. You best hasten before he grows distraught over your absence," Tru suggested, eager to be rid of the woman.

Mrs. Lawrence inclined her head with a disdainful sniff and then moved on to join her waiting husband.

"I loathe her," Rosalind muttered.

"What is not to loathe?" Valencia quipped with a mild shrug. "She is rich, still quite handsome—"

"Must be from all the innocent debutantes she devoured back in our day," Tru chimed in.

Valencia continued. "And married to a lovely gentleman."

"Not to mention she is about as sweet as an adder," Rosalind added.

"An apt comparison." Tru nodded. "And from all accounts, her daughter is a miniature version of herself."

"Splendid. Precisely what the world needs." Rosalind rolled her eyes.

"Poor Delia. She will have to contend with a Betsy Childs-Rutgers replica next season." Valencia shook her head in woe.

"Oh, she already is," Tru announced grimly.

"Already?" Rosalind blinked. "You mean the girl has come out? Is she not a year younger than our Delia?"

"Indeed. Her mother did not think she needed to wait another year. She deemed her ready at seventeen." She fluttered her fingers dramatically. "The young Miss Lawrence is just that polished and that sophisticated, a veritable diamond of the first water."

Rosalind shook her head in disgust. "Mere babes on the Marriage Mart."

"'Tis nothing new. Mama pushed me out of the schoolroom and into the ballroom at seventeen, too."

Rosalind shook her head in disapproval. "God in heaven she did not inflict such torture upon me."

"Yes, some girls have all the luck," Tru replied, careful to keep her voice level and not appear resentful.

It was not Rosalind's fault that she was the baby of the family, the cosseted one their parents preferred to keep them company amid their twilight years. Rosalind was in possession of an excellent reading voice. With their weakening eyesight, they relied on Ros more and more to read to them—Mama her Austen and Papa his horticulture texts.

Rosalind looked at Tru almost warily, a hint of apology in her eyes. "I suppose the pressure is less for the thirdborn."

Tru smiled back, willing herself to look genuine. She did not blame her sister. She did *not* resent her. Why would she have wanted Rosalind to suffer an arduous path? She was living a carefree existence, a life with choices. Free will. More than Tru ever experienced, and she was glad of that. Truly. "Of course."

"Mrs. Lawrence was not lying though," Valencia chimed in, staring after the lady appraisingly. "Look at the way her husband dotes on her. How does the likes of Betsy Childs-Rutgers land such a devoted husband? Especially all these years later? One would think he had sufficient time to become acquainted with her true nature." She shook her head with a tsk.

Tru looked away, not about to waste time bemoaning how Betsy Childs-Rutgers managed to capture such a loving husband whilst the rest of them had husbands . . . Well, they had husbands born of necessity, born of alliance and convenience. Never affection. Never devotion. Certainly not love.

It was an exercise in futility. Best to fixate on matters within her control, such as finding a way to spare Delia from an untenable match so that future Delia might *not* one day reflect on *her* life and all the shortcomings of *her* marriage.

There was quite a bit of squabbling among guests to see who would occupy the remaining coveted chairs surrounding the table. Mrs. Lawrence managed to slide into the seat her diligent husband had secured for her.

Tru spotted Lady Hollings, one of Mama's friends, elbowing the Bishop of Winchester's wife as though they were two little girls quarreling over a toy . . . except in this instance the toy happened to be a spot at Madame Klara's table.

Everyone stilled and a hush fell over the guests as their hostess entered the room. As one they tracked the veiled lady's progress toward her designated seat.

A footman held out an ornate chair that was more reminiscent of a throne for Madame Klara. A fireplace, large enough for a person to stand within, crackled and popped at her back, framing the veiled woman in a halo of fiery orange that felt fairly biblical.

Tru swallowed at the resplendent sight. Another surprise tonight. She had not expected the woman to be so young. Even through the hazy film of her veil, it was obvious she was scant years out of the schoolroom.

Madame Klara took London by storm a few months earlier,

quickly gaining notoriety as she gave her readings and conducted séances for the most esteemed members of Society. The Duchess of Wellington herself had called upon the woman, forever sealing her approval among the *ton*.

Madame Klara's upswept hair, dark as tar, matched her gown, a daring black ensemble with a plunging neckline. Long lacy sleeves clung to her slim arms, the fabric reminding Tru of a spider's web. Her chest gleamed milk white beneath the edge of her veil, like so much snow abutting a black landscape.

Altogether she was striking, and not just in appearance. There was a presence to her, a compelling aura. Even through the gossamer veil, her eyes were something otherworldly and all-seeing as they looked over the room and its inhabitants. Tru glanced at her sister. Rosalind clearly felt it, too. She was mesmerized.

Tru felt an inexplicable chill. She chafed her arms with her gloved hands, hoping to imbue warmth into her body and chase away the coldness. She did not believe in the supernatural. Ghosts were the stuff of bedtime stories. They weren't something conjured around a table with a roomful of onlookers. There was no truth to any of it. It was not real.

Thankfully there was a shortage of seats. She certainly felt no haste to become subject to that intense stare. She was quite content to remain standing and watch the performance unfold from a distance. She hung back, letting others dive into the sought-after chairs.

Her friends, however, were not of like mind.

Rosalind grasped her hand and attempted to guide Tru down into one of the last open chairs.

"No," Tru murmured, tugging her hand free. "This is not for me."

"This is precisely the thing you need," Valencia encouraged, bracing her hands on the back of the seat she clearly wished Tru to occupy, staking claim to it lest someone else snatch it. "A happy distraction could provide you with insight."

"Oh, no." Tru shook her head. She needed this in her life like she needed her husband, which was to say: not at all.

Clairvoyants were purportedly able to talk to spirits. How was that of any help to her in her current plight?

She had not asked for this. She came here to satisfy Rosalind, and to perhaps catch a moment alone with Hazel if the opportunity arose. So far Rosalind appeared happy, but Tru had not yet managed to steal a word with Hazel.

She supposed this evening might be a diverting distraction. Something to take her mind off her current distress. She expelled a heavy breath. Although there was no cure for her present distress. She had not taken a peaceful breath since Chatham's visit this afternoon.

Tru motioned insistently to the chair. "You best take it, Ros, before you lose it to someone else."

With an exasperated huff, Rosalind dropped into the chair.

With the final chair at last taken, Tru released a relieved breath. She was spared.

The seats surrounding the table were now fully occupied with over twenty ladies and gentlemen, whilst another thirty people remained standing, filling the corners of the room and peering at the unfolding spectacle with rapt expressions.

Tru stood behind her sister, with Valencia beside her. To Tru's right, a safe distance away, with three people between them, Hazel caught her eye. Hazel was always careful in that way, circumspect and conscious of the fact that Valencia could not abide her. Tru leaned forward and sent her a small, encouraging smile.

She was well aware of who Hazel was . . . *who* and *what* she had been before she married the Marquess of Sutton. Everyone knew.

But it had been five years now. The Marquess had made it clear she was to be accepted and received alongside him. She was the Marchioness of Sutton. It was hardly worth remarking upon anymore as far as Tru was concerned.

Valencia would not agree.

She still remarked upon it. Relentlessly.

Rosalind twisted in her chair to give them an excited smile.

Everyone else in the salon seemed to wear expressions of equal enchantment. Tru tried to return the smile, but she felt little excitement and managed only a tightening of her lips.

Why had she let her friends talk her into this nonsense?

Valencia whispered beside her, "I'm starting to wish I had snared a seat myself."

"Are you?" she asked idly, wondering at that wisdom. If Valencia believed that the lady truly possessed the power of sight, did she really want someone peering inside her and into the details of her life? It seemed a risky endeavor given all the things she harbored.

Tru buried her gloved hands in the folds of her skirt, her fingers twisting anxiously as Madame Klara turned her veiled face to survey all who surrounded her, nodding regally as she assessed them. Tru fought the urge to shrink back into the wallpaper—as though she could disappear, as though invisibility was possible.

Rosalind thought this night's adventure quite the lark.

Only Tru perceived how wrong it could go.

She did not wish to feel vulnerable or exposed. She had cultivated a sterling reputation. Her husband may very well be a cad, but no one could say she was anything less than a pillar of Society.

Madame Klara indicated that they should all hold hands. Rosalind eagerly obliged and took the hands of the lady and gentleman on either side of her. Holding hands with strangers. One of whom was a gentleman. Strange, indeed.

Not that her sister appeared affected to be connected so intimately with strangers. No, the whole of Rosalind's quivering attention was focused solely on the woman at the head of the table.

Tru watched her, too, raptly, unable to look away as the woman lowered her head and began whispering in a language Tru did not understand—presumably from Madame Klara's country of origin.

Madame Klara lifted her head and Tru startled a little. Her eyes gleamed so much darker than moments before. Almost onyx in the flickering light of the salon.

Tru glanced around the chamber, sensing a . . . change. The room itself felt darker, as though someone had snuffed out several of the candles in the space. No one had moved though. In fact, no one seemed to breathe. All eyes were trained, mesmerized, pinned on the woman holding assembly. Tru had to admit it. She was quite the showman. She belonged on the stage.

And yet was this not that very thing? A grand performance worthy of the stage? The donations and sponsorships she accumulated no doubt paid for this grand house with its many liveried servants and fashionable appointments. Her particular skills plumped her purse more than a career as an actress treading the boards, to be certain.

Yes, Tru was a cynic. It simply never occurred to her that the woman was the genuine article because the genuine article did not exist. Tru did not believe in mediums or clairvoyants or seers. That was the stuff of superstition and Tru was much too practical for that.

She shifted her weight on her feet and forced her attention away from the lady, taking another look about the room, tracking all the other guests and marveling at their reactions of varying delight and anticipation. They reminded her of children on the morning of their birthdays when they knew presents loomed imminent.

She knew several of Madame Klara's guests. They traveled in the same circles. Even those she did not recognize were fashionably dressed, the ladies impeccably coiffed and bejeweled and some even bewigged. The gentlemen wore dazzling signet rings and fobs that winked in the light of the chandelier.

Her gaze suddenly stopped its assessment, arresting on the face of someone, a man, a stranger to her. His hooded gaze reflected a degree of bored skepticism that could only be as great as her own. She wondered if he, too, was contemplating how he might presently be somewhere else and putting his time to better use.

Of course, it was not only this reflection of her attitude that captured her attention. He possessed the type of face and physique that ensnared and held one's attention.

He lurked on the fringe of the room, attired sharply in unremitting black, unlike so many of the other men in the room who chose more flamboyant colors—lavender was the signature color of the season, after all, and fully embraced by both ladies and gentlemen alike.

Lurking on the perimeter or not, he was striking; the manner of man that commanded attention wherever he went, which was unusual. If he was a gentleman of means, she should know him. She *ought* to know him. As a mama of a daughter of marriageable age, it was a necessary condition.

With some astonishment, she realized he was gazing back at her with deep, inquisitive eyes. His eyes could rival Madame Klara's for all their intensity. They were not quite as dark as that mysterious lady's but no less potent. No less affecting. No less . . . *magnetic*.

She was frozen. Even when he cocked a dark eyebrow at her, she could not look away. She could not blink. She could only hold her breath and stare back.

Chapter 5

Notoriety and popularity are two sides of the same coin. Where the ton is concerned, there is no distinction.
—Madame Klara, renowned clairvoyant and mesmerist

It was not like Tru to be caught gawking. She had carefully and painstakingly built a reputation of dispassion and composure in all social situations. She stoically endured the crowds and maintained a calm and cool mien. Staring overly long at a strange man conveyed the wrong message. She never wished for any gentleman to think she might be unduly interested in him. She was a mature woman. A respected matron. Not the manner of lady amenable to entanglement of a romantic nature no matter how intriguing or handsome the gentleman.

Breathe. Just breathe.

She blinked and wrenched her gaze away, focusing again on the back of her sister seated before her . . . and the riveting Madame Klara emitting her whispery song. The demonstration continued. Tru was not certain what else to call it. It certainly felt like a well-rehearsed production.

"We begin," a gentleman standing very stoically behind Madame Klara intoned.

We begin.

Tru's stomach dipped for some reason, and she glanced around uneasily, uncertain *what* was beginning and what her role might be, as the gentleman had used the inclusive *we.*

Madame Klara abruptly ceased all sounds. Her head drooped as though someone had just pricked her with a pin and deflated all life from her. It was as though she had departed her body. Her head hung limply. Only her chest rose and fell in laborious breaths, verifying that she was still well and truly alive.

Tru leaned slightly into Valencia beside her. "Er. I did not know participation would be required."

Valencia whispered back, "Fascinating, is it not?"

Not, she thought, but kept that word tucked tightly behind her teeth.

Again, she shifted her weight uneasily between her feet as though her slippers were too tight.

Whispers and light conversation murmured throughout the chamber, coming to a sudden halt when Madame Klara finally spoke. "Silence."

A hush instantly fell over the room. All eyes fixed on the veiled lady, awaiting her next move. Her low hum permeated the air. No words this time. A lyrical drone. At last she lifted her head, killing the sound. Her gaze tracked over each and every one of her guests surrounding the table.

She stopped, pinning her attention on one diminutive lady. "Marie."

The woman jerked, the ostrich feather in her turban quivering. "How did you know my name?"

Klara spoke again, but in a voice not her own, a voice heavy with a French accent. "Marie, *ma cherie*."

"Grand-mère!" the lady exclaimed, trembling with excitement but not releasing the hands of the people at either side of her. Marie, presumably, clung fast, even as her wide eyes devoured the woman at the head of the table. "Is that you? Why did you leave us? Why did you leave me?"

The gentleman with thick muttonchops beside Marie murmured dryly, "She was nine and eighty, Marie. Did you expect her to live forever? She had already outlived Moses."

Marie ignored him, instead pelting Klara with more questions. "Are you well? Are you . . . at peace? Sometimes I catch a whiff of your rose water soap and feel you with me. Is that you? Tell me I am not mad in those moments, please, Grand-mère!" It was difficult to take her seriously whilst the ostrich feather bounced before her nose.

"I am with you," Madame Klara confirmed in that same accent, and Tru was hard pressed not to roll her eyes.

"I knew it!" Marie exclaimed, and cast a triumphant look at

the man beside her, presumably her husband. "I told you I can smell her."

He sniffed, looking unimpressed.

Klara continued, her dark eyes slicing as sharply as knives through the veil. "I cannot leave until I say this to you, Marie . . ." She paused.

"Yes." Marie leaned forward eagerly.

"How is Chauncey faring?"

The elated look on Marie's face vanished. "Chauncey?"

"*Oui*. I left him to your care and I fear he is quite morose. Have you been feeding him as I instructed? He prefers his lamb finely chopped. Minced, Marie, minced!"

The woman's face reddened. "You're returning to speak to me about your infernal dog!"

There were several titters and laughs around the room. One woman muttered behind her fan, "Bloody French."

"Calm yourself, Marie."

The lady released her husband's hand, flinging it away in disgust so that she could press a palm to her heart. "Grand-mère . . . what of me? Do you not miss me?"

Madame Klara rolled her head on her shoulders as though stretching her neck, not answering the distraught woman. She resumed humming.

Perhaps that was what she did to call forth spirits. Not that Tru was believing any of it. Clearly there was a process, a methodology to this charade of hers. As far as Tru was concerned, nothing had been proven. The woman had divined nothing she could not have learned through minor inquiries.

Moments ticked by. No one spoke. All waited with breathless anticipation as she hummed.

Suddenly the humming ended. Klara's head snapped upright again and she stood abruptly, nearly toppling her chair back but for the footman who captured it.

There were gasps before that ominous hush claimed the room once more.

Ah. So Madame Klara was done playing the role of Grand-mère. What, or who, was next? Tru felt her lip curl. She cautioned her face to reveal none of her sneering disbelief.

Madame Klara began walking around the table, passing guests with steady steps, her veil fluttering around her shoulders like a rippling wave. The seated individuals twisted around in their chairs to follow her progress.

As she approached, Tru held her breath, willing the woman to keep going, keep walking away from her. Her chest ached, easing once Madame Klara passed her, moving on, gratefully away in a whisper of black silk and bombazine.

Tru released a pent-up breath, and then gasped as Madame Klara backed up a step, her attention dropping on Rosalind.

"You."

"Me?" Ros squeaked.

Madame Klara pointed a long, slim finger at her. "I see you." The voice coming from her sounded somehow older, a rasp to it that shook with years the young woman clearly did not possess.

"You see me?" Ros repeated.

"You were always so sly and sneaky, but I've *always* seen you, gel."

A long pause stretched on the air as Ros seemed to digest this. "Miss Hester?" She finally breathed out their long-dead governess's name. Miss Hester had seen to their eldest sister, Caroline, Tru, and Ros. It had been Ros, however, to put her in her grave. Granted she had been over sixty, but Ros, with her antics, had run the woman ragged.

"You think you're so clever, but your time is coming."

"My time?" Ros echoed in a voice tinged with panic.

Madame Klara nodded jerkily in a manner strongly reminiscent of their long-dead governess. "You thought you escaped responsibility and obligation. But your turn is coming when you must do your duty."

Ros looked desperately to Tru, clearly hoping for some kind of help. The exciting adventure she had been anticipating suddenly faded into the ether.

The séance had most definitely taken a turn.

Valencia patted Ros's shoulder, clearly hoping to comfort her through the awkward moment. At that simple motion, Madame Klara snapped her attention to Valencia, honing in on her like predator spying prey. "And you, my dear . . . have a care near the stairs."

It was Valencia's turn to look startled. "Stairs?"

"It is quite easy for someone to take a misstep and meet with dire consequences."

Tru blinked. Now, that felt vaguely threatening. "Oh, this is rubbish," she muttered, quite at the end of her tether.

Madame Klara's head snapped up, her gaze fixing on Tru. Regret instantly assailed her for attracting notice. She glanced wildly around as though a hole would materialize through which she could escape that black-eyed gaze. No such luck.

Their eyes locked, clashing through the gauzy veil between them. The barrier did nothing to lessen the shock of the seer's attention fixed so determinedly on Tru.

Madame's slim, bare fingers snatched Tru's gloved hand in a vise-like grip. "Gertrude," she whispered in a different voice yet again. She no longer sounded like Miss Hester.

Tru's stomach bottomed out. *How?* How did this woman know her name? Any of their names? They had never been introduced. Had she investigated all her guests?

Tru tried to pull her hand free, but it was pointless. The young woman had a powerful grip on her.

"Y-yes?"

"You must not do it." The woman's dark gaze scored her through the veil.

Her fierce clasp on Tru, her strange words—all combined, it was alarming. She was decidedly *not* enjoying her evening, and if she could tear her gaze—or hand—away, she would make haste for the exit.

"Whatever do you mean?" Tru gave a small nervous laugh.

"Listen to me, Gertrude," the woman said, using her full name again. Something about her manner of words, her crisp cadence of speech, reminded Tru of her grandmother. An impossibility, of course. Grandmama was long dead and not for one moment did she think this fraud had summoned her from the grave. "You must not do it."

"Do what?" she asked in bewilderment.

"Do not confess to him."

Confess? Now she knew the woman was a grand trickster. She made no sense. Tru had done nothing that required confessing. She harbored no secrets. She was one of the dullest creatures in existence.

"Very well," Tru muttered for lack of anything to say. Hopefully it satisfied the lady so that she would move on and leave Tru alone.

Sadly, the woman did not move on. She clung to Tru's hand and continued to drill her with those impenetrable eyes.

With great effort, Tru managed to free her hand. She stumbled back a step from the charlatan, pressing into the paneled wall even as she felt all eyes in the salon shift to her. Too many eyes.

Breathe. Just breathe.

Unfortunately, Madame Klara was not finished with Tru.

"Heed me," she continued, pointing a finger at her. "You are in danger. Say nothing. Confess nothing."

A shiver chased down Tru's spine. This was a mistake. Coming here had been a mistake. Tru's gaze skittered beseechingly to her friends, as though they might save her from this awkward predicament.

Ros was fully turned in her chair, looking at her in wide-eyed silent apology, correctly reading Tru's mortification. She managed a quick glimpse of Valencia's and Hazel's faces before she turned and fled the room, leaving Madame Klara and her prophetic words behind.

And yet the lady's words followed her, chasing her, echoing in her ears. *You are in danger. Say nothing. Confess nothing.*

Of course it was a sham. A grand swindle. As with the others, Tru had been targeted in this night's charade, embarrassed in front of a roomful of people.

She hastened down the corridor, past the watchful gazes of footmen, until she found a set of French doors. She burst out into the night, stepping onto a wide balcony that spanned the width of the house.

She breathed in. And out. In. Out. *Breathe. Just breathe.*

Her chest felt too tight. Her skin clammy and itchy. It was not the first time such sensations had overcome her. It had begun after her debut. The most notable attack had occurred on her wedding night as she waited for her husband to join her and fulfill his conjugal duties.

She had thought she might expire from the absolute dread of it all. She had burrowed beneath the counterpane of her bed after consuming the glass of brandy Hilda forced upon her. She'd let the drink relax her, falling asleep and waking at dawn to the arrival of her husband and his fumbling lovemaking. In his inebriated condition, it had been thankfully brief and rather underwhelming. His conjugal visits had always been brief (and underwhelming), even when he called upon her sober.

She braced her gloved hands on the railing before her and lowered her head, taking calming gulps of fresh air, wondering what on earth she was doing here, in this place of all places, when her life was on the verge of unraveling.

Another breath in. And out. That was how she managed this. That was how she coped with crowds, with moments of panic. She breathed until the tightness in her chest began to ease.

She stared into the night and flexed her grip on the stone balustrade. She could still feel the imprint of that woman's hand clasping hers with the ferocity of a lioness as she spoke her strange words.

Tru should be doing something to save her daughter from her husband's machinations—not being dragged into some woman's grand swindle on London Society.

She sent a glance of reproach over her shoulder into the house where Madame Klara was continuing the séance. The lady had rattled her, and Tru felt foolish that she had been so affected. She had played right into the charlatan's little hands. The woman was a brilliant actress. Tru would acknowledge that.

Fleeing from the room had likely only added to the drama and tomorrow it would be on everyone's tongues how Madame Klara had sent the cool and composed Countess of Chatham running from her salon. Not so cool. Not so composed. And certainly not dignified.

You are in danger. Say nothing.

Tru shook her head, exasperated at herself—at that woman, at all of this. This entire night. It was utter drivel. Rubbish.

She should have brushed it off with a witticism and a laugh. She should have stayed in the salon, clung to her composure, and held her ground instead of stammering and fleeing like a frightened child.

"Are you lost?"

Chapter 6

There are far worse names to be called than the "Cold Countess." Just ask any lady who has made a fool of a gentleman.

—Gertrude, the Countess of Chatham

Tru whirled around with a gasp at the unexpected voice, deep and soft as the rumble of distant thunder. She had thought she was alone on the balcony, but the gentleman from the séance, the one she had first noticed watching her as she watched him, stood feet away, intruding on her moment of weakness. His gaze had been palpable earlier. As tangible as the stroke of a hand to her skin. Impossible not to feel. Just as it was impossible not to feel right now.

Presently, he leaned against the wall of the house with an idle air, watching her as before, with dark and intent eyes that belied the seeming nonchalance of his body in repose.

Men did not typically stare at her. Not like they stared at her friends. Admiring glances followed Valencia and Hazel everywhere. She did not merit such attention. She was Lady Gertrude, the Countess of Chatham. She married at eighteen. After that she was done. Finished. She was not a creature that stirred men. She had been unable to stir her own husband in well over a decade. She certainly had never stirred *other* gentlemen. She was not an object of admiration. She floated through Society with the aplomb and austerity of the most dignified and doyen of dames.

"Are you lost?" he repeated, the dark slash of a single eyebrow lifting in inquiry.

This man was a contradiction. She marveled at that, at how he could project both a great predatory cat ready to spring and one on the cusp of succumbing to a nap.

Telling herself to tread carefully with this man, of whom she knew nothing, she replied, "No. I am not lost."

Her hand floated to her throat, resting against her exposed décolletage as though she could calm her suddenly galloping heart. His gaze followed her hand and a warm flush crept over her. Her gown was no more daring than any other woman's present in that salon tonight. In fact, she was attired quite sedately in comparison to most, the simple heart-shaped bodice revealing only a modest amount of cleavage.

He did not reply, and she felt compelled to fill the silence. "I merely needed some air. Have you"—she stopped and swallowed—"did you follow me out here?"

"You seemed flustered in there."

Flustered was a gentle euphemism. She could not summon a denial though. She had been flustered. Uncharacteristically so. Not that this man would know what was characteristic of her. He did not know anything about her. Not her identity. Nor that she was known as the Cold Countess in many circles.

She opted for vagueness. "Did I?" she queried with a slight hike of her chin, calling forth her usual poise.

She was discomfited by the unconventional gathering, to be certain, but he need not know that. She feigned ignorance . . . whilst trying not to feel flattered that he had been aware enough of her to follow her out here. She was not a giddy girl, free to surrender to euphoria at snaring the attention of a handsome gentleman.

She was a married lady. A virile young man with smoldering eyes should not affect her. She was much too upright to have her head turned. She was not some skittish miss to simper when cornered by a solitary man. As the Countess of Chatham, her reputation was faultless. Other ladies came to her for advice on a multitude of topics—from how to manage their fractious children, to how they should best outfit their daughters to ensnare a husband, to how one should redecorate their drawing room.

Simpering was not her area of expertise. She was too advanced in years for that. Simpering was for young girls like Delia and other debutantes.

She was a matron. A grand dame of the *ton*. Her days of flirting and simpering were long past.

Oh, she knew ladies in her position entertained lovers. Ladies who had done their duty, delivered the requisite sons and now lived separately from husbands who were engaging in their own indiscretions. It was not even fodder for the gossip mill when those ladies stepped outside their marriage for a bit of . . . diversion. Heavens knew Tru had spotted enough wives disappearing into alcoves with men who were *not* their husbands.

Discretion was expected, but people knew. It was simply nothing extraordinary enough to fill the scandal sheets.

And yet if Tru—the *Cold Countess*—were to suddenly take a lover, there would be more than a few lifted eyebrows, but only because she had abstained from such peccadilloes all these years.

She had decided years ago that she would be nothing like Chatham, who cared so little for his marriage vows—or for her.

He had shamed her by taking a mistress not even a fortnight after their wedding. In truth, his indiscretions had begun sooner than that. She had walked in on him with a chambermaid only days into their honeymoon. The girl had been scarlet-faced as she straightened her apron and cap and climbed off Tru's husband and out of their newly christened marriage bed. That had set the tone for the rest of their honeymoon. And marriage.

Chatham had lounged against the pillows, a languid, unapologetic smile on his face. She had never forgotten. Not his face, not his expression. The image of him had imprinted on her, taking residence in the deep recesses of her mind, tucked into that part of her that formed and shaped all future perceptions. The notion of marital accord and fidelity obliterated. The ability to trust another forever a point of challenge. The hope that her married life might be a thing of happy satisfaction gone. Vanished. Never to be revived.

She had known then that theirs would not be a marriage of affection or even a modicum of courtesy.

"Your first séance, I take it?" he inquired.

She huffed a little, bemused at the idea that séances were a normal occurrence for anyone. "It is. And you?"

He nodded, pushing off from the wall of the house and stepping forward. "And likely my last."

She released a small laugh. "You are not impressed with the theatrics then?"

He smiled and her stomach tightened oddly at the sight of those curving lips. They were remarkably sensual for a man. Wide-mouthed and full. Oh, he was lethally attractive. It was quite a good thing this man had not been unleashed on the ballrooms of the *ton*. All the debutantes would be quite undone with him in their midst.

"It was quite the performance, indeed," he said slowly, his mouth hugging the words in a way that made her feel decidedly warm inside. "Now I understand why Madame Klara has established such a reputation for herself."

"If you're not a believer, then why did you come?"

"My friend persuaded me."

She smiled then in understanding. "My friends dragged me here as well."

"Ah. Friends. What would we do without them? I can imagine

the arguments employed. Did they tell you Madame Klara would be diverting? And perhaps provide some *useful* direction for your life?"

She could not help herself. Laughter bubbled free. "You are unerringly spot-on. They said those very things." She nodded. "As though a clairvoyant is some manner of clergyman, trained in offering consult."

"Well, I have never had much use for a clergyman either."

Her laughter subsided and her smile slipped away. She fell silent, reminded that this man, this self-proclaimed blasphemer who advanced on her with measured steps, was a stranger.

He was a stranger with a wicked light in his eyes and she was alone with him.

"Have I offended?" He stopped before her. "Do you see me as a heretic now?"

They were standing much too close. He angled his head as he looked down at her, still wearing that tantalizing smile. Did he practice it before a mirror? It was much too beguiling and she was not one to be beguiled. She moved further away, sidling along the stone railing, her fingers grazing the balustrade as if needing the solid contact for reassurance.

"Hardly," she lied. She did see him as something like that. A heretic. And perhaps a seducer. Definitely a rake. Not that she would admit any of those things to him. "I don't even know you, sir. I would not deign to judge you."

More lies. She did judge him. That was what she did. Judge gentlemen and keep them at arm's length with the exception of a select few that she allowed into the same space as her daughter. A *very* select few. She did not expect this handsome, young Lothario to fall into that category.

She had believed in the charm and honor of a man once before, long ago, and she was still paying for that today. She no longer trusted.

He halted his advance on her, and she breathed a little easier. He studied her for a long beat before saying, "Indeed, you are wise to do so. Judge me as you will. We are but two strangers."

She considered him warily.

He continued. "But then a stranger is sometimes the best person to meet in a darkened garden."

She did not think she was imagining that his voice had dropped to a husky pitch. "I beg your pardon?" Did he mean to sound provocative? She was not the manner of woman propositioned in a darkened garden or anywhere else.

Again with that lethal smile. "The night need not be a total waste."

She felt a little light-headed, as though she had imbibed too freely of the claret at dinner. "I beg your pardon?" she repeated.

She could not seem to say anything else. She was having difficulty thinking rationally. The man was encroaching on her space with a decided *look* in his eyes. If she did not know any better, she would have thought it was appreciation of the carnal variety.

The mere thought made her feel a fool. She must be mistaken. She had to be. She did not evoke such emotions in men. She could not even tempt her husband into her bed, and he was not precisely discerning about his bedmates—at least from all the accounts she heard, and Society gossip regrettably kept her apprised.

Tru was a mother of two who was old enough to begin planning for her own daughter's wedding. She was not the manner of woman to get propositioned at parties by men younger than her thirty-seven years.

"I noticed you across the room earlier."

Startled at that, she turned and looked over her shoulder as though to find another person standing behind her. As though he was talking to someone else and not Tru. When she looked back at him he appeared wholly amused.

"Did you?" She scarcely recognized her voice. It must belong to some other breathless woman.

"Of course."

Of course? Of course? Why should he say that? As though it were obvious. As though she were so very remarkable. She took a sliding step back, bumping into the balustrade. She was not remarkable. She was an average woman, neither very young nor in her dotage, but undoubtedly a very uninspiring matron.

"Of course. How could I not?"

It was almost as though he was flirting with her, but she must be mistaken. It had been years since she found herself subject to flirtation.

Even when she was a young debutante, she had not been extraordinary. Not nearly as lovely as Delia now. Oh, she had been fair enough, but then youth was its own special attraction—as had been her considerable dowry.

Now she was well past the blush of youth. That time in her life was over. She had her chance at flirting and butterflies and dalliance. It was her daughter's and this season's fresh crop of eligible ladies' turn.

In the gloom of the balcony, his eyes glittered as they roamed her face. "You're lovely."

She was lovely? He must think her gullible. Had he not noticed Hazel? Or Valencia? He thought her so simple-minded that she would accept his compliment. Indignation prickled over her. "You mock me."

He looked startled. "Mock you?"

"Indeed. It is quite unkind of you."

He shook his head and looked at her as though she were quite the conundrum. "I am not trying to be unkind, madame. Quite the opposite."

She blinked. She was accustomed to being addressed by her title. Of course, he did not know that. He did not know anything about her at all. Not her name. Not her title. Not that she was too wise for the likes of him. The Cold Countess was immune to flattery.

"You do not think it unkind to feign interest in me?" she demanded. He chuckled roughly and the sound rippled over her skin. She felt only humiliation. "Do not laugh at me, sirrah."

He sobered. "My apologies. It only strikes me that *interest* is such a mild word for the feelings you are inspiring in me."

"What *word* would you use then?"

"Something not nearly as polite."

She swallowed against the thickness in her throat. She told her feet to move, to carry her away, but she remained firmly planted where she stood, riveted to this outrageous man and all he projected.

Oh, he was indeed a rake.

He leaned forward then, all levity absent from his features as he looked her over solemnly. "What is the *word* for wanting to remove you from this place . . . take you to the nearest bed and strip you of that gown?"

"Madness," she whispered hoarsely.

The word would be *madness*.

Chapter 7

There are clever women and then there are the lucky ones. It is far better to be lucky.

—Valencia, the Duchess of Dedham

Madness, she said.

A smile stretched Jasper's lips at the woman's response. Bloody hell, she was a hoyden. Clever *and* attractive *and* artless—not a usual combination. His smile felt a bit rusty and he resisted the urge to touch it with his fingers, to test if it was real there on his face. She would think him truly mad then.

Madness.

He liked that he had discomposed her. He liked that her whispery voice floated on the air between them as shaky as a warbling bird call.

He had begun to make the rounds in Town, sitting through teas and dinner parties and even an insufferable musicale where a pair of young ladies had, in tandem, murdered a pianoforte—and his ears. He was easing his way into Good Society. Unfortunately, most of the ladies he had thus far encountered were either callow chits fresh from the nursery or crafty-eyed, matchmaking mamas. This woman, however, was neither of those things and for that he was heartily grateful.

A nice reprieve, momentary as it was, for tomorrow he would be back in the trenches, attending his first ball. In fact, Jasper was so delighted and appreciative that he wanted to seize hold of this reprieve—of *her*—knowing he would be deprived for quite some time.

In his short time in London Society, he had learned one thing: no one was authentic in this glittering world. Every smile, every word, every laugh was a calculation. And yet this was the world he had chosen to make his own. He had infiltrated it and he would conquer it. He must.

The moment his gaze had met hers in the salon, he had sensed there was something more to her. Unlike everyone else in the room, she was not sucked into Madame Klara's charade with a rapturous expression on her face. He'd caught sight of her skepticism, and then later, she had clearly been horrified to be singled out by their hostess in so bold and theatrical a manner.

When she fled the house, he had been helpless to resist the urge to follow her out onto the balcony. He had not planned his brash behavior. He had not set out tonight to seduce a woman, but alas, he had done that very thing—was doing it. *Attempting* to, at any rate. What else could his words be described as? He'd told her he wanted to strip her naked and take her to bed. Not even his bed. The nearest one would do.

She looked aghast at him. She was suitably scandalized, and she was not wrong to be. She was clearly a lady, and he was coming at her as subtly as a battering ram.

It was indeed madness.

His mother had warned him that he was too direct in nature and that he would need to learn reticence if he was to join Good Society as a proper gentleman.

Proper. Gentleman. Two words that he was not accustomed to in application to himself. And yet he was in possession of wealth enough that he could at least pass himself off as one or entice the doyens of the *ton* to turn a blind eye to his less-than-genteel upbringing.

Far too many of the noblesse existed on the fumes of bygone wealth, their papas and grandpapas having frittered away their legacy. Whilst he might not possess the proper pedigree, Society blue bloods had no choice but to include him in their ranks, hoping that he might marry one of their daughters and refuel their coffers. The drawing rooms of Good Society were open to him—or rather, to his deep pockets. Certainly without them he would never be granted admittance. Hellfire, he had to pay to even step foot in *this* house. As a boy, he could not have fathomed spending so much for a single night's diversion. Of course, as a boy he had never envisioned he would be the man he was today and able to pay such an exorbitant sum for a night's diversion.

He was accustomed to hard work, to surviving by his wits and the strength of his back. Whilst blue bloods were taught the quadrille, he had been repairing the roof on his father's inn. Amid the toil, amid growing his father's business into what it was today, he had spent little time wooing the fairer sex. There was no time for that. Fucking was more his style, when the opportunity arose. A pretty shop girl, a lively laundress, a good-natured chambermaid. These were the women of his station whom he had always enjoyed.

He'd taken his pleasure in the storeroom of his father's inn more times than he could count. Hasty and satisfying encounters as uncomplicated as the women with whom he trysted. They used him as he used them, departing satisfied and with a promise to soon meet again.

This woman before him was something else entirely, rousing all his basest instincts. He wanted to enjoy her. He wanted a hasty and uncomplicated encounter with her.

Even as he knew she was not his usual variety—or even the variety he was on a quest to find—he could not stop himself from flirting with her as he did with any woman he wished to bed. With appreciation. With directness. When he wanted a woman, he did not mince words.

Life was short. His own father had expired a month before his fortieth year. His father's father had not even reached that age, falling into a creek after one too many pints and drowning when he was only thirty.

Life indeed was precarious, and he did not see the sense of indecisiveness when it could all be gone in a blink. He acted with swift purpose. He had made his fortune by the age of twenty-five guided by such philosophy. When he wanted something, he went after it without dithering about.

His mother had advised reticence as he ventured out into Society, but it was not in his nature. She was driven by fear for him. A mother's fear was a consuming thing—for the mother. And a yoke about the neck of the child—in this case, him. Ever since she became a young widow her fear of something befalling Jasper had been at the forefront of her life.

She had been very vocal in her wish for him to live cautiously, modestly, and humbly in the village of Leighton. Her hope for him had been simple. She wanted him to remain at the inn his grandfather had built, living and working in a steady and predictable manner. Safely. She had wanted him to marry the local miller's daughter. Dorcas was fine enough, but she was not the wife Jasper needed. Not for himself and not for his daughter. His mother insisted the miller's daughter, one of nine children, would sail through the rigors of childbirth. She was the safe choice. That would be the safe life.

And yet he could not accept it.

When he moved to London to expand his father's legacy, his mother had begged him not to go, convinced he would contract some fatal disease or be struck down in the street by the reckless driver of a curricle or be robbed by footpads and left for dead in a gutter. Her vivid imagination conjured all manner of dire fates. He ignored her words of caution.

He had not married Dorcas. He had not remained in Leighton. He had not been content to live as a simple innkeeper. He had opened another inn, and another, and another. Until he possessed eight in total all along the North Road. And now he had opened his grandest establishment yet, a luxury hotel in the midst of fashionable London, ignoring all his mother's cautions.

All except for one.

He was cautious as he entered the *ton*. It was a battlefield, or so he was told. And he was not versed in the many paths and turns and dips of it. He had but one friend helping him maneuver through it: Lord Theodore Branville. Theo had appointed himself Jasper's guide through all matters of Society. The man actually echoed Jasper's mother, prompting him to be more prudent in the ballrooms of the *ton*. Reserved. Coolly polite. At all costs, he should not behave hastily and recklessly.

Apparently Jasper could not simply pick out a bride from this year's crop of debutantes. He wished it was that simple. Attend a few soirées, survey his prospects, meet with the girl's papa, and sign a marriage contract. Done with a snap of his fingers.

It was not to be done that way, however. Theo insisted that was not the way of it. There must be a courtship.

You can afford to be selective. Your deep pockets alone guarantee that, to say nothing of that handsome face of yours. I refuse to permit you to rush this. You will find a lovely wife, someone who will be more than ornamental. She will be all you seek. Everything you wish and more. Your heart shall be most content.

Jasper had tried to explain to his friend that he was not on a quest for a love match. He would save that for the poets and dreamers of the world. Jasper was about building empires, not romances.

But this was Madame Klara's garden balcony and not a ballroom. It was a place for eccentrics, where he might make the acquaintance of someone amenable to a dalliance, a place where *madness* might prevail, where he was free to be himself and behave as he wished. After all, this woman was no debutante. No simpering miss banging away at a pianoforte until his ears bled. She was something altogether different and he felt completely at ease as he approached her.

He neared her, lifting a hand involuntarily to touch her, to stroke the curve of her cheek, run the backs of his fingers against her luminescent skin. "Have you any notion how wildly attractive you are?"

He felt as much as heard her gasp. Those cognac eyes of hers widened and blinked several times. She took a few staggering paces back, sliding further down along the railing and putting herself steadfastly out of his reach, her gloved hands gliding over the balustrade as she thrust out breasts that would spill over delightfully in his hands were he to seize them.

"Wildly attractive . . ." she echoed, as though she were speaking words of another tongue.

He nodded, his gaze crawling over her, devouring all he could observe of her in her modest gown of cranberry silk. Modest or not, he would wager that she was no untried virgin, which was more than fine with him. Not that it was his right to have a say in the matter, but virgins were overrated. He would soon have his fill of untried maids. They were never very excited about—or *during*—the bedding. He always felt as though he needed to apologize profusely throughout the whole process instead of simply surrendering and reveling in the act.

This woman was delicious. Curvy and ripe. She would be soft and luscious and eager against his hardness.

"Indeed," he agreed and repeated. "Wildly attractive."

She stopped her retreat, her eyes still fixed widely on him . . . and suddenly laughed.

He blinked.

She tilted her head back and exposed a delicious arch of throat as the airy sound escaped her lips. "*Wildly* attractive?" She wiped at one eye as though a tear of mirth escaped. "That *is* rich."

His compliments did not usually elicit this manner of reaction. "You seem unaccustomed to such flattery."

"I am. It is nonsense."

He squared his shoulders in affront. "I do not lie about such things."

He had only ever dealt with the women in his life honestly. Not that he had devoted much time to the fairer sex in these many years. Business came first. Work had consumed him, but never had he invented words to ingratiate himself with any woman.

He continued. "Why should I lie?"

She shook her head. "I haven't the foggiest."

"Shall I prove it to you then? My sincerity?" He pressed on.

"Let us leave this place for somewhere more comfortable and I will show you just how very truthful I am."

Her levity faded. There was no trace of laughter in her features now. Strangely she appeared almost . . . regretful. "I cannot do that."

There was no imagining it. He detected regret in her voice. "Because it is madness?" he asked, echoing her earlier declaration.

She nodded slowly. "It is."

"Then you have not the slightest wish to leave this place with me? Join me somewhere where we might both explore each other at leisure?" His gaze flicked beyond her, to the house. "Without fear of interruption." His attention then dropped to her lips, to the mouth he craved, the lips he longed to taste. "Indulge in each other and all the delights to be found in each other's arms?"

"You are incorrigible." She shook her head but never lifted her eyes from his face. She stared at him as though he were indeed a lunatic. A stranger and a lunatic. Evidently gentlemen did not seduce ladies with whom they were *not* acquainted. In her eyes, he had overstepped. In the eyes of many, he supposed, he overstepped.

He inclined his head in acknowledgment of this. And yet he did not regret his bold and direct manner. It was what led him through life, informing all his decisions. Decisions that had prompted him to turn his father's humble inn on the outskirts of London into a vast empire of coaching inns and more. It was what had led him to London, after all. The *more* was what he worked to continue, to build and grow even still.

Soon he would be in the ballrooms of the *ton*, mingling with the blue bloods he had only read about in the papers.

He expelled a breath. In this night, in this moment, he would be as he was. He would not think of his quest to find a bride among the *ton*'s pure and lily-handed maids. That could wait. For tonight, he would be only himself and not feel an ounce of regret in doing so.

Chapter 8

No ghostly apparition could be as horrid as the apparition of your own husband at your bedchamber door.

—Gertrude, the Countess of Chatham

They say when you die, your life flashes before your eyes in a whirl of images. Slices of your life captured in memories. Presumably these were the most significant and memorable moments of one's life. Tru imagined she would see her wedding day. No one said the memories had to be *good*, after all. The birth of her children. A summer afternoon spent frolicking in a field of gossamer-soft grass, young Delia's and Charles's cherub faces as they all sat together and made flower crowns from bluebells and poppies and honeysuckle. Those were the sort of memories she suspected she would recall as she departed this life and left her earthly tethers behind.

She was certain this would be one such of those moments, too, included in the kaleidoscope of colors comprising her existence. She had no great love in her life. Not even a great *like*. But there was this. A moment in which a handsome gentleman reminded her that she was a woman again. A woman *still*.

Tru fought for breath, feeling as though she were choking, an impossible thickness filling her throat, making it difficult not only to make speech but to move air in and out of her chest with ease. "You say the most wicked things, sir."

And yet she knew that every time she rested her head on her pillow at night she would hear those words. She would recall them, *him*, see this moment when she stood in a shadowed balcony with a handsome man who was offering her pleasure.

You have not the slightest wish to leave this place with me? Join me somewhere where we might both explore each other at leisure? Without fear of interruption. Indulge in each other and all the delights to be found in each other's arms?

There was no mistake. No mistaking his intent.

This was more than flirtation. At least it was more direct and brazen a flirtation than she had ever experienced. Granted, that would have been roughly two decades ago, but she would not have forgotten.

He canted his head to observe her. "You look quite surprised. Has no man attempted to seduce you before?"

"No," she huffed, scandalized at the mere suggestion. The Countess of Chatham did not endure such advances, and every gentleman of the *ton* well knew it of her. "I am a married woman."

"Oh." It was his turn to look surprised now. "I did not have that impression of you."

"No?"

"No."

"And what impression does a married lady convey?" And why had she somehow failed to convey that?

He considered her for a moment, evaluating her from head to toe. "A married woman strikes me as someone bedded with regularity. I would wager that is not you."

Her hand lashed out and delivered a resounding slap to his face.

His head jerked to the side, but he quickly righted to stare at her, no worse for wear. He looked calmly and unaffectedly back at her and that was most vexing. Calm and unaffected was not what she felt.

"How dare you?" she managed to get out even as she asked herself what most outraged her. His bold question? Or that he was correct? Or that he had provoked her into losing control?

One look at her and he knew she was not bedded with regularity? Heat crawled up her throat to her face. Was there a sign hanging about her neck proclaiming that to the world? The very notion mortified her. How could he determine that merely by looking at her?

"You asked. My apologies that my answer offends you so."

"H-how do you . . . Why do you think . . ." Her voice faded, words constricting in her throat. She could not ask him. She lacked the forthrightness he possessed.

No man had ever been so blunt with her. Discounting Chatham, and his forthrightness had only arrived following their wedding day, when he spoke to her with cruel candor, revealing his true colors.

"One can always tell if a woman is well and often pleasured."

Often pleasured? She had never been *once* pleasured.

The way this stranger looked at her with his hooded and darkly intent eyes made her think about that. Think about being *well* pleasured.

Blood suddenly rushed to parts of her body that had not felt anything of note before. Her face. Her breasts. She pulsed hotly between her legs. That assuredly had *never* happened before.

"Are you happily married?" he asked.

What manner of question was that?

Her voice escaped in a squeak. "Happily?"

"Yes. Are you content with your marriage, madame?"

She blinked. No one had ever asked that of her before. And why should they? It was not something that mattered. Marriages happened all the time without that consideration. Happiness or prospective happiness was rarely a factor at any point.

He went on to repeat, "Are. You. Happily. Married?"

Were there *any* truly happy marriages within the *ton*? Love matches were an anomaly.

"That is irrelevant."

It was his turn to blink. Nodding, he rocked back on his heels. "So there it is then. You are *un*happily wed."

"I did not say that." Outrage simmered anew through her. How dare this stranger ask such prying questions!

"Only an *un*happily married woman would reply thus."

How had she entered into so intimate a conversation with a man she did not know? "Why should you care about my happiness, or lack thereof?"

"Well, I would not proposition a *happily* married woman. That would be ill mannered." He was concerned with manners now? "But we both know you are not that."

Not happily married. Again, that stung. And again, she was not certain what offended her most. His words or that he was proclaiming the truth.

"How dare you, sirrah. You know nothing of me." *Except that you are trapped in a hollow union.* He knew that, it seemed. She took a gulping breath. Apparently she was that transparent to him. He did not know her name, her identity, her status, but he saw her for who she was—a prisoner in a gilded cage.

"I am sorry if I cause you distress."

She lifted her chin with as much indignation as she could muster. "You do not."

For all that she had slapped him—and she regretted that, she did; she regretted losing her temper and composure—she could not claim that he gave her distress. Not precisely that. She felt a tumult of emotions, but distress was not among them. She felt outrage. Exhilaration. *Temptation.*

"We can change one thing though."

She should not react, but she could not help inquiring. "What do you mean?"

"You can be well pleasured. If not in your marriage, then tonight at least. With me. I vow I will work most diligently to that end."

She stared at him with unwavering incredulity. He was not jesting. *I vow I will work most diligently to that end.* She believed he would.

Warmth flushed through her. This dreadfully attractive man was offering her a night. With him.

He lifted one shoulder in a shrug. "Or not, if that is your choice."

Everyone knew her to be too upright, too much of a prig to ever step outside her marriage. But this man did not know that. He did not know that about her and the invitation in his eyes was so very blasted compelling.

"And who knows?" He grinned then in a wicked manner that made her stomach tighten. She shifted on her feet as though that somehow might ease the not-unpleasant tension. "If we have a good time, then I am happy to offer more than one night. Let us not rush to any decisions on that score."

Oh. He was a cheeky devil. She would do well to slap him again. It would be more than warranted . . . and yet touching him struck her as exceedingly ill advised.

"You don't know anything about me," she whispered, and it was as though she were talking to herself—telling herself these words and not him. As though she needed the reminder.

"Need I know more than what I see? Than what I feel on the air between us? It needn't be any more complicated than that." He shrugged yet again. "It can be quite freeing, liberating, to take one's ease and release with an attractive stranger."

She released a hissing sound between her teeth and shook her head. *No.* She could not.

"How old are you?" he asked suddenly.

She squared her shoulders, indignation burning hot and heavy in her chest. Had she said or done something that made her look suddenly old and feeble to him? "What does that matter?"

"I am merely"—he lifted one shoulder in a shrug—"curious."

"Curious." She fairly sneered the word. "I don't suppose you've heard that it is impolite to inquire a lady's age?"

He chuckled. "We are beyond such social niceties, are we not? I thought we were being honest with each other."

She exhaled. Age was merely a marker of time. No sense being embarrassed or ashamed that she was no green girl anymore. No nubile virgin to be judged and, ultimately, humiliated. "I am thirty-seven." There. That should have him retracting his offer. She stared at him expectantly, ready to hear his excuses as he pardoned himself from her company.

No such thing happened.

He remained where he stood, canting his head to the side inquisitively. "Should that shock me and curb my craving for you?"

"Why, yes. Yes, it should. You are much too young for me."

One look at him and she could see he was younger than her thirty-seven years. He was a man. Men took young women—certainly young*er* women—to bed. As their wives. As their lovers. That was the way of things.

"I am younger than you," he admitted, "but not by much. I am thirty-three."

He was four years her junior. There was a greater age difference between Tru and Chatham. Only Chatham was her senior. It should not feel very different, and yet it did.

"Well. There you have it. Another reason you should rethink your proposition now that you know I am a *mature* woman."

"Mature?" Smiling, he looked her up and down with what she could only read as approval. "You say that as though it is an unnatural thing. Something . . . bad. Am I to pursue only women who have fewer years than myself? Nonsense. That would cancel out an entire swathe of women I should like to be free to . . . meet."

Meet? That was a gentle euphemism. He meant to dally with, to tup, to copulate.

"Oh." She shook her head. "You are incorrigible."

"So I've been told." His grin widened and her stomach gave another treacherous little flip. "By you, in fact. Tonight."

She fought back a smile. "I am certain I am not the only woman to lay such an allegation at your feet."

"Ahh," he murmured vaguely, not agreeing, but he might as well have been.

"I take that as agreement." Of course, rake that he was. She smirked. "Enticed many a married lady from darkened gardens into your bed, have you?"

"Ah. Are you saying I am enticing?"

"Obviously you are." She surprised both herself and him at her quick and honest rejoinder.

He blinked and then his smile turned slow and languorous on his features. "Shall we do something about it then?" Evidently he thought she was softening toward him. "I can call for my carriage."

He would be wrong. She had not softened. She was not free to do so.

"No. We cannot." She looked him up and down, taking in the impressive length of him, the breadth of his shoulders that was not disguised in the slightest by his fine jacket.

"We cannot," she repeated with a resigned sigh, and then confessed, "More's the pity."

He looked at her curiously. "So you are rejecting me, but you are . . . sorry to be doing so? That feels rather encouraging, as though I should not give up on you yet." Again with that dangerous smile.

He was offering himself to her for whatever mystifying reason. He was offering himself and a single night where she might have all the things denied to her. Passion. Connection. Intimacy. *Feeling.* A break from the numbness, the *nothing* she felt when alone in her bed at night staring into the dark.

"Oh, no." She shook her head emphatically. "You definitely should give up."

"You do not strike me as very convinced of the matter."

"I may be unhappily married," she admitted. No sense lying about what he already knew. "But I am faithful."

His expression only grew more curious as he gazed at her. "And is he? Faithful to you?"

A choked sound of surprise erupted from her mouth. She pressed her fingers to her lips. She could not help it. It was so ridiculous a notion. "Oh." She swallowed and cleared her throat, fighting for her composure. "No. No, he is not." Not by any stretch of the imagination did Chatham reciprocate her loyalty. She had lost count of the number of mistresses he had kept over the years—and those would only be the ones about which she knew.

"So why must you remain true for him? It does not appear he deserves your faithfulness. Or *you*, for that matter."

She rocked back on her heels a bit. No one had ever said such a thing to her before. No one told her that she might expect more for herself in this life, that she might *deserve* better. Indeed, the topic of what she deserved never rose on anyone's lips or even entered her mind—and that suddenly struck her as wholly flawed.

Not even her closest friends had uttered such words. Not her own mama, who, above all, should have cared for her contentment.

Oh, they certainly pitied her for being married to such a cad—Mama and her friends alike—but none of them had ever said those words to her before. Perhaps because they were caught up in their own less-than-idyllic marriages. Or perhaps because it did not matter. It would not serve a purpose other than to make her feel regret and long for an escape that could never come.

Although she could not help wondering what might have been if she had met someone like this man when she was seventeen. Would her life have taken a different direction? Would she still even be the Countess of Chatham?

She shook her head, chasing away the useless fantasy. It was futile. He was a rake. Rakes did not look for wives and that was the only thing she could have been to him. A potential wife. Just as that was impossible then, it was impossible now.

"Because no matter how tempting I find you," she said slowly, carefully arriving at her own answer in her head before she spoke it out loud, "I cannot be what he is. I cannot be him." She moistened her lips. "I will not be anything like him at all."

He nodded slowly as though understanding that. "More's the pity."

His choice of words was a deliberate echo of her own, of that she was certain, and for some reason she felt them, a dull throb at the center of her chest.

Indeed. *More's the pity.*

Everything about him was delicious and tempting, but perhaps the greatest temptation was the fact that she was unknown to him. A stranger. He did not know her. She did not know him. He did not move in her circles. He had somehow obtained an invitation to tonight's séance, but he did not navigate the ballrooms and drawing rooms of her world. He knew nothing of her husband, nothing of her parents or her children. Nothing of the Cold Countess. He was correct. It was a liberating prospect—to be someone other than she was.

She sighed and stepped back. If only she could be someone else, however briefly. Someone younger. Someone free. Or even one of her friends who engaged in liaisons outside the bounds of their marriage. Someone accustomed to entanglements.

And yet she was none of those things.

"Good night, sir."

He stared at her a long moment, barring her path before inclining his head and stepping aside, waving her to pass him. "Good night, madame."

She returned his gaze for a few beats more and then lifted her skirts, striding ahead swiftly, past him, as though afraid he should attempt to stop her. And, truth be told, a small part of her afraid he would not. Afraid that this chance, this temptation would slip away like particles of sand through her fingers, never to return, lost to wind as though these moments had never happened at all.

Then she would only be as she was forevermore. A grand matron of the *ton*, of solemnity and dignity and sterling reputation . . . but not a woman as a man might see, a woman who was a woman. A woman desired beneath the sheets, beneath a man, in his bed. She would grow old and die and break to dust, never having lived knowing passion wrought by the hands of another.

He did not stop her. He let her go and she returned to the salon.

Madama Klara was still caught up in her performance, holding everyone in rapt attention, but Valencia spotted her immediately. She put a hand to Rosalind's shoulder, and her sister's gaze lifted to collide with her own. She at once understood that Tru was ready to depart.

With the barest of nods, Ros rose from her chair, permitting someone else to slip into the coveted seat she had occupied.

Tru fought to keep her attention from straying to the seer, Madame Klara—a witch, many would allege. Whatever she was, she did possess some influence, and Tru was powerless to resist. She looked at her. One last time before departing, their eyes locked and Tru read those same words from before in the dark depths.

You are in danger. Say nothing. Confess nothing.

The words were still there, alive in her eyes, a warning to be heeded just as before . . . and just as nonsensical as before.

Gathering her composure with a steady breath, she led the three of them from the room. She caught no sight of the man from the balcony as she took her leave of the house. She imagined him still out there, gazing into the night, perhaps thinking of her as she thought of him. That was her vanity at work, but she told herself it was allowed if only just for a moment. She had made the right and proper choice, after all, and was going home to a lonely bed like every other night.

"Are you well, Tru?" Rosalind asked, patting her hand as the carriage rolled beneath them, the wheels clattering over the pavers.

"Yes."

"You look as though you've suffered a fright."

"Did she not? That was quite dramatic," Valencia remarked, peering at Tru sharply. "What do you think Madame Klara meant?"

"It was rubbish." She waved her hand in dismissal. "Pure fabrication. It meant nothing."

"Well, she sounded very convincing." Rosalind nodded with assertion, still giving Madame Klara's abilities far too much weight.

"That would be a requirement of her profession, I am sure," Tru said wryly.

"Well, she scared the stuffing out of me." Rosalind gave a little shiver.

"A good thing I am not the superstitious sort."

Rosalind made a snorting sound and folded her arms across her chest. They fell into silence the rest of the way, each lost in their own thoughts. Tru deposited them at their houses and then settled back, traveling the rest of the way home alone.

Only, instead of Madame Klara's prophetic words following her home, it was him. His face, his voice, his words.

They followed her as she entered her own house. As Hilda helped ready her for bed. As she climbed alone into her bed . . . and wondered *what if.*

What if she had said yes? What if she had joined him in his carriage and allowed him to take her home with him and surrendered, for once in her life, to wickedness, to wanton selfishness?

She would never know.

Tru was almost asleep when the slight creaking of hinges on her bedchamber door had her eyes flying wide open and alert. Soft footsteps followed, padding lightly over the floor in their race toward her bed.

Tru smiled. "Cordelia? Why are you from bed?"

Her mattress dipped with her daughter's weight, and Tru rolled to face her.

"How was your night, Mama?"

Her night? Her night was fraught with mischief and words of vice from a corrupt gentleman. "Fine. And your evening?"

"I heard Papa called."

She tensed. Of course she would have heard that. News of his visit would have been burning on the tongue of every servant in the house. "He did."

She paused before saying, "I heard he has selected a husband for me." Of course she would have heard that, too. The house had ears, after all. The staff would have wanted to know what motivated his visit.

"Mama?" she pressed. The fear trembling in her voice served to remind Tru how very young she was. She had scarcely lived a life outside their family seat in the Lake District. Oftentimes, when Tru came to London, Delia preferred to stay behind, favoring the country to Town.

Delia was not ready for this. No matter how much Tru had tried to prepare her . . . she had also sheltered her. She was not ready. Not ready for marriage to a stranger—to a man personally selected by Chatham. That was the lowest of recommendations.

Tru took a bracing breath. "He has chosen someone, yes."

"Who is he? My betrothed?"

It pained her that Delia was so blithely accepting. She took her daughter's hands in her own and gave them a comforting squeeze. Tru would not accept this. She could not. And yet she did not need to fire her daughter with outrage. She would be outraged enough for the two of them.

"Mama? Who is it I am to marry?"

"I do not know," she admitted.

"How can you not know?" Delia looked both perplexed and disappointed.

Because Tru was Tru. The Countess of Chatham. She knew every eligible gentleman in Society. The fact that she did not know this one man was a grave concern, indeed.

"Have no fear. I shall soon know everything there is to know about him."

Chapter 9

You may think my life dull; I would say rather that I have chosen safety and security. Only the very young and the very foolish prefer an exciting life.

—Gertrude, the Countess of Chatham

Jasper Thorne settled into the comfortable squabs of his carriage as he ventured home alone. Theo remained behind, enraptured as all were by Madame Klara.

Only one woman, however, had enraptured him tonight and it was not Madame Klara. A woman with fine eyes that reminded him of his favorite cognac. From across the salon those eyes had snapped in annoyance. She was clearly irked to find herself in the midst of a séance, and that had amused the hell out of him. He felt an immediate sense of kinship with her.

He lifted his hand to part the curtain and peer out at the

swiftly passing night. Already things were not going according to plan—the plan he himself had devised.

When he'd followed her out onto the balcony, he had thought to acquaint himself with the lady and escape the utter folly occurring inside the house. It had not been his intention to so earnestly offer himself to her on a platter, and yet that was precisely what he had done. He'd offered himself to her for the night—and longer if she were inclined.

An evening in her company struck him as a more interesting way to occupy himself than watching Madame Klara swindle a roomful of fools. He shook his head and chuckled to himself. Blue bloods. There was no limit to their senselessness—or the ways in which they might waste their money.

Theo had insisted he attend tonight. As Jasper had opted to follow Theo's advice on the matter of how to spend his time whilst in Town, he'd scarcely uttered a protest when his friend told him they would be attending a séance. Theo was doing him a great service by introducing him to London Society, after all. He had not the heart nor the will to refuse him. He owed much to him.

The coach rocked him in a comfortable motion. He was relaxed by the time he reached the hotel, if not disappointed he was spending the evening alone and not with the woman from the séance. He'd likely never see her again. Just as well. The last thing he needed at this moment was a romantic entanglement. He did not need the distraction.

He crossed the threshold into the grand marble-floored foyer of his hotel. He knew he needed a proper home for his daughter. For now, Bettina resided with him in his quarters. She adored it. The hotel staff doted on her . . . and at four stories high, the view of London was spectacular from their rooms.

He was content to stay in his own private chambers, but he was well aware that a young lady should not be brought up in the top floor of a hotel, no matter how fine the establishment. Never mind that he had been brought up in a roadside inn. That was him. Bettina would have better. She deserved as much, and he had promised.

There would be time enough to change residence after he married. He would let his bride pick out a fashionable house in an appropriately lavish neighborhood. She would be the one to spend her time there with his daughter, after all. He would be busy. He had plans for more hotels. London was just the start. He, however, would keep his quarters at the Harrowgate.

He ascended the stairs to his quarters on the fourth floor of the hotel. A footman stood at the outside doors to his rooms, as always. His daughter slept on the other side of those doors. He would not leave it unguarded. He always carefully chose the men to guard those doors. They each weighed well over fifteen stone and possessed hands the size of hams. In a hotel full of guests, strangers, he made certain no one entered his rooms who should not do so.

With a nod, his man opened the door for him.

Ames, his butler, greeted him on the other side, taking his coat.

"Ames, you should not have waited up for me."

"It is not so very late. How was your evening, Mr. Thorne?"

"Quite well. Thank you, Ames. How is my daughter? I hope she did not plague Miss Morris into letting her stay up late."

"Miss Morris and Miss Bettina played a very lively game of chess before retiring for bed."

"Ah. Who won?"

"I don't believe they finished. They plan to reconvene tomorrow."

"Well, that is something." He nodded in approval as he tugged his cravat loose. "I recall when Miss Morris could beat her in a half dozen moves."

"Those days are long past, sir. Miss Bettina is quite clever. A most worthy opponent."

He nodded, pleased. She was an intelligent girl, to be sure. That would serve her well in life. She would need that to navigate the waters of the *ton*, which would be rife with fortune hunters. Hopefully, her future stepmother would be a solid arbiter to help direct her through those decisions, but it was a comfort to know she possessed a keen mind.

"Shall I help you ready for bed, sir?" Ames never ceased to make that offer. It horrified the butler that Jasper did not have a valet. Jasper had no need for one. He was not a child. He'd been dressing and undressing himself for years.

"No, thank you. I can manage."

He ascended the half dozen steps that led to the bedchambers, but not before checking in on his daughter. Bettina's door was the last on the left at the far end of the corridor. He placed his hand on the latch and listened for a moment. Sometimes he would catch her awake, up playing with her dolls instead of sleeping as she ought to be.

It was silent on the other side. He eased the door open and peered into the still room. A small mound occupied the middle of a great canopied bed. His daughter's slight figure lifted in the softest of breaths beneath the counterpane.

The damask drapes were pulled back, letting the glow from the outside world creep into the room. He strolled silently across the chamber to stare out. Streetlights dotted the city, the oil lamps with their reflectors effusing the night with a warm glow that saved the bedchamber from blackness.

That was the thing that most startled him when he first came to London. There was no night. Not truly. Not as he was accustomed to at home. At home, the moment you stepped outside at night, infinite darkness swallowed you. Here, the world never slept. There were always people and bustle and sounds and light.

Somewhere out there was his bride. The future stepmother of his daughter. The woman who would lead her through life, specifically London Society, and into a future of contentment and ease—to the security and happiness he had vowed to her mother she would have. It was for Bettina he did this. Not himself. No other reason would prompt him to bind himself to a woman again.

Turning, he strode back toward his daughter, where she slept, oblivious of his presence—or anything else in her midst. Her fair hair fanned out on the pillow around her, only a few shades darker than the cream-toned linens. She possessed Eliza's rounded features, right down to her pert little nose. It was only right that she should look so much like her mother. Her mother, happy and laughing despite her humble beginnings and callused hands that stood testament to her life of toil.

Jasper glanced around at the shadows of the well-appointed chamber supplied with all the trappings of privileged childhood: toys, stuffed animals, and a very impressive dollhouse he had commissioned for her last birthday. Ten years old. Ten years since Eliza died. In that time he had become a very wealthy man. In a mere ten years, he had amassed a fortune.

Eliza would have wanted this life for her daughter, if she could even have imagined it.

When Jasper met her, she was a simple seamstress's apprentice. Jasper's father was since deceased, and he spent his time running the inn. He'd already begun the work of opening another lodging house in the neighboring village. He had no time for a proper courtship. Tupping, however, was another matter. He'd made time for that.

He would meet Eliza in the evenings, clandestinely, often in one of the stalls in the stables behind the house. Not the inn. Never the inn. Jasper's mother lived there, so he could not very well entertain a lover beneath that roof. Perhaps he could. He simply never did. He would see that a stall was clean and fresh, with sweet-smelling hay, ready and waiting for Eliza.

Marriage had been the last thought on his mind, but he had offered it to Eliza when they learned she was with child. He'd offered and she'd accepted, and they had wed before Bettina was born.

He believed they would have been happy enough. Content. Eliza was uncomplicated and undemanding. She wanted only him and their child. Sadly, she was not permitted even that. She died a few days after bringing Bettina into this world, never recovering from the rigors.

And yet before she died, she had extracted the promise that drove him today. The promise to see Bettina well provided for in life, happy and loved.

He'd given her a happy childhood and would continue to do so, but now he had to look toward the future. Her future. She would not be a little girl forever. Childhood would end as it did for all. He could not bring her up in obscurity at a roadside inn, even if his mother was there to tend to her. There was no opportunity in that. She deserved the life of a lady. He was working toward that goal. With Theo's help, he'd already been introduced to a few notable fathers. Notable fathers of notable daughters. Daughters who would be fine role models . . . stepmothers who could make certain his daughter was the toast of the season years from now. The toast of the season with her pick of fine young men. Choices. She would be a lady with choices, which was far above what many women had in this life.

That would well and beyond fulfill his promise to Eliza. He would see it done.

Even if that meant he must buy himself some blue-blooded toff in marriage.

Chapter 10

In matters of marriage, there are two sets of rules: one for the husband, and one for the wife. Hazard a guess as to who comes out ahead on that score?

—Valencia, the Duchess of Dedham

The hour was late, but not late enough.

Valencia stared after the carriage carrying her friends away, watching as it rounded the corner and wishing she were still with them. Wishing she were being carried off, too. A futile wish. She was bound to her life—to this house and the man inside it.

With a sigh, she faced forward and eased the door carefully open, feeling like a thief entering her own home. It was not truly *her* house, after all. It had been a long time since this place felt like her house. Not since the early years of her marriage. The grand Mayfair mausoleum belonged to the Duke of Dedham. It was *his* home. She was merely the wife with whom he permitted to share it. The wife he had once loved and bedded with all the passion of a youthful and hopeful heart. And yet those days were gone, his heart gone with them. All lost in a vagary of fate.

Unlike Tru, Valencia was forced to endure her husband day in and day out. Dedham did not reside elsewhere. Nor did he allow Valencia her own home. She was forced to see him, the shadow of the man she had wed. They slept beneath the same roof, but not in the same chamber, not in the same bed. That, too, was a thing of the past.

In *ton* marriages it was not unusual for couples to live apart. She had suggested it once to Dedham. Carefully so. She had suggested that he might like his privacy . . . and prefer to live apart from her. It had been a mistake, of course, and she had suffered for the misstep and never dared mention it again.

She exhaled in relief when the hinges failed to squeak. She regularly directed the staff to oil the hinges of all the doors, so there would be no unnecessary noise to disturb Dedham. Disturbing Dedham was a thing to be avoided—his temper was a thing to avoid.

A footman snored lightly from where he sat in a chair in the foyer. She held her breath, careful not to alert him of her arrival as she softly closed the door behind her.

Tru's husband was a spendthrift and a philanderer. He was unkind, but she rarely endured his company. His recent visit was only to inform Tru of his decision regarding Delia. Otherwise, he would have continued to ignore her and leave her in blessed peace.

Valencia envied her that peace. Not that she said as much to Tru. To do so would be to reveal the extent of her misery with Dedham. And no one knew that. No one could ever know that. The shame was too great, the suffering hers alone to bear.

Bending, she removed her shoes. Gripping her slippers with one hand, she held up her skirts with the other. Carefully, she tiptoed across the smooth floor of the foyer, grateful for the silence of her stocking-clad feet.

Dedham had hopefully imbibed enough spirits and laudanum to slumber well into tomorrow. Like most nights. That was his preferred after-dinner custom.

She ascended the stairs in silence.

Her maid always made certain to keep the wall sconces lit for her, so that she was not fumbling about in the dark. She was not the only one wary of his tempers. No one wished to disturb Dedham. He vented his spleen on anyone.

She was halfway down the corridor to her bedchamber when a voice spoke. "Where have you been? Out whoring?"

She whirled around to find her husband making his way toward her, disheveled in his dressing gown. He was in need of a haircut—his hair shot up in every direction from his skull—but she dared not mention it to him and risk his unpredictable mood.

"Dedham," she breathed, the pulse at her throat hammering to wild life. "You're awake," she said rather dumbly.

His ashen face shone with perspiration. That, and the sound of his ragged breaths, signaled this was not one of his better nights.

"Inconvenient for you, I am sure," he sneered, his eyes gleaming like glass from the effects of the laudanum he had consumed. "You were doubtlessly hoping you could return home after fuck knows what—and whom—you've been doing."

She flinched at his harsh words.

He pressed. "Whom were you with this night, wife?"

"Tru and Rosalind . . . and H-Hazel was also—"

"Hazel? That whore?" She only mentioned Hazel because Dedham still respected Valencia's father, and Hazel was her father's wife, for whatever else she might be. If Dedham wanted corroboration that she had not spent the evening engaged in an illicit affair, he could simply verify her activity through her father. "I don't believe you. You cannot abide her . . . although I imagine you have a great deal in common."

"Dedham, please."

"Who did you wrap your thighs around tonight?" He had grown obsessive and irrational. Since the accident, he was convinced she cuckolded him at every turn.

She tried to reason with him again. "Dedham, please—"

"Come now. You expect me to believe you've not let another man into your bed all these years?"

She stared up at him beseechingly, searching his face for the man she had married. She had loved him once, and he had loved her. It had been real.

The hour was late. His pain was keen. Arguing with him was fruitless. The more she attempted to convince him that she was a loyal wife, the more irate he would become. That was the pattern. She knew it well.

Sighing, she took another step closer. "Come, Your Grace. I will help you back to your bed." The last thing she wanted was to wake the household with an altercation.

She rested a hand on his sleeve, gently so as not to do anything to push him over the precipice.

He lowered his head and exhaled, his shoulders lifting and falling with deep breaths.

"Dedham?" she queried softly.

Slowly, after long moments, he lifted his head to gaze down at her. Glassy, dead eyes stared back at her. "Think you can waltz in here after spending the evening on your back and then tuck me to bed as though you've committed no wrong?"

She shook her head. "Dedham, I did not d—"

The rest of her words were cut off with a sharp gasp that twisted into a scream as he brought his hands up to her chest and shoved her.

The world spun in a violent kaleidoscope of colors. Bright lights burst across her vision as she fell. The hard embrace of the floor rose up to meet her, striking her body seemingly *everywhere* as she collided with bone-jarring force.

A strange mewling filled her ears that she dimly realized came from deep within her chest. Pain was in the air she breathed. It was taste, sound, color. It was all . . . before the blackness settled and she saw color no more.

Chapter 11

I long for the days when one only had to ring for the nursemaid or governess. Dealing with adult offspring is far more taxing.

—The Right Honorable Lady Rosalind Shawley

The following morning, Tru sat in the drawing room of the most renowned gossip of the *ton*—her mother.

Information began and ended with Lady Shawley. If Tru wanted the particulars on the man Chatham had chosen for Delia, the baroness would certainly have those details.

"Well, Mama?" Tru lowered her teacup to its saucer with a crisp click, gently prodding the lady to answer her. "What do you know of the man?"

"Mama, Mama, Mama!"

Tru glared at the gray parrot as it bobbed along the back of the settee behind her mother. The beast loved to mimic everyone but no one more than Tru. She loathed that bird. Unfortunately, she could not have a moment alone with her mother without its hovering presence.

The baroness reached for a thin slice of apple and offered it to her pet. "Calm your feathers. Here you are, my love." She cast Tru a chiding glare. "You're ruffling Athena."

"Me?" Shaking her head, she ignored the parrot's judgmental stare and pressed on. "Mama, this is for Delia. What do you know of the man?"

As much as Tru had her fingertips on the pulse of Society, her mother knew all. Knowledge was power, her mother oft told her. The baroness had risen in the ranks for that very reason. There existed no lady in the *ton*, even those of greater station, who did not give her proper deference.

Of course, calling on Mama would have its cost. Rather than readying herself and Delia for tonight's ball as she desperately needed to do, more so than usual, due to Chatham's dictates, she would be stuck here, paying homage to her mother. It was necessary though. She needed as much information as she could gather on the mysterious Jasper Thorne. Tru would have to stay at least half the day and listen to all of her mother's many and varied quibbles. Mama would torment her only as she knew how to do if Tru left too soon.

"Do you know your difficulty, Gertrude?" Lady Shawley began in much the manner she began most of their conversations. With criticism.

"No, Mama," she said with what she hoped was little to no

inflection in her voice. It never served her to lose patience with her mother.

Mama fed Athena one more apple slice and resumed flipping through her correspondence swiftly with deft fingers, separating them into two piles: one for her secretary to decline and another for her to accept. Her mother was invited to everything. It took a great deal of strategizing to decide which invitations to accept and which to decline.

Her mother continued in her typical long-winded fashion that indicated she was just getting started. "I shall tell you then, my girl."

"Please do," she murmured, even though she did know. She knew all her mother's chief complaints. Tru had heard them all before. She could recount them perfectly. And yet she knew her mother wanted to list them, and she would not appreciate Tru robbing her of that pleasure.

"You do not know how to manage your husband."

Tru nodded. Yes. That was one of them.

Mama continued. "You should have had more children."

Ah. Yes. That was another one.

"More children! More children!" Athena chanted in her warbling voice.

Tru glared at the parrot, and it seemed that Athena's beady white eyes narrowed back at her. From the moment the bird arrived in their lives, she had fixated on Tru. "Oh, hush, Athena," she snapped.

"Gertrude, be kind to your sister."

She gnashed her teeth. "Mama, I don't know how many times I have to tell you, that bird is not my sister."

It was an argument she had been waging ever since Papa had bought the parrot for Mama twenty years ago. The creature was older than Delia, and Tru feared it would live forever.

Mama sniffed and stroked the gray feathers ruffling along Athena's neck, pausing to straighten the bird's gem-studded collar. Mama insisted it was a necklace and not a collar. Collars were for pets and Athena was family. The parrot had quite the jewelry collection. There were ladies with fewer trinkets. "She's only agreeing with me. You should listen to her. She has more sense than you."

Tru pointed to the feathered abomination. "Athena? Has more sense in her bird brain than I do?"

Mama nodded and went on. "Entice your husband back to your bed and have another baby."

Athena squawked. "Another baby! Baby! Baby!"

Tru took a breath. "It's too late for that."

"Not too late." Mama wagged an envelope in her direction.

"Yes," Tru quickly rebutted. "It is."

Her mother sent her a reproving look over her reading spectacles. "Your aunt Philomena delivered your cousin Warwick when she was thirty-nine years."

Rather than argue that point—procreation was a requirement, after all, and Chatham had not visited her bed in years—she said yet again, "I do not know why we are discussing this." She paused for a beat and gave a single shake of her head.

"My girl, children are commodities. More children would give you greater leverage with Chatham. That is why we are discussing this."

Of course, Mama would know. She had birthed four babies—three daughters and a son—and she managed her husband quite effectively for nearly forty years. Although Tru doubted her fertility had anything to do with her successful handling of Papa. It was simply a matter of providence . . . and perhaps a bit of luck.

Papa was a very placid man. He cared only for his dogs and the hunt. As long as Mama left him to that, he was happy to let her rule their little world, and rule it she did. Not only had she guided her four children through life but she managed Shawley House and Papa's accounts with a judicious eye. She had not depleted his fortune. On the contrary, it had grown under her careful supervision.

She was not wrong, of course. Chatham had wanted more children. Sons to marry the wealthy daughters of Society's elite and daughters to marry the social climbers with deep pockets. Anything to advance himself. He had never minced words on what he deemed Tru's duty. That was her lot, her burden, her sole purpose. The purpose of every eligible young woman. Aside from her generous dowry, it was perhaps the thing Chatham had wanted *most* from their union. That's what *ton* marriages were about, after all—calculated investments and favorable yields.

Marry the earl and provide him with the progeny he required. Her assignment had been clear, and she thought she had done that, but not well enough evidently. Over the years, he had made his disappointment abundantly clear.

He had continued to visit her bed after the birth of Charles, very vocal in his wish for a second son. Every heir needed a spare, he was fond of saying.

For a couple of years after Charles, he had worked toward that, visiting her every fortnight. He would materialize in her chamber at night, oft deep in his cups, and wake her from a dead sleep so that they could perform their conjugal duties. Eventually, however, his visits had become less frequent. As his visits decreased, his disdain for her only grew.

She would never forget his last visit to her bedchamber.

He had stood at the foot of her bed, pulling his trousers back up in agitated motions. He had not bothered to remove his boots. Why should he? It never took him long. A half dozen thrusts and it was over. There was that, at least. It was always brief and rather perfunctory. Not painful. Simply undignified. She did not need to fully undress even. He never did. Never had.

"I haven't the foggiest notion why I even bother with you anymore. You're about as useless as a rag doll . . . and as enticing."

His cutting words had flayed her. She flinched and curled up into a ball. Those were the days when he could still hurt her. The days when she thought he might remember himself, remember them, and how lovely it had been during their courtship.

She could only stare at her husband on that long-ago night, struggling to rationalize *this* man with the one who had courted her so sweetly. She felt a fool for being taken in so completely by a man who now obviously despised her.

They had been married almost five years at that point. The man he was during their courtship, during their betrothal, was gone. He had not been real. He had never existed.

"I assumed you would be as prolific a breeder as your mother," he charged with a shake of his head as he yanked his jacket back to rights. "Such a waste. Bloody hell. I could have had the Houghton chit. Last I heard she's given Claremont five sons. Five!" He looked her over in contempt where she sank deeper into the bed.

He had made her feel useless in that moment. She had been terribly green, still so very young. She had naively thought she married a gentleman who harbored affection and fondness for her—at the very least. If he had cared for her, he could never have treated her so cruelly that night or in the years to come.

That was the last time he ever crossed the threshold of her chamber, and for that she was heartily grateful.

Eventually she recovered from that indignity and grew self-possessed enough to not blame herself. The love of her children, the comfort of her friends and family, had helped in that endeavor. She refused to blame herself. All blame rightfully belonged to Chatham.

Now she knew him for the cad he was, and she would do everything in her power to save her daughter from his machinations. She had not been able to protect herself from him, but she would protect Delia.

"So then." Tru sighed. "You know nothing of the man." That was disappointing. She'd made this visit for naught.

"I did not say that."

"You have not said *anything*," she retorted, her patience fraying.

Mama picked up her quill and made note of something on the parchment resting on her writing table beside the settee, likely a directive for her secretary to address later. Or a note to the housekeeper. Even though Tru sat across from her, determined to speak on an important matter, she knew she had only a fraction of her mother's attention. Athena held more of it than Tru.

Setting down her quill, she announced, "I have indeed heard of this Jasper Thorne. That new monstrosity of a hotel, the Harrowgate? It belongs to him." She wrinkled her nose.

"He's in trade?"

"He's a proprietor. A most successful one. He owns a string of inns along the North Road. The man has very deep pockets."

"Deep pockets," she murmured. "Of course." He must be in his dotage to have accrued such an empire. It was an awful notion—her beautiful young daughter bound to an old man.

Mama wrinkled her nose again. "A self-made man, as they say. Terribly uncouth, I know, but at least there would be another person for Chatham to pester for funds. Not all the responsibility would fall to me and Papa any longer."

It was cold comfort. Delia was worth more than that. Tru would not sacrifice her daughter's chance for happiness so that her wastrel of a father could continue his spendthrift ways.

"I will not accept this."

“No?” Mama lifted an eyebrow in mild interest.

“No,” she pronounced.

“Hm.” Mama placed another envelope on one of the ever-growing piles.

“So what should I do, Mama?”

“About Chatham choosing Delia’s suitor?” she asked as though needing clarification.

“Yes.” Because she certainly couldn’t stand aside and do *nothing.*

“What can you do? You have never been able to control Chatham. If you could he would not be running like a wild stallion all over England. Nor would he still come begging me for money every few months.”

She shifted uncomfortably in her chair. She was well aware that her husband came to her mother for money, just as she was achingly aware that Mama rued the day she and Papa had ever blessed their union. The earl had burned through her dowry in record time. Mama was the only reason the creditors stayed at bay. She helped keep Chatham out of Newgate . . . and Tru and the children free of shame and scandal.

“So we should simply accept this man, this *stranger* that Chatham has chosen?”

“At least meet him. Perhaps he is not that bad.”

Not that bad.

Such a ringing endorsement. She had wanted much more for her daughter. So much more than *not that bad.*

Mama leaned forward, lowering her voice as she cast a glance to the maid standing stoically near the doors of the parlor. Mama was always mindful of speaking when ears were present. She insisted the staff and their wagging tongues were responsible for most of the gossip to flow through London. "If it comes to it, and you and Delia find him so very objectionable, there are ways to discourage a man from offering marriage." Her lips twisted in a grimace. "I could direct you to any number of spinsters who are expert at repelling gentlemen. They could provide you with tips. Just ask your sister."

"Indeed?" Tru queried, thinking about that—about the fact that her mother would offer her this advice now and not years ago. Mama had never imparted that particular suggestion to her when she had been a young debutante. But then Tru had not opposed Chatham's suit. She had been a dutiful daughter, willing to wed, and Chatham had been charming. Her mother would not have needed to offer such advice.

"Oh. Indeed," Mama confirmed.

Tru considered that for a moment more. Delia was perfectly lovely. The most obvious impediment was that she had a less-than-generous dowry, thanks to the earl's wild spending habits, but apparently this Jasper Thorne already knew that. No doubt he was counting on it to give him an advantage.

"It is all about discovering what it is the gentleman hopes to gain with marriage," Mama explained, "and then showing him that he will not be able to gain *that* with Delia as his wife."

"Oh." It was so simple that it was . . . brilliant. "I see."

"I shall make inquiries." Mama gave her hand a reassuring pat. "And find out what motivates this Mr. Thorne."

"I would appreciate that, Mama."

"Of course, dear. The last thing I want is for my granddaughter to be as miserable as you are."

She stiffened. "I am not miserable," she said in a small voice.

"Missserable. Missserable," Athena echoed on cue, and Tru resisted clubbing the beastly bird.

"No? You mean you are happy with Chatham?" Her mother settled a look of skepticism on her.

Happy with Chatham? Of course not.

And yet Tru had long ago learned not to rely on Chatham for her happiness. As she and her husband moved in different circles—she did not frequent gaming hells, bordellos, or Tattersalls—they rarely crossed paths. She claimed happiness for herself away from him.

She took delight in other aspects of her life. Her children. Her friends and Ros. Her charities. Her position in Society. She enjoyed spending time in the country. Fortunately, Chatham spent almost no time there. Indeed, her life was good, even if she did have a wretch of a husband.

She held her mother's stare. "I am happy enough, Mama."

"Hm. Happy enough."

She nodded stiffly. "Yes."

Mama continued. "Strange, is it not? That *happy enough* is not adequate for *your* daughter?"

"What are you implying?"

"I am simply saying that perhaps you should demand the same things for yourself that you demand for Delia."

"There is a difference, Mama. It is too late for me."

"Please." She scoffed and shook her bewigged head. Mama enjoyed alternating wigs. Today she wore a vibrant red, the artificial tresses piled atop her head in ringlets. "You are still young. It is not too late." She leaned forward and whispered indiscreetly, "Take a lover, Gertrude."

She stared agog at her mother.

"Take a lover, take a lover, take a lover," Athena echoed, and Tru snatched a biscuit from the tea service and flung it at the bird.

The maid beside the door snickered.

"Do not vent your spleen on dear Athena . . . and do not look at me as though this is a wild suggestion. Women do it. Not me," she qualified. "But *other* women. Women married to a maggot as you are."

"Mother!"

Mama shrugged. "Oh, we know what he is. Unfortunately, we did not know it before the wedding. He charmed us all, I fear. Now do not be so missish. Find yourself a handsome rake."

She did not even *know* the woman sitting across from her. She was suggesting Tru take a lover like she might test a new flavor of ice at Gunter's.

"What is the harm?" She lifted both shoulders in a prolonged, careless shrug. "You can be discreet. You deserve some pleasure, Gertrude."

She sucked in a breath. It was passing strange to hear her mother use almost the same words as the gentleman from last night.

"Mama . . ."

"You needn't look so scandalized. I can suggest a few handsome rakes that would do the trick—"

"I don't need your suggestions!"

If she ever wished to take a lover—and she did not—she did not require her mother to see to it for her.

"Oh? You have someone in mind already then? Who is he?"

"No, no! I haven't anyone in mind."

At least no one she could give name to because she did not even know his name.

Tru shook her head, pushing the memory of the dark-haired stranger with the velvet voice from her head. It mattered not at all that an anonymous man had offered her a night of anonymous pleasure. It would have been the height of discretion, but she did not feel a flicker of regret for refusing him. Truly. Not at all. Not even a little.

She was not that woman. She could not do such . . . acts. She was not like the earl. She could not do the very thing he had done to her, the thing she had condemned him for, betraying her time and again. It was not her character to be so bold, so reckless. Besides . . . she had never found physical congress particularly enjoyable. It had been a necessary deed and naught more.

Rattled by the sudden turn of conversation—it was certainly one topic she never expected to talk about with her mother—she pushed up to her feet. If she incurred her mother's wrath for departing prematurely, so be it.

"I really must hasten home. I have much to do to prepare Delia for tonight. I will see you there."

"I would not miss it, my girl . . . or meeting Mr. Thorne."

Mr. Thorne, indeed. Tru came forward to press a kiss to her mother's cheek. "Until tonight."

In the foyer, a servant proffered her gloves and pelisse as her carriage was brought around. As she stood there waiting, shrugging into her pelisse and fastening the row of tiny silk-covered buttons up the front of her bodice, Athena's halting voice reached her like something from a nightmare. "Take a lover, take a lover, take a lover!"

Chapter 12

No soirée, ball, or assembly begins until I arrive.
—Maeve, Mrs. Bernard-Hill

What manner of name is Thorne anyway?" Tru grumbled, fanning herself vigorously as she scanned the packed ballroom.

Jasper Thorne. It sounded fairly piratical. For all she knew that was precisely what he was. A pirate. She could not put such a thing past Chatham. He was mercenary in that manner. A tiger stalking the fattest calf. A little thing like an unsavory past would not deter him.

"And," she added, "why is it so blasted warm in here?" The steamy air felt thin and she took careful breaths, willing her burgeoning sense of panic to remain at bay. *Breathe. Just breathe.* She had known there would be a mad crush tonight, but that did not stop her from wanting to run from the room and find a space that was hers alone, where the air was fresh and blessedly free of people.

Tru scanned the crowded ballroom, searching for a patch-eyed marauder of waning years who smelled of seawater and rotting fish with a knife clenched between his teeth strolling amid the rainbow of silks and brocades.

Dramatic, perhaps, but Chatham was recommending the man. Try as she might to be optimistic, she could not disregard the source of his entry into her world, into her daughter's life. Not when that source was Chatham.

"I do not find it particularly warm. Perhaps you are going through the change of life," Maeve leaned in to whisper.

Tru whipped her gaze to glare at her friend. "Pardon me?"

Maeve shrugged. "It is a possibility."

She did not bother explaining to her friend that she was overly warm because she was overwrought. Tonight could go wrong in so very many ways.

Chatham had been clear in his instructions. Tonight introductions were to be made to Jasper Thorne. Also clear: they were not to disappoint the earl. Above all, Tru and Delia were to impress Mr. Thorne. They must win him over or face Chatham's not-inconsiderable wrath.

"Some women begin the change young," Maeve continued, ever reasonable as she extended her own working fan so that Tru might receive the benefit of more air.

"How young?" Hazel inquired, as though truly intrigued by the subject and wanting to know for her own edification.

"She is not going through the change," Rosalind interjected with a fair amount of indignation. "She is but thirty-eight."

Thirty-*seven*. One would think her sister knew her age. She would not be thirty-eight for many months yet, but Tru did not bother correcting her. She had no wish to prolong the conversation.

Presently, she only had the time and energy to focus on ending this courtship between Delia and Jasper Thorne before it even began. She would have to act quickly. She would not put it past the earl to draw up a marriage contract without her knowledge. Clearly, he did not need her consent. Why would he apprise her of his next steps? They did not have that manner of marriage.

"There is nothing to be offended about. It is a normal female condition." Again, this came from Maeve, the ever-practical one. As a diplomat's daughter, she had lived all over the world before marrying. Her husband was an agent well positioned in the Home Office, not to mention the third son of a very prominent viscount.

She was a fount of information on all manner of subjects and had the ear of everyone in the British government. She was fluent in four languages and versed in different cultures and customs. At times, her tongue was a little too free with her colorful anecdotes, such as now, but she was never left off a guest list. "My cousin was not yet forty when it happened to her."

Tru did not have the time or inclination to debate that she was *not* going through the change of life with Maeve. There were greater issues at hand. She had to repel this Jasper Thorne, and it had never been her goal to *repel* anyone. It was going to require some creative stratagems, to be certain.

"Do you have any notion what he looks like, Hazel?" she asked, craning her neck to catch a glimpse of her husband, certain that Chatham would be in close proximity to his quarry. Whether Jasper Thorne realized it or not, he was her husband's quarry. He and every other matchmaking mama in the room. "What is his age approximately?"

"Oh. I have only heard of him. I never met him," Hazel replied with an innocent blink. "I heard mention of him when one of my friends was, ah . . . keeping company with him with some frequency." Even though she chose her words carefully there was not the faintest blush to her face as she disclosed this, and Tru imagined she had ceased to possess any sense of shame over her past.

Valencia, however, possessed shame enough for the both of them. From the tightening of her lips, it seemed she was struggling to refrain from letting her disdain surface. In truth, she had a pinched look about her face tonight, ever since she had arrived at the ball. She was not in her usual high spirits. She'd been rather muted, and Tru wondered if she was not feeling well.

"When one of your friends was keeping company with him . . ." Rosalind echoed, canting her head as though attempting to decipher that. Her sister was naive. A condition perhaps attributed to her unwed status. She knew nothing of men—of their foibles and behavior. Her guileless nature was an anomaly in the hedonistic landscape of the *ton*.

The meaning of that remark, however, was not missed by Tru or Maeve or Valencia. They understood perfectly and all shared significant looks. One of Hazel's friends, a fellow member of the *demimonde*, had shared a bed with the man. Perhaps she had even been Thorne's mistress.

Tru blew out a breath. *Brilliant.* Another ringing endorsement for Mr. Thorne. Although what else could she expect of this stranger? He was a man, after all. Her own husband had never been without a mistress. It was the way of things, no matter one's rank in Society. Gentlemen did as they pleased. They knew nothing of abstemiousness.

"Of course this is how you know of the man," Valencia muttered. "From one of your *friends*."

Hazel looked at her crossly. "Yes. From one of my friends. Before your father, Tabitha and I actually shared a room together. Not all of us grew up a spoiled little girl. Some of us were not born with a silver spoon in our mouth."

Valencia's expression only tightened further.

"Ladies," Maeve chided, as she usually did, ever the diplomat. She had been the first to warmly wave Hazel into their midst tonight. It was a trait of her worldly upbringing. She was very accepting of others.

When Hazel first married the marquess, Maeve hosted a dinner party in their honor, forcing Valencia to mingle with her new stepmother, a woman whose existence she would have preferred to ignore. From then on, if not precisely one of them, Hazel was allowed into their orbit.

"I am certain you shared your room with many people," Valencia tartly replied. "Would that you still did, instead of occupying the bedchamber that belongs, by rights, to my dear mother."

Hazel released an exasperated breath. "Oh, stuff it, Valencia. Your mother died over a decade ago."

Tru blew out a breath. It was the usual. There were not many fetes where Hazel and Valencia did not spar words. This had been the case for years now. Tru heartily wished the two women could get along, so that they might all enjoy themselves without the taunts and insults.

"Tabitha never mentioned his age . . . but I cannot imagine him too ancient. She would have likely remarked on that."

"I can imagine him ancient," Rosalind said sharply. "I would not put it past Chatham to attempt to attach our Delia to an old man with one foot in the grave."

An uncomfortable look passed over Hazel's face at that. She lifted her glass of ratafia and sipped as though it were much needed in that moment. Understandable, Tru supposed, since the woman was married to a man well fitting that description.

The marquess was practically a walking corpse, and Hazel was his third wife. He liked young brides . . . and he somehow had managed to outlive two and make it to his third wife. To Hazel.

Valencia happened to be the daughter of his first wife. That made Hazel her stepmother. Six years younger than Valencia . . . and her stepmother. A real sore point for Valencia. That and the fact that Hazel had been his mistress before he decided to make her his marchioness. It had shocked the *ton* at the time, but no one wanted to offend the Marquess of Sutton. Now, years later, no one even talked about Hazel's less-than-respectable origins. It seemed mostly forgotten . . . except for Valencia. She would never forget.

"Ah!" Hazel exclaimed. "There is Chatham." She nodded toward some distant spot across the ballroom. "Delia's beau must be with him."

Tru's entire being seized, her heart stopping. She did not even bother correcting Hazel. Mr. Jasper Thorne was not Delia's beau *yet*. Not ever, if she had anything to say about it.

She followed Hazel's gaze, instantly spotting her husband, garbed splendidly in evening attire. There were multiple gentlemen around him. Her gaze skipped over each of them, identifying them as her husband's usual cohorts—most ne'er-do-well husbands such as he, all overly fond of the gaming hells.

All except for one.

He stood with his back to her, but she did not recognize him. Perhaps when she saw his face, she might know him. Attired all in black though, he was different from the other men in her husband's orbit, who embraced the colors of the season and wore dove gray or peacock blue or lavender.

"Is that him?" Tru whispered, so quietly she was not even certain the words were audible to those around her.

She could scarcely speak. She could not move at all. A stillness came over her as she stared, her utterance directed more to herself than her friends, but they knew, too. The chatter faded around her as they all stared across the room, through the colorful whirl of dancing figures.

Delia was in there somewhere, hopefully not yet spotted by Chatham . . . and the mysterious Mr. Thorne. Any potential seeds of doubt she could plant in that man's mind about her daughter, all the better then. For once he clapped eyes on lovely Delia, he would want her. Of course he would. She was lovely and charming and *titled*. All the things a gentleman sought.

She gulped.

Her husband laughed heartily at something said, clapping a hand congenially on the stranger's shoulder, as though they were lifelong friends. Oh, yes. It was him. Certainty took hold of her. It was Jasper Thorne. This was the man she must defeat. The man who would have her daughter, if she did not do something to stop him, to steer him in another direction. She swallowed thickly. He was taller than Chatham, than most of the gentlemen around him.

He had not turned yet, but that did not stop the gnawing ache in her belly. Even without seeing him, she felt slightly ill. It was inexplicable and unwarranted.

He was just a man. Like any other . . . except perhaps with a bit more money. And size. He filled out his jacket with his broad shoulders in a decidedly uncivilized fashion. She moistened her lips. Of course he made her feel uncomfortable. Her daughter's fate rested upon him.

"He does not appear old," Valencia murmured.

No, he did not. He appeared virile and strong . . . his body powerful in his gentleman's garb. More powerful than the many dandies surrounding him.

"How can you tell that from the back of him?" Rosalind asked, frowning.

"Perhaps Delia will like him," Maeve offered, her gaze bright and hopeful.

"Oh, indeed. Perhaps," Valencia agreed with a hint of something sharp in her voice. Bitterness perhaps? "As we *all* liked our husbands. In the beginning." Her expression went tight again.

Tru understood her meaning perfectly.

Valencia's story was much like her own. Perhaps worse. Or better. It depended on how one viewed the fact that she and her husband had once loved each other. Truly. Deeply. They had been that rare thing among the *ton*. A love match.

Valencia and Dedham had enjoyed each other beyond their courtship, beyond their wedding night and honeymoon. Their enjoyment of each other had lasted years. Even without the blessing of children, they were happy and in love. Up until the accident. Until Dedham had been thrown from his horse.

He had recovered. Somewhat. The physician first predicted he would not survive. That he would never wake. For days he did not open his eyes. Then he did. At that point, the physician said Dedham would not walk again. For weeks he did not step from bed. Then he did.

He didn't die. Miraculously, he walked again. But not without crippling pain. He rarely left his house anymore, too afflicted. He was no longer himself. No longer the man who loved Valencia.

No longer the man Valencia loved. He loved nothing. Nothing save his constant companions: whiskey and laudanum.

"That must be him, no?" Rosalind baldly demanded as she ducked a hand inside her reticule to retrieve a small bejeweled flask of brandy. She quickly uncapped it and furtively poured a healthy nip into her glass of punch.

"I think so. Yes," Tru murmured, her stomach churning uneasily.

"Well, what does he look like?"

Valencia sent her a chiding glance. "That is what we are waiting to see."

Rosalind playfully pushed her as she sipped from her glass. Valencia staggered a bit, as though caught off-balance. A grimace passed over her face. Just for a moment. Then it was gone, a mild and cool expression back in place as she regained her poise.

Tru opened her mouth to inquire if she was perhaps not feeling well and needed a respite from the crowded room when Maeve suddenly gasped and seized hold of her hand, squeezing her. "There! Look! He's turned around!"

Jasper Thorne, *presumably* Jasper Thorne, turned, and they were all granted the full view of his face.

A general exclamation of delight rippled through their group as they assessed the gentleman.

Tru squeezed Maeve's hand back. Perhaps too hard. Her friend winced. With a muttered apology, she released her friend's hand, and buried both of hers into the skirts of her gown, clenching her fingers tightly in the folds of fabric.

"Well, now. I say, that is unexpected." Rosalind nodded as though she were not the spinster of the group who had disavowed marriage. "He is not so very bad." She took a slurp of her brandy-laced punch. "Not bad at all. This could work out nicely for Delia."

"Indeed. Our Cordelia is quite the fortunate girl. He is very handsome," Maeve agreed as only one who was perfectly happy would. Maeve was living her best life with her perfectly behaved husband and perfectly behaved children. Tru was happy for her, if not a little irked in moments like these. Living a charmed existence precluded her from seeing the potential flaws in this situation.

Maeve could not fathom what it would be like to be wed to a man like Chatham. Or Dedham, for that matter. She saw only a handsome face when she looked across the room at Mr. Thorne. She could not imagine anything else. Unlike Tru. Tru had no difficulty imagining the bad . . . the ills that could accompany marrying a handsome man. It was a lesson she well knew.

"And he *is* young," Rosalind chimed.

Valencia snorted. She, aside from Tru, of course, appeared the least impressed. A pretty face would indeed not impress her. She had married a pretty man. She would understand that beauty was not everything. Sometimes it was not even anything. It did not signify kindness, or potential happiness. It guaranteed nothing.

"Tru?" Maeve queried at her continued silence, an uncertain smile on her lips. "Do you not think so? It appears as though you were worried for naught."

She was *rightly* worried. Worry and fury and fear bubbled up inside her as she stared at him. It was worse than she feared.

Please. God. No. It could not be him.

The suitor Chatham handpicked for their daughter could not be the handsome wretch from last night. He could not be the same man who had propositioned her and promised her pleasure.

It was a mistake. It had to be. Surely it was some manner of jest.

"That is not *him*," Tru murmured even as she did not believe her own words. It could not be. It *must* not be.

"No? Who is he then? I've never seen him before. It must be him. Look at the way Chatham is fawning over him."

Dear heavens. He could not be at this ball, standing beside her husband as though he had every right to be here. As though he had every right to court and claim her daughter. As though it was *his* decision and she would have nothing to say about it.

And yet it was him. The man who burned hotly through her mind since yesterday was Jasper Thorne, the man intent on claiming her daughter.

Chapter 13

The only weapons at a lady's disposal are her beauty and her dowry. A family history of breeding healthy, strapping sons does not hurt either.

—Gertrude, the Countess of Chatham

It was something out of a nightmare.

Tru's life was far from perfect, to be certain, but things like this did not happen to her. This was truly awful. She could not be *this* unlucky. *This* cursed.

For some reason Madame Klara's face flashed across her mind, which was absurd. The woman had not predicted this. Her warning had been something else. Something about confessing. Or rather, *not* confessing. Whatever that meant—and Tru still believed it was all nonsense—it did not apply to him, to this man, to this dreadful scenario.

No. This was just a terrible coincidence.

Jasper Thorne was apparently the same man who had haunted her thoughts and given her an uneasy rest last night. He was the man who stood across the ballroom from her now, rubbing shoulders with her husband. The man she had thought never to see again. The man she had thought about with a flicker of regret after speaking with her mother today, wondering if maybe she had been too hasty to reject his offer.

"Tru, you look pale. Can I get you something? A drink? Canapé?" Food had somehow found its way into her sister's hand and she now waved the savory bite beneath Tru's nose.

Tru swatted at it distractedly but did not tear her attention away from Mr. Thorne. No, nothing short of gale-force winds would wrench her attention away from that man. "No . . . no."

The earl waved a hand, motioning about the room as he talked. The gesture was inherently searching, as was his gaze. And she knew. He was looking. Not for her, no. She was of no importance to him. Merely his wife. He was scanning for his target, for the one whom he did value. Cordelia.

Tru's stomach twisted tighter.

In his search, her husband's gaze alighted on her. She was caught, snared. He paused, studying her. She could read him thinking, contemplating. She was not Cordelia, but she was the next best thing. The one who might lead him to his daughter. He nodded to her and motioned her over with a beckoning flick of his fingers.

"Uh-oh. He has seen you." Rosalind tsked.

Indeed. And he was not the only one. Jasper Thorne followed

Chatham's gaze and looked across the room. His eyes collided with hers. She was spotted. *Identified.*

His eyes widened. Her heart seized and she panicked. Turning, she fled. It was a futile exercise. She could not run from this, from him, from her life. And yet she could not seem to stop herself from lifting her skirts and pushing past revelers, shoving through the ballroom.

She knew she must look ridiculous to watchful eyes. Chatham would vent his wrath upon her later for her defiance. She had been given specific instructions to impress Mr. Thorne, and here she was ignoring her husband's summons and escaping the room.

She heard her sister call after her, but still she kept moving, kept going.

She passed through the open French doors leading onto the veranda and plunged outside, gulping greedily the fresh air. And yet it was not far enough away. The sounds of the ball were still too near. The music, the revelers, Chatham, Mr. Thorne . . .

She hastened down the steps into the pulsing garden and into the maze of hedges, seeking distance and privacy.

Of course, she was not the only one on such a quest. The maze was a haven for trysting couples. She chose her turns carefully, mindful to avoid moving in the direction of any whispers and sighs and groans and gasping giggles.

She rounded one hedge and collapsed against the firm, scratchy wall of leaves and branches. Moonlight glowed overhead. She pressed a hand to the center of her chest as the night engulfed her, trying to still her pounding heart that threatened to burst free.

Alone, her gasps eased into even breaths as the foolishness of her behavior washed over her. Immediately, her mind leapt, searching for reasons to give for her hasty departure. She strategized potential excuses. Her husband would demand an explanation for ignoring his summons and fleeing like a frightened hare.

Thorne had seen her.

He would know by now who she was.

She nodded reassuringly, telling herself all would be well. It would be an easy matter to expel Thorne from her life. Once he realized he had propositioned the mother of his prospective bride, the shame of it would repel him. He would turn his attention elsewhere, to some other more suitable debutante of the season. He would be rightly embarrassed and long to forget all about her and Chatham and Delia. He would find other quarry.

A deep voice rumbled across the air. "It is *you*."

She straightened, stepping away from the hedge as though fire lit her backside.

He had found her.

His dark eyes glittered in the night, appearing pleased at the sight of her. She ignored the flicker of warmth in her chest at that look from him. That look was not hers to enjoy. He should not be pleased.

She forced her gaze away and stared beyond him, half expecting the earl to be trailing after him like the fawning puppet he was. No sight of him, however. That was a relief. It was simply this man. Only him. Stranger no more though. Jasper Thorne had followed her. He had haunted her thoughts, and now he haunted her in reality. Blast him.

"And it is *you*," she countered hotly.

"Why did you run away when you saw me?" His forehead furrowed as though truly confused at her behavior.

"Why? Why?" she echoed at a shrill whisper. "Is it not evident?"

"Apparently not. Please explain."

She shook her head, marveling that he did not yet realize. "Did you think I wished to greet you in the company of my husband?"

"Your husband?" He blinked, and she tried not to appreciate how ridiculously long his lashes were over his intense eyes.

She stilled. He did not yet know. Prickles chased up her spine. Somehow he had not learned her identity.

He stepped back and dragged a hand over his mouth, as though seeking composure.

"Yes, my husband," she hissed, wondering why admitting that, this truth that had been her existence for almost twenty years, should now, more than ever, bring her such deep regret.

She was the Countess of Chatham. She had long lived the role. For half her life. Regret was not something she felt anymore. It was a wasted emotion. And yet locking eyes with Mr. Thorne with full knowledge of their identities . . . she felt regret. And not a little ill. She pressed a hand against her suddenly churning stomach.

"Your husband," he echoed, consternation writ all over his features as he digested her words. "Chatham?" he asked, pointing in the direction of the house. "That . . . *sod*?" He stopped himself at her wince. "That man is your husband?"

She nodded stiffly, afraid to open her mouth to speak lest she cast her accounts all over her slippered feet.

His features tightened, a muscle feathering in his jaw. "Now I realize why you are unhappily wed."

She flinched. Squaring her shoulders, she folded her hands before her with more composure than she felt. "This is a most awkward situation."

"Awkward? Would that be because I very nearly bedded you last night?"

"*Nearly?*" she cried in affront, and yet warm tingles ran over her skin at the image of her with him, locked together on a bed. "Ha! You did not even come close, sir!"

"Oh, you were considering it," he replied with surety, his voice dropping to a husky pitch. "As I am sure you have considered it since. As I have been."

As I have been.

She shook off the wicked thought. It was neither here nor there. Astonishing though that he would *still* proposition her after learning of her identity. He was a reprobate through and through who deserved another slap to his face.

"Your arrogance knows no bounds, sir. I vow to you there was no chance of an indiscretion between us."

He nodded, stepping closer, allowing her to better see his face. Tension ticced in his cheek. She did not know why he should feel angry with her. She should be the offended party here, not he.

He stopped directly in front of her. "Deny all you like, but I distinctly recall your words."

"My words?" she asked warily.

"'More's the pity,'" he quoted with emphasis.

She pulled back, startled at the echo of her words from last night. *More's the pity.* The words she had used to express her regret that she could not—would not—take her pleasure with him. Her guard had slipped for that moment.

She closed her eyes in one long blink, keenly embarrassed at revealing her longing to him. "None of this matters now. You are here to find a bride."

"Yes. I believe I have."

She stared. He could not mean . . .

"My daughter?" She inhaled thinly through her nostrils. "Whom you have never even met?"

"I will soon. Tonight. Your husband is intent on that."

"You don't even know her."

"Marriages are founded on less."

She could not dispute the truth of that.

"And that is what you seek?" She would try a different approach. "You wish to marry a stranger?"

"She meets my needs."

"And what are those precisely?"

"I need a lady."

Tru gestured in the direction of the house. "There are plenty of those here tonight. Look elsewhere and take your pick."

"I seek a young lady well positioned in Society."

Ah. A young lady of high rank. That did narrow it down a bit. "As I said. Look elsewhere. There are others that meet those criteria."

"Chatham has been quite persuasive."

"Meaning?"

"He insists that Lady Cordelia is my perfect match."

Perfect match? Ha! Her husband was a *perfect* ass.

He continued. "And he insists no lady will be more amenable to my suit."

Apparently Chatham had been campaigning most diligently, and he was doing so by making Mr. Thorne feel like Delia was his only option—as though others might be turned off by his lack of rank and humble origins. Whilst she supposed not every blue-blooded papa would readily sell his daughter off to the highest bidder, plenty of them would. This was the *ton*, after all.

"There are other young ladies here that will suit your needs, I promise you." Plenty of fathers were as mercenary as Chatham.

"And yet your husband is so very insistent that it be Lady Cordelia. He's already offered her hand. I could end my search now."

Her ears went hot. "After what transpired between us . . . you cannot mean to seriously court my daughter."

"I have been invited to dine with your family tomorrow."

She jerked as though struck. Of course this was the first time she heard mention of this. "You must not—"

"I have already agreed."

She shook her head, wondering if her eyes appeared as wild as she felt inside. "You must renege."

"I would not be so rude—"

She surged a step toward him, certain he mocked her. "What game are you playing, sir?"

"No game. I am most serious about finding a suitable wife. I have a daughter that needs a mother to teach her how to be a lady and guide her through Society." He motioned about them with a flick of fingers. "She will have this world. She will be part of this glittering . . . spectacle." It was strange, but she detected equal amounts disgust and awe in his voice as he uttered this. "I vow it."

His daughter?

That effectively silenced her. She had not considered this as his reason for seeking matrimony. He had a daughter of his own? That was what motivated him? Mr. Thorne . . . a *father*. That led her to another jarring and uncomfortable thought.

Delia? A mother? She was still a child herself. It did not seem fair to thrust her into both wifehood and motherhood simultaneously when she had yet to fully mature herself.

He continued. "Tell me. Your daughter. Is she very much like you?"

She shook her head, bewildered a bit. "I—I . . . A little." In truth, they did not resemble each other in appearance. Delia was fair-haired with cornflower blue eyes. She more favored Chatham. Her temperament, however, matched Tru's. At least Tru's in her youth.

Debutante Tru had been timid and unsure of herself, easily influenced by others. Not as she was now. Now she possessed a voice. Now she was not afraid to fight.

"I look forward to making her acquaintance."

The words were innocent enough, but she recalled him last night, seductive and wicked . . . and now he was intent on her daughter. She would not tolerate it.

"Stay away from my daughter, Mr. Thorne."

"Want me for yourself, do you?"

She sucked in a hissing breath and resisted slapping him as he soundly deserved. Oh, the man was arrogant! She curled her fingers inward on her palms, digging them into the tender flesh, letting the cutting slice of her nails stay the impulse in her. He really did provoke the worst out of her.

Lifting her skirts, she circled him, giving him a wide berth as she strode away with swift strides.

She was a good many paces from him when he called out, "Until tomorrow night, Countess."

She stiffened, halting in her tracks. She nodded once without turning around. *Tomorrow night.* With a careful breath, she resumed her strides, vowing she would be ready for him.

Chapter 14

Would that papas love their daughters more than they love their cards, whiskey, and courtesans.
—Gertrude, the Countess of Chatham

Jasper waited in the shadowed garden several moments, resisting the urge to follow directly on the Countess of Chatham's heels. That would create some buzz among the *ton*. A man like him trailing after the very married, very proper, very prominent Countess of Chatham.

The Countess of Chatham. *Bloody hell.*

He could not have developed an attraction for a simple scullery maid or an independent widow. Oh, no. Nothing as uncomplicated as that. He had to have met the mother of the debutante he'd set out to court. Met her and flirted with her. *More* than flirted. *Join me somewhere where we might both explore each other at leisure.*

He had propositioned her and not in any subtle manner. And then when he'd just seen her tonight, he could not help himself. He had *still* flirted with her.

He supposed he ought to quit his pursuit of the Chatham girl—as the countess had insisted. It would be the sensible thing. Lady Cordelia was not the only blue-blooded princess of the *ton* out there shopping for a rich husband. He could find another. In time.

However, Chatham was amenable to his suit. The earl had called upon him a sennight ago, surprising him in his quarters. They'd never met before, but Theo had laid the groundwork, putting information about him out there, like a spray of dandelion fluffs on the air. Apparently the seeds Theo had planted on his behalf throughout Society had taken root. Chatham had learned Jasper was seeking a wife among Society, and he did not mince words.

"My daughter is available to the highest bidder this season, and word has it that man is you."

Jasper had shown no outward reaction, simply remained in the chair of his office, his fingers tapping on the arm in a seemingly indolent manner despite the tension he felt as he stared across his desk at the pompous earl.

Of course he had heard of Lady Cordelia Chatham. She'd been mentioned in the papers, and he'd made special note of her, putting her on the top of his list. Only, he had not imagined her father would appear on his doorstep. Or that he would be so plainspoken.

Jasper thought fathers were supposed to be more protective and wary of men when it came to their daughters. He could not imagine tossing his daughter at any gentleman without a thorough look into his background and spending time with the man, becoming familiar and confident of his good character.

With a cool expression, he murmured, "Thank you for your consideration, Lord Chatham. I look forward to meeting your daughter."

"You should do that and soon. She won't be available next season, Mr. Thorne." His gaze had locked on Jasper then, full of intensity and caution. "That I can promise you. If you want her, do not dally." He moved to take his leave then, pausing only to add, "We will be at the Lindley ball Friday evening. If you like the look of my daughter, join us for dinner Saturday night."

It had seemed almost too easy. He had only recently determined to meet Lady Cordelia Chatham, and then her father had appeared as though summoned by magic, offering her to him on a silver platter. If she was even half of what the scandal rags professed, she was exactly what he was looking for. He might find her father distasteful, but the man could be managed.

Jasper knew men like him, ruled by their vices and the weight—or lack of weight—of their pocketbooks. As long as Chatham was fed a steady allowance, he would be tolerable. Blunt would keep him in check.

Lady Cordelia's mother, however, would not be nearly so easy to manage. A woman like her was not ruled by money. Jasper knew that at once. She would not be willing to release her daughter to him, and he could not fault her for that. Not after their tricky start.

He should forget all about them—the entire lot: father, daughter, mother. The situation was already more complicated than he needed it to be. He was seeking a wife to be a mother to his child. This was not about love or affection or even fleeting lust. This was about finding someone for Bettina. Not for himself.

Except he had *every* desire to follow the countess. Normally he would. Normally, he would behave as he had last night. If he *wanted* a woman, he would make certain she knew it and *normally* he would have her.

Except this was not his world.

This was their world. *Her* world. The countess's world. He was simply attempting to learn it. To infiltrate it. Or perhaps not so simply. There were rules. Ways to do things, conduct and behavior he must heed. He was certain stalking a married woman, the mother of the young debutante he courted, did not fall in with those rules.

He looked skyward, studying the bright moon. It was the same moon he'd looked upon as a lad living in the back room of his father's inn. And it would be the same moon wherever he went in the future. There was some comfort in that. Some things never changed. He would always be Jasper Thorne. Callused-palmed, unrefined, not bred for ballrooms or fit for ladies that smelled of rose water. Only his blunt was good enough. Not him.

The sooner he found his bride, the sooner he could be done with all this. He could get back to his life, his business, whilst his lady wife traveled these ballrooms and saw to it that his daughter was brought up so that she could glide among peacocks and not be deemed a fraud in their midst.

Lady Cordelia Chatham could be that bride.

He started from the gardens, his tread steady but unhurried.

"Thorne! There you are. I've been looking for you." Chatham appeared at his side the moment he entered the ballroom. Clearly the man had been looking for him. He clapped him on the shoulder as though they were lifelong friends.

"I just stepped out for some air."

Chatham turned and waved to someone in the crowd, his beringed fingers glinting as he beckoned the person closer.

Jasper followed his gaze, scanning the impeccably dressed revelers. The silks and brocades sparkled beneath the lights of the chandeliers. Near him a woman laughed like a braying donkey as she drank heavily of champagne. Her gaze alighted on him and her eyes turned fairly lecherous. Her tongue trailed her lip suggestively. She leaned toward a friend, their heads touching as they eyed him, giggling and whispering to each other.

He detected a few snatches of their words: *Coarse as a yeoman . . . Big all over, I wager . . .*

He must have a sign about his neck that declared him not one of them. It was a needed reminder of what he was to them. A novelty. Someone for them to use, but never would he be one of them.

"Ah, there she is! My delightful girl."

Jasper dragged his attention back to Chatham . . . and to the young girl in a gown of virginal white arriving in their midst like some manner of angel.

"Papa?" she murmured, looking up at Jasper as she stopped beside her father.

"Cordelia, meet Mr. Thorne."

She lowered her blue eyes demurely and dipped into a flawless curtsey. As she rose, he took her gloved hand and bowed over her fingers very correctly, understanding at once why this young lady was so feted this season among the *ton*.

"Lady Cordelia," he greeted. "I've been looking forward to making your acquaintance."

"As have I yours, Mr. Thorne." Her words trembled a little, lacking conviction. Whether those words were true or not, she made a pretty picture with her fair ringlets and creamy skin. Young and fresh and innocent . . . and untried. He recognized that at once, and not with any real excitement. She was barely more than a child. She did not stir him in the least, and he was certain her mother would be glad to know that.

Bloody hell. He could not shake the thought of the countess even now when faced with her daughter. He could only search the girl's features, looking for the slightest echo of Lady Chatham there. And yet there was very little that reminded him of her mother. Something in the shape of her eyes perhaps. The arch of her eyebrows.

He lifted his gaze and glanced about, peering over Lady Cordelia's head. She would not abandon her child to him. To her credit, she was a dedicated and protective mother. He knew she was near, watching from somewhere in the ballroom right now, likely staring daggers at him. He knew because he knew her. Already, he knew her.

His pulse quickened at the thought of the countess's eyes on him. There was nothing demure in her gaze. Only directness. Those warm brown eyes sparked and started a fire in his stomach. He scanned faces, seeking with no luck.

The earl's voice drew his attention back to him. "We look forward to having you to dinner tomorrow. Our cook . . ." The earl pulled a rapturous expression and kissed his fingertips. "You are in for a treat."

Jasper nodded, but he couldn't care less about the meal to come. He did care, however, about seeing the countess again. *Bloody hell.* He should invent an excuse, take his leave, and find another eligible young lady.

Instead, he heard himself saying, "What time should I arrive?"

Chatham beamed. "Brilliant, brilliant! Let's say, oh . . . eight?" The earl looked from Jasper to young Cordelia triumphantly, as though it was done, as though they were already bound and betrothed.

Jasper nodded, a grim weight settling over him for some reason. The earl excused himself then, moving off to talk to some obviously affluent lady, if the number of jewels at her throat and in her tiara was any indication. Chatham's attention did not stray fully, however.

The earl sent his daughter a rather pointed look and a significant nod toward Jasper from where he stood. The young lady cleared her throat and smiled apprehensively at him.

He decided to spare her and speak. "Are you enjoying yourself, Lady Cordelia?"

"Oh, very much, Mr. Thorne—" She was cut off from saying anything more by the arrival of Theo.

"Lady Cordelia." He bowed over her hand with a smile. Theo was a few years older than Jasper but possessed a perpetually youthful mien, with his boyishly round face and impish grin.

"Lord Branville," she returned, looking almost relieved at his arrival. Clearly she had not been comfortable left alone with Jasper.

Theo clapped him on the shoulder. "What do you think, Thorne? Have you ever seen so many elegant and beautiful ladies in one place?"

"Never," he replied dutifully.

It was as though the addition of Theo to the group signaled others to join them. Lady Cordelia was soon surrounded by a bevy of young gentlemen, proving, in case Jasper harbored any doubts, that she was indeed a much-sought-after debutante.

Theo stepped closer, murmuring for his ears alone, "Did I see you follow the Cold Countess outside?"

He looked sharply at the man who had become his friend. "The Cold Countess?"

"Lady Chatham," he whispered with a nod. "That's what everyone calls her."

Jasper could not fathom why. There was nothing in the least bit frigid about the lady. On the contrary, she elicited the warmest of sensations in him.

"You were gone for some time, and when the lady returned she seemed quite flushed in the face. What could have happened to discompose the ever-unflappable Cold Countess? She looked quite cross. Did she have words with you? Does she disapprove of you so greatly? I can't imagine she is like her husband, judging suitors for her daughter by their pocketbooks. She would be harder to impress. But then it's Chatham with the final word on the matter." Theo shrugged as though this was simply the way of things, and Jasper knew it was, but that did not mean he felt good about it.

"I don't know what you're talking about."

Theo looked him over with marked skepticism. "Very well. Keep your secrets."

He would. Lady Chatham was a married lady. He would say nothing to sully her name or endanger her reputation.

Let her remain the Cold Countess to the world. He alone knew better. He alone knew there was more to her than that. Perhaps he preferred it that way.

Chapter 15

The ton, especially the Marriage Mart, is so full of masks, costumes, and people desperately hiding their true selves. It may as well be an opera house.

—Lady Cordelia Chatham

Delia stared at her reflection in the mirror of her dressing table. "I don't wish to go downstairs."

Mama came up behind her in a swish of silken skirts, her hips swaying in that natural womanly way that Delia envied. Mama had curves. Hips. Breasts. A deep décolletage that belonged in a Botticelli painting. *She* was not a twig that could scarcely fill out a corset.

Delia liked to think she would one day have those same curves, but there was little of her person that resembled her mother. She suspected she would never be voluptuous. A portrait of her mother the year she came out in Society graced the hall at her grandparents' home, and the evidence was there. Mama had always possessed a bounty of curves, whilst Delia did not, nor would she likely ever.

Mama placed her hands on her shoulders—shoulders that were uncommonly bare. Delia had been out for a few weeks now and was no longer wearing her girlhood frocks, but this crimson gown was something else entirely. Delia usually stuck to pastels and white like other debutantes. In this red gown, she looked like a woman, even though she still felt a girl, which summed up her general mood. She felt like a child playing at being an adult.

Mama had reservations when she was fitted for the gown, voicing her concern about the color and the deep cut of the bodice, but Delia had pleaded until Mama relented.

She had been beyond excited, imagining the places she would venture wearing the bold dress. Adventure had loomed ahead. When she first donned it in the modiste shop, she could not have fathomed that her first opportunity to wear it would be for a man handpicked for her by her father. Now the sight of herself in the dress filled her with unease, and she wished she could stuff the gown back into her wardrobe and pretend she had never asked for it in the first place.

Papa's sudden interest, when he had shown no interest in her whatsoever, did not bode well. He liked this Jasper Thorne for her. Why else would Papa himself have arrived early today to search her wardrobe and pick out this gown for her to wear tonight? When she had discovered him going through her gowns, he had explained: *You need to look like a woman tonight and not a little girl in those frocks your mother forces on you.*

"Cook prepared a pot of tea for you." Mama gestured to the service waiting nearby on the dressing table. As though a cup of tea could cure all ails.

Delia offered her mother a tremulous smile. "Is that meant to make the medicine of this evening go down better?"

It was what Mama had done when she fell ill as a child, after all. She would have Cook prepare a pot of tea and her favorite biscuits to entice her to take the necessary tincture.

Her mother's gaze softened, and she thought she detected pity there, and that was something to digest. Her own mother pitied her. The sympathetic way she looked at her was far from heartening.

Mama stroked one of the ringlets that fell heavily over her shoulder. "Delia, let us simply dine with this Mr. Thorne tonight and then—"

"I don't even know him," she cut in.

"It is only a dinner."

"He is . . . *old*." Handsome, she supposed, in an intense and brooding way that some women liked. She did not. She liked cheerful and lighthearted. Young men full of playfulness.

Mama smiled. "Thirty-three is not old." She then shook her head. "But that does not matter, because it is as I said . . . only a dinner. It does not mean that—"

"I spoke with Papa," she blurted.

Mama blinked. "Oh. When?"

"This morning whilst you were out." She nodded and fingered one of the puffed sleeves of her gown. "When he chose this dress for me to wear."

"I see." Mama looked uneasy. "What did he say?"

"This is not merely a dinner with Mr. Thorne as you insist. Papa made that abundantly clear when he selected this gown for me."

Mama looked her over anew with a narrowing gaze, her nostrils flaring slightly. "I did not realize your father visited your chamber and personally chose this dress for you."

Nodding, Delia went on. "He told me that I was to make myself especially accommodating tonight." Delia stopped for a fortifying breath. "That I am to impress him no matter what it takes. He said Mr. Thorne is a very rich man and that we need him."

Hot emotion flashed over Mama's eyes before she put it in check, banking the embers. But it did not matter. Delia had seen it. It was always the same. Mama hiding that she despised Papa. Or rather, *attempting* to hide that she despised him. She never succeeded though. Delia knew. She and her brother both knew.

They knew and wished they could do something to help their mother, to save her because she deserved better than Papa. And yet there was no saving Mama. This was her life and there was no salvation from it. Delia hoped, fervently, that she would not be stuck in a similar situation. She did not want to find herself married to a man she could not abide. She did not think herself as strong as Mama. She would not survive it.

It was probably best Charles was away at school, even though she missed him and took comfort in his presence. He would not like this at all. He would want to save Delia from entering into a fate like their mother's. He would confront Papa and that would not go well at all.

Mama tightened her grip on Delia's bare shoulders and forced her to turn around on the cushioned bench before the vanity table. "I vow you this. You shall not be forced to marry anyone. You do not have to *impress* Mr. Thorne. Indeed not. Be yourself."

Delia gazed silently at her mother, willing herself to speak, to trust her mother in this, but the conviction did not emerge—nor did words. Her throat was too thick.

"I promise you, Cordelia. The choice will be yours." Her mother's warm brown eyes drilled into her, and Delia knew she meant what she said—she believed in it. Even if it was not true. Even if she lacked the power to save Cordelia from Papa's will. Mama believed she could.

Delia knew better, however. *She* did not believe it. The choice was not hers or her mother's. Papa held all the power. No matter what Mama believed, she could not keep such a promise.

Papa would choose whomever he wanted for her. And she would marry him.

TRU COULD NOT recall a time in the last fifteen years when she and her husband hosted anything together. The earl had moved into his own residence soon after their vows and lived his life without her. Together, *collaboration*, was not something that had ever applied to them.

And yet that did not stop Chatham from presiding over the dinner party as though he were king of her house and all those within it. Seated at the head of the table, he snapped his fingers at her butler and the footmen, indicating when each dish should be brought out and drinks should be poured and refilled.

The menu was also his invention entirely, heavy on the braised meats and gravies and butter sauces, light on the vegetables. No sherry for the ladies. Such consideration was not given. It was very different from the dinner parties she hosted at this table. So very different from the dinners she had *imagined* hosting in her married life. Her silly childhood dreams of presiding over a home, arm in arm with a doting husband, were just that. *Silly*.

She watched the earl in distaste as he used his fingers, seizing his lamb chop and using it to mop up the gravy on his plate. Tru reached for her glass of claret, lifting it to her lips for a sip. Stronger than sherry, but perhaps she needed something stronger this night. Over the rim of the glass, her gaze clashed with the man across from her. Jasper Thorne.

He cocked an eyebrow. She narrowed her gaze back at him, allowing him to feel her full wrath. He turned his attention to Delia seated beside him. Her daughter smiled amiably at him. She had been amiable all evening.

Despite their earlier conversation, Delia presented herself in a most pleasing manner. She did honor to her training, conducting herself with charm and ease. Her governess would be proud. Tru certainly was. Even Chatham watched on, beaming in approval, and Tru's fingers tightened around her fork, the urge to stab her husband with it so very overwhelming.

Would that Delia slurped her soup and brayed like a mule and commented inanely on the weather. Perhaps then Jasper Thorne would take himself away and forget about Delia.

With a fortifying breath, Tru forced her gaze away from them all. Chatham. Delia. Jasper Thorne. Observing them was simply too disquieting to her constitution. The longer she watched her daughter interact with Thorne, she feared her food might sour in her stomach.

She scanned the length of the table. Her husband had invited others. Valencia and her husband. And the earl's oldest friend, Lord Burton, a vile man. He and Chatham had attended Eton together. They loved to regale each other with reminiscences of the past—as though they each had not been present during those distasteful exploits, as though others cared to hear their sordid misdeeds. She could recount every unsavory tale, for she had heard them all. Countless times. The ugly pranks. The drunken revels. The barmaids they had shared. They really were a vulgar pair.

Valencia and her husband might not be vulgar, but their presence was troubling in another respect. Valencia was never herself in his company. She sat stoic-faced and tight-lipped whilst her husband conducted himself at half capacity, usually out of his head from spirits and whatever other remedies he relied on to alleviate his pain. Tonight, however, his remedies did not seem to be working. He looked rather green, perspiration dotting his skin as he lifted a shaking fork to his lips, attempting to eat as one did at a dinner party.

Chatham had always approved of her friendship with Valencia. She was married to a duke, after all. It mattered not at all that the Duke of Dedham was merely a shell of the man he was before his accident. It did not signify that he sat in his chair looking rather peaked and ready to keel over at any moment. A duke was a duke. An important man, and Chatham always preferred to surround himself with important men. No doubt Chatham was trying to impress Mr. Thorne with evidence of lofty friends. He was not only selling his daughter . . . he was selling his connections.

The duke, no longer the robust figure he once was, suddenly swayed in his seat. Valencia reached out to steady him, seizing hold of his arm in a white-knuckled grip. He blinked and righted himself, yanking free of her touch and sending her a baleful glare. "I am fine," he muttered.

She withdrew her hand and nodded, dipping her dark gaze, doubtlessly embarrassed to be spoken to so sharply in front of company. A faint flush of color marred her olive complexion.

Tru's heart ached for her friend. She knew what it felt like to be slighted, to be snubbed and rebuffed by a husband—the man you took vows with, the man who was meant to be your partner in all things in life. It especially stung when it was done in front of others.

"Brandy going to your head, Your Grace?" the earl called jovially to Dedham. "It is fine stuff . . . Creeps up on you though. Let us know if you have a preference for something else. We have a fine Madeira." This was the charming Chatham, the one that had so fooled her as a girl.

Dedham lifted his glass in salute and then downed it. "Fine stuff," he agreed. "Nothing I cannot handle though, my lord."

Valencia gave her head a slight shake. Still keeping her eyes averted, she reached for her own drink as though needing something to do with herself—even if that was only sipping her drink.

Tru overhead Delia asking Thorne, "How are you enjoying the season thus far, Mr. Thorne?"

"I confess this might be the most delightful evening I've had so far, Lady Cordelia, in your charming company, of course."

Tru rolled her eyes and stifled a snort. *Of course.*

"Since you enjoy Cordelia's company so much, you should join us at Chatham House. We leave the day after tomorrow."

"We are . . . leaving?" Delia blinked bewildered eyes at this news.

We are? Tru refrained from echoing her daughter. She would not react and reveal how little informed she was of her husband's decisions. She did not wish to appear foolish and without authority, even if she was.

"You go to the country? But the season has just started," Burton exclaimed.

"Spring is lovely in the Lake District," Chatham replied as he sawed into his meat, this time with a knife and fork. "Everything so blindingly green. Gardens bursting with flowers. Excellent weather for fishing, riding, hunting. Join us, Burton. You've always enjoyed yourself there." Her husband pointed a fork in Thorne's direction. "And you, too, Thorne. We shall make a party of it. Nothing quite as merry as a house party."

Tru sucked in a breath, realizing at once what her husband was doing. He was trying to lure the man out of London, away from the season and all its diversions . . . all of its *many* young, pretty, and eligible diversions.

No doubt he believed sequestering Thorne away with Delia would increase opportunity for the two to court. Perhaps he would even have a signed betrothal contract by the end of the house party. Oh, he was indeed clever. Tru would not put it past him to maneuver the situation so that Thorne compromised Delia and was forced to offer for her. Heat scored her face as she imagined that. She knew firsthand that compromising women was not something beyond her husband's scruples. Was he so ruthless that he would orchestrate his own daughter's ruin?

"But the season has just begun," Delia murmured, her gaze moving to Tru questioningly, clearly wondering if she knew of this plan. Jasper Thorne followed Delia's gaze, resting his deep brown eyes on Tru thoughtfully.

She reached rather fumblingly for her glass and lifted it for another fortifying sip.

"Well, Thorne. What say you?" the earl pressed. "I cannot promise things won't become too . . . unruly. House parties often have that reputation, but only in the best of ways." He chortled and sent both Burton and Thorne a wink and a knowing grin.

Burton nodded and chuckled. "You do, indeed, know how to host a proper party, Chatham. I can attest to that."

A *proper* party. Her lip curled ever so slightly. She could not help herself. She did not attend the parties her husband hosted. Even so, she knew they were decidedly *not* proper.

The earl's gaze skipped to the duke. "Will you be joining us, too, Dedham? It has been some time since you graced us with your presence at Chatham House."

Some time, indeed. The last time would have been prior to his accident. She knew from Valencia that her husband spent most of his days suffering within their London home, unwilling or unable to endure the rigors of travel. Outings like tonight tested the extent of his energies.

He skirted the food around his plate with his fork. He was clever at rearranging the food on his plate so that it appeared he was eating. She recalled that trick from when her children had been young.

"My lord husband does not travel these days—"

"Hold your tongue, wife. I can speak on my own behalf."

Valencia fell silent, her dark eyes fixed on her plate, the high arch of her thick eyebrows more dramatic than usual set within her tense expression.

Tru waited, expecting to hear the duke decline the invitation. Of course he could not travel.

Dedham stabbed at a dainty bit of lamb and lifted it to his lips, chewing tentatively. "You know," he murmured, "I think I shall join you." He lifted his napkin to pat his lips and then his perspiring brow. "It will be nice to depart the crush of the city."

Valencia cut him a swift glance, her displeasure clearly writ on her face, and Tru understood why. The journey would be difficult for him and she would be the one to bear the brunt of his displeasure over his discomfort.

Valencia reached for his arm again. "You cannot think to make such a journey in—"

"I think," he said tightly, pulling his arm free, "that a country house party sounds just the thing, wife. We shall go."

Valencia withdrew her hand, tucking it beneath the table on her lap. She forced a smile, but her misery was there, behind the gleam of her teeth. Tru sent her a look that she hoped conveyed her apology. She hated that her husband's machinations reached her friend, too. Not only was her daughter affected but now Valencia was, too.

"Splendid. We have quite the party in the making. And what of you, Thorne? Shall you join us?"

Tru whipped her attention to Jasper Thorne. She held Thorne's gaze willfully, challengingly, almost daring him to accept the invitation. If he did, she would make his life hell, she vowed. She would make him regret the moment he decided to pursue her daughter.

"If another person would not be an inconvenience to your lady wife." He held her gaze as he said this, his warm eyes roaming over her face, almost as though he welcomed her dissent. What did he expect? For her to renege on her husband's invitation?

"My wife?" Chatham blinked and glanced around as though searching for her at the table, as though she were seated so very far away and not a mere two chairs from him. "What has she to do with this?"

Because Tru never had anything to do with the normal course of his life.

"I would not wish to impose . . ."

Tru fought to swallow as he continued to talk, wishing he would simply stop. She understood he was being polite, this uncultured gentleman. Ironic, she supposed. Her husband was born with a silver spoon in his mouth, and yet he possessed all the manners of a Barbary pirate. Whilst Jasper Thorne . . .

Well, he was altogether something else. Someone with dignity and wit and manners. Except when he was seducing ladies on terraces, of course.

Contrary to his appearance—he looked more like a yeoman accustomed to humble labor—he was the epitome of civility. Whereas Mr. Thorne was able to crush a person with his bare hands, Chatham crushed people with the bite and the sting of his words. With a vicious glare. A lip-curling sneer. These were the weapons in his arsenal, and she knew them all well.

"You need not concern yourself with my wife." Chatham fluttered a hand. "Gertie is of no account."

Tru flinched and looked down, hating the name he alone insisted on calling her, hating his words, hating *him* for a flash of a moment before she dispelled that dark emotion from her heart. Hating him accomplished nothing save poisoning herself. She'd forbidden herself from feeling that particular sentiment.

She concentrated on her plate and its contents rather than what her husband had just said. She was doubtlessly red-faced. Hopefully no one noticed her burning cheeks.

"Is that not right, my dear?" Chatham inquired.

It should not sting. Chatham never said a kind word about her or to her. Not in private. Not in public. Why should she expect otherwise? It did not matter if guests were present. Belittling her in word or deed was not so surprising.

Much like Valencia, she fixed a smile on her face and looked across the table at Jasper Thorne. "You must join us, Mr. Thorne. The more, the merrier."

He inclined his head. "How could I refuse such delightful company?" He motioned lightly about the table, but his intense gaze held hers.

"Splendid," Chatham proclaimed. "Are we all done here? Shall we retire to the drawing room?" He wiped his napkin at his mouth and then pushed to his feet whilst addressing Valencia. "Your Grace, perhaps you shall entertain us at the pianoforte? You play so beautifully."

Valencia nodded. "Of course, my lord."

They exited the dining room. Tru had just passed through the doors and stepped into the corridor when she heard her husband say behind her: "Mr. Thorne, have you seen our gardens? Cordelia, why don't you escort Mr. Thorne?"

Tru whirled around. "It is dark."

Her husband glared at her. "There are lanterns . . . and a moon in the sky." He looked back to their daughter and motioned her down the corridor to the French doors that led to the gardens. "Go on with you now, Cordelia. Be a proper hostess. Give Mr. Thorne a tour of the garden."

She would not let him cow her in this. She brought her chin up. "It is unseemly, my lord—"

He seized her arm then, his grip tight on her elbow as he walked them ahead, following after the rest of the party that was already en route to the drawing room. "Let the young people take some air, wife. They needn't be bored in our company."

She looked back over her shoulder and caught a glimpse of her daughter's wide eyes and Mr. Thorne's narrow gaze on her as Chatham pulled her roughly along. Then she was compelled forward and could not look behind her anymore.

"Have you lost all sense of propriety?" she hissed, thinking of poor Delia, tossed to the wolves—or in this case, wolf. A singular wolf in the form of Mr. Thorne. "How dare you?"

Her husband blinked mildly, clearly unperturbed at her outraged question. In fact, he looked bored. It was an expression he commonly wore when he looked at her.

"What are you talking about?"

"You know entirely what I am talking about. You just threw our daughter to that wolf . . . inviting him to take her unchaperoned in the garden—"

"Well, I did not invite him to *take* her, as you say. He's hardly ravishing her in the bushes. He does not seem the sort to do that. They merely go for a stroll. At the most, he may steal a kiss or two." He shrugged. "Perhaps a pat or a fondle. Nothing more than what most young men do when the opportunity presents itself." He shrugged yet again, as though the possibility of that scenario was of no account to him.

Her ears burned with hot emotion. "You are barbaric."

Her husband's face tightened. He did not like that. "Have a care how you speak to me, Gertie. I do nothing other than speed along this courtship to its eventual destination." His gaze fastened on her. "If he wants our daughter, he is free to have her. I will not oppose it and neither will you."

"Chatham." She tried for a reasonable tone despite the angry fire burning a hole through her stomach. "This is not the right—"

"You will not ruin this, dear *wife*, as you seem so very intent on doing."

She had thought he might attempt something like this when they ventured to the country for his impromptu country party, but she had not suspected he would be so bold as to do such a thing this very night.

"This is not the way to go about—"

"Leave this to me. I will not stomach your interference. Assuming he wants her, I *will* have Jasper Thorne for a son-in-law, and I will not hear one word against it from you." His fingers tightened on her arm. "Do you understand me?"

His fingers continued to squeeze her flesh, awaiting her agreement. She would likely have a bruise come tomorrow, but she would not need the marks to remind her of this moment . . . or of what she must do.

Chapter 16

My husband's opinion ranks somewhere below my dressmaker's in terms of importance.

—Gertrude, the Countess of Chatham

Jasper wanted the mother of the girl he courted. It was the most unfortunate predicament and one he must put to an end.

He was not some blue-blooded earl, snapping his fingers at servants with no thought to them or that they were people who worked all day and often into the night for very little wage, waking before sunrise to do it all over again—only to have some arrogant prig snap his fingers at them like they were no better than a dog.

Jasper was brought up in a humble coaching inn, mucking stalls, lugging water, sweeping floors, repairing roofs, fences, even cleaning the taproom floor, which consisted of vomit, piss, and other matter he preferred not to ponder. He would do any and all things that needed doing or suffer a cuff to the head from his father. He did not receive the things he wanted simply because he wanted them. His father had not been an indulgent man.

Jasper knew about want and wanting, but he knew more about denial. He was inured to it. Not getting his way should not feel such a hardship. Lady Chatham was simply another denial in his life that he must accept.

He strolled along the paved path with Lady Cordelia's hand tucked inside his elbow. His thoughts should be on the young lady beside him, but he could not stop thinking about the woman he left behind inside the house. He wanted to thrash her husband for the way he spoke to her, for the way he put his hand on her arm, dragging her off like a sack of grain.

Oh, that would have been a brilliant spectacle. It had taken every bit of his self-control, and the reminder that she was the man's wife, to stay his impulse. Attacking Chatham would not have helped her. It would have gotten Jasper tossed from the house and out of Lady Chatham's orbit forever, and he was not ready to quit the countess yet.

She was in the drawing room now with her snake of a husband and his equally vile friend. The duke, who looked ready to tip over in his chair and slip into unconsciousness at any moment, and his sad-eyed wife were in there, too, making conversation and reveling in the importance granted to them from the good fortune of their births. Well, perhaps not the duchess. She struck him as being as miserable as the countess.

And yet he itched to rejoin them, to plant his gaze on the Cold Countess again.

Gertrude. *Gertie*, her husband had called her. She did not like that. He had detected her flinch each time Chatham used that moniker.

He'd attended this dinner because of *her*. He'd wanted to see the countess again. Although face-to-face with her again, watching her with her husband and daughter . . . should have changed his thoughts and ideas of her.

It should have, but good sense had not struck him. On the contrary. He wanted her even more after enduring that wretched dinner.

Her husband was an undeniable bastard. Witnessing the dynamic between them, the way he talked to her, the way he did *not* talk to her and overlooked her entirely . . . only made him want to snatch her up in his arms and haul her away.

"What do you think, Mr. Thorne?" Lady Cordelia motioned around them.

"It is indeed a lovely garden," Jasper declared as they walked. "A peaceful spot. Almost as though you're not in the city at all."

"Mama likes gardens and fountains and the like." She gestured to the burbling fountain. "They are quite marvelous at our country home. She would prefer for us to stay there year-round, but Chatham House is a good bit away from Town and I need to be here for . . ." Her voice faded, but he knew what she meant to say. She needed to be here for the Marriage Mart . . . to entice a husband.

By the bleak look of her, she was not enthused at the prospect, and he could not help wondering if it were him specifically that left her dispirited or the notion of marriage altogether.

Of course, it mattered not at all. Not anymore. He could not marry this girl. Not after everything that had transpired between him and the countess. It would be perverse. He'd known it from the moment he'd discovered the identity of her mother. He was not *that* unprincipled. He would not court and wed this girl after attempting to seduce her mother.

Of course, he had not given such assurance to Lady Chatham when she begged him for it. He knew he should relieve her mind, but he rather enjoyed sparring with her and watching the color flood her cheeks when she was outraged. And he clearly outraged her.

Lady Cordelia bestowed on him a practiced smile. "But you shall see Chatham House soon and admire the grounds for yourself. I am certain Mama will wish to give you a tour herself, Mr. Thorne. She is very proud of her roses."

Oh, he wanted that. Longed for it. Time alone with the countess in her rose garden . . . or anywhere else. He gave his head a small shake, suddenly, grimly, fervently knowing this needed to come to an end.

He had come to London to expand his business, to find a wife, a mother for his daughter. Not for himself. He could find a woman for himself after he had accomplished that.

He needed to walk away from this family. There were other eligible ladies. This fascination he had with the countess was ill timed, to be sure, and he needed to put an end to it before it became any more complicated, before it distracted him any more from his task.

Perhaps after he was wed to someone else, he would meet her again, a chance encounter on another terrace with the Cold Countess. Perhaps then she would be receptive to his advances.

He cleared his throat and stopped to face the girl, determined to put an end to what had become a messy business.

"It has been a pleasure making your acquaintance, Lady Cordelia, but I do not think I am going to be able to join you on that trip to your country house, after all."

Her head snapped a little higher, her eyes fixing on him intently. "W-what? Why not?" She gave her head a small shake. "Forgive me for prying, sir, but my father is so looking forward to your visit with us." Desperation tinged her voice, and even a hint of . . . panic. "He will be most disappointed."

Jasper studied her for a moment and realized she was afraid. His stomach churned a bit at that. He did not like that this girl—for that was what she was . . . a *girl*—was afraid. He studied her features and understood at once.

She feared that if he returned inside the house and announced he had changed his mind and would not be joining them at their house party the blame would fall on her. Her father would be disappointed. Angry even. And he would fault her. Chatham would conclude that she had said or done something on their walk to lose his favor.

She might not wish Jasper for a husband, but nor did she want her father's wrath.

"My lady," he began slowly. "Permission to speak freely."

Her eyes widened and she glanced around wildly as though she might dive into a hedge. "Oh, I wish you would not. Please do not."

He grasped her newfound fear at once . . . She thought he was about to declare himself to her and she was terrified at the prospect. If there was ever any doubt, this confirmed it. The girl did not want him. Which was just as well, since he did not want her either.

"Settle yourself, Lady Delia. I have no intention of dropping on my knee before you and asking for your hand."

That silenced her. She gawked at him.

He continued. "You clearly do not see me as a potential husband."

At that, she stammered, "W-why do you say that? Have I offended you in some way?" Both her hands dropped to his arm to squeeze beseechingly. "Oh, please do not tell my father—"

He felt a colossal bastard in that moment. This young girl was clearly being coerced into courtship with him, and he had blithely gone along with it, considering Chatham's offer of her hand in matrimony as though her wishes did not bear consequence. He could think only of his own daughter in that moment and how he would never want her to feel forced into *anything*. Not because of him or any man.

Would he have even noticed if he himself had decided *not* to put an end to it because of her mother? Would he have continued to be that clueless and indifferent to her unhappiness . . . her unwillingness? It was a sobering and grim prospect.

"I promise you . . . I will say nothing of this to your father."

She bit her lip. "But he will blame me. And Mama. He will think it both our faults if you withdraw your suit and look elsewhere." She lifted her hands from his arm and pressed them to her cheeks as though the action might calm her.

"I vow I will not speak a word of displeasure to him. I will only sing your praises—"

"It will not matter. Your mere absence from my side will say it all, as will your rejection of his invitation to Chatham House." She blew out a great huff of breath. "And when you begin to court someone else. Oh, dear." She plopped down on the edge of the nearby fountain, indifferent to the spray of water at her back.

"Lady Delia," he began, using the soothing voice he adopted with Bettina when she was upset. "Do you want to marry me? Come now. You won't offend me. Be honest."

She looked at him almost shyly from beneath her lashes and shook her head. "No," she whispered.

"Then you should not feel compelled to marry me."

"Ha. Tell *that* to my father." She shrugged. "I might as well marry you. You seem a decent sort."

"Thank you?" he said wryly.

She continued. "I only wish I had more time. Unfortunately, Papa wishes for me to be betrothed already. There will be no delaying. If not you, it will be someone else by the week's end."

He sank down beside her. "And if you had more time, if there was no pressure or urgency . . . what would you do with it?"

She shrugged awkwardly. "Enjoy the season. Perhaps find someone who truly suits me. If not this season, then the next."

He nodded. "You should have more time. You're young. There should be no rush." He could not imagine ever hastening his daughter into marriage. He could scarcely even imagine handing her over to a man in marriage at all. He was in favor of putting that off for as long as possible.

"Would that Papa felt as you do."

"What of your mother?" he asked, attempting to sound casual.

"Oh, she would not force me to marry anyone. She wants it to be my choice. She said a woman should never be coerced and should enter into the decision with a fully agreeable mind and heart."

A smile played at the corners of his mouth. That sounded like Lady Chatham. He had not known her long, and yet he knew that about her already.

"Your mother sounds wise and kind."

"Oh, she is. The very best of mothers."

"What if there was a way to relieve yourself of your father's . . . pressure?"

She frowned slightly. "How could I do that?"

"Accept my courtship."

The panicked look returned to her eyes. "You said you had no wish to marry me."

"And I do not."

"I am sorry." She shook her head with an exasperated huff. "I do not understand."

"We can feign a courtship. For all the world it will appear we are romantically embroiled. You can take your ease and enjoy your season, safe in the knowledge that you will not be forced to wed anyone at the end of it. Certainly not me. This will give you more time in which to decide that for yourself. Your father will not pressure you—"

"Because he will believe we are courting," she finished.

"Yes."

She shook her head again. "You would do that for me? Why?"

Very good question. How could he tell her? The truth would scandalize her. It fairly scandalized *him*, and he had witnessed all manner of things spending his life at roadside inns. People committed acts of debauchery away from their homes . . . at coaching inns where they believed no one knew them. Anonymity was the great liberator.

"Tell me," she demanded, her gaze narrowing on him suspiciously.

Clearly she sought to know what was in this for him. He could not tell her, of course. Not when he did not rightly understand it himself.

"Suffice it to say it shall benefit me."

"How?" she pressed.

He opened and closed his mouth before finally arriving at,

"Like you, Lady Cordelia, I have my goals and wish for time to pursue them. I do not wish to be pressed on all sides as I move about my first season, too."

She smirked. "So we are alike, you and me?"

"It would seem so." He nodded slowly.

She studied him in silence, with keen eyes that reminded him a little of her mother's in that moment. "How do I know you are not lying? What if I go down this road with you and suddenly this fake courtship is no longer quite so pretend for you?"

"You mean what if I trick you?"

She gave a single nod.

He continued. "I will not. You have my word."

She still stared at him—hard.

He smiled in what he hoped appeared a coaxing manner and not at all threatening. "I realize I am a stranger and my word means little to you."

"You would be correct, sir."

He held out his arms at his sides. "I am harmless."

He was still met with her wary-eyed stare.

He continued. "What are your options, Lady Cordelia? Take me up on my proposition and we play at courtship for"—he shrugged—"a few weeks."

What are you doing? What are you promising? This would not be furthering his goal. A fake courtship with her meant he was courting no one else. *But you would be near her mother.* It was madness, but still he talked. Still he continued with this wild scheme taking form in his mind. "Or we end this now and we part ways. But you know as well as I do that your father will have you back on the Marriage Mart before the week is out and you will be betrothed before the season ends. He will pick someone else . . . someone who will not offer you a game of pretend. You will be a wife in truth before the year is out."

She blinked long, squeezing her eyes shut as though in pain, and then opened them as she nodded. "Yes. You are correct."

"I can offer you . . . the time you spoke of. A reprieve. What is it you decide, Lady Cordelia?"

"I would not mind a reprieve from the Marriage Mart. But what happens when our farce comes to an end? Would that not harm my reputation?"

"Not if you are the one to end it. We will make certain all of Society knows it is *you* rejecting *me*. That should raise you in the estimation of others."

After a moment's consideration, she lifted her chin. "I accept your kind offer, Mr. Thorne." She extended her hand. "We have an agreement."

He closed his fingers around hers and shook her hand. "Indeed, we do."

"I shall see you at Chatham House then."

He exhaled. "Yes." A country party, sleeping under the same roof as the countess. It was precisely what he wanted . . . and he was right mad for it.

Her eyes narrowed again as their hands slipped apart. "I confess, I am still suspicious of your motives. Do you not want a wife, Mr. Thorne? Is that not why you are here?" She motioned around them as though to encompass the entire city. "What does this agreement bring you?"

"In due time I will find a wife. For now, I will simply observe. Like you, this will grant me more time to decide what it is I want. *Whom* I want. Without pressure. Everyone will believe that I have settled on you, so all the mamas shall give me room to breathe." Even as he said the words, he realized they were not completely without merit.

"But you have not," she pressed sharply, still needing reassurance, wariness still shimmering in her eyes, "decided on me?"

"I promise." He bestowed an encouraging smile on her. "I have not decided on you."

I have decided on your mother.

Chapter 17

It is only a scandal if one cares about the opinions of others.
—Hazel, the Marchioness of Sutton

Tru could not abide it. Her daughter was out there. Alone with Jasper Thorne.

She knew just how seductive the man could be, and Delia was hardly accustomed to dealing with men of his ilk. Goodness, Tru was a woman grown and she struggled to contend with him.

Whilst Valencia played at the pianoforte—beautifully, as always—the Duke of Dedham's eyes drifted shut. No doubt the drink, laudanum, and whatever else he had consumed to cope with his constant discomfort had overcome him. His head fell back on the wingback chair and light snores rumbled from his throat.

The earl and Burton bent their heads together, lost in their conversation, oblivious to her where she sat. They were no doubt plotting which house of ill repute they would visit later this evening.

Her slippered foot tapped impatiently as she looked back and forth from her husband to the drawing room door, hoping Delia would soon stroll inside the room. She could not stomach it. Thorne was out there, in the night, with her daughter. Unchaperoned.

As moments slid into minutes, her anxiety grew. Simply contemplating what he might be saying or *doing* to her daughter made her teeth grind. She rocked a little where she sat, her fingers laced over her knees, and it had nothing to do with the lovely music emanating from the pianoforte. Tru knew the damage the man could do to one's senses. She was well familiar with the power, the impact he had . . . the temptation he could wreak.

She told herself it was concern. Fear for her daughter. Concern and fear and *not* jealousy. Not in the slightest. That would be wrong.

Enough was enough. Holding her breath, she eased up from her chair and moved stealthily to the door, heedful that she moved silently. At the door, she glanced over her shoulder, reassuring herself that no one noticed her departure.

The men were lost in their own world. Only Valencia watched her as she worked her fingers over the keys. Their gazes locked and held for a moment in silent communication. Valencia understood. She knew where Tru was going. With a parting nod for her, Tru slipped from the room.

Lifting her skirts, she hastened down the corridor.

She passed through the French doors onto the terrace. Leaves rustled in the wind. Her slippers rasped over the stone terrace as she hurried forward. At the balustrade, she wrapped her fingers around the top railing and peered out into the gardens. Chatham was correct. With the lamps and the moon overhead, the night was not lost to darkness. Peering around, her gaze rested on the burbling fountain with its silvery water.

"Mama?"

Tru whirled around. Delia and Thorne ascended onto the terrace from a side stair.

"Delia," she greeted, her gaze scanning her daughter in that scandalous gown that she was regretting adding to Delia's wardrobe. She looked her over from head to toe as though she could detect if anything untoward had happened to her out in the garden—whether this man had dared to touch her. "How was your stroll?"

"It was fine, Mama."

"Very good." She nodded, her gaze lifting to Thorne. He watched her in turn with an amused and faintly mocking expression on his face that served to make her feel ridiculous.

Of course he could read her mind and knew why she was waiting for them. *Of course* he knew she suspected he had inveigled her innocent daughter into doing something she was not comfortable doing.

"Your garden is lovely, Lady Chatham, but Cordelia informs

me that I will be quite impressed with the grounds at Chatham House." His deep voice rumbled on the air, stroking her like a physical touch. "I most look forward to your house party."

It was a distinct reminder that he would be joining them in the country. Distinct and . . . deliberate. He'd also been so bold as to address Delia by her Christian name. Tru had not missed that familiarity. She had not missed it . . . and she did not like it. It was simply another thing. One more point of aggravation.

"Ah. Yes. That." She motioned to the house, her hand cutting through the air. "Delia, if you would give me a moment with Mr. Thorne."

Enough of this nonsense. She would be putting an end to all of this directly. There would be no house party in the country with him. With anyone, for that matter. Once the earl realized Jasper Thorne would not be joining them, he would cancel it. They would stay in Town for the season like everyone else, amid all the many diversions.

Delia looked uncertainly between the two of them. "Very well. I will see you inside." She released Mr. Thorne's arm and started for the house.

Tru waited impatiently, watching her daughter disappear inside the house before it felt safe enough to turn and squarely face Thorne.

His gaze glinted devilishly. "You wanted me . . ."

He let the words hang between them, heavy with innuendo. *You wanted me . . .*

She blew out an exasperated breath. Of course he would be

inappropriate. He was a rake, unequivocally, and he reveled in it. He reveled in making her uncomfortable.

"A word with you, please." She nodded once, perfunctorily.

He set his features as though attempting seriousness. "A word. Very well. I am listening. Proceed."

She felt mocked. His eyes still taunted her, and she felt again that overwhelming urge to wipe the smug look off his face. It was unprecedented . . . this reaction she felt toward him. No one had ever provoked violence in her. She was always calm. Composed. Dignified. What was it about him that needled her?

She cast another glance toward the house, assuring herself that Delia was gone and they were truly alone.

She stood with him as before, alone on a terrace at night, the air alive and crackling between them. It was not a comfortable sensation and wholly new.

She shifted her weight on her feet as though that would serve to balance her. As though that would give her equanimity and she would not feel so discomposed around this man.

She had never experienced this before. Not even in her courtship with Chatham. There had been nerves, but nothing compared to the riotous butterflies waging war inside her stomach now. Quite truly . . . she felt one breath from casting up her accounts.

Was this attraction? That thing she heard other ladies titter on about . . . the racing hearts, the inability to breathe? She could do without it, thank you very kindly.

She was more determined than ever on rebuffing him, more

intent than ever to cast this man from Delia's life. Or most importantly . . . from her own life.

JASPER WAITED, WATCHING her.

The countess looked back to the doors through which her daughter disappeared, clearly requiring assurance that they were truly alone.

"She is gone. You may speak freely," he prompted, eager to hear what she had to say.

She was outraged. It vibrated off her body. Those luscious breasts quivered in her bodice, the creamy swells brimming above the neckline, drawing his gaze and making his mouth water. She was eager to vent her spleen on him, and for some reason he was eager, too.

He wanted her angry, he wanted hot emotion from her.

He did not care for that frigid creature she had been at dinner, speaking little, the fire in her eyes banked. If he had not already interacted with her at Madame Klara's séance, he would not be able to reconcile those two women as one and the same.

He wanted to see that woman again, the one he had met previously . . . and he would do whatever it took to draw her out of the shell where she hid.

"Have you no voice?" he prodded, stepping closer, circling her, pausing at her rigid back and letting his voice drift over her ear, rustling the fine burnished brown tendrils at her temple. "Or do you need your husband's permission to speak? Even when you're not in his company?"

He stopped directly in front of her.

Her eyes flashed, and he knew he'd struck a nerve. *Good.*

"You cannot want to do this," she announced, and her indignant voice gratified him.

Want.

The word conjured up all manner of thoughts and images . . . desires that had nothing to do with Lady Cordelia Chatham and everything to do with Lady Gertrude Chatham.

He angled his head and asked mildly, "I cannot want to pursue your daughter? Or I cannot want to join your house party in the country? Please be specific."

Her hands clenched into fists at her sides. "Both. I speak of both, sir."

He nodded slowly. "I see. Well, I have decided I want *both*. I will do both." He watched her face change varying shades of red as she digested that.

He was enjoying himself more than he should. He should not relish the fact that he provoked her. And yet he somehow suspected she needed this. She needed to be woken from her stupor of docility, shaken from her tedious and well-behaved life.

Her nostrils flared with her sharp inhales. Oh, she was in a fine temper. He could not help thinking she should direct some of this temper at her husband. The prig deserved her wrath. Then he quickly changed his mind at that thought. He would prefer she kept this fire between them alone and remained the frigid shell around that bastard. Chatham did not deserve to see her like this.

She shook her head. "It is of no account. My daughter will not have you." She smiled lightly, smug in this knowledge. "No matter what you say. No matter what my husband says. She has more sense—"

"It is done," he interrupted.

She stopped hard and blinked at that. "What do you mean?"

"She has agreed."

The color suddenly bled from her face, along with her earlier smugness. "I do not understand."

Oh. But she did. Or she at least had a general idea of his meaning. She simply did not like it.

"Cordelia has agreed to my suit."

"No."

"Yes."

She shook her head fiercely, her warm brown eyes widening. "I know my daughter. She did not even want to dine with you this evening. She would not have agreed to your suit—"

"She did." He shrugged. "What can I say? I must have charmed her."

The countess's mouth hung open at that. "You lie."

He stood taller, squaring his shoulders as though offended. "I assure you I do not."

She stared at him for a long moment, and in that time he read the precise instant she accepted he spoke the truth. Her shoulders slumped. "I don't understand this."

"I am sure you can if you try. If you recall, I have my . . . appeal."

The color returned to her cheeks in a flash. She indeed remembered. Which was all he wanted. He wanted her to remember. He wanted her to remember and to surrender herself to the feelings she would deny between them.

"What did you do to her?"

He held up his hands defensively. "Nothing."

She eyed him distrustfully. "You intend to do this," she whispered roughly, "despite . . ." Her voice faded.

"Despite what?"

"Despite what happened between us . . ." She waved a hand in the space between them.

He tsked. "But nothing happened between us." His gaze flickered over her, fastening on her mouth. "You declined my offer for a night together." He pronounced this last bit succinctly, tasting the words as he would like to thoroughly taste her. "Remember?"

She nodded jerkily.

He continued. "I suppose it's for the best now as I am courting your daughter. It would be perverse . . . to have the daughter when I already had the mother." He ended those outrageous words with a casual shrug.

She stabbed a finger toward him. "You shall not put a hand on Delia."

"The choice is hers. Perhaps she will be more accommodating than you. We shall see. Anything can happen at a house party."

"You wretch!" She surged forward, coming at him clumsily, her hands lifted like claws ready to tear him apart. If eyes could kill, hers would be slicing him into a million little pieces. A fierce dragon, ready to protect her young, and he was ready for her, for *this*. It had been his goal, after all, to rouse the little mouse, to set the Cold Countess on fire. He would take this dragon all day, every day.

He caught her wrists. She fell against him as she struggled to break her hands free. Her body instantly recoiled, arching away from him as though burned. She writhed, valiantly resisting contact with him, even using her feet.

Her slippers kicked at his shins, likely hurting her toes more than him. He backed her against the exterior wall of the house, away from the vantage of the windows.

"Oof." She glared up at him, ivy springing all around her head, snagging in her hair. "Release me."

"So you can attack me again?" He tsked.

"You deserve it!"

"So unladylike. What would your daughter think?"

Her chest heaved with fierce breath, and his gaze dropped to her impressive cleavage.

"Let her see," she hissed. "Then perhaps she will understand. Perhaps then she will see you for the unconscionable rake you are."

"You do not mean that."

Her chin jutted out. "I do."

"Oh, the unconscionable-rake part, yes. But you don't want her to see this." He pinned her hands to either side of her head, holding on to her wrists as he flattened himself against her, letting her breasts plump against his chest in a way that made his stomach muscles tighten and the blood rush to his cock. She released a breathy little gasp that fanned his lips. He swallowed and resisted closing the small gap between their faces and taking that tasty mouth in a kiss. "This would scandalize her. *You* would scandalize her."

"Me?" Her eyes grew round and luminous, glowing embers in the night. Despite the horror in her voice, a fair share of fascination gleamed there. Fascination and curiosity and hunger for more of what he was offering her.

"Yes. *You.*" His nose brushed her cheek, inhaling her sweet scent. "She would not even recognize you this way. All fire and wanton woman—"

Growling, she turned her face and attempted to bite him, her teeth snapping the air near his nose.

He didn't think. There was no restraint left in him. He reacted, turning his face in a blinding fast move. His mouth captured hers, seizing her lips, snapping teeth and all.

He kissed her hard, pushing them both deeper into the ivy covering the wall of the house.

He kissed her as he had longed to do since he first met her.

He kissed her as though he were a starving man and this was the last woman he would ever kiss, the last meal he would ever taste, the last drink he would ever swallow.

He kissed her as though this would be their last and only kiss . . . because he knew that was in all likelihood the truth.

Chapter 18

I am fortunate enough to be well acquainted with all of Polite Society. And I can tell you from experience . . . they are all dreadful.

—Valencia, the Duchess of Dedham

Tru did not bite him. She could. She most certainly *should*, but she did not.

Her lips stilled, a small startled cry escaping into his mouth. He drank the sound and took full advantage. Kissing her and kissing her and kissing her until she couldn't feel her lips anymore. He kissed her top lip. Then her bottom. He alternated . . . and suddenly his tongue was there, licking over the seam of her lips until she parted for him, opening up so that he could thrust inside her mouth in a smooth, easy glide that turned the blood in her veins to molten lava.

She was grateful for the wall at her back and his body at her front because she would not be able to stand against such sensual assault.

This was hardly her first kiss, but it seemed like it. She felt a novice, and in matters of passion she supposed she was.

She could not even recall previous kisses, and that was telling enough. Chatham had kissed her. In the beginning. Truthfully, he had never devoted much time to the act of kissing once they were married. He had always skipped to the finale. It—*he*—had been underwhelming to say the least.

There had never been *this*. No long, deep, blistering kisses that she felt to her very toes. No fusing of lips and tongue, where her mouth became its own entity—something that existed outside of herself, that pulsed and lived with its own desperate need.

She had been touched by only one man in her life and that was long ago. So long ago she could not remember anything about it except the certainty that it had happened. It had happened and it meant nothing. It had been quick and empty. Void of emotion. Nothingness.

This was not nothingness.

This was pleasure. Unbelievable pleasure. All of it astonishingly . . . *astonishing*. That it was happening at all. That it felt . . . that it *felt*. That *she* felt.

She was bombarded by sensations. His mouth was scalding. His hands fierce where they gripped her. She felt consumed, devoured. Undone.

She bit his mouth . . . and she wasn't certain where the impulse originated. Was it a wild bid for freedom? Or something *else* wild? Something feral and primitive that throbbed at her core?

He pulled back with a curse. Touching his lip gingerly, he glared at her with darkly brutal eyes.

Her breath fell in noisy blasts of air between them.

It was a fraught moment. She knew what she *should* do next.

She had bit him—stopped him. Now she should turn and flee from this wretched man who had kissed her as though it was his right. She should tell her husband—put an end to this and save her daughter in the process.

He had kissed her. Her chest lifted on another ragged breath. No man had dared such liberties with her before.

With a snarl, she rose on her tiptoes. One of her hands shot out, grabbing a fistful of his luxuriously dark hair. She dragged his head back down to her, planting her mouth on his once again.

She marveled that she could feel things everywhere when only their mouths melded. Every nerve ending was on fire, vibrating and singing and shooting sensation directly to the ache between her legs.

It was too much.

One of her hands was still pinned against the wall. Her fingers curled, lacing with his. Her nails dug into his skin . . . clinging to him rather than shoving him away.

He growled into her mouth and opened his hand wider, locking, fusing their palms together. Their hands, like their mouths, were bonded, and she relished every bit of it—the hard press of his length against her, the sink of him into her softness.

She whimpered into the ravaging suck and pull of his mouth. She felt eaten, devoured, consumed from a simple kiss. But there was nothing *simple* about it.

He bent, angling his head and venturing deeper with mouth, tongue, teeth . . .

She speared her fingers through his hair—tugging and pulling on those strands, wishing she could crawl inside him. She might lack the carnal experience, but instinct drove her and she knew what to do. He kissed her, and she kissed him back, her head lifting up off the ivy-covered wall, lunging for him, taking as well as receiving.

His mouth worked over hers, words vibrating against her tender lips. "I knew it would be like this with you . . ."

It was a splash of icy water, dousing the fire.

No. She pushed at his shoulders, severing the lock of their mouths. "This isn't going to be like *anything* with me because this is not going to *be*."

His hands flattened on the wall beside her head, penning her in . . . keeping her effectively caged. He looked down at her with infinitely dark eyes, the whites seemingly gone. "Why do you deny yourself—"

"Because I am not *this*," she hissed, her hand waving wildly in the small space between them.

His dark eyes crawled over her face and lower down her body.

"I think you are. You feel like it . . . You taste like it." His eyes dropped to her mouth again, and God save her, but she wanted to have him there again, for the delicious torment to continue. "I think you want to be this way. With me."

"Strange words coming from the man who seeks to court my daughter." He was a despicable man and she hated herself in this moment for enjoying his kisses.

Something passed over his features then. Something unreadable, but she felt a trickle of unease at the sight of it. He wanted to say it—whatever *it* was—but the words did not emerge. Whatever he thought he decided to keep from her.

Stepping back slowly, he gave her space.

She took advantage, moving several paces away from him, creating a respectable distance when nothing respectable existed between them.

Her hands still tingled from his touch and she rubbed where he had held her. "You cannot do this. Do not come to the country with us, I beg you."

He held her gaze for a long beat, and then came forward, his bigger body easily crowding her again. She swallowed her gasp, resisting shrinking away. She held her ground. She had to be strong and remember how dreadful he was. No more kisses.

He brushed a thumb over her swollen lips, and murmured with an idle air, "I like it when you beg. Your eyes turn so bright, so alive . . . and your mouth goes soft."

She moistened her lips, her tongue involuntarily brushing him. "Please. Don't."

He studied her lips as though mesmerized, still stroking the oversensitive skin. His stare turned scorching. "I cannot do that."

A rough breath escaped her and she didn't know if it was disappointment or relief.

His thumb dropped from her mouth. With a final look, he turned and strode from the terrace, leaving her alone, aching, her body humming, her lips tingling, her heart a hard-clenching fist in her chest.

What had she done?

TRU WAS A wicked, wicked, *wicked* creature. Without shame. Without conscience. Without any notion of how she was going to face Jasper Thorne again—especially in the company of others. How could she abide the sight of him with her daughter? One glimpse at her face and people would know.

Nausea churned her stomach and tears burned her eyes, blurring her vision as she stood alone on her terrace, pressing a hand to her middle and willing a return to herself, to the composed and dignified creature she knew herself to be.

For years she had held herself above the adulterers of the *ton*. She had prided herself on not being like Chatham, not being like any of them. And she was an arrogant fool. Not only had she kissed a man, she had kissed the man courting her daughter—and enjoyed it. What kind of person was she?

What kind of person was *he*?

After some moments, she felt collected enough to venture inside the house again. She had no choice. She was the Countess of Chatham. She must don her mask and face the world—Jasper Thorne included.

Breathe. Just breathe. She moved through the corridor on unsteady legs, grateful for skirts to hide her trembling limbs. She need only get through this night and then escape to her bedchamber, where she could scream into her pillow at the injustice of Jasper Thorne invading her life.

"Tru!"

At the sound of her name, she stopped and turned.

Valencia swiftly walked in her direction, her elegant skirts of blue silk shot with silver embroidery swishing at her ankles. It really was an exquisite creation—but all of Valencia's gowns were exquisite. She was a fashion icon among the *ton*. Whatever Valencia chose to wear, rest assured everyone else would be imitating it a sennight later.

Currently, her expression knitted in worry as she assessed Tru. "I've been looking for you. You did not return to the drawing room with Delia. And then Mr. Thorne was missing . . ." She pointed to her forehead. "Look at these lines. You're too much for my nerves. I'll become like Lady Newall with her smelling salts."

"Did Thorne return to the drawing room?" she quickly asked.

"Yes. That was when I came to find you." Valencia stopped before her, her gaze narrowing on Tru's face. "Is something amiss?"

"I . . . I'm well." She hoped, rather desperately, that she did not appear as though she had just been kissed senseless.

One of Valencia's dark eyebrows winged high. Apparently Tru

did not pass her keen-eyed inspection. "What has happened?" she demanded.

Tru shook her head fiercely. "I cannot—" Her voice choked in her throat, forcing her to stop.

Valencia looked around swiftly. Seizing hold of Tru's hands, she dragged her into the vacant music room nearby. Closing the door behind them, she whirled on Tru. "Tell me."

Her friend knew her too well.

She gulped, clearing her throat. "It has been decided. Chatham has decided. *He* wants it. Thorne will have my daughter, and for some reason she has not discouraged the man." She would have to get to the bottom of that once she had Delia alone. "In fact she has given Thorne every indication that she is amenable to his suit." She finished the words with a gaspy little breath.

"Tru. Could it be because she finds him attractive?" Valencia moistened her lips and spoke gently. "Is this so very terrible if it comes to pass?"

Tru's eyes widened. She felt an irrational stab of betrayal. "Yes! It is. It *is* terrible. Chatham cares not for our daughter's well-being. He only cares for his pocketbook."

"I will not dispute that. But Mr. Thorne does not seem so very villainous. He is handsome. Young and courteous." She winced and inclined her head. "At least on the surface. But is that not what we are only ever allowed to glimpse before we marry a man? What we see on the surface? How a gentleman presents himself is all we have to judge." She shrugged. "That being so, Mr. Thorne does not appear so very terrible."

Tru knew she spoke reasonably. She spoke from experience. Hers and Tru's. They chose their husbands because they had been trusting souls and they had been wooed by charming men. Because their families had encouraged the match. Because Society told them they would be mad not to. Because they thought they would have happy marriages.

Valencia continued. "At least she is not so misguided as to think she is in love with him. She is entering into this arrangement with her eyes open. That is more than either one of us can say. We thought we were marrying a pair of fairy-tale princes."

Tru winced and nodded. "You speak sensibly, but you do not know . . ." Her voice faded.

Valencia looked at her sharply. "What do I not know? If there is more, tell me."

Dare she say it? Even to Valencia?

On an exhale, she confessed, "I met Mr. Thorne before."

Valencia pulled back a little, squaring her shoulders as though bracing herself. "You did not mention that. When was this? Where did you meet him?"

"I met him at Madame Klara's séance." That night seemed so long ago and not mere days. That absurd séance where she was delivered that overdramatic warning. She *and* her friends, for that matter, all found themselves the recipients of vaguely ominous warnings. If Madame Klara was legitimate, why had she not forewarned of this? Of *him*? Jasper Thorne? Did his eruption into her life not warrant a warning?

"What? I did not notice . . ."

"When I went outside to escape Madame Klara. We had a conversation. We had words."

That was a delicate way of describing it.

"Why did you not say anything?"

She shrugged, twisting away slightly, unable to look at her friend in that moment, but Valencia was not having it. Her hands grasped Tru's shoulders and forced her to meet her gaze. Those keen eyes of hers scanned her features. "Did something *unseemly* happen between you and Mr. Thorne?"

"You could say that."

Valencia released a laugh, the sound a crack on the air. "All these years, Chatham cavorts with whomever he wants, but you remain steadfast. *Now* you decide to step outside your marriage . . . and it's with your daughter's beau?" Her friend made a hissing sound between her teeth that could have been awe or disapproval. Perhaps both. "You are a veritable scandal, Lady Gertrude."

"I am not," she denied hotly.

"Who would ever have guessed?"

Not me. "I did not plan for this. It was a mistake." A colossal one.

Valencia shook her head. "No one ever does."

"And I am not stepping outside my marriage. We just shared a kiss." A spectacular understatement, but she let that hang between them. "It won't happen again." Her eyes had been opened. He was a wretched man and she would not permit him to seduce her.

Valencia looked dubious at Tru's confession. "Will it not?"

"It will *not*," she insisted with an emphatic nod. "I told him to leave us alone, but he insists on joining us in the country."

"He kissed you," Valencia reminded, and Tru winced at that. "But he's courting your daughter. What is his game?" she mused.

"I do not know. I know only I have no intention of playing it."

"What will you do then?"

She thought about that for a moment and expelled a breath. She evidently could not get rid of Jasper Thorne herself, and Delia seemed unable to turn him away, for whatever reason.

"I have to go to Chatham." It was the only way. "I will convince him that a union between Delia and Thorne is not to his advantage, that Thorne is not the one for Delia."

"Because *you* are?"

She looked at her friend in horror. "No! I did not say that."

Valencia looked at her skeptically. "He is a handsome man and he clearly has eyes for you. It would not make you a bad person to find yourself attracted to him."

"Oh, but it would," she cut in, hardening her heart, refusing to let her friend soften her resistance with impossible words.

"Once he is turned off from Delia, perhaps you could engage in a dalliance with him. Perhaps then it would—"

"I would never . . ." She could not even finish the words. As far as she was concerned it would never be acceptable to dally with Jasper Thorne.

Valencia looked at her a little sadly then, shaking her head slowly, a fat ink-dark curl tossing lightly over the bare skin of her shoulder. “You have had so little joy in your life. It’s unfair. It should not be that way for you.”

It should not be that way for *either* of them. And yet Tru did not choose to wage that argument. Lamenting the unfairness of life would change nothing.

She lifted her chin. “I have my children.”

“They should not be your single joy. They will grow and claim their own lives, their own happiness, as is right. You should have yours independent from them. You deserve some happiness. Whether with Thorne or another man, what is the harm?” Valencia’s dark eyes searched her face.

She shook her head, denying that. Denying herself. “No.”

“I think perhaps you’re making a mistake.” Valencia’s dark eyes went soft as she uttered this, kind in a way only she could be, as someone who understood what it felt like to be bound unhappily to another person with no chance outside of death of ever becoming free.

“In this? How is that possible?” She shook her head with a small snort. There was no way she could accept Jasper Thorne into her life as a lover—even if he was not courting her daughter. She would not accept him or any man. And yet she must do whatever she could to distract him from his course. That would certainly require some creativity on her part. And perhaps some self-sacrifice, too. In the way mothers had happily been sacrificing for their children since the dawn of time.

Perhaps she would use his interest in her . . . and not resist him quite so much. For Delia's sake, of course.

She took a careful breath. "We should return to the drawing room."

Valencia snorted. "I doubt our husbands will miss us, but very well."

Arm in arm, they left the music room and marched down the corridor as friends, comrades . . . soldiers heading into battle.

—

Chapter 19

The marriage bed is always a messy business.
I am heartily glad to be done with it.
—Gertrude, the Countess of Chatham

Chatham and Lord Burton were gone when Tru and Valencia arrived in the drawing room. It was just the duke snoring lightly in his chair and Delia in conversation with Thorne near the fireplace.

"Mama," Delia greeted. "Papa and Lord Burton left for another engagement."

Of course they did.

"I see that." Tru imagined that the engagement involved gaming tables and fallen women and copious amounts of brandy. Their usual proclivities.

Valencia moved to her husband and gently shook him awake. He still bore a sickly pallor, but that was not unusual. She oft wondered if the duke's pallor was a consequence of the injury he suffered so many years ago or a result of the liberal amounts of spirits, laudanum, and other mystery tinctures he ingested.

"It is late," Tru announced, her gaze holding fast to Jasper Thorne. He watched her in turn, his dark gaze steady and much too perceptive. As though he knew all. She was rattled. Affected. Angry. *Furious*. Above all, she wanted him gone. He understood that quite well.

"Yes," Valencia agreed as her husband rose up from his chair, glassy-eyed, his back bent, moving like an old man instead of someone in the prime of his life. "We have much to do tomorrow to ready for our trip." She took Dedham's elbow, guiding him through the room, pausing to press a kiss to Tru's cheek on her way out. "We shall see you at Chatham House."

Then it was the three of them: Tru, Jasper Thorne, and Delia. The awkwardness was palpable as smoke on the air.

Delia cleared her throat. "I think I shall retire, too. Mr. Thorne." She faced him and executed a smart curtsey. Her daughter had very pretty manners, but in that moment Tru wished she did not. She wished she were anything other than appealing to this man so that he might quit this house . . . and quit the both of them. "I look forward to spending time with you in the country."

Tru donned a tight expression, hopefully masking the emotions churning through her.

Thorne took Delia's gloved hand and kissed the back of it. Tru bristled, loathing that, loathing the sight of him touching her. Her gaze tracked her daughter as she departed the room.

Then it was the two of them again. She had not imagined she would be alone with him, suffering his presence so soon.

"I will arrive the morning after tomorrow with my finest carriage. I am sure your daughter will find it very comfortable for the journey."

She had not even thought that far ahead. She had been struggling with the idea of being trapped with him at Chatham House. She had not even thought about the journey that would take them there.

"I wish you would not. We can get ourselves to Chatham House."

"I am certain your husband would prefer if I travel with you and your daughter."

Of course Chatham would prefer that. Their carriages had not been replaced or refurbished in years. Perhaps not since they had been married. They were quite shoddy. Chatham would want to pass the time en route upon the finest, most luxurious of squab seats. Oh, dear. And Thorne owned coaching inns. No doubt Chatham would wish to avail himself of Mr. Thorne's hospitality at his establishments. It was quite lowering to be married to such a leech.

Tru opened her mouth to plead with him again, and then remembered what he had said. *I like it when you beg.*

Her mouth closed with a snap. No. She would not do that again.

He approached and bowed before her much in the manner he had bowed before Delia, and she did not like that. She did not like to consider that he was doing any of the same things to her that he was going to do to her daughter. That led to a whole host of uncomfortable imaginings in her mind. "I will see you soon."

Why did that feel like a threat?

She watched as he left the room, not breathing fully until he was gone. Then she moved, collapsing in a nearby chair, covering her pounding heart with her palm and determining that she had much to do over the next day. Her lips still tingled . . . along with the rest of her. She felt alive, humming and vibrating, quivering from that kiss.

It would not make you a bad person to find yourself attracted to him. Valencia was wrong. It would indeed make her a bad person. She could not dally with her daughter's suitor . . . but another man? *What is the harm?* Perhaps Valencia was right on that score. Once she put this business behind her, it might be time for her to take a lover.

TRU HAD NEVER visited her husband's residence in Gresham Square before. It was a lively and busy area of the city, populated not only with homes but with fashionable shops, theaters, and playhouses. She had visited a well-esteemed gallery one block down just a sennight past. It felt a lifetime since she strolled those parquet floors and admired the sculptures and paintings.

She had never possessed the desire or brazenness to call on Chatham at his private residence before. She felt only relief that the earl pursued his own life away from her. Once it became clear that her husband was a faithless wretch, she was glad to be spared him.

It was a short carriage ride. A mere ten minutes, but it felt interminable as she thought ahead to the encounter to come.

She was well aware that at different times he kept a mistress with him. That alone was reason enough to stay away. Wives and mistresses should never intermingle. It was an unspoken rule known by all. She imagined that was for both their sakes. It seemed in poor taste to do so. And yet as she stared at the two-storied brick edifice, she knew the bigger reason she stayed away from Chatham was that she simply had no wish to be in his company. She had no desire or need to ever see him.

Until now.

For Delia's sake, she would do anything—even something as detestable as this.

After last night, she had to see him.

After breaking her fast and directing Hilda and Stella on what to pack for the country, she'd asked for a carriage to be brought around. It was precautionary. In case she failed and was unable to budge Chatham on the matter of this house party.

She prayed Hilda's and Stella's labors would be for naught, however. Hopefully, she would be able to reason with the earl and then she could set the lady's maids to the task of unpacking their luggage.

She didn't bother to knock. Her pride kept her from doing that. She was the Countess of Chatham. She might not be known to the staff, but she certainly would not knock on the door of her husband's residence. She strode inside the foyer, glancing about curiously as she tugged off her kid gloves, dropping them on the round table at the center of the foyer.

A gawking butler appeared, looking her up and down with a critical eye at her temerity to enter the house unbidden. Clearly he thought she was some tart come to put herself forward to the earl.

Before he could speak, she saved him from embarrassment and intercepted whatever insult he would have delivered unto her, saying with polite crispness, "Please inform the earl that his wife awaits him in the drawing room."

The man blinked, looking her over again with new measure. "Yes, my lady." He motioned her to the nearby drawing room doors. "If you would care to wait, I will alert him to your arrival."

Nodding with the same regal air she had seen her mother demonstrate over the years, she took herself to the drawing room. She remained standing, inspecting the room curiously. She wondered if her husband had managed the decor himself. She had never realized he was quite such a devotee of the color peach. The furniture, the gilt-framed art, the rug beneath her feet . . . Everything was in varying shades of peach.

She turned at the agitated shuffle of his steps. He was coming. She recognized his tread. She was almost surprised at how quickly her husband joined her. He was not an early riser. He usually slept well into the afternoon. Her arrival must have really confounded him.

"Gertie? Is it you?" he asked from the threshold, his thinning hair disheveled without its usual pomade. He peered at her in naught but his elegant dressing robe. Clearly they had roused him from bed to see her. "This is unexpected."

He did not wait for her response. Turning, he addressed the waiting butler. "Fetch me breakfast, Baxter. I'll eat in the drawing room whilst my wife tells me what brings her here at such an ungodly hour of the day when she undoubtedly knows I had a late night last night."

He strode deeper into the room and dropped unceremoniously on a sofa before the fireplace. Propping his elbow on the arm of the chair, he pressed two fingers to his temple as though enduring a headache . . . or boredom. Perhaps it was both. "Well? Explain yourself and why I should not be irate with you for rousing me. You overstep, wife, coming here."

She swallowed. "I am aware—"

"Are you?" He stretched his legs out in front of him. His robe parted a little wider, exposing a great deal of calves and thigh, which was more of her husband than she had ever seen—or wished to see. He looked her over with interest. "Are you aware? Because I would not wish to offend your matronly sensibilities with what you have walked into."

Since when had her husband ever cared about offending her sensibilities? She would have guessed that he went out of his way to do that very thing.

She began again. "I am aware that this is your house."

"Bloody right it is. It *is* my house, and I live here and do whatever I see fit beneath this roof."

She nodded once. "Yes."

Chatham pointed to the ceiling. "My mistress is in bed upstairs, sleeping off a rather vigorous evening. At any moment she could wake and venture downstairs looking for me, more than likely wearing very little garments. Fatima does not possess a great deal of modesty. I would hate for the *Cold Countess* to suffer affront."

From his unapologetic manner and the way he flung her moniker at her, she did not think he would hate that at all. She did not think he would care. More than likely he worried about offending his opera singer with the unwanted presence of his wife.

"I will stomach any . . . affront without complaint," she promised.

Of course, she had always known of his indiscretions, but he had never admitted to them so boldly before. She did not know that she could dislike him any more than she already did. She thought her dislike of him went just about as deep as it could run. Apparently she was mistaken.

He smiled. "My dear starchy prig of a wife, I doubt that." His smile slipped. "You should not have come."

"Rest assured I would not have felt compelled if it were not exceedingly important."

"Well, then. Have out with it, so that you might take your leave. I imagine you have a great deal to do before we depart tomorrow."

"It's about Jasper Thorne."

"Ah." The vague interest in his gaze dimmed then. He was officially bored. With a sigh, he rose to his feet and turned his attention to stirring the fire in the hearth, his robe flapping loose and dangerously close to the flames. "What about the man?"

"I think we must rule him out for Delia."

He whirled back around to face her. "We have already gone over this."

"I agreed to meet with him."

"And you have. You and Delia both did. You cannot possibly object. I know ladies find him attractive as they were all aflutter for him at the Lindley ball. He is no old man. I spared her that. Not to mention he is in possession of all his teeth. She will be the envy of all her friends. He will provide for her well beyond her dreams." She almost snorted at that. What did Chatham know of Delia's dreams? "What can conceivably be your complaint?"

The man kissed me and makes me uncomfortable in my very skin.

Chatham continued. "He will make a fine son-in-law."

Son-in-law? Perhaps she should have considered that, but she had not thought of him in those terms and the notion made her ill. If Thorne and Delia married, he would be her son-in-law. She swallowed back the surge of bile.

"Delia does not favor him and wishes to keep looking for someone more suitable."

"He is utterly suitable. And what do you mean she does not favor him?" He shook his head with a grunt. "She is fortunate, indeed, that she has me looking out for her. Daft-headed chit. Clearly she lacks sense."

"We should respect her wishes—"

"Rubbish."

A maid entered the room then, pushing a cart laden with food and a steaming pot of tea. Chatham eagerly returned to his seat on the sofa, allowing the maid to stop the cart before him and then snap a linen napkin free before draping it over his lap.

"Chatham?" a voice called.

Tru turned. A woman stood in the threshold and she knew instantly this was Fatima, if for no other reason than she wore a frilly dressing robe that did little to conceal her abundant curves. The robe was only loosely belted, revealing the plump swells of her impressive breasts.

"Ah, my dear." He invited her closer with a flick of his fingers. "Come join me for breakfast. I'm certain you've built an appetite."

The woman did not simply walk into the room, she moved with carnal prowess blatant in her every step.

Chatham nodded to Tru. "This is Gertie, my wife. Fatima, my dear, meet my countess."

Fatima inclined her head, seemingly unaffected at the presence of her lover's wife. "Lovely to make your acquaintance, my lady," she replied in a lyrical voice. She seated herself beside the earl, tossing her dark, lustrous hair over her shoulder. Studying her, Tru could detect only sincerity in the greeting.

Fatima began eating from Chatham's tray with sensual movements. The woman was not merely beautiful. She was mesmerizing. She ate a grape like she was making love to it, placing it on her tongue and then chewing slowly, savoring it. With an arched eyebrow, she pointed one elegant finger to a sweet bun, asking without words if Tru would like one.

Tru shook her head in refusal. "No, thank you."

Chatham joined Fatima, digging into the repast with gusto, feeding himself and allowing her to feed him as well. He did not bother to invite Tru to partake. Not that she would have. Even if she had not eaten yet, her stomach was rioting. She would not be able to stomach a morsel of food in this strange situation.

Deciding to ignore the fact that his mistress had joined them, Tru continued. "We should remain here in Town where Delia can circulate the Marriage Mart. Why should we isolate her from such a surfeit of eligible gentlemen?"

"It is *Thorne* I am isolating from other eligible girls."

"I am not so certain she can win him over with her present disinterest . . . and we will have wasted time better spent pursuing other opportunities."

At that, her husband stopped chewing. He stared hard at Tru before stabbing his fork several times in her direction. "That girl better not muck this up, you hear me?"

"That is not a guarantee I can make. As you said . . . he is a handsome man. Wealthy to boot. Who can say if he will even be interested in our Delia once they become better acquainted? She is a bit green and not the most sophisticated of young ladies." At this moment she would say anything about her daughter if it would dissuade her husband from this path.

"I say! I *say* because he *is* interested. We have already spoken.

We have an agreement, he and I. This courtship"—he spun his fork in a little circle in the air—"is merely a formality."

Her stomach bottomed out. "You act as though it is done. As though they are betrothed," she whispered.

"They may as well be. Now fall in line like a proper wife should and get our daughter into compliance. Remind her of her duty and tell her she may thank me for not saddling her with some hideous man."

She stared at him in silent entreaty even as she realized it would do no good. He returned his attention to cutting into his ham steak. Fatima watched her with mild interest, saying nothing as she popped another grape into her mouth.

He wanted her to be a proper wife? If he only knew how very improper she was. Sadly, even if she were to confess that to him, it probably would change nothing.

He wanted Thorne for his deep pockets. He was not looking out for his daughter's happiness or comfort. He certainly was not considering Tru's peace of mind. That meant the business of that fell to her. She alone would have to remedy this.

Chapter 20

There is nothing so tiresome as a debutante.
Except a debutante's mama.
—Gertrude, the Countess of Chatham

The carriages were every bit as comfortable as promised, and Tru was reminded again that Jasper Thorne was a very wealthy man. Not that she had ever forgotten that. Her husband would not have bothered with him otherwise, and they would not now be sitting in his opulent carriage. She would not have spent a sleepless night recounting the taste of him and attempting to invent ways to avoid hosting this house party.

"Gor!" Chatham's eyes boggled as he settled into the seat across from Tru, his hand roaming the rich upholstery like it was the body of a long-lost lover. "I say, Thorne, I've not seen so fine a conveyance. Is it French?"

Fine pashmina blankets sat folded on the seats, ready for

use—along with a carafe of lemon water and a basket of iced biscuits and tiny cakes. Delicately embroidered linens sat folded in the basket as well, just in case the bite-sized wonders left crumbs.

Chatham wasted no time indulging. He leaned across his seat and snatched up a few, popping them into his mouth one after another, grunting in approval.

It was the height of luxury, and she could not help feeling awe at the evidence of such opulence. Not only opulence, she realized . . . but courtesy. Humble, low-born beginnings or not, Jasper Thorne knew how to treat his guests well. He was a consummate host. Not even King George's royal mews could boast better.

She smoothed a hand over the mahogany panels with cream and gold inlay beside her head. It seemed too beautiful for a carriage. The walls belonged in the finest of parlors.

Mr. Thorne stood outside the carriage, peering in through the open door. "A Scotsman in Glasgow builds them. I ordered a pair of them."

"A Scotsman? You don't say?" Chatham dragged a hand over the sumptuous velvet squabs. They were well padded with extra springs for maximum comfort. A feature that would be much appreciated in the long journey ahead. "Who knew the Scots were good for something?"

She closed her eyes in forbearance. He really was a wretched man.

When she opened her eyes it was to find Mr. Thorne staring at her intently, as though he had not heard her husband at all. He gazed at her as though she were the sole focus of his existence, a meal to be devoured, and her chest tightened—her breasts suddenly swollen and aching and pushing at the edge of her sprigged muslin bodice.

She could not look away from those molten brown eyes of his if her life depended upon it. And perhaps it did in a manner. Her husband sat two feet across from her. It was most perplexing. Chatham cared nothing for her, but she could only imagine his rage if he were to learn that she and Thorne engaged in . . .

She could not even finish the thought.

Chatham was not the type of man to look the other way at his wife's indiscretions. At least in this instance he would not. He had chosen Thorne for Delia. He would be incensed and humiliated if he learned that Thorne was more interested in bedding his wife than his daughter.

She inhaled. And who was she to say Thorne was not interested in bedding Delia, too? That was a sobering and rather revolting thought. He was courting Delia with marriage in mind, after all. Perhaps he expected to bed them both? A wave of nausea overwhelmed her and she pressed a hand to her stomach, where her breakfast suddenly threatened to rebel.

She did not like the notion of that at all, but she would cling to it. It painted Thorne in the worst light, and as long as she kept that at the forefront of her mind, then she could not possibly find him attractive.

Her husband was still marveling over the fine carriage and not looking at either one of them, thankfully. He did not see the long look between them, nor did he feel the tension.

Mr. Thorne would not be riding with her. There was that, at least. It was already decided, and for the best. Close proximity to him for hours would not do well for her constitution. The risk was too great all around. What if Chatham detected that something existed between them?

"It really was kind of you to provide two carriages, Mr. Thorne," she said.

He inclined his head in acknowledgment. He was not wearing a hat and the morning sun lit his dark hair, turning it a glossy chestnut.

"He is courting us as well," Chatham chortled, and that gave her a jolt.

"Indeed," Mr. Thorne murmured, his gaze warm and feasting on her.

She shifted anxiously on the comfortable seat. How could Chatham be so oblivious to that look? She felt fairly stripped naked before his gaze, and all jesting aside she felt the truth of his agreement. His *indeed* rumbled through her like a growl of thunder under her skin. He was truly courting her, too. Well, perhaps not *courting*, but he was waging a campaign of seduction that was not without effect.

It was unconscionable.

What perverse manner of man was he to openly court her daughter and pursue her? He was a libertine. He ranked right up there with her husband as the most repugnant man she knew.

She was grateful to be spared sitting beside him on the journey north. Truly. There would be no charged looks. No accidental brushing of hands or legs. Except that left Thorne riding with Delia in the second carriage.

She would be worried if not for Rosalind. Her sister would be with them as a chaperone. There was that at least. Ros would just as soon smother him with one of those pashmina blankets if he dared to make an inappropriate advance on Delia.

Surprisingly, Chatham had made that decision. Tru had not realized he sent word to Rosalind, inviting her to join them, until she appeared bright and early this morning. Apparently even he realized there needed to be a semblance of propriety, and Rosalind would certainly be the one to see that no lines were crossed.

Rosalind's voice rang out impatiently from somewhere outside. "Are we leaving yet? I should like to reach Chatham House before the season ends!"

Tru's lips twitched.

Thorne's gaze lingered on Tru for a moment before he turned and called to her sister politely, "Indeed. Let us depart now, Miss Shawley."

At least her parents were not joining them. Mama insisted that Athena did not travel well in her advanced years. Whatever the case, it was a relief. Mama always had a way of looking right through Tru. There was no possibility she would *not* detect something awry between Thorne and Tru. Chatham might be oblivious, but her hawk-eyed mother would not be. Indeed not.

Another reason to put an end to this courtship. Mama must never see Tru in the vicinity of Jasper Thorne or she would know at once that they had shared . . . intimacies. She would take one look at Tru's face and instantly recognize that.

Thorne turned back to look at her sitting so cozily inside his sumptuous carriage. Not Chatham though. Chatham was still preoccupied, availing himself of the lemon water. No doubt all the drink and food would be gone before they ever left the city.

"Lady Chatham," Thorne murmured, reaching for her gloved hand. "I shall see you at the first stop when we change horses." Still watching her, he lowered his lips to the back of her gloved fingers. She ceased to breathe, watching him watch her with those liquid-dark eyes, watching his mouth descend and swearing that she could feel the singe of those lips through her fine kid glove.

She nodded rather dumbly, wondering why that should feel like an intimate promise and not a casual remark. *Yes.* He would see her at the next stop. It meant nothing, and yet she felt the dark promise of those words slither through her in a ribbon of heat.

Naturally she would be seeing him a great deal over the next few days until they reached Chatham House . . . and once they arrived there, she would see him even more because she would certainly be doing everything in her power to limit his time with Delia, even if that meant throwing herself in his path and providing herself as an obstacle.

There would be other guests and responsibilities to attend to, but she would neglect them. Her attention would be on him.

She swallowed the sudden boulder forming in her throat at that thought, seeing those scenarios in her mind, envisioning herself with him at every opportunity. It would not be easy: enduring him, resisting him . . . and yet subjecting herself to him so that her daughter would be spared. She would persuade him though, through whatever means necessary.

As the carriage door closed and started making its way from Grosvenor Square and out of the city, she settled back against the squabs and contemplated that and just how far she would go to save her daughter.

Was she so determined to lure him from her daughter that she would use her own dubious wiles on him? She had hours to ponder that and ask herself if that was truly such a sacrifice. Hours to wonder if perhaps it was no longer only about saving her daughter . . . and that perhaps a small part of it was also about pleasing herself.

THE TWO CARRIAGES traveled together, following each other north, deep into the Lake District, one after another, making a good pace along the well-traversed road. For all the beauty of Mr. Thorne's fancy carriages, they were lightweight and fast. The countryside moved past her window in a blur.

The rest of the guests were to depart London a day after them, giving them time to arrive first. Tru had sent a note to the housekeeper that they would be coming with a large group and to have all chambers readied, but she still needed to arrive earlier and make certain everything was in order.

As Tru had no hand in this country party, she was only informed of the guests en route. Chatham finally deigned to speak to her and share his plans then. There was little else to do in the enclosed space, after all, except talk.

Even so, such conversation lasted only an hour, but they covered all pertinent details related to the upcoming house party: what activities might entertain these guests, what they should feed them, who might be given which bedchamber. All was discussed and decided.

Aside from the Duke and Duchess of Dedham and the repellant Lord Burton joining them, Chatham had invited another dozen people. It would be quite the frolicsome gathering, with only the crème de la crème of Society in attendance. Titled blue bloods all, but none of them with marriageable daughters. Chatham had been mindful on that point. There would be no competition for Delia.

It would take four days to reach Chatham House, and Tru realized within the first hour that they might well be the longest four days of her life.

She was unaccustomed to spending so much time with her husband, and she was now acutely aware of what a blessing that had been all these years.

The first hour, whilst they talked, he ate and drank with gluttonous abandon . . . passing wind and belching, filling the space with such noxious fumes that she had to practically hang out the window. When he slumped to the side and dozed off, she was most grateful for it.

He slept most of the first day, not waking even during their stops until they called a halt for the night. When the carriages arrived in the yard, he woke with a noisy yawn. Of course he roused then, for it was the dinner hour.

He ate with gusto and stayed up all night, having slept all day. He kept to the taproom of Mr. Thorne's Harrowgate Arms, where he played cards with other patrons and flirted with the serving girls. Perhaps he more than flirted. She did not know. Tru kept to her room, getting a good night's sleep in order to continue the rest of the journey with a modicum of good-naturedness.

The following day and night passed in much the same manner.

They spent the nights at lodging houses all owned by Thorne, where they were treated like royalty and given the most comfortable of chambers with the most luxurious of beds and delicious food and exceedingly attentive servants.

"I could grow accustomed to this, Thorne," Chatham groaned as he dropped onto the squabs across from her on the third day of their trip.

Mr. Thorne had helped him inside the carriage, practically carrying him. Chatham still did not seem quite sober yet at dawn. She should feel embarrassed. Except she had long ago ceased to allow her husband's behavior to affect her. She could bear responsibility only for her own actions.

Thorne stood at the door. "And why is that, my lord?"

"I never knew spending my evenings in a coaching inn could be so enjoyable."

"Clearly you have been staying at the wrong coaching inns, my lord," Thorne amiably replied.

She rolled her eyes. More than likely the other coaching inns demanded he settle his account the following morning. That likely made all the difference.

Thorne did not fail to notice her expression. One corner of his mouth kicked up and he asked her, "And how are you enjoying my coaching inns, my lady?"

"Very comfortable, Mr. Thorne. Your staff has a keen eye for hospitality and attending to the comfort of guests."

He inclined his head in thanks. "I am sorry I cannot extend that hospitality to you for another night."

"No! No, no, no. The Harrowgate Arms is the only coaching inn for me." Chatham twirled a finger in the air rather ridiculously whilst reclined on his back on the bench seat. He was clearly still feeling the effects of his cups.

"We must depart the North Road and move west to reach Chatham House," Thorne said ever reasonably as though the earl did not already know this. "There is no Harrowgate Arms en route."

Chatham huffed, resembling a pouty child. "You clearly need more coaching inns."

Thorne chuckled. "I am working on that."

The earl shook his head. "Not soon enough, ol' boy. No other coaching inn will be good enough. We will be treated as—as—"

"As everyday mortals?" Tru supplied.

Thorne chuckled, and she tried not to preen because she had managed to amuse the man.

Chatham nodded, taking her question seriously. "Yes."

"Perhaps the innkeeper at the next inn will be keen to court our daughter, too, and then he will pamper your whims," she said unthinkingly.

A tense quiet fell.

Chatham appeared decidedly sober in that moment and decidedly unhappy with her. "Sarcasm does not suit you, *wife*." He muttered *wife* as though it were the foulest of titles.

Even Thorne looked unamused, staring at her almost reproachfully, the approval shining in his eyes moments before now gone. As though *she* had offended *him*. Men! She'd had enough of the lot of them. Enough of being forever at their whim and mercy.

With a huff, she turned and stared out the window, willing for Thorne to leave and for this carriage to get on its way.

Only one more day and she would be at Chatham House. Then she would not have to spend so much time in the company of her unbearable husband. She would have her own chamber to escape to when she needed refuge.

A sudden frown took her as she had a thought. She doubted they would be afforded their own rooms at the next inn as they had been these last two nights . . . but hopefully she would share a room with her sister and Delia and there would be no expectation of sharing a chamber with Chatham. A small shiver racked her. She simply could not do it. Sharing a carriage with him was bad enough. A bedchamber . . . a *bed*. Never. Never again.

Chatham curried Thorne's favor so much, and Thorne was so blasted determined to court Delia. The two men could share a chamber, if necessary. They could be bedmates. It would serve them both right to be stuck with one another without reprieve. At least that was the rather desperate plan she was devising in her mind.

She assuredly had nothing to fret. The earl would more than likely stay up all night playing cards in the taproom with other patrons. She doubted he would even bother coming to bed, even if they were forced to occupy the same room. It would be exactly as it had been the last two nights. Why wouldn't it?

Soon, she heard the carriage door click shut. Thorne's deep voice called up to the driver from outside and the vehicle rolled forward. They were on their way again and she determined to give this night's sleeping arrangements not another thought.

Chapter 21

If only husbands were like ballgowns—a new one for every occasion.

—Valencia, the Duchess of Dedham

They were a few more hours from their final stop for the night when they halted to change horses and take luncheon at a small village.

A groom helped Tru down from the carriage, and she was glad to stretch her legs about the yard. Her sister and Delia took themselves in search of the water closet whilst the gentlemen went inside to see about luncheon. Tru looked skyward, letting the sun kiss her face, enjoying its warming rays after being cooped up with Chatham.

"There is a wishing well, if you would care to see it, madame?"

Tru whirled to face a maid who was emerging from the inn.

She balanced a basket on her hip as she waved toward the rising hills beyond the inn.

A wishing well? Was there a sign about her neck that proclaimed her a superstitious fool? First the séance and now this. She started to shake her head, to deny interest in such a silly thing as a wishing well . . . and then she stopped herself. *Why not?* It was not such a poor idea. Why not take a stroll and view the countryside and this bit of local lore? She would not mind the fresh air, especially after being trapped in a conveyance all morning with Chatham.

She nodded agreeably. "Yes. That sounds a fine idea. Would you mind directing me the way?"

"Aye. Just follow me." The girl led her around the inn and behind the stables, pointing to a winding path that led through the trees. "Down the path. Straight that way. You can't miss it. It's a right lovely spot."

"Thank you." Lifting her skirts, she started down the path. She did not have far to travel before she reached the well. The girl was correct. It could not be missed. It was something out of a storybook with its mossy gray rock. Green ivy and flowers sprouted from the stone cracks. She stopped and peered down over the wide circular rim. An endless dark stared back at her.

"Not considering jumping, are you?"

At Jasper Thorne's voice, she turned and smiled slowly, reaching for her well-tested composure. "I do not wish to avoid you that much, Mr. Thorne."

"Ah. That is heartening news."

"Do not mistake me. That does not mean I like you or want you here."

He nodded and smiled. "Of course not."

"Why do you smile?" she demanded. She had insulted the man and he smiled at her? She did not understand him at all. Chatham would not react thusly. Not with a smile and not with such even temper.

Instead of answering her, he replied, "You *do* like me. I know it."

She could not find the words at first. She blinked at him in astonishment. "Your arrogance knows no bounds."

"Confidence is a virtue."

"Not in abundance."

Levity eased his handsome expression. "Ah, you do bring out the lightness in me."

"I do?" She blinked and tried not to let that go to her head . . . or her heart. She ought not to care that she did anything to please him.

He was a young, handsome man whose company was most coveted by the *ton*. Chatham was not the only one flocking to him, smiling and laughing at everything he said whether it was amusing or not.

"Quite so. You make me smile, Countess."

She stared at him in consternation, waiting for him to add that he was jesting with her. She was not amusing. She possessed no sparkling wit. She was merely a watcher, an onlooker, a player that maneuvered chess pieces on a grand board. She had long ceased to be one of those chess pieces herself. She was no longer in the game. No longer one to flirt or with whom *to* flirt.

"I should not make you smile. It is certainly not intentional." She gave an awkward laugh and looked down at the toes of her shoes for a moment before looking back up at him with, hopefully, more certainty than she felt. "I am quite dull, I assure you."

"Dull? Hardly. Charming is more like it."

Charming? She?

She was the serious one of her set, the mama bear, as Valencia liked to call her. She mediated. She offered direction and advice. She did not charm.

"No one would say that."

"No?"

"No." She nodded with certainty.

Perhaps it would not be that difficult to lure him away from Delia after all. Not if he found her so charming. It had seemed like a solid notion before—tossing herself at him so that she could spare her daughter. Faced with that scenario now, however, she felt a ball of nerves and misgivings.

His gaze crawled over her features. "Then perhaps they don't really see you," he said softly.

But he *did?*

She was breathless to know what else he might glimpse when he looked at her, but she would not ask. She would merely appear to be fishing for compliments, hungry for his approval. She did not need her ego fed. That was shallow. Not to mention unimportant and irrelevant.

"Because," he continued, "I have been accused of being somewhat taciturn in the past. And you do make me smile." He shrugged as though it were a simple test that she had passed, but what that test signified she could not fathom.

"You? Taciturn? I would never apply such an adjective to you."

His smile widened and she felt the allure of it deep in her bones. "I feel different when I'm around you, when I am with . . . you, Countess."

A strange fluttering started in her stomach.

"You make me feel different, too," she admitted, even though she dared not permit herself to feel that way. She glanced around at the peaceful calm of the rustling trees and verdant foliage, as though someone might overhear her confession. She knew she should not have said the words . . . *especially* because they were true. And yet he made her *feel*. It had been a long time since a man had done that—if ever.

She shook her head once, hard, as though that would jog some sense back into herself. *When I am with you*. That was not right. It could not happen. They could never be *with* each other. There was no chance, no opportunity in this world, in the whole of the universe, for them to be *with* each other. Such freedom, such *choice*, did not exist.

She looked around, over her shoulder, the worry creeping in that they should be seen, spotted together, and the wrong assumptions be made.

"What are you so afraid of?" he demanded.

"Is it not obvious?" she whispered.

"That you want me as much as I want you? That it will be good between us? Quite possibly better than good and—"

"Stop." She held up a hand. "Bite your tongue." She darted another glance over his shoulder down the path she took to reach the charming little well. "You must not say such things."

"Why not? We are alone."

She bit her lip and released it to mutter, "And we should not be."

He snorted. "No one would suspect anything amiss. You're not in need of a chaperone. They believe me here for Delia . . . not you."

"You *are* here for Delia," she insisted, her voice flying like a whip. "You are not here for me."

"Yes," he agreed mildly. "To all the world I am here for Delia."

To all the world. A strange way to phrase it.

"And your daughter—you are doing this for her, too," she reminded. "My daughter and *yours*."

He had confided as much, but perhaps he needed to hear the reminder of his motivation so he would cease to be out here with her, tempting her and driving her to distraction.

"Yes. Of course. My daughter, too." He nodded, resolve entering his deep gaze.

She cleared her thickening throat. "I don't believe you ever mentioned what happened to her mother."

The moment she asked, she regretted it. It was prying. Invasive.

A shutter fell over his eyes, a door slamming closed on the gleaming dark depths that had been open a moment before. His lips compressed, his jaw locking as a muscle ticked in his cheek.

"I am s-sorry," she mumbled. "I did not—"

"She is gone. Died in childbirth. Or rather . . . as a result. She lingered for a couple of miserable days."

"Oh." She swallowed at the halting declaration and squeezed her eyes in one tight blink. She had known he was likely a widower. Divorces and annulments were nigh on impossible. Or perhaps he never even married. She would not be so indelicate as to question the legitimacy of his daughter. Chatham certainly had not mentioned it, and she wondered if Chatham even knew. She didn't suppose it would matter to her husband. Daughters generally did not. Unless they carried an advantage.

"I am sorry," she whispered. "That must have been difficult." His daughter never knew her mother. She would be left with only the legacy of her death—and the grim knowledge that her mother's life ended so that hers could begin. It would be a burden, to be certain. "It still is, I am sure."

"It was ten years ago."

"I doubt the years have erased the pain."

"You assume much." He peered at her rather reproachfully, clearly resenting her prying. "Would you feel pain if your husband died on you?"

Heat flared in her face at the impertinent question. "You are not me," she quickly rejoined. "And you know nothing of my relationship with my husband."

"I know enough," he retorted. "I have eyes. I can see. I see you. I see him." His lip curled, indicating his distaste.

She shook her head and smiled humorlessly. "That's clever."

"What?"

"Distracting. Deflecting from the real conversation. We are talking about you, Mr. Thorne."

He sighed. "*You* are talking about me."

"Attempting to, yes. About your wife . . . er, your daughter's mother?"

He shrugged and an expression passed over his face that resembled a wince. "I was young and stupid . . . I did not know . . ."

"What did you not know? That bringing a child into the world could be dangerous? That some women do not survive it? How is that your fault?"

"I should have . . ." His voice faded and he expelled another breath, this one heavier, deeper.

"Sometimes bad things happen to good people. There is no reason for it. No fault. And your daughter is fortunate to have you."

He inhaled. "I'm not her mother though, am I?" He shook his head and dragged a hand through his hair. "A girl needs a mother. She's gone long enough without one."

And he was considering Delia to be his daughter's mother? That jarred her. It was much to absorb. Too much. Her daughter of eighteen years, who was scarcely a woman herself . . . could become this man's wife and mother to his young daughter?

She shook her head once as though to dispel the very notion, to cast it away from her in its intolerableness.

Of course her daughter could have children someday. More than likely. And Tru would be happy for her when that happened. But the idea of her becoming a mother overnight was passing strange. To this man's child? Married to Jasper Thorne, sharing his bed, raising his daughter as her own, and giving him more babes. It was too much to contemplate.

He continued. "My mother has done the best she can. She is a good grandmother, but she is getting on in years and she can't give Bettina all that she deserves. Nor does my mother know Society. She is not like you. And Bettina deserves more than a governess to care for her." His voice faded here.

She reached for his arm. She could not stop herself from touching him in that moment, giving encouragement to a matter that most gentlemen would not give a second thought. Most gentlemen had no trouble passing their daughters off to be raised by others.

He looked down at her hand on his arm. His gaze fixed for a long moment to that spot, as though a bug had landed there. Her hand flexed involuntarily over his forearm. It was spontaneous. She couldn't stop herself. Her fingers acted with a will of their own, needing, desiring the sensation of his tightening flesh bunching beneath her touch.

He lifted his gaze back to her, permitting her to glimpse the anguish there for a flash of a moment. It was just a glimpse but it went deep. She felt the echo of it inside herself.

"Your touch is a comfort, Countess."

She snatched her hand away and flushed. "Well. I suppose so. I am a mother, after all—"

"You're not *my* mother, Countess. And your touch on me is decidedly not *maternal*."

She folded her arms across her chest, tucking her hands to her sides as though she needed to restrain herself from touching him. She nodded toward the path. "We best go. They're likely waiting luncheon on us."

He stepped aside and motioned for her to precede him.

She moved ahead, taking long, unladylike strides down the path, eager to put him behind her. Would that she were able to put the memory of him behind her with equal ease.

Chapter 22

It does not matter what is. *It only matters how it looks.*

—Gertrude, the Countess of Chatham

This time Tru fell asleep before Chatham did, the rocking motion of the carriage getting the best of her. She recalled only watching her husband consume snacks and the carafe of whatever drink had been provided from the courteous staff of the Harrowgate Arms, marveling that the earl should be hungry so soon after taking luncheon, and then . . . nothing. She nodded off.

She was jolted awake by the sudden hard stop of the carriage. She fell forward, her face striking the edge of the seat across from her in a cruel return to reality. Her nose burned where it made contact with the squab and she furiously rubbed at the tip.

Unfortunately, reality would only become all the more cruel.

Chatham lurched to one window and then the next, peering

outside, leaning far enough that his shoulders hung out the window.

"What is it?" she asked, righting her skirts as she lifted herself back onto the seat. "Why have we stopped?" *And so suddenly?* "Is there something obstructing the road?"

The horses neighed wildly outside over the shouts of the driver. Hoofs stomped. Harnesses jangled.

Chatham dropped back inside, his face flushed, eyes panicked. "We must stay here. Do not reveal yourself." Her husband made a shushing sound, motioning to his own lips as though to quiet even himself.

"What is it?" she demanded.

"Quiet! 'Tis highwaymen."

Her stomach sank. *Dear. God.*

They both fell silent. She strained to hear, listening for any sounds over the horses' whinnies and the clink of harnesses.

A break in the silence came at last. "Stand and deliver!"

"Bloody fuck," Chatham cursed, his arms stretching wide, palms flattening on the inside walls of the carriage as though he could will himself somewhere else, as though he possessed the ability to disappear.

"Stay calm," she snapped, reaching for her reticule. "We shall give them our valuables and they will depart." She was shaking despite the calm of her words. "That is what they want."

"I'll not give such vermin *anything*." He tugged violently on his signet ring and wrenched his fob watch from his vest. "Here."

Before she knew what he was about, he was reaching for her and stuffed the objects down the front of her bodice.

"Ow!" she exclaimed, slapping at his hands.

"Cease your wiggling, you stupid woman." He reached for his pocketbook and slipped the few notes he had out of it. He lunged for her again and she dodged him.

"Enough!" She swiped a hand through the air when he moved to add them to her cleavage. "Hide them in your own undergarments. Do not use me!" She dug out his ring and fob watch and tossed them at him. The last thing she wanted was to be discovered hiding valuables from a bunch of brigands. She had no desire to anger them. Certainly not for Chatham's sake.

"Silence," he hissed as he fumbled to gather up his things and stuff them down his trousers.

She rolled her eyes. "What? You think they do not know we are here?" she snapped. "We cannot hide."

What was the fool thinking? They were two carriages traveling in tandem, one behind the other. There was no hiding.

Multiple shouts carried from outside the carriage. The highwaymen presumably, shouting and issuing instructions. She strained to hear, flinching when she thought she heard a woman's voice. It had to be Delia or Rosalind. More than likely her outspoken sister.

"It sounds as though they are at the other carriage," Chatham volunteered, mouthing more than speaking the words. "Perhaps we can slip away undetected and hide in the woods."

"The other carriage holds our daughter!" With a shake of her head, Tru reached for the latch.

The earl stopped her, covering her hand with his own, squeezing tightly to the point of pain. "What are you doing, you daft woman? Do not go out there!"

She wasn't hiding. She wasn't leaving her daughter and sister out there, or even Thorne, to the mercies of ruthless villains.

"They know we are in here, and our daughter is out there. She is defenseless!"

"She is not defenseless. She has Thorne and your sister. Your *sister*." He stared at her rather pointedly at that. "She is a terrifying creature, that one. They will likely kill her."

And that was meant to make her feel better?

"I will not remain here hiding with my tail tucked as God knows what befalls them." She fought against his grip, forcing the latch down and pushing open the door so that she stumbled out onto the road.

The masked ruffians were indeed at the other carriage. Her daughter, Rosalind, and Thorne stood outside, hands aloft before them in a gesture of submission.

One scoundrel waved his pistol about in a most reckless manner. It did not ease her mind to see that he stood much too close to Delia. That pistol could easily go off. Lifting her skirts, she hastened ahead, determined to put herself before her daughter, ready to protect her.

The blackguard caught sight of her—well, perhaps not sight.

Perhaps he perceived only the motion of her, the blur of movement as she hastened forward.

He swung his pistol wildly upward in her general direction, discharging it with a loud blast. The ball hit the carriage, sending a spray of splinters into the air, one striking her and slicing into her cheek. She scarcely registered the sting, still charging ahead over the shouts and chaos erupting all around her. Her heart pounded in her throat.

"Martin! Ye daft fool!" one of his cohorts cried out even as Thorne suddenly broke away from the group and flung himself on the man holding the pistol, bringing him down hard to the ground.

Cries went up as the two bodies thrashed in the dirt, wrestling for the pistol.

Tru reached her daughter's side, wrapping an arm about her shoulders even as she stared in dismay at the scene unfolding.

Three other scoundrels seized Jasper, tugging him off the man he attacked.

Thorne breathed raggedly, his hot gaze scouring the men before landing on Tru. Her chest tightened at his feral expression. With his arms restrained at his sides, he looked her over as though verifying for himself that she was unharmed.

Tru flexed her fingers against Delia and tucked her behind her. She glanced around, praying fervently help would come from somewhere.

The earl failed to emerge. He would not risk himself. Not for his daughter or wife or Jasper Thorne. Nor for honor's sake. The coachmen and groom came no closer either. Clearly there would be no help coming. From anywhere. They were well and truly stranded with these armed and dangerous men.

Martin, the one who'd fired the pistol, was now fully exposed. His mask had come askew when Thorne attacked him. He sniffled and wiped at his bloody nose, glaring balefully at Thorne.

Thorne paid the young man no mind, his gaze still pinned to her. "Are you hurt?" he demanded in a hard voice, his eyes frightening in their intensity.

She could only stare at his fearsome visage, her voice impossible to retrieve, stuck as it was somewhere in the vicinity of her feet.

"Woman," he barked. "Are you well?" He radiated power and command, even when restrained. She was not the only one to think so either. The brigands eyed him in wariness, clearly cognizant that he was no milksop to discount.

She jerked and nodded swiftly. "I—I am fine."

His gaze held fast to her face. "You bleed," he growled.

Her hand flew to her face, touching where her flesh stung. She pulled back her fingers to see them coated with blood.

Delia turned to look at her as well. "Mama! You are hurt! Were you shot?"

"*Mama?*" One of the brigands looked her over in astonishment. "She doesn't look like any mother I've ever seen."

"Aye," Martin chuckled. "I would swive that."

All the men sniggered at that. Except Thorne. He surged

against the hold of his captors, whether to reach her or have another go at the offender holding the pistol she could not say.

Tru stepped forward, letting her daughter fall into Rosalind's waiting hands. Hoping to dispel some of the intensity of the moment, she extended a reassuring hand to Thorne where he struggled to break free. "'Tis only a scratch, Mr. Thorne. The bullet did not reach me."

"See there! She is fine," one of the highwaymen proclaimed, waving a hand in her direction. "Hale and hearty. Ease yourself."

Thorne snapped his gaze to the man. "She *bleeds*."

The highwayman's jovial air faded a bit, his ruthless nature surfacing at last. He was a highwayman, after all. Kindness could not be expected. "She is well," he insisted. "Let it go lest you want this to become more than a simple matter of robbery."

"It already is no longer a simple matter." Mr. Thorne nodded at the man who would have shot her. "Your man Martin there nearly put a bullet through her."

"He would not do that."

"And yet his poor aim is the only reason that she lives."

At this, Martin surged forward, puffing out his chest, his face red with indignation. "I am not a poor shot. Shall I show you just how—"

The rest of his speech did not finish.

Thorne broke loose in that moment. He moved in a blur, striking the other man directly in the mouth, putting a stop to whatever bold words he would have spewed.

Everyone gasped as though struck collectively.

"You little whelp," Thorne growled. He struck him again, his fist punctuating his words. "You dare too much. I might have overlooked the indignity of a robbery, but never this." He jerked his head in her direction. "She bleeds. You think I should ignore that?"

Martin looked up at him, holding his bloodied nose, and whining in a nasally voice, "I should carve out your heart." He looked at his cohorts. "You're going to let him strike me? He cannot treat us like this!"

The other highwaymen all glanced at each other questioningly, none looking particularly moved to intercede.

"He has not put hands on *us*," one chimed. "Just you."

Another volunteered, "And you did nearly kill his woman and then talked about swiving her."

Tru blinked. *His woman*.

She opened her mouth to correct that misstatement and then thought better of it. This seemed a moment where it was best not to correct the scary criminals. She did not see Mr. Thorne jumping to do so.

"Uncle," Martin beseeched, looking at one of the marauders.

His uncle, presumably, shook his head in disgust. "Go wait by the horses," he snapped. "I'll deal with you later."

Martin stood and dusted himself off, shooting another glare to Thorne before tromping away.

"Apologies." The uncle addressed them with far more dignity than one might expect from a criminal. "Youth can be so . . . fractious."

Thorne grunted and then moved to stand before Tru. Her heart swelled. Blood pounded in her ears. Chatham cowered inside the other carriage, but here this man stood, gallantly protecting her and her kinswomen.

With slow movements, Thorne reached for his pocketbook inside his jacket and held it up. "I have several pounds here, more than you could earn in a week at an honest occupation. I offer this to you in exchange for you riding on and not accosting these ladies further."

The man considered him carefully over the edge of his face mask. "What's to stop me from taking that and anything else we want?" His gaze skipped over Thorne's shoulder, scanning Tru, Delia, and Rosalind. "We can search the ladies. I'm sure they possess valuables."

"It will serve you well to leave these ladies alone. Put even one finger on them, and I vow that I will spend my considerable resources hunting you down."

The highwaymen all looked to one another, hesitation suddenly rife in their movements.

Thorne continued. "I know young Martin's name. I've seen his face. It won't take long to locate him. And then I shall ferret out the identities of the rest of you within days."

Silence fell.

Thorne held the lead brigand's gaze, seemingly indifferent to the fact that multiple weapons were pointed at him.

The highwayman tipped his head to the side, considering Thorne's words, judging them for the threat they were. At last, he lifted his pistol, pointing it away, skyward. He took several easy steps forward and plucked the pocketbook from Thorne's hands. Still holding his gaze, he removed the notes from inside. "Very well."

Thorne inclined his head and accepted the return of his pocketbook.

"Have a care, sir, on the rest of your journey," the brigand advised. "These roads can be treacherous."

Rosalind snorted at that but held her tongue. Surprisingly.

They all stood, watching as the brigands turned and departed for their waiting mounts.

No one moved until they disappeared into the surrounding foliage.

"Well," Rosalind declared. "That was an adventure."

"I could do without such adventures." Tru released a breath.

Mr. Thorne faced her, his dark eyes angry. "Why did you leave your carriage?"

He sounded like Chatham! "Did you expect me to cower in the carriage whilst my daughter and sister were forced to endure those ruffians?"

"I expected you to keep yourself safe."

She shook her head. "Would you have remained in your carriage if *your* daughter had been outside in the company of highwaymen?"

Tension feathered his jaw. "That is not the same thing. I'm—"

"What? A man? A father?" she scoffed. "Spare me your prejudice."

He blinked, startled at her words.

She arched an eyebrow. "Am I to love less? Feel less? Because I'm a woman? Should I not seek to protect those I care about? My own child?" She scoffed.

He exhaled, his nostrils flaring as his gaze crawled over her face. "You confound me, woman." With a muttered expletive, he reached for her cheek. She flinched at the pressure of his touch on her stinging cut. "This could have been a bullet piercing your face," he growled, "and not a shard of wood."

She covered his hand with hers. "But it was not."

They stood like that, gazes locked, her hand covering his whilst his fingers caressed her cheek.

Gradually, she became aware of the others. Rosalind and Delia. She turned her face to find them watching her and Jasper Thorne with keen interest. She cleared her throat and stepped back, dropping her hand from Thorne.

"Is everyone unharmed?" she asked in a shaky voice.

"You seemed to have borne the worst of the damage, sister," Rosalind said with a tsk. "I hope you do not scar."

Thorne glanced back toward the tree line as though he wished nothing more than to give chase to the fleeing highwaymen and deliver upon them the thrashing of their lives.

"I am fine," she insisted, reaching for Thorne's hand and giving it a reassuring squeeze. "All is well. 'Tis only money they took."

He blinked at her, looking startled. "I don't give a bloody damn about the money. It's you I care about."

"Oh." It was her turn to blink in astonishment. Again, she was conscious of her sister and daughter watching, hanging on their every word avidly. "I am not harmed, Mr. Thorne. I'm alive and well and no worse for wear." She took a step back, hoping she appeared only circumspect.

A voice called out then: "Are they gone?"

They all turned as one to spot Chatham hanging from the window of the carriage.

"Yes, my lord," Rosalind called back. "No thanks to you."

"Then what are we waiting for?" He waved an arm. "Let us press on." He disappeared back inside the carriage.

The three of them all exchanged varying looks of disgust.

"I suppose we should do as he says." Rosalind lifted her skirts and started for the carriage. "No sense hanging about here, I suppose, waiting for those highwaymen to change their minds and return."

"They won't be back," Thorne announced, his mouth set in a grim line.

Delia looked wide-eyed between Tru and Thorne before following her aunt.

They stood together then, alone in the light of day, seeing each other as they had never looked before. Thorne with his mussed hair and wild eyes fresh from brawling. Tru, still unable to properly catch her breath, her face bleeding.

Thorne reached inside his jacket and fumbled a bit until he pulled out a handkerchief. Gently, he pressed it to her face, blotting at the wound to stanch the bleeding.

She did not move, did not so much as breathe under his tender ministrations. They stood so close that his body heat reached her, enveloping her. She felt connected to him, pulled closer as if by an invisible thread.

A light gleamed at the center of his eyes, a torch in the night that beckoned. Her lips parted on a small breathy sigh and she inhaled. His scent filled her nose.

"Are we going yet?" Chatham shouted from the window again, impatience rife in his voice. "What is the delay?"

She stepped back hastily, smoothing a trembling hand down her skirts as she inhaled a ragged breath. "We should return to the road."

Thorne did not appear affected in the least as he returned her stare. He nodded once, his lips compressed into a firm line that did nothing to detract from the splendor that was his mouth. Really, it was unfair. A man should not be in possession of lips so fine. She could study for hours his wide mouth, making a memory of that bottom lip, so full, and yet the top no less enticing with its sharp dip at the center. She could imagine kissing that mouth—*again*. Kissing him back. Spending time loving his mouth with her tongue, tracing and exploring that little dip.

She must have given something away. A look. A flicker in her eyes.

He clearly had an inkling of her thoughts, for his gaze deepened, sharpened on her, and his hand lifted at his side as though to touch her. "Tru," he whispered, and the familiarity of that—of all *this*—felt too much. She blinked, shook herself, and stepped away.

With a final lingering look at him, she turned and hastened to her waiting carriage.

Chapter 23

If you wish to test the true mettle of a gentleman, you need only place him in the path of a highwayman's pistol.

—Gertrude, the Countess of Chatham

The coaching inn where they were to spend the night was less than spectacular, but it was adequate. It would serve their needs, even if it was not as fine as Mr. Thorne's establishments, a point Chatham made certain to announce as soon as they arrived, standing in the foyer with his hands on his hips as he critically swept his gaze about the small space with narrow, quivering nostrils.

Tru still felt a little dazed from their roadside debacle. Her cheek had stopped bleeding, but she still felt the sting—both physically and emotionally.

Jasper Thorne had stuck his neck out for her in a way her own husband had not. Not that she expected anything remotely altruistic from the earl, but she had expected nothing so noble from Thorne. She felt shaken from it.

She could scarcely bring herself to look at him, too fretful that he might see something in her face that she did not wish him to see. Something beyond gratitude. Something like infatuation, adulation . . . longing.

The earl had already moved on, putting the day's events behind him. And why should he not? It had not quite been a debacle for him. He had not even come face-to-face with a highwayman, after all. No pistol had been pointed in his direction or waved in his face. Indeed not. He had been quite safe with his valuables tucked into his trousers for safekeeping.

Their group took a quiet dinner together in the taproom. There were a few other people, other patrons, boisterous and in high spirits as they dined at the nearby tables. Tru picked at her food, lacking her usual appetite, grateful when the meal was over and their plates were collected.

They were given separate rooms for the night. She suspected Thorne had something to do with that. He might not be the proprietor of this particular lodging house, but he seemed to speak the language—or perhaps his purse was simply hefty enough.

From the moment they arrived, they were well attended by staff, each escorted to their individual rooms and promptly delivered basins of water and soap to refresh themselves. Even the meal they were treated to was bountiful. Not the tastiest fare, but there was no lack of it.

Thorne might have emptied the notes from his pocketbook, but he clearly had money stashed elsewhere. She noticed him generously tipping staff members at various times throughout the evening. Never once did she see Chatham pay for anything, even though she knew the highwaymen had taken nothing from him.

In any event, she was grateful for the conclusion of their dinner. As usual, Chatham remained behind in the taproom, eager to settle into a game of cards with any willing patron.

Thorne disappeared with an excuse about seeing that his men were settled in for the night. Tru, Delia, and Rosalind took the stairs to their bedchambers.

"As comfortable as this journey has been I cannot wait to reach Chatham House tomorrow," Rosalind announced. "I will not miss the season at all. Perhaps we can stay away for the duration of it."

"I would not expect that," Tru murmured as they approached first Delia's room.

"And why not?" Rosalind asked. "You cannot mean to say you actually miss Town. I know how you hate the crowds."

That was true. She did hate the press of bodies, the din of people and parties, the endless routs and gatherings where she had to remind herself to breathe. But her daughter was out in Society now. There was no avoiding it.

"We will stay at least a week, I am sure." She shrugged. "Chatham certainly will not miss all of the season. He enjoys its amusements far too much." No doubt he would only stay away long enough to further his own ends and secure Delia as Thorne's betrothed. The notion sent a familiar surge of bile to her throat.

With murmured good nights, they each parted at their separate rooms, following Tru's instruction to bolt their doors.

Alone in her chamber she opened her valise and lifted out her nightclothes. She was exhausted. The day had been long and fraught. She should sleep hard and deep the instant her head touched the pillow.

And yet she did not move toward the solace of the bed. She could not even manage to undress herself yet. She paced the small space, stopping before the window and peering down into the yard.

She caught sight of Thorne leaving the stables, his long strides carrying him back in the direction of the inn. He wore a cape and the wind whipped it about his legs.

Before she knew quite what she was about, she was turning and hastening to the door, intent on intercepting him. To what purpose, she was not certain. To thank him for today? For being nothing like her husband? She shook her head. No. Comparing the two of them would achieve nothing. It would only breed disappointment and discontent in her heart and longing for what could never be. They were clearly different men. One honorable and one . . . well, one Chatham.

She had thought, or rather hoped, she could appeal to her husband and persuade him to end this courtship between Delia and Thorne, but that now struck her as foolish. She should have known better. The earl was self-serving. Stubborn and without empathy. Today left her with no doubt on this matter.

Clearly Thorne was the man to hear her appeals. She could beseech him and perhaps persuade him. Now more than ever she believed that. She *hoped* for that. He was honorable, capable of reason and compassion.

She stepped out into the dim corridor, looking up and down its length, searching for her quarry. Far down the corridor, in the direction of the stairs, it was dark and shadowy. Assuming he would soon emerge from the bottom floor, she started that way with cautious steps.

"You should not be walking these corridors alone late at night."

Gasping, she whipped around to find him, a looming wall behind her. She had not heard his approach.

"Coaching inns aren't known to house the most respectable and honorable of gentlemen," he added.

She supposed he, above all, would know that to be true, but it did not make her appreciate his advice. She was a woman full grown and unaccustomed to anyone telling her what to do. It was one of the advantages to finding herself neglected and overlooked by her husband—at least until recently.

She pressed a hand to her galloping heart. "You gave me a fright."

"Better me than an unsavory brigand."

She released a nervous laugh. "Indeed. I have been subjected to enough brigands for today, thank you very much."

"Then allow me to escort you to your chamber, where you may

no longer be at risk." He took her arm, not bothering to confirm if that was what she wanted.

"Must you always be so solicitous?" she snapped.

He released her, staring down at her in consternation, so blasted attractive with his deep gaze and his wind-tossed hair and imposing figure that smelled of the night air and something else. Something inherently male and potent.

She rubbed her arm where she could still feel the burning imprint of his touch. Not that he had grasped her very firmly. He had not, and yet that did not matter. His touch was like a brand. It was vexing. *He* was vexing. He was a good man, but not for her.

It was suddenly too much. Enduring his nearness, suffering his kindness, his protection, whilst the one man in her life who should seek to protect her would not weep over her corpse.

Why should she not wish for such a man to court her daughter? She shook her head in frustration. "Why must you be so . . . *you*?"

He blinked. "Now you have me completely confounded. Are you angry? With me?"

"Yes!" Yes. She was angry. Furious. Insensibly enraged. She had set out to appeal to him to abandon his suit of Delia, but now she could feel only the simmer of resentment in her blood.

"Why?"

"I did not ask for your protection. Or your stupid nobility. I do not need it. Nor do I want it!" She did not need these emotions . . . these *feelings* for him swelling inside her.

It was his turn now to look angry. His nostrils flared. His eyes glinted. "Am I simply not supposed to care?"

"About me?" She nodded doggedly. "Yes. You should not care. You should not give a bloody damn about me."

It was what she needed—what ought to be. She needed him to be as uncaring and heartless as her own husband. She needed this desperately. She needed him not to care so that she could in turn not care about him. So that she could hate him for her daughter and cast him from their lives in good faith.

"Well, too bad," he growled. "I give a bloody damn about you. Did you think I would do nothing today? Did you think that I would stand there and let you be accosted, let you be hurt . . . let those men look at you and talk to you in that manner . . ."

A lump of emotion welled up inside her. "Stop," she choked. "Stop saying these things." She felt the childlike compulsion to cover her ears.

His hot gaze scalded her, roaming her face, seeing past skin and bones, seeing everything beneath. Seeing all of her.

She shook her head. It could not be. She could not have this. She could not feel this way about *this* man. It was much too dangerous. *He* was much too dangerous. She no longer needed him out of her life for the sake of her daughter.

She needed him out of her life for *her* sake.

He is not here for you. He is here for Delia. Not you. Not you ever.

The mantra rolled over and over in her thoughts because it

was necessary. She needed to believe it. She needed it to influence her, to make her stop wanting him so very much.

She realized she had moved. So had he.

He had backed her against the wall of the corridor. He was fire, and she recoiled, desperate not to get burned.

He was chaos. Life. Vitality. So much raw power and energy fueling her, waking her from what felt like a decades-long dormancy.

She lifted her hands to push him away, her palms flattening on his impressive chest. And there she failed. There she halted. There she succumbed, surrendered, her palms absorbing the solid sensation of him.

Her fingers flexed, kneading into his chest like a purring cat. She was lost. She bit her lip, attempting to quell the whimper of yearning that rose up from her throat. She felt as much as she heard the growl emanating from him.

"You say these things you do not mean," he husked, his mouth so very close to her face that she could taste the hint of sweet whiskey on his breath.

She lifted her chin defiantly. "I say only what I mean." It was an unequivocal lie. But it was necessary. It was a lie to save herself.

"Oh?" He cocked a dark eyebrow. "You don't wish me to care? You don't want me to protect you should the need arise? You want me to be precisely like that weasel you are married to?"

A sob choked in her throat. And yet she continued to nod her head emphatically.

"Liar," he rasped, his dark eyes impossibly furious. "You want me to be like this, as I am. You need me to be this. You want me exactly this way."

She stopped nodding and shook her head now. Refusing. Rejecting. Her life depended upon convincing him he was wrong. Persuading him that this was wrong.

And yet her hands betrayed her, moving over his chest, feeling him, luxuriating in the sensation of his strong body beneath her hands. This strong body that would put itself in harm's way for her. Protect her. Care for her . . .

He was the greatest of aphrodisiacs. Just him. Only him. Himself. And her guilt was immense. But that did not stop her from wanting to lean into him, disappear inside him, absorb him fully until they could not be distinguished separately. It was madness. Nothing she had ever felt. Nothing she had ever thought possible.

"Why?" she whispered, at once miserable and elated. "Why are you doing this to me?"

He shook his head, looking down at her a little bit sadly, but with a great deal of bewilderment and regret. "I do not know. I know I should stop. I know it is not right. I know—"

She kissed him.

She kissed *him*. The distinction mattered.

Perhaps it was his regret—hearing him agree that he should stop, that he should step back from her, that he should end this and walk away. It filled her with such a bleak sense of loss that she could do nothing except drive her mouth into his.

He was everything she did not have, everything she never had.

In this fleeting moment, she would take it, revel in it, have it for herself. It would not last, so she would make this enough because it had to be. Because it would be all she ever had.

Her hands climbed up his chest and over his shoulders, her arms wrapping fully around him, mashing her breasts into him.

As though lit afire, his hands went everywhere, frenzied at her back, her hips, pulling her closer, grinding himself into her belly. The ache was unbearable. She felt him through the barrier of their clothes. That hard, swollen prod that pushed her over the edge.

His hands squeezed her derriere, then swept up along her shoulders, skimming her throat, diving into her hair. His fingers speared the thick locks, dislodging pins and scattering them, sending them falling to the floor like leaves in a storm.

Her hair tumbled loose and then he was grasping handfuls of it, clenching the unbound waves with a fierceness matched by the sudden pulse between her thighs. He bent her neck, angling her head for the deep thrust of his tongue, his ravaging lips bruising hers in the most consuming way.

The heat was searing. The passion debilitating. She could scarcely remain upright. If not for the wall at her back and his body at her front she would fall, collapse into a heap of silk and bones and flesh at his feet. *From dust . . . to dust.*

She should be afraid. Demoralized. But there was no fear.

No fear of falling. No fear of anything. It was as though her entire life had led to this one kiss.

She was certain, positive, seized with such clarity that upon the moment of her death this would be one of the images that burst across her mind, that told her that she had lived. That she *knew* life. That something meaningful had touched her.

Could a single moment make a life? She knew in this instant, in a blinding flash, that it could.

Chapter 24

There is no better place to start—or end—a romance than a country house party.

—Gertrude, the Countess of Chatham

She was kissing *him*.

It was the damnedest thing. The most spectacular thing. Even if she was not *his*, in this moment she was. In this moment Jasper could forget she was married . . . and that the world thought he was courting her daughter.

It was a fine mess, but a mess he was presently enjoying.

The lady pulled his hair in both fists as she stretched up on her toes, her lush mouth devouring his like he was her favorite sweetmeat.

His hands slipped down, grasping her ass through the folds of her gown, and he was rewarded with her moan in his mouth.

He had begun to worry he would never crack her shell. That

she would keep him at arm's length and hold him in disdain forevermore, and he was simply wasting his time feigning a courtship to someone he had no intention of taking to wife all simply to be near a woman who wanted nothing to do with him.

He kissed her back with equal fervor, releasing all his pent-up longing. His only regret was that they were in a corridor and not in a bed.

He cradled her head, his fingers lost in her wild mane of hair as he pushed her into the wall and consumed her mouth as though it fed him life-saving nectar.

She melted against him, her body every bit as pliant and sweetly yielding as he recalled. In the back of his mind he contemplated moving them, walking them somewhere else, relocating to someplace more comfortable, somewhere more conducive to what came next.

And yet he was loath to move, loath to stop, to put a pause on this magical thing happening between them even for a moment. They kissed and kissed and kissed.

It was inevitable, he supposed, that they would be discovered. They stood in the corridor of an inn. It was not even very late. Anyone could stumble upon them. And one did.

The sharp gasp did not immediately penetrate, but the loud clattering of dishes did.

They jumped apart.

A serving girl stood at the far end of the hall, her wide eyes riveted to them. "Begging your pardon. I did not mean to . . ." Her voice faded.

Jasper gave his head a small shake as though attempting to return to his senses.

The girl bent to retrieve the tray she had dropped, gathering up the dishes and crockery—many now broken.

Before he could say or do anything, Tru hurried forward to help her. He watched for a moment, marveling at that. His countess was not too good to help a humble servant girl and he liked her—wanted her—all the more for it.

"Oh no, madame. I can do this." The girl darted a nervous glance Jasper's way as though fearing reprisal from him for the interruption. "I do not want to bother you."

"'Tis no bother."

Once the girl had returned everything to the tray, she stood and made a hasty retreat.

Once again Jasper was alone with the woman who had become his sole fixation. It truly was a bitter and unpalatable thing. She belonged to another. Someone unworthy and undeserving of her, but that did not change the fact that she could never be his. Anything he had with her, anything she gave him, anything he took, would be stolen.

She watched the serving girl flee. Hands clasped before her, she turned to face him with all the dignity of a queen. The Cold Countess had returned. Not the passionate, feral hellcat who kissed him only moments before.

He let loose a small sigh, sorry to see her go, wondering what it would take to get her back, and suspecting it would not be this night.

She stared at him with cold reserve in her cognac eyes. "You need to call this off. End it. Return to London."

He did not need her to explain her meaning. "You expect me to simply go? What about the house party?"

A flash of hope crossed her features and he felt a ripple of disappointment. She thought him relenting and considering her command.

She spoke quickly, hurriedly, as though fearing he might change his mind and she needed to get ahead of that possibility. "I will make your excuses. It won't matter. No one will be offended . . ." She stopped abruptly and made a small snorting sound. "Even if you were to offend, why should you care?"

Her advice was sound. It was a mad scheme, this charade he was playing with young Delia. He could simply leave and put an end to it all.

She shook her head. "Why are you doing this? Chatham is just using you because of your deep pockets."

He pressed his hand to his heart in mock exaggeration. "You don't say? You mean to tell me that I am not the man the haughty members of the *ton* envisioned for their precious daughters?" He shook his head with a rough laugh. "I am fully aware that the wife I marry will have been one bought."

She flinched. "And that does not bother you? You don't strike me as the manner of man agreeable to such a marriage."

He shrugged. "Are you really one to lecture me on the state of matrimony? How fares *your* union?" The words escaped him before he could think better of it.

Her spine shot ramrod straight and he knew he had lost her then. Her walls went up. Her armor back in place. Whatever softness, whatever hunger, he had inspired in this woman vanished.

"Good night, Mr. Thorne."

"Jasper." He angled his head, staring at her intently. "I think we are well beyond the point of formality, Tru."

Her chest lifted on a swift inhalation. There was no mistaking her scorn for him in that moment. Perhaps, however, there was even some scorn reserved for herself. "Good night, Mr. Thorne."

CHATHAM HOUSE WAS everything he expected the country seat of an earldom to be. A sprawling stone and brick monstrosity replete with duck ponds, a maze-like hedge garden, and an impressive lake dotted with swans that looked like something out of a storybook.

The place was more like a castle than a house and it served as a reminder of why he was even bothering to enter Good Society. It was the kind of home he wanted for his daughter. This was what Bettina deserved, what he had promised her mother he would get for her. Only the very best. Nothing less.

On the afternoon of their arrival his countess disappeared. *His* countess. *His.* He knew that was inaccurate. She could never be his, but in his mind she was. He could not look at her, could not think of her without the word *mine* burning through him. She was a contagion, a poison in his blood for which there was no cure.

He knew she was caught up in preparations for the impending party. The house was a whirlwind. Staff buzzing around. Guests were scheduled to arrive on the morrow, but her avoidance felt a deliberate move on her part. A definite choice.

She was dodging him.

After their last encounter, after he flung in her face the fact that her marriage was less than admirable and far, far less than ideal, he could not blame her.

Unfortunately that left him almost exclusively in the company of Delia with her aunt serving as a chaperone, dogging their heels everywhere. Tru's sister might be of like age to him, but she was a veritable dragon, as vigilant as any old dame. She watched him with distrust and a certain *knowing* in her gaze that prickled his skin, and he could not help wondering if she could see inside him, into his very thoughts. If she somehow knew the truth—that he was here for Tru and not Delia at all.

It was not the situation he had envisioned when he agreed to this house party. He had done this to get closer to Tru. A miscalculation. Clearly that was not happening. Clearly he'd erred, not estimating how complicated and messy matters would become the more embroiled he became with the countess. He'd not felt this before . . . this infatuation. *Infatuation.* For that was all it could be.

When the guests arrived the following day, Tru finally surfaced, forced to play hostess publicly, all the while avoiding his eyes.

Over dinner that very night, seated at a table large enough to accommodate thirty, she charmed and chatted and laughed gaily and saw that everyone was replete and satiated with fine food and drink.

She was the consummate host, fulfilling her role whilst giving him no acknowledgment. It was the height of subtlety. No one else would notice except perhaps that shrewd-eyed sister of hers.

After dinner the party moved itself into what was called the Little Ballroom. A group of musicians waited there, local talent acquired from the neighboring village.

The earl led off the dancing with his daughter, stopping halfway through the merry reel to hand her off to Jasper.

The rest of the evening passed in a blur. He danced with Delia and a few other ladies. The Duchess of Dedham, the Marchioness of Sutton, and Mrs. Bernard-Hill—it was a chore not to become mesmerized by that lady's sparkly silver wig. Then Delia again. The girl always seemed to end up in his arms. Definitely not a coincidence. The earl was behind each of those maneuvers, to be certain.

He bided his time, never not aware of where the countess was in the room at all times. When he saw his moment, he took it, cutting a direct line across the room.

With a slight bow, he asked, "Lady Chatham?" Straightening, he motioned to the parquet dance floor.

She hesitated and he knew she was contemplating how to decline. How might she avoid dancing with him without attracting attention? He had trapped her. There was no way for her to refuse him without raising eyebrows and well she knew it. With a stiff nod she accepted his hand and joined him on the dance floor.

He had deliberately chosen a country waltz for their dance. Any excuse to hold her in his arms again.

She moved like a dream. Natural and graceful. She was created for this. For him. They moved together like they were meant for each other.

"You have been avoiding me, Countess." He wore a mild smile as he said the words, so that anyone watching them would think they did nothing more than exchange polite conversation. And yet as he looked over her head, he realized that might not be working. Miss Shawley watched them, and she wasn't the only one. There were others standing beside her sister. The Duchess of Dedham, the Marchioness of Sutton, and Mrs. Bernard-Hill. Something akin to speculation gleamed in their eyes.

"I have been preoccupied. There's much involved with hosting a country party."

"I have no doubt. And yet you *are* avoiding me."

The skin around her eyes seemed to tighten. "No."

"You would not be dancing with me if you did not have to be."

The smile on her face turned as brittle as glass. "You are here for my daughter. I've asked you to stop, to end this courtship . . . to leave, but here you are."

"Here I am," he agreed. But not for her daughter. For her.

As though she heard his thoughts, her gaze lifted from where it had been scanning the room, over her guests. Her eyes locked with his, and he saw something there in those melting depths. A softness. A longing. A heat. It was the thing that held him here, bound him to her, made him forget that his purpose was to find a wife.

"Feel free to leave at any time," she murmured even as those damn eyes of hers belied her words, even as her fingers increased their pressure on his shoulder.

"Oh, I am not going anywhere," he vowed.

The music slowed, the waltz coming to an end. He stopped. So did she. Their hands fell away from each other.

He bowed very correctly before her even as everything that burned through his mind was decidedly incorrect. This. Him. *Them*. What he felt and wanted was wrong, but that did not mean he could stop wanting it. Wanting *her*.

Her soft brown eyes gleamed with challenge. Words passed between them, unspoken and yet no less heard.

It was time, he realized. It was time he told her he was here for her and no other reason.

Mrs. Bernard-Hill, with her improbable silvery wig, suddenly approached, quivering with excitement. "Oh, Gertrude, dear!" She shot Jasper a coy smile. "I just learned you were set upon by brigands! How terrifying that must have been!"

Tru sent him a wry glance. "We are grateful to emerge unscathed, Maeve."

The woman waved her hand as though their safety was irrelevant. "The brigands though! I imagine they were something straight out of one of Mrs. Radcliffe's novels. Come, you must tell me everything."

She tugged Tru off the dance floor. He followed at a slower pace, knowing he should find Delia and alert her that he intended to let her mother know that their courtship was a farce, but he was intercepted by the lady who sat across from him at dinner tonight.

"Mr. Thorne." She seized his arm, brushing her impressive bosom against his sleeve. "My patience is at an end. I've been waiting for you to ask me to dance all evening. Is it not yet my turn?"

He smiled politely. "It is, of course, Lady Ashbourne." He was not certain who, at that point, guided whom back to the dance floor, but soon he was caught up in yet another waltz.

Chapter 25

I am convinced that most rakes secretly crave a wife to tell them what to do.
—Maeve, Mrs. Bernard-Hill

The waltz ended and Valencia permitted Lord Burton to escort her back to where her friends stood at the edge of the dance floor.

"Thank you, Your Grace." Burton bowed over her hand, permitting his lips to brush the back of her gloved hand in a lingering caress that was decidedly *im*proper. She wore gloves, but she thought she felt the graze of his tongue against the back of her hand.

She snatched her fingers free of his, tucking it into the folds of her skirts as though that would wipe it clean.

When Burton lifted his gaze, his eyes possessed a devilish

taunt that matched the wickedness of his earlier proposition. The man was incorrigible. Naturally. He was a close friend of Chatham, after all. Tru's husband would only consort with gentlemen as debauched as he.

It was not the first time the man had propositioned Valencia. It was, however, the first time he had done so whilst her husband was beneath the same roof. She supposed that signified how unthreatening he found her husband. Not surprising, she supposed. The duke looked ready to expire.

Her cheeks warmed as she recalled Burton's flirtatious remarks. He was not *un*attractive. She would be lying to herself if she claimed indifference. It was nice to know a man appreciated her—even if it was a libertine like Burton. And yet she would be lying even further if she pretended that his advances were something she could ever entertain. Other ladies were free to take ballroom flirtations to the next stage. She was not. Unlike Burton, she found her husband very threatening.

"May I fetch you a drink?" Burton asked, clearly not ready to quit her company.

"That would be lovely." Anything to have a respite from the man. At least Dedham had retired for the night. The journey here had taken its toll. He'd consumed more than his usual dose of whiskey . . . of *both* laudanum and whiskey.

Burton inclined his head and turned on his heels for the refreshment table. She watched his retreat, studying the back of him. He cut a handsome figure, but it did not matter. Even though his interest was evident, it did not matter. She and the duke did not have the manner of marriage where they took lovers. Not before the accident and certainly not after.

She might not have shared her husband's bed in years, but he had not shared the bed of anyone else either. His condition precluded him from enjoying such activities. His condition precluded him from enjoying . . . anything. The good-natured man she had married died when he was thrown from his horse. The fiend she lived with now had taken his place.

She looked away from Burton with deliberation, reminding herself that if she were ever to risk the considerable wrath of her husband and take a lover . . . it would not be for the likes of Burton. Even if she found him appealing enough to take the risk, the man would make sure everyone knew of their affair. There were men who loved to boast of their conquests, and he was one such man. She was smarter than that.

With a sniff, she smiled at her friends, bestowing on them her full attention. She did not need anyone to think she was interested in Burton and carry such a tale to her husband. She had no wish to further aggravate Dedham. He was far too easily provoked.

It was not that Dedham was jealous of her because he loved her. Indeed not. He was jealous that she lived a life free of pain, that she enjoyed herself in a way he no longer could . . . that she might find someone to give her the happiness he could no longer claim for himself.

As though the thought of Dedham had conjured him, Rosalind sent an elbow swiftly to her side. "Val? Your husband is over there."

She shook her head and sent Rosalind a hushing smile. No. It could not be. He had scarcely been in a fit condition at dinner. Simply sinking down in his chair had pained him. He had retired to bed as soon as dinner ended. She had accompanied him, making certain he was settled as comfortably as possible for the night. He would assuredly not leave the comfort of his bedchamber and rejoin them for dancing. The pain of these last few days' travel had been too intense. Her last glimpse had been of him lost in a deep laudanum-induced sleep.

He had met with many a physician, and they had all said the same thing. It was a miracle he still lived after being thrown from his horse. Witnesses said it was over twenty feet. It appeared he had landed oddly, very nearly on his head. Not only was it miraculous he lived, it was a marvel that he could still walk at all.

He lived. He walked. And his every breath was an agony.

After the accident, the surgeon who tended to Dedham had warned him to be cautious and to not over-imbibe on the laudanum, but her husband had long since stopped heeding that advice. As his pain increased, so did his reliance on anything to mitigate the pain.

Maeve inched closer to Valencia, a worrisome expression on her face. "Valencia," she said quietly. "It is true. Your husband is here and he looks quite cross."

A cold wind rushed over her skin. Valencia quickly turned and scanned the room, searching despite her doubts.

She spotted him across the room, looking back at her with displeasure sharp in his gaze. Maeve had not exaggerated. Cross, indeed.

Somehow he had roused himself. Disquiet beset her. She knew that look. Had he seen her dancing with Burton? He could not have heard their exchange. He could not know the man had propositioned her.

That did not mean he would not suspect, of course. He suspected her of everything. Ever since he took to his bed, he distrusted her and often accused her of infidelity.

His eyes blazed at her, hot with disapproval and hungry for retribution . . . all beneath the glaze of his usual pain, of course.

She had done nothing wrong, but that did not stop him from finding fault with her. Her simple existence seemed to infuriate him. If she should look happy or to be enjoying herself . . . that made things all the more difficult for her.

It was strange to think he had once loved her, that he had ever teased her and treated her with kindness and courtesy. It had been a lesson, to be sure. She would never trust her heart again. People changed. Fortunes changed. Affection . . . *love* could be lost—could vanish far quicker than it arrived.

What was he doing here? She was shocked that he was even well enough to stand, much less stroll through a ballroom on the strength of his own two feet. She had not thought him capable of leaving his bedchamber.

She had worried the cost of this journey would be too high. The pain of it would plague him for days, likely the entire week of this house party, but he had been insistent on attending. He was stubborn that way, refusing to accept that he was not the same virile man he once was.

"Yes." She exhaled a shuddering breath, adding unnecessarily, "It is Dedham."

"Should he not be abed?"

She understood why Rosalind would ask the question. He did not look himself. He was wan. Gaunt. Lines bracketed his mouth, cutting deeply into his cheeks. She knew this pitiable sight of him, but the others did not.

"Oh, heavens." Tru approached, looking to her in concern. "Should he be here? He looks as though he ought to be in bed."

She sighed. *Try telling him that.*

"Oh. He must be feeling well. He looks . . . better than the last time I saw him," Rosalind kindly lied even as her expression revealed she did not think the duke looked well at all. Indeed not. In fact, he looked close to death.

The group fell into an awkward silence as they watched the Duke of Dedham maneuver his way through the ballroom in a less-than-steady line.

Despite the torment he oft inflicted on her, she felt a stab of pity. She knew why he was doing this. It was his valiant attempt to keep claim on his life, to be himself again . . . even if that version of himself had vanished years ago.

"I thought you put him to bed," Tru murmured.

She nodded. "As did I."

"Well, it is good to see him out and about," Maeve cheerfully, *ridiculously*, inserted. A brief grimace twisted her features before she masked it. She was well meaning. Always well meaning, and tonight, unfortunately, that grated.

No good would come of this. Even across the distance, Valencia could read the tension lines in his face. His pain was great, but he battled it. This little excursion would cost him.

And, as always, she would be the one to pay the price.

His gaze locked with hers, and she saw at once that he had not forgotten his anger. It still burned bright in his eyes.

It burned for her.

TRU HID HER frown behind her glass, drinking deeply as she gazed out at the half dozen couples on the dance floor. Jasper Thorne had moved on from Delia and was now dancing with Lady Ashbourne.

Truthfully, she would prefer to see him dancing with Delia rather than that particular lady. Lady Ashbourne was a beautiful woman. Her husband ran in Chatham's set, which meant he was as vile as Chatham. His wife boasted her own similarly lascivious proclivities as well. Wherever she went, she had a retinue of young bucks trailing after her, enraptured of her flawless skin and blue eyes that seemed to taunt and promise untold wicked delights.

Lady Ashbourne was wildly notorious for selecting one lover from the handsome young bucks panting after her every season. One lover per season. That was her routine. As this season was just beginning, she likely had not made her selection yet.

Jasper Thorne was certainly her type. He possessed youth, beauty, and deep pockets. She grimaced. He was *every* woman's type.

Tru knew she should not have a preference when it came to Thorne's dancing partners. So what if Lady Ashbourne flirted with him. She should feel only relief that he had turned his attention away from Delia, even if it was simply to dance with another woman.

Chatham may have been careful in selecting guests with no marriageable daughters, but he had clearly not given much thought to the wives in attendance. A definite oversight considering Lady Ashbourne's reputation—and Chatham's goals.

As she danced with Mr. Thorne, her hand roamed his shoulders and back in an overly familiar manner. Tru's stomach cramped as she observed them in what she hoped was a surreptitious manner, but even if it was not, even if she failed to appear disinterested, what did it matter? The man was supposedly courting her daughter and here he was being pawed at amid her country party. She had a right to look offended.

"You think Lady Ashbourne has made her selection yet?"

She started a bit and looked askance at her husband as he sidled up beside her. He customarily ignored her at these things. She did not bother to ask after his meaning. She understood perfectly and she was in no mood to play coy.

Lady Ashbourne tossed her head back in a burst of gay laughter at something Thorne said.

Tru forced herself to look away, giving the earl her full attention.

"It is quite possible. It is that time of year when she chooses her paramour."

He grunted in displeasure. "Lady Ashbourne appears taken with our Mr. Thorne."

"He is not *my* anything," she was quick to retort. "You chose him."

"Indeed. *I* have chosen him, which is why I don't care for what I am observing."

"You invited her," she reminded.

"Lord Ashbourne is a good friend."

"Hm." She grunted, well aware of what made them *good* friends—a penchant for vice and debauchery.

Chatham watched the dancing pair for several more moments with an aggravated air and then shrugged. "She is married. He still looks for a bride. He can enjoy the delights of Lady Ashbourne and still do right by me."

Right by me. Because this was about Chatham. Delia was merely a pawn. A chess piece to be moved about on a board played by men. Played by Chatham and Thorne. As far as her husband was concerned, this marriage business began and ended with him. That was his mistake. She inhaled through her nose, her chest lifting with resolve. Dismissing Tru as thoroughly as he dismissed Delia would be his mistake. He never once thought that his wife might do something to circumvent his authority, but he would be wrong to underestimate her.

"And they dance again," Chatham volunteered with a twinge of annoyance to his voice.

Her gaze shot back to the dance floor. It was true. Lady Ashbourne and Thorne engaged in yet another dance. Two in a row. It was beyond the pale.

"No doubt he will find his way to her bedchamber tonight." He snorted. "As I recall, she and Ashbourne do not share a bedchamber . . . even at house parties. *Especially* at house parties. It gives them the freedom to, ah . . . entertain."

"Do you not want more for our daughter than a philandering husband? She deserves someone better."

"You are such a romantic, Gertie." He tsked and shook his head disgustedly. "I had forgotten that about you. I hope you haven't planted such foolish ideas in our daughter. If so, marriage shall be a struggle for her. She will expect romance and affection and a man who never strays from her bed." He gulped back the remaining whiskey in his glass, still studying the dancers. "Such wives are a bore."

She glared at him coolly. "You would know."

He glanced at her with a small smile. "Quite so." Without the courtesy of a farewell or bow over her hand, he turned and left her.

Valencia approached then, joining her. "He seems in good spirits," she murmured.

"And why would he not be? All this is his doing." She waved about them. "It's precisely what he wanted."

"Even that?" Valencia nodded to where Lady Ashbourne flirted with Thorne. "That can't please him."

"He is not concerned. A man has oats to sow, after all. It has naught to do with marriage." Somehow she managed to get the words out even as they tasted like poison in her mouth.

"Of course," Valencia murmured with a distracted air as her dark eyes swept the room, searching, doubtlessly, for the whereabouts of her husband. She had been inordinately quiet ever since Dedham arrived in the Little Ballroom a short while ago.

Before his arrival, Valencia had danced and laughed and made her rounds in the room, chatting with everyone. Now she watched her surroundings with a much more subdued manner. It was always that way. She was distracted and quiet when her husband was present—lively and smiling when he was not.

"Valencia? Are you . . . well?"

It was a foolish question. Tru knew she was not. What wives, forced into marriage and then managed cruelly or indifferently (sometimes both), were ever truly well?

Her friend had not been well in many years. Not since her husband's dreadful accident. The day Dedham broke his body, she, too, broke. She was married to a man sick in body and spirit, who made certain his wife suffered right alongside him.

Rather than answer her question, Valencia said, "Take heart. I do not think the shift of his attention to Lady Ashbourne pains your daughter in the least."

Tru considered that as she studied her daughter sitting on a chaise near the open balcony doors. Valencia was correct. She did not seem affected. She laughed and chatted enthusiastically with Rosalind, oblivious to her beau flirting with another woman. She did not care.

Watching her daughter, she saw the truth of this. It was a curious thing. For having agreed to his suit, Delia did not find Jasper Thorne appealing. Whilst, to her discredit, Tru did.

"She is not taken with him," she mused, then added wryly, "unlike her father, who is quite taken with him. Unfortunately."

"Is that not always the situation?" Valencia asked. "It is forever the papas who are more impressed with the suitors of their daughters than the daughters themselves." She rolled her eyes. "My own father would have married Dedham himself, were it done."

They both laughed lightly . . . bleakly.

Suddenly weary of the subject of heartlessly mercenary fathers and husbands, Tru excused herself. "I need to speak with Mrs. Carson and see that everything is in order for tomorrow." A likely excuse, of course. This was a house party. There were a great many matters that required her constant attention.

She simply needed to remove herself from the room so she did not have to look upon Thorne flirting with Lady Ashbourne for another moment. And that disturbed her. Inexplicably so. A flirtation with another woman meant he was not solely fixated on her daughter, which was precisely what she wanted. She should be rejoicing in that and not feeling this misplaced sense of . . . heartache.

She found her way to her favorite drawing room, around the corner from the Little Ballroom. It was smaller than the main drawing room where she usually received callers. Full of creams and pastels and comfortable settees with fat cushions she could sink into, it was a true refuge.

She made her way to the tray holding her favorite claret and poured herself a sizable glass. She took a healthy swig just as the hinges of the door she had most definitely shut behind her creaked open. Tru turned to see who had followed her, expecting it to be one of her friends, but not very surprised to see Jasper Thorne there. He had a way of sneaking up on her. It would not be the first time he'd sought a private moment with her. She forced her suddenly leaping heart to ease in her chest.

Presenting him with her back, she poured yet more claret into her glass. Without facing him, she asked, "Have you finished dancing, Mr. Thorne?"

"Would you believe I am not one for dancing?"

She laughed once, a light, brief sound. "No. I would not believe that." She sent him a scathing look over her shoulder. "One would not at all think that after observing you this evening."

"Oh, I am *able* to dance, but I could think of other things I would *far* more enjoy doing with a desirable woman in my arms."

If she did not imagine it . . . his gaze rested on her with hot speculation. Warmth crept over her face, reaching all the way to her ears. The man was insufferable. He thought he could court her daughter, flirt with Lady Ashbourne, and then come at her with veiled innuendo and a lewd gaze.

"You seemed quite merry in the company of Lady Ashbourne." Try as she might, she sounded accusing. She could not hide it.

He approached, closing the distance between them. Her heart beat faster, accelerating as he bypassed her entirely, stopping before the tray of claret to pour himself a glass. "Do I detect a bit of scorn in your voice? Judgment?"

"However I sound . . . I have a right to sound it."

He released a growling breath. Straightening, he faced her, and his very wearied nature pricked at her already fraying temper.

What did he have to be so aggrieved about? He was a man. A man with money and power and the blessing of good looks. He was in possession of all his own teeth and had his pick of any wife he chose. No one controlled him. No one pulled his strings as though he were a puppet to be maneuvered. That was Tru. That was her life.

Tru took a bracing breath. She had never been like this before . . . never so fractious, never so quick to enrage. Never *anything* that involved an excess of emotion. Histrionics were not her custom. She was not that. She was a woman who spent a lifetime carefully crafting her image, cultivating a well-respected reputation as a grand dame of the *ton*. A hot temper was not in her nature—nor ought it be.

Why did he do this to her and turn her into someone else, some version of herself she barely recognized?

"Permit me to give you some advice as you navigate Society this season."

"Please do," he encouraged.

"You should have more care for the feelings of the ladies you court, or rather, the lady." *My daughter*. He had made it evident that he was not interested in anyone else. He had proclaimed that he courted Delia—blast him.

"Feelings?" He blinked as though he had never heard the word before . . . and perhaps he had not. He was about as sensitive as a brick, after all. It was the only explanation for his behavior . . . for the fact that he courted her daughter whilst flirting with someone else. Whilst looking at her in a way that made her feel naked beneath his gaze.

"My daughter deserves better. If you're going to cavort and flirt with other women, at least do not do it in the presence of my daughter. Have that much respect." *Do not do it in the presence of me.*

He shook his head. "What are you talking about?"

"I saw you. We all did. You danced with Lady Ashbourne two times. Twice. Back to back. And your manner—"

"My manner?"

"Yes," she snapped. "Your *manner*, sir, was most shameless." She needn't say more than that. He should understand.

He held her gaze for a moment, the brown of his eyes shifting from amusement to annoyance and back again. It was almost as though he could not decide how to feel about her.

His eyes brightened with enlightenment. "You were making quite a study of me then?"

She squared her shoulders. "I was hardly spying on you. You were in plain sight of all."

He rolled his eyes with a snort.

He thought her nosey. A busybody. That was fine. It was natural. She was a mother. A mother would do anything for the sake of her child. As a parent he should understand that.

She continued. "If you must be a philanderer, I beg that you exercise discretion."

"If I *must* be?"

"Come now. I'm not a green girl, and you're a man of the world. We needn't pretend we don't know how these things happen among gentlemen of the *ton*." It was how things had happened to her. She had hoped it would be different for her daughter, but the world had not changed since then.

She took an unladylike swallow of her drink.

He shook his head. "You bloody blue bloods. You can't help yourself, can you?"

What was that supposed to mean? She lowered her glass. "I beg your pardon?"

Whatever he meant, from his scoffing manner, she was certain it was not complimentary.

He stepped closer, pressing in, a great wall of heat radiating at her front. "Need I remind *you* that I am not a gentleman of the *ton*? I would appreciate you not lumping me in with the rest of them."

"Indeed, you are not, but you clearly wish to be. Why else are you here, tossing your hat into the ring and courting my daughter? You want to be one of us," she accused.

His stare scoured her, swept over her face. "Is that what you think?"

It was as though her words sparked a fire in him. His eyes burned molten as they glared down at her, and she felt something ignite in her as well. Heat unfurled in her belly, blossoming out, spreading, sizzling along her veins. Her breasts felt heavier, hot and heavy as though a fever had settled in her blood. She knew the sensation. She'd felt it before with him. Only him.

"I want many things in this life, Countess. Fine whiskey. Good food. A warm bed every night." He paused, took a breath as his gaze slid over her face, looking from her eyes to her mouth and then back to her eyes again. "The soft cradle of a woman's thighs on occasion."

Her breath caught at that particular image, her pulse quickening.

He continued, his voice flowing like honey. "This bloody world"—he flicked his fingers contemptuously around him—"has never been something I wanted, but I promised that I would give it to Bettina." He inhaled, lifting his chest on a great breath of air. "*That* is why I am here."

She studied him for some moments, fighting against the relenting of her wrath, the give of her heart. He might have a daughter whom he was looking out for . . . but so did she.

So did she and so *would* she.

She need only conjure forth the image of Lady Ashbourne plastered indecently over him—of him smiling down at the woman—to sustain her earlier outrage.

"Might I suggest that you hunt for 'the soft cradle of warm thighs' elsewhere?" she flung out. "Rather than here, beneath the same roof as my daughter?"

He crossed his arms and studied her in a way that made her

strangely and suddenly want to crawl beneath a rock. "It seems you have decided to believe the worst of me."

He wanted her trust then? Mirthless laughter bubbled up in her throat. She was not a naive girl anymore. She knew better than to ever lower her guard with a man again. After all, what reason did he give her to trust him?

He waved behind him, in the vague direction of the Little Ballroom. "You misunderstood what you saw. I've no designs on the Lady Ashbourne. I promise you that I do not intend to be a husband who shames his wife."

She inhaled a seething breath. Why did that feel so very pointed? Was it because he believed Chatham shamed her? Because he had witnessed himself how very little the earl thought of her?

Heat flushed over her face. Of course Chatham knew nothing of honor or discretion when it came to her. She knew that to be true. She felt it every day, but it stung her that Thorne saw it, too.

I promise you that I do not intend to be a husband who shames his wife.

It was more than what the earl had ever promised her.

Her lips worked. "I only seek to protect my daughter from making a mistake—"

"As you have?"

She pulled back slightly. "I beg your pardon."

He stepped closer. "Clearly you and your husband do not have the manner of marriage anyone would aspire—"

She reacted unthinkingly. Her hand shot out and cracked him across the face.

They stared at each other in astonishment.

She knew instantly that she struck him for daring to speak the truth. For unerringly speaking the stinging truth and shame that she lived with every day. "I—I," she stammered. "I am—"

He reached for her and she was certain he meant to deliver recompense. Shake her or slap her back. What did she know of him, after all?

His hands landed on her shoulders and he yanked her close. Brought her against him. She caught a flash of his eyes, the brown darker than usual, before his head descended and his mouth landed on hers. Claimed her. Kissed her with a ferocity that matched her slap. It was punishing. It was delicious.

It was madness.

She tossed herself into the maelstrom, into his arms, kissing him back as though it were her right to do so. As though a house full of guests did not buzz outside those doors. As though scandal did not live and breathe as a beast beside them both, ready to devour all.

Chapter 26

There is nothing a prospective husband could offer me that shines brighter than the promise of independence.
—The Right Honorable Lady Rosalind Shawley

Jasper knew he should stop.

This was not the place for it. It was not the bedchamber, or the bed, he had envisioned. Certainly there was no guarantee of privacy. It was the height of indiscretion. Despite coming to this house party because of her—for *her*—he did not seek to ruin her. And yet when it came to the countess, he lacked all sense and good judgment. He could not keep his hands or lips to himself.

Their kiss turned furious, wild, a seething frenzy. Their tongues mated. One of his hands gripped her face, the other dragged down her throat, seizing her breast through her bodice. She gasped, and the sound tore through him, inflamed him.

He palmed the generous flesh and her gasp turned to a moan.

"Do you like that, love?" he growled against her lips, dipping two fingers inside her bodice. He brushed her nipple, unerringly finding the distended tip. He swept his fingers back and forth over the aroused bud until catching it and squeezing.

Her head fell back with a choked cry, and his hand came up, gripping the back of her head and guiding her mouth to his, smothering the sound as he played with her breast beneath the tight fit of her bodice.

They kissed like that, mouths melding hotly, bodies writhing together, against each other, with his hand buried down the front of her dress.

"Stop," she groaned against his mouth, and he stilled at the single word. He opened his eyes to look down at her. The sight of her kiss-bruised lips and anguished face tore at him.

But there was not only anguish there. There was still desire. Hunger. Want.

"I cannot." She braced her hands on his chest as though needing sudden leverage. "I cannot do this *with you*."

The way she emphasized *with you* gave him pause. He covered one of her hands with his and asked directly, "Am I not good enough for you, Countess?"

Her eyes flared wide. "It is not that. It is everything else. You are here to court my daughter. You are her beau despite all my efforts to persuade you not to be. That is reason enough, but I can certainly recount more." She pushed past him with surprising speed.

She was almost to the door before he reached her. He caught up with her and whirled her back around to face him. "Tru, wait—"

"No!" She tugged free and swiped her hand through the air in a cutting motion that bespoke finality. "This has to stop. You cannot look at me like that . . . talk to me, touch me, kiss me whilst you are here for Delia . . ."

I'm here for you.

He held both hands in front of him. "I apologize if my actions have made you uncomfortable—"

"Uncomfortable?" She released a shrill little laugh. "That is putting it lightly. These encounters are becoming much too frequent. It is only a matter of time before we are caught. Or at the very least someone begins to suspect."

She spoke the truth. The way her clever sister watched him, he was beginning to wonder if someone already did. They had not been behaving clandestinely by any means, but it was frighteningly easy to lose sight of everything else when she was in his arms.

"I don't care what others think," he said.

"Well, that is convenient for you. I cannot afford to turn a blind eye. I have to care what others think. I have a reputation to consider. I cannot risk doing"—she fluttered her hand between them—"*this*. A scandal would harm both my children." She held out a hand as though to ward him off from approaching her. "You can never touch me again."

Her words felt like a physical blow. *No.*

From the cradle, she was taught to care about Society and the way others perceived her. From the cradle, he had no thought for anything other than his survival, for finding his foothold in this world and strengthening it, bettering himself. He had taken his pleasures whenever and wherever he chose with no threat to that ambition. Whilst pleasure appeared to be something she could never seize for herself—not without threat, loss, and dire consequence.

They were two entirely different creatures.

She continued. "For God's sake, you're courting my daughter." She shook her head with apparent self-disgust and muttered something unintelligible. "You are here for her."

"Sweetheart, don't you realize yet? I am here for you."

She startled. "What?"

"I'm not courting Delia."

"B-but . . . she said—"

"It is a lie. A sham. We agreed to pretend, so that she might have a reprieve from the Marriage Mart and the endless swarm of suitors, and I might have an excuse to be around you."

She stared at him uncomprehendingly. "How . . ."

"We agreed. Before we came here. She confessed she did not wish to marry me, and I no longer wished to marry her after . . . well, after you."

"*Me?*" she whispered.

"Yes, you." He smiled. "From the moment I met you, I wanted to see you again. I knew if I walked away after the Lindley ball, I would have no reason to be in your company again. I could not bear the thought of that."

She pressed her fingertips to her temple as though suffering an aching head. "You and Delia concocted this scheme? This lie?" Her eyes widened then. "Does she know about . . . us?"

"No, of course not." He paused, wincing a bit. "At least *I* have not told her, but she is a bright girl. She might wonder what my motivation could be for perpetrating a sham of a courtship. What could I possibly have to gain?" His gaze crawled over her features.

She nodded slowly, clearly considering his words. "Indeed. What could you possibly have to gain?"

"You," he answered simply, lifting one shoulder in a shrug that seemed to say: *Obviously*.

Tru's expression became pained. "You've done all this . . . to be near me?" Emotion thickened her voice and it broke him. She might strike him again, but he reached for her and drew her to him, pressing her against his chest.

"I ache for you," he confessed, his lips brushing the fine tendrils at her hairline. "Ever since I spoke to you in that garden."

"Jasper," she breathed against his throat, her lips an enticing graze against his skin, and it undid him to hear this, the very first sound of his name on her lips. *Jasper.*

The hinges on the door gave a creaking alert and they sprang apart.

TRU TURNED TO watch Rosalind enter the room. Her sister stopped abruptly, assessing them with narrowed eyes as they stood awkwardly away from each other. "There you are, Tru." She sent Jasper one of her usual distrustful glares. "I wondered where you got to."

Tru forced a smile that felt brittle as a leaf on her face. "Just having a word with Mr. Thorne."

Rosalind nodded in a knowing manner, and Tru could only

imagine what she was thinking. Hopefully she thought Tru was merely warning him off her daughter and not indulging in her own indiscretion with him. "I've come to fetch you. Everyone has moved to the Little Ballroom for parlor games."

"Games?" Tru echoed as though she had never heard the word before.

"Yes." She looked to Jasper. "Come along, Mr. Thorne. You must play, too."

"Oh, must we?" Tru appealed. "It is getting late."

"Come now." Ros's eyes glinted in rebuke. "Attend to your guests."

"Very well." She could not help thinking how odd it was that Ros was lecturing her on her responsibilities. Usually it was the other way around.

"Ladies." Thorne waved for them to precede him out of the room.

Tru fell in step beside Ros, advancing to the Little Ballroom, but she was achingly aware of the man trailing at her back.

Ros stopped before they entered the room, taking Tru's elbow and pulling her to the side. She smiled tightly to Jasper and inclined her head, indicating he should move ahead without them. "We will join everyone in a moment, Mr. Thorne."

His gaze snared and held Tru's for a moment, and warmth flushed through her as she watched him take his leave and return to the party.

Ros nodded to Thorne's back as he disappeared into the room ahead of them. "What are you about?"

"What do you mean?" Even as she asked the question, she recalled his husky voice. *Sweetheart, don't you realize yet? I am here for you.*

Was that true? Did others suspect? Did her sister?

Ros considered her for a long moment. In the background, the voices in the Little Ballroom grew boisterous. "Do you regret it?"

"Regret what?"

"Choosing Chatham . . . choosing this life?"

It was a strange question—almost as strange as the concept of *choice*. She had never felt this life was of her choosing. But perhaps even *more* strange was her sister asking that of her right now. In this moment. Coincidental when Tru did not believe in coincidences.

Tru peered through the open door, her gaze landing on her daughter. "I would not have my children had I lived a different life, so . . . no."

Ros smiled indulgently. "Of course, but . . . that aside?"

"We all have our paths to travel." She shrugged, hoping to inject some flippancy into a conversation that suddenly felt too serious. "And what of you, sister? Do you have regrets? Not marrying, staying with Mama and Papa?"

Ros released a brief huff of laughter and then sobered. Moistening her lips, she asked, "Do you recall that séance?"

Tru huffed. "I've tried to forget it."

"I haven't forgotten it. Or those words Madame Klara said to me. *Your turn is coming when you must do your duty.*"

"Rubbish," Tru pronounced. "You should think on it no more."

Ros shrugged uneasily. "I don't know. She sounded so much like . . ."

She sounded like their old governess. *Miss Hester.* Ros didn't need to finish her words. Tru knew.

"Do you think it could have meant anything?" Ros pressed.

Tru scoffed. "I think Madame Klara was a charlatan who reminded us of our old governess. Nothing more than that."

It couldn't mean anything. If she was to believe those words to Rosalind actually meant something, then she had to believe the words Madame Klara spoke to her meant something, too. *You are in danger. Say nothing. Confess nothing.* And what could she make of that? It was simply theatrics. Drama for the hungry audience who had paid for entry to Madame Klara's salon.

Ros looked as though she wanted to say more, but then a burst of lively laughter erupted within the ballroom and Ros glanced through the door. After a moment, she looked back to Tru, thoughtfully assessing, her gaze lowering to her lips that still felt bruised and tingling. "You asked if *I* had regrets, sister?"

Tru resisted lifting her fingers and touching her mouth. "Yes."

"That would be absurd, would it not? I have my freedom. Mostly." She shrugged. "What else could I possibly long for?"

Tru nodded. "That is so. You are free."

"You are correct. We all have our paths in this life." Her nostrils flared on an exhale. "I suppose my path seems trivial."

She flinched. "Ros, I would *never* say that."

Her smile turned faintly sad. "I am a spinster. *Everyone* would say that. Everyone does."

Tru linked arms with her sister. "You're being unusually morose tonight. Come. Let us be silly and join the games."

Together they entered the room just as Lady Ashbourne was holding out her arms and declaring to enraptured guests, "Let us begin!"

Chapter 27

Always remember, even the very most depraved rake begins life as a squalling, red-faced infant.

—The Right Honorable Lady Rosalind Shawley

Everyone was already arranged in a rough semicircle, seated in chairs that had been pulled out from against the walls. Apparently Lady Ashbourne had matters well in hand. A few gentlemen remained on their feet. Tru's gaze landed on Jasper standing near the large hearth with Lord Ashbourne beside him, both wearing rather bemused expressions at the proceedings.

Maeve was the first to start, sitting very properly with her hands in her lap. "How is the weather in *Bristol*?" She cocked her head to the side, her silvery wig glinting beneath the chandelier light as she waited for her husband's response.

"*Crystal* clear, I am *told*," Mr. Bernard-Hill replied with a wink for his wife. The room applauded. The affable gentleman then turned to Delia on his right.

Delia paused, biting her lip in contemplation as she now searched for a word to rhyme with *told*.

Ros clapped heartily, cheering her on. "Come now, Delia. You can do this."

Delia's eyes lit up. Clearly inspiration had seized her. "*Scold* me not, for I disagree, *sir*."

Delighted cheers went up. Delia inclined her head at her triumph.

Old Sutton caressed the gem-studded head of his cane and leaned forward, his milky-eyed gaze gleaming as he swept it over everyone in the room. He licked his lips with anticipation just before his rasping voice got out "*Purr*"—he paused to emphasize his accomplishment at finding a rhyming word, and then continued—"kitten, *purr*."

Cricket silence met the nonsensical phrase. The object of the game was not only to rhyme, but also to state something logical.

Individuals in the room blinked in the silence, and Hazel's elderly husband roughly cackled, repeating, "*Purr*, kitten, *purr*."

More awkward silence.

The brash Lady Ashbourne finally spoke. "Perhaps we should switch to a new game!" She gave a cheerful clap. "Something more *exciting* than a rhyming game."

"What manner of excitement did you have in mind, my dear

lady?" Chatham asked with a lecherous leer. He was clearly in a randy mood. He lounged indolently in an armchair, his ankles crossed and stretched out in front of him.

Lady Ashbourne moved to the center of the room with a swish of mulberry silk skirts. She brandished her hands, her beringed fingers splayed wide for dramatic effect. "What if we play . . . Kiss the Candlestick?"

Several gasps, giggles, and titters met the wicked suggestion.

Chatham clearly loved the idea. He launched to his feet, hastening across the room to fetch one of the candlesticks on the great mantel above the fireplace.

Tru stepped forward, hoping to keep this house party from turning into an orgy. "Oh, I don't think so . . ."

Her hope was dashed.

"Oh, stop being a prude," Chatham reprimanded, not even looking her way.

A current of excitement undulated over the room as people stood, moving into what they deemed to be more advantageous positions. Clearly people wanted to kiss . . . as long as they had a choice in the matter of partners.

"Well, then." Valencia stepped beside her and murmured, "It has become one of *those* house parties."

Tru could not hide her dismay. She shook her head grimly.

"Mama?" Delia sidled next to her, looking confused. "What is Kiss the Candlestick?"

Of course her innocent daughter would not know this particular parlor game. Tru sent her husband an exasperated look and approached him. "Chatham. Need I remind you that your daughter is in attendance?"

He turned from where he was positioning himself between Lady Ashbourne and Hazel, certainly two of the most attractive women present this evening.

"Well, she has had her coming-out already. She's not a child anymore, Gertie. Best she learn how the *ton* plays. Let her join in." He nodded his head in the direction of Jasper near the hearth. "I am certain our Mr. Thorne would not mind playing Kiss the Candlestick with our daughter." He waved a hand. "And with many of the other fetching ladies we've in attendance tonight."

He was a libertine. He would not blink an eye if this house party turned into Sodom and Gomorrah. In fact, he would revel in it.

He quit her then, turning his attention to the room at large as he held the candlestick aloft. "Who should like to begin?" He scarcely waited for anyone to answer before saying, "Very well! I will." He held the candlestick up to his face and eagerly turned to Hazel.

Cheers went up as he yanked the candlestick away and planted a kiss on her friend's lips with a loud smack. He stepped back and held up his arms as though a grand victor.

Hazel looked on tolerantly with a slight roll of her eyes. She was undoubtedly accustomed to suffering men's advances. Still, Tru could not help thinking that did not make it right. Hazel wiped a hand to her mouth as though to rid herself of his kiss, and Tru wished she could have spared her that.

The game went on. Kissing. And cheering. And more kissing. Everyone was enjoying themselves—especially the men.

"I predict there will be a great deal of bedchamber hopping this night," Valencia whispered from beside her as they observed the revelry. "The halls will be like Bond Street the morning after Boxing Day."

"I fear you are correct," Tru grumbled.

They observed a while longer, and then Valencia wryly inquired, "Is it just me? Or is *no one* kissing the candlestick?"

As though to prove her wrong, long, plaintive *boo*s went up as Ros, who had taken her turn and held the candlestick, permitted the Marquess of Sutton to kiss the actual candlestick and *not* her lips. The old man was visibly disappointed. Ros looked only determinedly stalwart.

Valencia chuckled. "Papa thought he was going to get a treat from your sister."

"Not a chance of that. He best rely on his wife for kisses."

Valencia's lips tightened at the mention of her stepmother. The expression was short-lived. She was tapped on the shoulder and spun around to greet the candlestick being brandished by Lord Burton. *Of course.*

The crowd cheered at this pairing. Everyone knew exactly the manner of man Burton was . . . and he would not settle for kissing a candlestick. Not when he had an opportunity to kiss lovely Valencia.

The color bled out from her friend's face. Her head turned, searching the room. Tru knew at once whom she was looking for.

Tru followed suit, also seeking a glimpse of the Duke of Dedham. She spotted him sitting in a chair looking his usual weary self. Only his eyes showed life, sparking with fury as Burton yanked the candlestick away at the last moment and planted a kiss on Valencia. Not just any kiss either. The man pulled her close and bent her over his arm as he kissed her long and hard in a spectacle worthy of the stage. The onlookers went wild.

When Valencia was released she looked shaken and equally furious. She glared at Burton and wiped her mouth in a rough motion.

The man chuckled and faced the crowd with a boastful air. "Try to outdo that!"

Valencia distractedly accepted her turn with the candlestick amid the hollers and applause. Turning to Tru, she pulled the candlestick clear at the last moment and pressed a quick kiss to her cheek. A boring demonstration, to be certain, but the crowd needed taming as far as Tru was concerned.

Then it was her turn. Tru held the silver candlestick, still frowning over her friend's obvious upset. Turning, she faced . . . Jasper.

He had moved somehow beside her without her notice.

Chatham called out, "Sorry about that, my good man. I know you would have preferred someone else."

She shot a glare at her husband. Clearly another man kissing her did not bother him.

The crowd hooted. Someone called out Delia's name, directing her to: "Switch with your mother!"

Annoyance burned in her chest. It should not have felt like a slight. She should have felt no shame. Of course the guests would want to see such a pairing. They believed the two of them were courting. No one knew it was all a sham. No one knew that Jasper wanted her. *Clearly no one would believe it.* And that stung. Wrong or right of her . . . she could not crush her indignation at being deemed somehow unworthy.

Lady Ashbourne sidled near. Her low and throaty voice whispered for Tru's ears alone, "If you don't know what to do with this dazzling specimen, I bloody hell do. Hand me the candlestick."

That spiked something else in her, adding tinder to the fire the others had already ignited within her.

She was not *nothing*. She was someone. A woman. Still alive. Still with a heartbeat and still of value.

Before she could reconsider how this might be a mistake, how she would most certainly regret it later, she yanked the candlestick from between their faces and kissed Jasper full on the mouth in front of God, the devil, and present company.

There was a moment of stunned silence. She digested this even amid the scorching kiss she delivered upon him. He kissed her back, his lips moving in a way that was becoming all too familiar—hopefully no one else noticed the familiarity.

Theirs was not a kiss for performance. It would be no difficult task to forget that they even had an audience. She could lose herself in this kiss, in this man, if she allowed it.

Gathering up her will, she broke the kiss and staggered back breathlessly.

Several guests applauded, looking her over with seemingly new estimation.

"Well done," Lady Ashbourne proclaimed behind her. "Not at all what I would have expected from the Cold Countess. Chatham, you're a fortunate man!"

Laughter met this. Tru smiled slightly.

Thorne stared down at her with an unreadable expression, his dark eyes intent and hungry as a wolf on her.

She looked away and her gaze snagged on her husband.

He stared at her in confusion—as though he had never seen her before. She could relate to that. She did not quite know herself anymore either.

Chapter 28

No one cares whether a rumor is true so long as it is titillating.

—Gertrude, the Countess of Chatham

Tru tossed and turned.

She was unable to forget Jasper's words. *From the moment I met you, I wanted to see you again . . .*

She could not set aside the shock of that. Nor his kiss. *Kisses.* Especially the one she had bestowed on him in front of the entire house party. In front of her husband. In front of her daughter. In front of—

She forced herself to stop recounting all the individuals who had witnessed her debauched demonstration.

It was still a wholly untenable situation. Perhaps in some ways, Jasper pursuing *her* and not Delia was even worse. Jasper Thorne was not here to court her daughter. He was here to seduce her. That should not endear the man to her . . . and yet it did.

A soft scratching sounded at her door.

She bolted upright in bed, wondering if she misheard. Perhaps it was a mouse. Or a ghost. The Chatham family seat had a long, winding history and it was rumored there was more than one ghost skulking about the place. Perhaps Madame Klara should be called forth to expel them.

The sound came again.

She roused, flipping the coverlet back and lighting her lamp, filling the room with its soft glow. Crossing her chamber, she waited a moment at the door, listening, her heart pushing hard against her rib cage.

"Who is there?" she whispered, pressing the flat of her hand to the door, almost frightened it was a ghost and not who she longed it to be.

There was no answer. Merely a turning of the latch. She stepped back, watching that latch, holding her breath as she waited . . . fearing . . . hoping.

Above all else, hoping.

The door opened with nary a creak. There was that at least. Not so much as a whisper of sound as Jasper's considerable figure entered her chamber and closed the door behind him.

"Tell me to go and I shall."

Instead of telling him to leave, as she should, she moistened her lips and said, "You should not have placed yourself next to me during Kiss the Candlestick."

"Do you think I would stand by and watch you kiss another man?"

Her husband would. Her husband *did*. It was strange that this man felt bound to her whilst her own husband did not.

His chest lifted on a deep inhale. "Tell me to go and I shall," he repeated.

The choice was hers.

She approached him with slow steps, holding his gaze as she lifted her arms and slid her hands inside his dressing robe, pushing the garment off his shoulders.

He assisted her, his hands unknotting the belt at his waist. The robe fell to his feet in a puddle.

He was naked beneath the robe. He stood naked in the center of her bedchamber.

It should scandalize her. By rights she had never seen a man fully unclothed before. There had been no chance of that with Chatham and his hasty fumblings in the dark. Even so, she suspected no man would appear to her eyes as this one did.

He was the very image of robust health. Tall and broad-shouldered. His chest and stomach boasted interesting ridges and hollows that made her mouth water. He bore the evidence of a life spent at toil and labor. There was nothing soft about him. She could not help thinking his was a warrior's body. Like a Viking or knight of old. Not like the thick-bellied gentlemen of the *ton*. Indeed not.

Her fingers ached to trace the lean lines of him, curling open and closed at her sides as she battled that impulse.

Her gaze drifted lower. Down from that very fascinating abdomen with its trail of hair arrowing directly to his manhood.

Her gaze shot to his face. "You're . . ." *At full-mast for me.* And they had not even begun yet. Not really. "You're ready for me."

"I have been ready for you since the moment we met." His hands reached for her, circling her waist, and she refused to contemplate how her waist was thicker and softer than that of the ladies most gentlemen preferred.

She permitted him that. Just as she permitted herself to forget why this could not be.

He picked her up as though she were naught more than a feather and dropped her unceremoniously down on the bed.

She chose to forget who she was.

She forgot that he was not for her—a man younger than she, bent on finding a bride, a wife. The one thing she could not ever be to him.

"Now come here, lass."

She was lost. The moment he opened his mouth, the moment he said those words . . . she was his.

He was here for her. He wanted only her.

Her body knew this. She responded and arched and opened to him like a flower to sun.

I have been ready for you since the moment we met.

Perhaps it was a lie, a fabrication meant to feed an older, gullible, and unappreciated matron such as she, but she did not think so. Her heart told her he did not deceive her in this. And yet if she was mistaken . . . she would take that risk.

They came together on her bed, sinking into the soft mattress. She reveled in the weight of him over her as they kissed. He held her, both his large hands spanning her face, palms over her cheeks, fingers spearing through her hair. She felt his very heartbeat through his palms, boring into her through her skin.

After a time she rolled, coming atop him, straddling him as though it were the most natural thing to do in the world. Her hair fell over him, curtaining him as she kissed him.

She sat up after a time, breathing heavily as she looked down at him, feeling very much empowered, a veritable queen.

She took his hands and placed them on her, over her breasts, molding his palms and fingers to her through the thin fabric of her nightgown. She did not need to guide him further. He clearly knew what to do. His hands instantly began fondling, squeezing, his thumbs finding and tweaking her nipples through the thin barrier of cotton.

She flung her head back with a gaspy cry. Moisture rushed between her thighs and she set an urgent pace, rocking over him, riding the hard prodding ridge of him.

His hands went to her nightgown, feverishly gathering the fabric, his fingers clenching in the voluminous material, clawing it upward until he met her flesh.

He gripped her for a moment, long fingers pressing, sinking into her hips, and suddenly it was all too real. He froze as though sensing she was having a moment, thinking, weighing this in her mind and coming to a decision.

Reaching down, she grabbed fistfuls of her nightgown and yanked it over her head in one smooth motion.

"There," she breathed. They were both naked now, nothing separating them.

"Sweet hell," he choked, hungrily drinking the sight of her.

"Do you like what you see?" she asked, pleased that she managed to sound flirtatious in an enticing and not silly manner.

She was older. Older than him. And hers was a body that had brought two children into the world. She was no nubile virgin. And yet insecurity did not rouse itself. It was impossible with the way he looked at her. With the way his hands kneaded her flesh.

"I want to do filthy, improper things to you," he growled, his hands flexing on the swells of her hips.

"Then do them."

He answered her by surging his hips upward, rubbing the ridge of his manhood into the seam of her.

A languorous lick of heat curled low in her belly, squeezing and tightening until she grew wet between the legs.

She moaned into his mouth, pressing herself against him, desperate to relieve the insistent ache throbbing at her core.

His hands went lower, seizing her bottom.

Her head fell back, her neck was weak, unable to support her head. She was melting against him, atop him. A boneless heap.

Growling, he sat up and dragged his lips down the column of her throat, nipping and sucking at the cords of her neck before arriving at her breasts. His breath fired against her skin. Then the hot suction of his mouth closed over her nipple, drawing first one and then the other in deep, fierce, wet pulls that had her shaking.

Her head rolled to one side, a hoarse cry ripping from her lips. "Please, Jasper!"

His hands tightened, his rough palms deliciously chafing her sensitive skin. His touch felt almost reverent . . . but in no way gentle. Even as cherished and worshipped as she felt, he did not handle her like she was something precious. He handled her with all the need and desperation she felt inside herself.

He lifted his head from her and took her nipples between thumb and forefinger, rolling the pebble-hard tips until she thought she would fly apart into a million pieces. She arched over him, closing her eyes as shards of pleasure and pain exploded through her.

She looked down, opening her eyes to his.

In the shadows of her bedchamber, they appeared almost black. Fathomless pools drowning her. He growled her name. "Tru."

His hands continued to explore her, his fingers teasing the inside of her thighs. There was no fear. No recoiling. No pulling away. Instinctively, of their own accord, her thighs parted wider in welcome, ready to take him inside her.

His fingers drifted higher, stroking her, one slipping inside, pushing and easing in with tormenting slowness until she was panting, tears leaking from the corners of her eyes.

He applied his thumb, finding and rolling that little nub at the top of her sex in hard, swift circles. "That's it, my love. Let go."

She shuddered against his hand, a cry bursting from her lips.

Overcome with the sensation of release, her body dropped heavily over him. Once again she was a boneless heap.

He caught her up in his arms, holding her tightly as he lifted her, raising her up just a fraction higher above him.

The shudders continued to rock her, ebbing in waves as she felt him, big and prodding at her entrance.

Their eyes locked, his burning with a dark fire that she felt all the way to her toes. It scalded her. Touched her. Changed her forever. In that one look, in this one moment, she knew she would never feel alone again. Come what may, this would sustain her through life's lowest and most cheerless moments.

"Jasper." Her voice was not her own but some other wild and wanton creature's.

His hands pressed deeper into her, against her body, his fingers digging into her skin as he shifted, entering her in one smooth thrust, burying himself deeply inside her, filling her, stretching her in a way that was more than physical. It went beyond a physical act. It was more than anything she had ever felt before. It was true intimacy.

Emotion clogged her throat. Even in the throes of what she was feeling, she did not let herself think *it*. She did not let herself dare form the dangerous notion.

He continued to gaze at her. She gazed right back. He sat up then, adjusting slightly but not dislodging himself from her.

Arms wrapped around each other, holding each other, they began to move together.

She had never felt so equal, so very connected and in true union with another human being. He rolled his hips and she responded, moving with him, against him, rocking until they were both panting and working and straining against each other for the same goal.

His groans and pants melded with her own. His hands moved from her bottom to her back to her shoulders. It was constant touching. A constant embrace as his cock stroked in and out of her. Again and again and again for a pleasure so intense, so sweet. The incredible friction drove her right over the precipice.

The ache that had started at their very first kiss tightened every nerve in her body until everything snapped in a great release.

His mouth caught hers, swallowing her cry as she exploded into pieces, his cock thrusting harder, faster, stoking the fire even as she squeezed and climaxed around him.

She was past movement and they both became still in the sudden shocking aftermath.

They remained just so for several moments, locked together, chest to chest, gazes connected.

"Wow," she breathed against his lips. "That was brilliant."

He grinned. "I knew it would be."

She laughed lightly. "Did you?"

His boyish grin faded slightly, turned into something serious and sincere and lovely. "Yes. Tupping is always better when you feel something for the other person."

Her chest squeezed, her heart tightening at that. "That makes sense."

"Some men would deny that, but it's true." He shifted then, lifting her off him and tucking her into the bed against his warm, solid side.

"We can't stay like this all night." It was the only thing she could bring herself to say. She hated to shatter their lovely spell, but they could not stay like this and risk being caught. What if Delia came to her bed in the middle of the night as she sometimes did? She didn't do it as much as she once did when she was a little girl, but it still happened on occasion.

"I know." He wrapped an arm around her, pulling her in and enveloping her in a great cloud of comfort and security. "Just a little longer."

"A little longer," she mumbled in agreement, lethargy stealing over her.

This, she realized dimly as the cloud surrounding her grew more dense and her thoughts loosened . . . must be what love felt like.

THE PEACEFUL SLUMBER of Chatham House came to an abrupt end.

The screams were loud enough to be heard in the nearby village, so most certainly Jasper and Tru were not the only ones bouncing up from bed, startled awake.

Hastily they dressed themselves. "What is the hour?"

"Not yet morning," Jasper replied.

Tru shook her head fiercely, her hair brushing over her bare shoulders, reminding her that she was naked. With a man. A man not her husband. A beautiful man who made her forget things like duty and responsibility and her very role as the Countess of Chatham. "I cannot believe I fell asleep," she muttered in full chagrin with herself.

"I can," he said with smug approval. "You quite tired yourself."

"It does not appear you slept," she accused, staring at his bright and alert gaze with tender reproach. Either that or he was the manner of person who could wake immediately fresh and alert. She would like to know, she realized with a pang. She'd like to know how he behaved in the mornings. Did he take a tray in his rooms or venture to the dining room? Drink tea or coffee? Eat an enormous breakfast of eggs and sausages or simply content himself with toast? She gave herself a firm mental shake and cast off such futile musings.

"Indeed I did not," he said as he slipped on the dressing robe he'd worn to her chamber. "I was quite appreciating the beauty sleeping beside me."

She snorted, even as she felt a warm flush of pleasure. He discomfited her, to be certain, addling her thoughts . . . but it was not something she disliked. It was rather exhilarating. Everything he had made her feel since they first met could be characterized that way. She could not help but wonder if it would always be thus with him. Not that she *should* wonder. It was not something she could ever know. Not beyond this night.

Her fingers attempted to set her own robe to rights, but she was not certain she even wore it properly. The ribbon piping did not seem to line up correctly at the front, but there was no time.

The screams had not abated. Additionally, other sounds emerged: doors slamming, rushed footsteps, and overlapping voices in the previously silent house. The longer she remained in her chamber, the greater the risk of someone coming to fetch her—and discovering Jasper in the process.

She glanced to him again. "I shall go first." Motioning for him to wait behind, she opened the door and stepped out, joining the chaos.

Guests poured out of their chambers in their bedclothes, all on the hunt for the source of the harrowing screams. They flowed in the direction of the stairs. She was scarcely given a glance, even by her own daughter and husband. Everyone was too fixated on discovering what was afoot.

Tru hovered in the threshold of her door, waiting, watching. Once everyone had passed her bedchamber and it seemed no one else would emerge from their rooms, she quickly stepped aside and shooed Jasper out from her room.

He stepped out in the corridor, and together they followed in the rear, merging seamlessly into the crowd. Fortunately everyone was distracted. No one looked to them. No one had noticed Jasper slipping from her bedchamber. There was that at least.

The screaming stopped, as did the mob of houseguests, stalling at the top of the stairs. A general murmuring took over—scandalized whispers of which she could not yet decipher.

As politely as possible, she pushed herself to the front of the group—she was the hostess, after all—and peered down the long staircase to the bottom floor.

There, at the base of the steps, sprawled the Duke of Dedham's broken, mangled body. Unmoving. Lifeless. Her hand flew to her mouth, muffling her cry.

She looked around wildly, searching for her friend. She spotted Valencia in the group, a stricken expression on her face, her olive skin pale as milk. Bloodless. As though she had seen a ghost. And in this case that may very well be true.

Valencia's dark, haunted eyes looked down the many, brutal steps to where her husband lay still, and there was little doubt.

The man was dead.

Chapter 29

Marriage is forever. Death is the only escape. Mine. Or his.
—Valencia, the Duchess of Dedham

The funeral of the Duke of Dedham was a grand affair attended by all of Society. The Right Reverend Howley himself presided over the service. The procession congested the streets for hours. There was not a member of the *ton* who failed to pay their respects, and not a citizen who didn't gawk from the sidewalks at the black-creped carriages pulled by Belgian Blacks adorned with black-ostrich-plumed headdresses as they rolled down the streets, trailing after the bell-tollers and the featherman.

Tru had scarcely had a moment alone with Valencia since it all transpired. She wanted to be there for her friend through this terrible tragedy, but there was all manner of family that had surfaced, reminiscent of circling vultures. Not to mention the solicitors and agents of the dukedom that pressed on every side of her. Their union had been childless. In the early days of their marriage, it had almost happened. Twice Valencia had increased and then lost the babes. All hope for a child fled after Dedham's accident. He left no heir. There would be a new duke now. Tru fervently hoped whoever was next in line would be kind and generous with her friend. She deserved that after all her trials.

Valencia, the newly minted Dowager Duchess, sat through it all in her starched bombazine, a heavy fog about her. She still wore that same haunted expression Tru had noted the night the duke died. Her dramatic arched eyebrows seemed all the more stark set in her uncommonly pale face. Her dark eyes gleamed, strangely glassy, blank, as though she were somewhere else and not inside herself at all.

At least the house party was over and she was back in London. She had never wanted it to happen, after all. It ended, scarcely before it began, the night they discovered Dedham deceased. As house parties were wont to do, she supposed, with the appearance of a dead body.

Following making arrangements for the duke's body to be returned to Town, they had all departed, guests included, leaving in a great exodus from Chatham House.

One very necessary thing, at least, was achieved with their departure. Things had come to an end with Jasper. He and Tru had their time together, fleeting as it was, and now it was over.

Fortunately a somber mien was the order of the day, because that was all Tru could manage upon returning to Town.

Jasper was no longer under the same roof with her. Their indiscretion would only be singular. There would be no repeat of it. No further risk. No threat of scandal. They had not, thankfully, been discovered in the chaos of that night at Chatham House.

All this was a relief . . . and a grave wound simultaneously. Tru felt the pain of it keenly. Hopefully it would dull with time. The memory, the glimpse, the short-lived taste he had given her of what it felt like to be with a man for whom you felt desire, affection—*and perhaps even love*—would certainly fade.

This was all the more probable if he continued to keep himself away and out of sight. She had not seen him since they returned to Town over a week ago.

The flurry of the funeral had come and gone and he had not called on them. She had already suffered a visit from Chatham, and it was his very loud and leading complaint.

"Where in the bloody hell is Thorne?"

She and Delia had borne the indignity of Chatham's visit together. The earl had raged and paced up and down the length of the drawing room, demanding to know what they had done to repel Mr. Thorne. Because it must be their fault. Of course.

"Chatham, the funeral was only four days ago." Tru had attempted to reason with him. Perhaps a foolhardy plight, but she nonetheless attempted it.

"Dedham was not part of this family or Thorne's family. We are not bound to mourning. Where is the man?"

"Papa, perhaps he has simply decided that he and I do not suit?"

Tru did not mistake the hopefulness in her daughter's young voice. How had she not noticed before how perfectly disinterested she was in Jasper?

"Blast it! I gave you both one task!" He waved his finger rather violently in the air. "One bloody task! How difficult can it be to win over a lowborn bastard hunting for a blue-blooded debutante? I already told him he could have you! You needn't have done anything. You only had to keep him on the hook. I snared him for you and yet you scared him off." He muttered a foul curse and stopped to glare out the window.

Tru draped an arm around Delia's shoulders and gave her a comforting squeeze, disconcerted to feel that her shoulders were slightly trembling.

"It is not the end of the world, Chatham." Tru addressed his back. "There will be other opportunities. Other chances for Delia."

He spun around, looking much calmer than she expected. He nodded on a sharp inhale and smoothed his hands down the front of his jacket, as though that restored him to order. "Indeed. No time to waste about it. We will all go to the Fairmont ball tonight."

"Tonight?" Delia squeaked.

Tru nodded. "We had not planned on attending—"

"They will be thrilled to have us. They will be excited to hear all the details of Dedham keeling over at our house. It is quite the *on dit*. Everywhere I go, it's all anyone wants to talk about." He switched his gaze back to his daughter, stabbing another threatening finger her way. "And you, my girl. You will *shine* and be all that is charming and come away with a score of new suitors."

"Yes, Papa." The only thing that *shone* in that moment was the misery in her daughter's eyes.

Chatham swung his gaze to Tru. "And you make certain of that."

She nodded as always, feigning obedience. It felt quite normal to suffer another one of her husband's demands. It also felt quite normal for her to plan to do whatever she felt was necessary and right, and to bloody hell with Chatham.

She didn't have to obey him—and neither did Delia. This was what she told herself as she readied for the ball that night.

Later, when she and Delia arrived and entered the Fairmonts' grand ballroom together, she squeezed her daughter's hand and reminded her, "Do whatever you like. Dance with whomever you want—or no one at all. Go find your friends and enjoy yourself. Don't worry about anything. I promise you . . . all will be well."

"Yes, Mama." Delia hugged her abruptly, fiercely, before hastening away into the crowd to be with her friends.

Tru stood alone for a moment, watching Delia and wondering how she might keep that promise. Chatham held all the power. She could think she didn't need to obey him, but in the end he would have his way.

A deep voice sounded suddenly behind her, turning her skin to gooseflesh and tightening her chest almost to the point of pain. "What would I have to do in order to embrace you like that?"

Instead of delivering a properly discouraging setdown, she

turned and smiled with longing in her heart at the man standing closely before her, so closely she could mark the amber striations in his brown eyes. "Why not ask me to dance, Mr. Thorne? We can begin there."

THE FAIRMONT BALL was always a popular event of the season, but it was a mad crush tonight, and Hazel suspected it had everything to do with the fact that it was one of the first social gatherings since the Duke of Dedham's funeral.

Whilst it was no surprise the man had died—he had been wasting away since his accident all those years ago—no one had imagined he would perish in so spectacular a way. To be found at the bottom of a flight of stairs at a house party and not in his bed? Everyone wanted every gory detail. And of course there were rumors that the sickly duke had not fallen and lost his balance at all. Wild speculation, naturally. There was no evidence to the contrary. Certainly nothing would come of it. They were only rumors, after all, a bit of juicy gossip with no foundation. The type of thing that always abounded in the *ton*. No one with good sense gave such conjecture merit. She, especially, knew that.

The surplus of people all slavering for salacious details seemed to make the crowded ballroom especially frenetic tonight. More than one gentleman had been overly handsy with her. Given her history, she was accustomed to licentious gentlemen. Although tonight they seemed to behave even more coarsely than usual.

Hazel cowered behind a group of potted ferns, grateful for her emerald green skirts that allowed her to blend into the foliage.

At least she hoped she blended in and did not look like what she was—a woman hiding from unwanted attentions.

It was cowardly, to be certain, but she needed a respite.

She was accustomed to gentlemen from her past approaching her. They abounded in the ballrooms of the *ton*. She had been married to the Marquess of Sutton for years now. Long enough that they should accept her as one of them and treat her without long and lingering glances.

They *should*.

Unfortunately, memories ran deep in the *ton*, and once a mistress . . . always a mistress.

Oh, no one disrespected her directly to her face. She was now the Marchioness of Sutton, after all. No matter who, or *what*, she had once been, she had married *up* and escaped the world to which she had been assigned.

And yet wives oft glared at her whilst their husbands . . . Well, it was safe to say their husbands did not treat *other* men's wives with leers, winks, and whispered suggestions for her to meet them in the gardens for a tryst. No, it was singularly Hazel forced to endure such boorish behavior.

She knew the talk. Wicked gossip was the lifeblood of Society, after all. She was not an adulteress. Contrary to what was believed of her, she had taken no man to her bed since she married Sutton. Valencia, however, believed such talk, and that same talk only encouraged the bolder men of Society to regularly pursue her.

Burton was one such of those gentlemen. More aggressive and

persistent than most. She had not missed him when he had gone to Chatham House. Unfortunately, Dedham had finally expired and that house party had been cut short. Now Burton was back and pursuing her again with his customary doggedness.

Tonight he was especially bothersome. She peered through the fronds to see if he was still searching for her amid the ballroom.

She did not spot him. In fact, she could see little else besides the two gentlemen standing in front of the ferns, blocking her view.

"Surprised to see you here, Chatham. You don't generally enjoy these types of affairs."

She eyed the pair of gentlemen who stared out at the ballroom, immediately marking Chatham. She could not see enough of his companion to identify him. He was merely another gentleman—a nobleman, more than likely—in an impeccably tailored jacket of peacock blue.

"Yes, well. I've a daughter to marry off, so I will be making the rounds until I have that settled to my satisfaction. Soon, hopefully. I've a man in mind for her. It's all but official."

"Oh? Well. Congratulations then."

"Thank you, Crawford." Chatham inclined his head in acknowledgment, and Hazel wondered if Tru knew this . . . if she would agree that her daughter's betrothal was all but official.

"Is that your wife there, Chatham?"

"Eh. Where?"

"In the red gown?"

Hazel peered out at the ballroom, catching a glimpse of Tru, looking especially lovely tonight as she whirled around the dance floor in the arms of Jasper Thorne.

"Ah. Yes, it is."

"She's rather fetching tonight. You're a lucky man to have that in your bed whenever the mood strikes you."

"Am I?"

"Indeed. Look at her. That's a fine woman."

Hazel peered thoughtfully at the back of Chatham as he considered his wife, canting his head as he studied her. For some reason, she felt a stab of misgiving. She considered Tru a friend. She and Valencia might be thick as thieves, but that did not stop Tru from treating her kindly.

Hazel knew Tru's marriage was not a love match. Those were few and far between in the *ton*. Hazel doubted she was interested in piquing her husband's interest, but Hazel suspected Crawford's words were presently achieving that very thing.

She knew enough of men to know that nothing attracted one's notice as when another identified a woman as desirable.

Crawford continued. "I've been married as long as you and my wife is not nearly so enticing. After the children . . . well, she's never been the same. Not a problem for your wife, I see."

"I suppose not," Chatham mused.

"Who is that she is dancing with?"

"That is Jasper Thorne."

"That is Thorne? I've heard of him. He just finished that grand hotel in Town, did he not?"

"Yes."

Crawford whistled lightly. "Deep pockets. That hotel of his is cracking." The man laughed then. "From the way he's looking at your wife, I would say he thinks she's a fetching piece, too."

"Indeed," Chatham murmured.

"Holding her rather closely, is he not?"

"He does appear to be."

Hazel followed their gazes, assessing for herself. Tru and Mr. Thorne did look quite the cozy pair. The man was holding her closely, his lips at her hair.

"Cannot blame the man."

"I suppose not."

"At least you're the lucky one who gets to take her home. That privilege is yours alone."

"Indeed." Pause. "Indeed, it is."

Hazel bit her lip. Except it wasn't. The two had lived separately for years. She knew they did not share a bed . . . or anything else, for that matter.

Hazel shifted uneasily behind the ferns. Something about the entire conversation made her uncomfortable. Yes . . . she was eavesdropping and that alone should make her uncomfortable, but there was more to it than that.

They were discussing Tru in a manner that would mortify her. Also . . . this was Tru's husband. Her neglectful and indifferent husband. Chatham devoutly ignored his wife, and Tru preferred it that way. She had never said those words directly to Hazel, but she knew. She had not made it this far in life without observing the actions of others closely and letting those actions inform her own decisions.

"If you will excuse me," Chatham said. "I think I will go reclaim my wife."

Reclaim my wife.

Uh-oh. The words unsettled Hazel. She was quite confident that Chatham had not *claimed* his wife in a good many years.

Hazel shifted, peering through the bright green fronds of the fern as he cut across the dance floor. Never since she had been frequenting the gilded ballrooms of the *ton* had she seen the Earl of Chatham take to the dance floor. She had especially not seen him talk to his wife, much less dance with her, at these events. He usually occupied himself in the card room.

Now he was stopping beside Tru and interrupting her waltz with Mr. Thorne. The handsome gentleman very properly handed Tru over to her husband, but there was something in the hard set of his jaw, in the possessive glint of his eyes. He did not want to release Tru to the man—to her very own husband.

Chatham *dancing* with Tru was quite the unusual event, and Hazel knew Tru thought so, too. One glimpse of her strained expression as she waltzed past in the arms of her husband confirmed that she was rattled at the entire exchange. She wore a pretend smile though. She was much too proper and accomplished to drop her guard completely. She looked every inch the grand and contented lady as she waltzed in the arms of her husband. Only, Hazel knew better.

Chapter 30

I've never had a lover. Only benefactors.
—Hazel, the Marchioness of Sutton

"What are you doing, Chatham? We don't dance," Tru demanded between her teeth, a polite smile straining her lips, in case anyone glanced her way. She would not wish to appear anything other than pleasant and unaffected as she danced with her husband. Not only that. He had interrupted her dance with Jasper, and Tru didn't need anyone noticing how much *that* disappointed her.

Jasper.

She had not expected to see Jasper here tonight . . . and she most assuredly had not expected to be pulled into his arms and flooded with memories of their night together and a longing for him that was so acute it made her chest pinch and ache.

"Jasper, why are you here?" she had asked him as soon as he swept her out onto the dance floor.

"I am here, naturally, because you are here."

She shook her head slightly before she caught herself. No need to appear contrary, after all. Anyone might be watching. In the *ton* everyone was always watching. "How did you know I would be here?"

"A well-placed coin in the palm of a footman, my lady."

She felt her eyes go round. "You bribed one of my footmen?"

A smile played at his lips. "You sound so horrified."

"You bribed my footmen." She repeated this yet again, as though it was the sticking point she could not comprehend.

"One of them, at any rate."

"Which one?" she demanded sharply, intent on exacting proper and deserved retribution.

He inclined his head slightly. "That would not be very gentlemanly of me. I should not wish to compromise his position."

"But what if he were to talk of your unseemly interest in me to someone else? I am certain he wondered at your inquiry."

"I did not say why I wanted to know . . . I am certain he assumes it is for your daughter."

"Ah. Yes." She breathed a little easier. Of course that would be the natural conclusion. Who would suspect he had a yen for the Cold Countess? She could hardly fathom it herself. It would only be thought that he was after the younger, pretty Delia. "Assuredly that is what he assumes. You are correct, indeed."

That settled over her for a few moments, a grim reminder that she *should* have no interest at all in this man. He was not for her. She was not for him. No one would even imagine he was interested in her. No one would even suspect they were lovers. She was firmly established as a woman a man would not pursue.

He frowned slightly as he looked down at her. "Whatever you are thinking, I do not like it. Remove it from your head."

She blinked up at him, sniffing in affront. "You are capable of reading my thoughts now, are you?"

"I know you, Tru."

She blinked again.

Those simple words put forth a shiver because she suspected they were true. Somehow this man knew her. In a short time, he had come to know her. Not only intimately—though there was that, of course—but he *knew her*. In a way perhaps no one else did.

Her heart gave a painful little squeeze at the impossibility of it all. She could long for it, she could dream of it and fantasize it, but it could never be.

"You do not know me, sir," she insisted, still wearing a politely distant smile on her face in case anyone observed them.

He chuckled lightly. "I know you. I know you lie to me right in this moment. And you lie to yourself."

Her gaze shot to his face. His dark eyes looked down at her.

"You have denied yourself your whole life. You have denied yourself love. Happiness. Pleasure and passion in bed. All the things you deserve. The question is, how much longer will you deny yourself? Forever?"

She took a careful breath. "I cannot ask you to cease coming out in Society, but you needn't speak to me. Certainly you should not dance with me." All interactions between them should stop altogether. "I understand you have a quest to find yourself a bride, a mother for your daughter. You should focus your energies on that." *And leave me be.*

"I believe I have found her."

He looked down at her then, his eyes darkly gleaming beneath the slash of his brows. The determination she read there elicited a small gasp. "No." She gave her head a single hard shake. "Do not be foolish. That is ridiculous."

"I have found her," he insisted, so unruffled, so matter-of-fact.

More head shaking. "No. It can never be."

"I want you."

Impossible and he well knew it. "Stop it." Tru looked about wildly as they moved around the dance floor, fearful someone might have overheard.

Of course, he spoke quietly, but she would not have those words out there, floating in the air of this roomful of people with the power to ruin her and destroy her family. It was panic inducing. Suddenly she caught sight of Hazel's face, her gold-red hair a bright flame against the ferns where she seemed to skulk. Her eyes were narrowed thoughtfully and rather speculatively on Tru, tracking her as she spun about the dance floor.

"There must be a way." His hand splayed wider at the small of her back, each finger a burning imprint, branding her through the fabric of her gown. "We can find a way."

"There is no way." She nodded in greeting to the Portuguese ambassador's wife, who made eye contact with her over the shoulder of her dance partner. The woman had a son she was looking to marry off, and Tru knew she was a great admirer of Delia. "Not even your wealth can forge a path for us—"

"Do not underestimate the power of money."

"That's a cynical sentiment."

"Nevertheless true."

She felt a treacherous little niggle of hope that she quickly squashed. He was wrong. They could not legitimately be together. Not even with his influence and machinations.

"Even this you cannot buy."

"I should like to try."

She shook her head. "You cannot buy *me*."

He glowered as he whirled them about the dance floor. "I did not mean that. I do not see you as property. I don't believe Chatham would say the same, however."

She flinched. There was a truth in that she could not dispute.

He continued. "You deserve better."

"It will ruin me and all those close to me—"

"I am not ready to give up." The pressure of his hand on her back increased, and he pulled her closer yet. "I am not ready to give *you* up." That simple clarification fogged her thoughts—as did the sensation of him, his bigger body radiating like a fire grate at her front. "Are you?"

She moistened her lips. "I must."

He brought his face closer, his cheek nearly touching her own, his mouth a hairsbreadth from her ear. "That was not the question I put to you, my love."

He twirled her and she felt a little dizzy . . . and not from the dancing. It was him. His words. His closeness. His warm breath fanning her ear.

He went on weaving his spell. "Come now, Tru. Did you think just once would be enough? For either of us?"

"It's all we're ever going to have."

"You still want me." His breath tickled her ear and sent delicious chills through her body. She could not speak right then, even if she knew the words to use to convince him, to convince herself—which she clearly did not.

"You want more," he added in that maddeningly confident way. The puff of those words on the whorls of her ear turned her knees to jam and brought forth the memory of being entwined with him. Their bodies locked together, joined, rocking . . . bare skin to bare skin. Her fingers clenching his shoulders, clinging to him for support. As if sensing how close she was to crumpling, he pulled her flush to his chest, his arm a hard band encircling her.

His seductive voice continued. "Are you willing to walk away? Are you done with me? With us?" A challenging glint entered his eyes. His gaze roamed her face and then dipped down, skimming her bare shoulders and décolletage.

Her breasts tightened within her bodice. Suddenly breathing no longer became a simple matter. She could manage only a nod of affirmation.

His lips moved to her ear again. "I wager I could have you panting and begging for my touch within thirty seconds."

Thirty seconds? She gulped. Unfortunately, she believed that boast. Not that she would dare reveal that to him. Pride as well as survival demanded she remain stalwart in her resistance.

"You go too far."

"With you? Yes. That always seems the case. You bring out the daring in me."

"Begging your pardon, Thorne. I think I shall take over from here."

Tru had flown out of her skin at the suddenness of her husband's voice so close and unwelcome, shattering the intimate moment. *Blast the man.*

What had transpired next was the height of awkwardness.

She'd looked between Jasper and Chatham, trying to determine if her wretched husband had overheard any of their exchange.

Jasper faced Chatham with a coolly unreadable expression, only very gradually lowering his arms from around her as he stepped back. "But of course." He inclined his head, but his eyes sparked defiance.

Chatham had not seemed to notice—or perhaps he simply did not care.

He swept her into his embrace, tossing out to Jasper, "Why don't you dance with our Delia? I saw her looking rather forlornly at you earlier." A blatant lie. "She has missed you since we returned from the country."

Tru winced.

Jasper nodded stiffly, sending her a lingering look that promised there was still more to come.

What are you doing, Chatham? We don't dance.

Her question hung in the air, a palpable thing between Chatham and herself. She was beginning to wonder if he would ever answer. He gazed at her in the most peculiar and unnerving manner. Assessing and calculating. As though he had never seen her before.

"Perhaps," he began, "we should though." Another waltz started, but her husband kept her firmly in the circle of his arms.

Jasper moved to the edge of the ballroom, not taking Chatham's advice. Indeed not. He stood there with his gaze fixed on Tru despite the fact that Delia and any number of ladies stood in want of partners. She silently willed him to stop, urging him to turn his attention elsewhere, away from her.

Her husband moved her about the dance floor with ease. As they circled the floor she caught a glimpse of both her sister's and daughter's astounded faces. She knew they were realizing the rarity of Chatham dancing with her, too.

"I've forgotten how gracefully you move, wife."

A compliment? A slap would have jarred her no less.

"Th-thank you?"

"I suppose I do not always appreciate you."

"Uh." What was happening?

"I shall endeavor to do better."

She looked at him sharply. Either Chatham had been taken over by an imposter or he was toying with her.

"That is kind of you, my lord," she said carefully.

"Kindness. Yes. It's something that should exist between us."

"Are you foxed?" she demanded, staring in disbelief at his earnest expression.

He chuckled and that convinced her. He must be in his cups.

"Life is too short to live it in misery. Dedham's passing has only made that all the more clear to me, my dear."

They continued to dance then, Chatham wearing a placid smile, the likes of which she had never seen on him before. Her gaze drifted over his shoulder to the blur of faces as they moved about the floor. Jasper, stony-eyed. Delia and her sister, still agape. And even Hazel. That lady's eyes appeared to be full of something that looked akin to a . . . warning? Tru could not decipher that right then. She was too preoccupied with this change of attitude in her husband.

"Your words hearten me, my lord," she said cautiously.

"As they should." He pulled her in a little closer. "I want only your happiness, Gertie. You must believe that."

She didn't know if she *must*, but she *wanted* to believe him. She *wanted* to think that he had been struck with the sudden advent of a heart.

Her gaze drifted back to Jasper, who still watched her intently from the side of the room. His words came back to her. *We can find a way.*

Hope fluttered in her breast. Perhaps if Chatham cared enough for her happiness . . . there might be a way after all.

Chapter 31

There is nothing so full of wisdom as a daughter who is aware of her mother's most embarrassing mistakes.
—Gertrude, the Countess of Chatham

"Oh, I must have left my gloves in the retiring room. I will be but a moment, Mama."

"Very well." Tru nodded and watched briefly as Delia hastened back inside. The nearby groom offered her a hand and assisted her up into her waiting carriage, closing the door behind her with a resounding and satisfied click.

Tru settled into the squabs with a sigh to await the return of her daughter. She was quite eager to reach her own bedchamber. Eager for her own bed and a night where she might gather her thoughts about this most extraordinary evening.

She was a fool to consider that her husband might have changed, that he might have suddenly become generous in spirit toward her and wish for her happiness, especially at cost to himself. The dissolution of their marriage would certainly be at great cost to him. It was tempting to believe it possible, but she knew the likelihood of that was naught.

She was suddenly torn from her thoughts as the opposite door of the carriage opened and Jasper slid onto the seat beside her.

"Jasper!" she hissed. "What are you doing? You must not be here. My daughter will return any moment and you—"

"You will just continue then?" he charged. "Existing as you are? Not happy? Not fully living when you can have this? When you can have me?" His hands seized her face between his hands, holding her cheeks, his thumbs sweeping over her skin with a tenderness that made her ache. His deep brown eyes stared at her, *into* her . . . so intently that she felt his gaze like a touch—as palpable as his big hands cupping her face.

She closed her eyes in a long blink, luxuriating in the sensation, in the feel of his hands on her skin. Her chest hurt as she looked at him, feeling him, hearing those words.

"Why?" she choked. "Why did I have to meet you? Why could I have not continued . . . never knowing . . ." Her voice faded.

"Never knowing what?" he whispered, a desperate urgency to his voice.

"*You*," she breathed. "Never knowing you." *Never knowing love.*

"But now you do know me," he murmured, and then his words fell in a torrent. "You know this. You know how it can be between us, and you cannot think we can ever go back. I will hire the best solicitor in London. We can live abroad. Whatever it takes . . ."

He shook his head as though the particulars did not matter. "The world will not end if we love each other—"

The carriage door opened and they were confronted with Delia's shocked gasp. "Mama! Mr. Thorne!"

Tru sprang back from Jasper as though a bolt of lightning split the earth between them. Misery washed over her as her daughter faced her, discovering in that moment that *her* suitor was more enamored with her mother. The shame of it scored Tru like a whip.

Delia might not have wanted to wed Jasper herself, they might have had a secret agreement to pretend at courtship, but it must still come as a shock to find her mother in the arms of a man thought to be a good match for her.

Delia gaped, unblinking, from the open door of the carriage, the groom somewhere behind her, thankfully not able to see inside the confines of the carriage.

Jasper still held her. Could he not see they were on the brink of scandal? Delia had discovered them and from the look on her face she was quickly drawing the proper conclusions.

Tru lifted his hand from her arm. "Go, now, please."

He stared at her, the stubbornness glinting hard in his eyes. Evidently he did not worry about Delia discovering them. What could he be thinking? Was he *that* ready to cast them both to scandal? Or did he simply feel that Delia was trustworthy?

"I shall think on your words. Now go, Jasper," she pleaded. "Please."

Tension feathered his cheek. "Very well." Turning, he slipped back out the opposite door.

Delia watched him take his departure before ascending into the carriage. The groom closed the door behind her and she settled across from Tru in a rustle of silk skirts, her movements stilted, her expression wary as she folded her hands in her lap. That alone felt like a knife to Tru's heart. Silence stretched between them. Her daughter looked at her as a stranger. "Jasper, is it?" she asked archly.

Tru grimaced, regretting that slip, as it revealed the intimacy between them. "Delia, please allow me to explain." She reached across the seat for her hand.

Delia dodged her touch. "Please, no," she said stiffly. "I would rather you not."

"Do you . . . hate me?"

She sighed. "I could never hate you, Mama. I—I just . . . I don't know quite what to think yet." She paused and bit her lip. "But I do know you deserve to be happy. More than anyone I know, you deserve that. Does he make you happy?"

Tru hesitated for a moment and then decided on the truth. She nodded once, a lump of apprehension thickening in her throat, but also something else. Something akin to relief. Relief at finally admitting the truth, not only to her daughter . . . but to herself.

Happiness was just one of the things she felt with Jasper. Desire. Excitement. A sense of comfort and safety. There was an ease with him. He made her feel beautiful. He made her feel valued. She wanted that. She wanted that for all of her days.

"Well, then," Delia said in a manner that sounded very final and rather accepting.

Her daughter, one of the most important people in her life, knew of her relationship with Jasper and the world had not ended. She did not hate Tru. She even seemed to almost . . . understand.

Perhaps Jasper had been right. Perhaps they could find a way.

Perhaps the world would go on spinning if the truth about them came to light.

THE HOUR WAS quite late when Tru's carriage pulled up before her husband's residence. It was a strange thing . . . this skulking about to pay a call to her very own husband in the calm of night. Strange, indeed, that it should feel so secretive, so very clandestine and forbidden . . . like everything else in her life lately.

Soon, hopefully, that would be over.

Tru was led into the drawing room whilst a footman left to fetch the earl. The butler remained, surveying her as though she were some manner of beggar come to call for scraps and not the Countess of Chatham. It was a strange set of circumstances, indeed. Her staff was well versed in welcoming guests. And she could not even be called a guest, could she? She was, regrettably, the man's wife.

Chatham soon arrived in his dressing robe, looking fairly rumpled. "Gertie?" he inquired, much more polite than the last time she had called upon him in this very room.

"Chatham, forgive my late intrusion."

Her husband motioned almost solicitously toward an armchair for her to take a seat. "What is this about?"

She remained standing, too anxious to sink down into the chair. "I've given some thought to our conversation earlier this evening. Your concern for my happiness, as you said, was very touching."

He smiled. "And that has brought you running here to see me tonight?"

She frowned and shifted uneasily. "I was eager for a conversation—"

"Eager?" He fairly leered at her now. "You don't say."

"Yes. To discuss . . . my happiness, as you said."

"Your happiness," he said slowly, lingering over the words as though he could taste them . . . staring at her as though he would like to taste *her*. It was quite disconcerting. He'd viewed her as a sexless creature all these years. The sudden interest in his gaze was troubling.

"Yes." She swallowed. "We have lived apart for so many years. We have not even been . . . together in over fifteen years now. We have made neither one of us happy. Ever."

His grinning leer slipped away. "What are you at, wife? Why did you come here?"

"We do not live together as man and wife—"

"Yet we are man and wife."

She shook her head, staring intently at him in a silent plea. "Yes. But perhaps we should not be."

His eyes turned glacial, all the generosity of earlier gone in a flash.

She sucked in a gratifying breath. "I don't want to be married to you anymore."

There. She had said it, and it was not nearly as difficult as she had imagined.

In truth, getting the words out was a colossal relief. It felt as though she had been released from a cage and allowed her first breath of fresh air. Finally. Her first clean, unfettered breath in close to twenty years.

He stared at her a long moment, doubtless surprised at her uncharacteristically direct manner. She always relented to his bullying ways. She determinedly held his stare. Looking away would be a weakness and she had to be strong now—in this. She could not crumble.

Then, to her astonishment, he laughed lightly. "You do not think I have felt the same way over the years? I could still be siring children with any number of younger, more fruitful women. I could have a half dozen sons by now if I were married to *anyone* else. Instead I am stuck with you."

That did not even produce a flinch. Chatham married to someone else would be a blessing. Although she pitied any woman who might wed him succeeding her, she welcomed him the freedom to do so, as it meant she would be well rid of him. She would be free.

"Then," she suggested, "let us dissolve this farce of a union, so that you might move on and find yourself in a happier situation."

He tsked. "You know that is not done. Not for people like us. It is impossible."

"It would be difficult, yes. But not impossible." She moistened her lips. They could find a way, as Jasper had said.

He nodded slowly. “I see you have looked into this matter.”

Hope fluttered in her chest that he was at least listening. He had not exploded in a temper. Perhaps Jasper had been correct and he would indeed agree to this.

He continued. “I hope you exercised discretion when you conducted your sleuthing. I would not wish for all of London to be gossiping about the state of our marriage. This idiocy of yours should not become common knowledge.”

She opened her mouth to assure him that she had spoken to no one but stopped herself. That would be a lie. Jasper. Of course there was Jasper. She was not alone in this. He was the reason for all of this. Well, not the *only* reason . . . but she had found the courage to make such a demand because of him. Jasper had shown her she was worth more, that she did not have to suffer unhappiness and a dreadful husband who treated her ill.

No woman should have to endure that.

She had spent almost two decades in a miserable marriage. That was enough time wasted on a loveless and cheerless union. It was time to let their unholy union go. She did not have to waste another decade of her life on Chatham.

“You’ve gained a backbone, wife. Never would I have thought it of you. Perhaps that is why you suddenly appeared so attractive tonight.” His eyes narrowed on her. “Your glow was remarked upon.”

She inhaled. “I do not know what you mean.”

His hand lashed out and seized her face. His fingers dug cruelly into her cheeks. "Do not lie to me." He leaned forward, his nose burrowing into her hair with a sharp inhale. "Do I smell another man, wife?"

Panic rippled along her skin. It was only conjecture, of course. He could not *know*. He could not *smell* Jasper on her. He was simply attempting to scare her and she was quite finished being afraid of him.

"Unhand me." She yanked her face free of him and took a step back. She lifted her chin defiantly, struggling to show composure.

"You think to escape me?" He took a menacing step in her direction. "When we married it was for life. There is no escaping me. We are in this together. Until the end." His pale blue eyes glinted down at her. "Until one of us dies."

Perhaps it was her imagination, but those last words felt vaguely threatening.

"I want out."

He angled his head sharply. "Are you stupid? Did you not hear me—"

"It is you who does not hear me. This is finished, my lord." Her voice rang out with admirable force. "We are done."

His hand lashed out then, wrapping around her throat this time. He exerted only the slightest pressure. "I don't know what—or who—has gotten into you to give you these ideas, but you are my wife and that is not going to change. You will not leave me. I will not endure the scandal. I would kill you first. Is that clear enough for you to understand?"

She did not know what she expected. She had known this could turn ugly, but she had not expected this threat on her life. She had not thought him capable of that.

She nodded jerkily, with his fingers still wrapped about her throat, and found the strangest burst of courage. Or stupidity. Perhaps both.

She'd endured enough from this man. Cowered and hid herself away from him for so long, and now he had threatened to kill her.

Come what may, she would stand her ground. She would hide no more.

"There is another man," she confessed baldly.

His eyes bulged, his fingers tightening yet more. "I knew it. I knew as much. Tell me, my harlot wife. Who is he?"

"You should approve," she flung out, her voice strangling in her shrinking windpipe. "You found him so very impressive."

His pale eyes flitted over her features, discerning, searching. They flared wide as he sneered, "Thorne."

She gave a single nod. "He wants me as you never did," she choked. "He's kind and respectful . . . and doesn't treat me like something to be used and discarded."

He gave her neck another slight squeeze and for a moment she wondered if this was it. Spots danced before her vision. Would he finish her now?

A strange calm settled over him. His fingers eased, softening on her skin. Sweet air flowed through her, filling her lungs. "You know, Gertie, I think you might stay here for a bit, a penance for whoring yourself. Clearly my long absences have made you wayward."

She cried out in dismay, "No! I don't need to stay here, please."

He released her throat. "Oh, I think that is best." His voice had adopted a frighteningly serene quality. "It's clearly time for me to reassert myself as your husband."

She shook her head vehemently, staggering back a step. How could this be happening?

She had hoped to dissolve their marriage, and now he was threatening to keep her here in his private residence. He likely had his mistress upstairs.

She attempted once more. "You were so very kind to me this evening. Very human." The most human she had ever seen him. "Where did that man go?"

He laughed harshly then. "Oh, Gertie. That man never existed."

She swallowed down a little whimper and moved to leave, giving him a wide berth as she darted for the door.

"Baxter," her husband intoned.

The butler materialized from the hall outside the drawing room, blocking her escape. She blinked at the suddenness of his appearance. He no doubt heard their entire exchange.

She sent a mortified glance to Chatham, who now stood behind her.

He shrugged and lifted an eyebrow. "Baxter, would you please escort my wife to the attic room?"

She gasped and looked back to the grim-faced butler. He was the very image of stoic and loyal servitude. Looking straight beyond her, somewhere over her head, he said, "Of course, my lord."

She shook her head. "No!" She started past him, but his hard hand clamped down on her arm.

"How dare you! Unhand me!" She glared at the man.

Baxter sent a mildly questioning look to the earl, clearly seeking final approval. She followed his gaze to her husband, her chest squeezing tightly with breathless hope.

Chatham gave a single nod. "Take her upstairs, Baxter. See to it that she does not leave this house."

Everything within her sank. Her stomach dropped to her toes. "Chatham, no. You cannot keep me prisoner."

"*I* can do whatever I choose with you. You are my wife, *my* property."

Then, from somewhere buried deep inside, she heard the echo of a voice, as though emerging from a deep canyon. *Do not confess to him.*

She flinched. God in heaven. Had Madame Klara seen this coming? Had Rosalind been right to worry about the woman's strange words?

Whatever the case, Tru knew then. She had made a grave mistake.

She should never have confessed. Never come here. Never confronted Chatham. *Never* put herself in so precarious a situation. She had been an anxious, lovestruck fool, made desperate and optimistic by Jasper's words this evening. She had foolishly hoped. Foolishly thought she had seen a softness in Chatham tonight. That he might perhaps relent and give her her heart's wish.

She stared helplessly after him as he strode from the chamber.

She took a step toward the door, desperate to flee. Her legs felt as substantial as jam, shaking and trembling, but she attempted to escape at any rate and dodged around Baxter. She didn't make it.

The butler caught up with her, sweeping her into his burly arms. She cried out and struggled, her legs kicking wildly against her skirts. "You can't keep me here! Chatham, do you hear me? You can't keep me here!"

"Oh, shut her up, will you, Baxter?" the earl called from beyond the drawing room. "I've heard enough from her tonight."

Panicked, she fought harder. Twisting in the butler's arms, she glimpsed a thick fist coming toward her a moment before it made crushing contact with her face.

Then nothingness.

Chapter 32

I wish men knew what it felt like to be a woman. Perhaps then they would not be so hasty to inflict their will upon us.
—Gertrude, the Countess of Chatham

Pain.

She woke with a pitiably hoarse cry in a darkened room, instantly alert to the fact that every inch of her body ached, but no part more than her face. Closing her eyes, she lifted a shaking hand, tenderly touching, probing her throbbing, hot cheek, and whimpering for her efforts.

She lowered her hand from her face and curled herself into a small ball on the cold floor. At least she assumed she reclined on the floor. She held herself still for a moment, fear freezing her motionless as she gradually reopened her eyes to the dark, blinking them slowly, struggling to acclimate.

Her mind was a fog. She could not recall what happened . . . or where she was, but fear coated her tongue as bitter as vinegar, and she knew she was not safe. The pain radiating through her body told her as much. It told her everything.

She shifted slightly. Burning agony flashed through her, and another thin whimper tore from her throat.

The leaden weight of her eyelids pulled them shut again, dragging her back under, where there was no pain and no fear.

Only blackness.

PAIN AGAIN.

Her eyes flew open and she released a stinging hiss.

Thin, feeble light slipped inside the space she occupied. It was either dusk or dawn.

She flexed her fingers, dimly cognizant that she was not anywhere familiar. The surface beneath her was hard. She lifted her cheek with a mewling cry, blinking slowly until her vision ceased to blur and she could adjust to the murky air swimming around her.

She recalled everything then in a swoosh. Chatham. His hand on her throat. The butler. His fist bearing down on her face.

She was a prisoner in her husband's house.

Her limbs trembled as she placed her palms down on the grimy floor, pushing herself up and taking in her surroundings. It was a tiny attic room. A dresser and narrow bureau. A cot. The butler had not bothered to deposit her on the bed. Her entire body ached and she imagined he had just flung her on the floor like a sack of potatoes.

Her hopelessly wrinkled skirts pooled around her as her new reality settled over her. Birds chirped outside and she suspected it was morning. A new day. A new day trapped in this hell.

Last night she had dared to confess the truth to him. She had asked for her freedom. Had she foolishly thought she had a chance? That perhaps she could be free? A woman free to give her heart to someone else? Free to be with Jasper?

Not even close. She was not free. Chatham would never grant her that.

The shackles that had always manacled her only tightened further now. There would be no escape.

She was a prisoner.

JASPER WONDERED IF he had pushed Tru too far.

He rotated in his desk chair, staring out the window at the city spread before him. His daughter slept down the hall in her room, peaceful and undisturbed by life's troubles, which was as it should be. It was the very thing he had promised her mother. He realized now that it would mean so much more to his daughter if he, too, lived a happy life. A happy life in love with his wife. Bettina would learn something from that. That would be a lesson she would carry with her forever, guiding her expectations, shaping her future.

He spent the day recalling everything he had said the last time he was with Tru: his desperate words to win her over, to convince her to be with him. Perhaps he had demanded too much. And yet he could not accept that there was no chance for them to be together.

He wanted more than an affair. He wanted more than prowling about the shadows with her. He wanted to love her honestly, truly, openly. He wanted to live in the light with her. He was not yet ready to accept that it was an impossibility.

A soft knock at his office door had him looking up from his desk. His man, Ames, entered the room at his behest.

"Mr. Thorne, there is a woman to see you. She is waiting in the entry—" Ames paused at the suddenness with which Jasper lifted up from his chair. "And I am to assume you wish to see her."

Jasper strode ahead, his pulse hammering at his throat. Indeed. She had come. She had come to see him. She had considered his words and she was here.

Tru was here.

He could not reach the entry quickly enough. And yet when he arrived, he did not find standing there whom he had expected.

He stopped abruptly and stared. "Lady Delia?"

She was alone. That did not bode well. The last thing he wanted to do was find himself compromised with the girl. He looked beyond her shoulder, searching, hoping . . . "Is your mother not with you—"

"I have not seen her since yesterday."

Yesterday? He started at that. "What? What do you mean? We were all together at the Fairmont ball."

"We came home together last night, and then—" She shrugged helplessly. "I did not see her after we arrived home and I did not see her this morning. When I looked in on her this afternoon and discovered that her bed had not been slept in, I thought she might be—" Her chin went up. She looked him squarely in the eyes. "Well, I thought she might be with you, sir."

"No." Of course she would think that after discovering them together. "I have not seen her."

She continued, shaking her head fretfully, "I cannot find her. I questioned the staff. No one has seen her all day."

He moved then, striding across the entryway. He opened the door and motioned for her to precede him.

She stepped hesitantly forward. "Where are we going?"

"We are going back to your house to question the staff more thoroughly. Someone has to know something. Did you ask your coachman? Unless she left on foot he would have taken her somewhere. We will learn where."

She shook her head, her eyes widening. "You? You will go with me? But won't people wonder why you are there? They will think . . ."

"I don't give a bloody damn what anyone thinks," he growled. "Your mother is missing and we're going to find her."

Chapter 33

There is nothing more freeing than widowhood.

—Valencia, the Dowager Duchess of Dedham

A slight scrabbling at the door brought Tru lurching to her feet. She stood, braced tight, one of her hands curled into a fist at her side. Her other hand clutched a candlestick she had taken off the top of the dresser during her earlier investigation of the room. She buried it in the folds of her skirts to keep it hidden. She would require an element of surprise if she hoped to use it successfully.

Clearly Chatham was beyond reason. She could not assume herself safe. He had threatened to kill her and she had to believe him capable of it. She had to get out of this house. Her gaze darted around her. She had to get out of this *room*. Her hand flexed around her would-be weapon, ready to swing, ready to defend herself. She would do whatever necessary.

No one had bothered to feed her yet. She imagined that would happen eventually. Unless the intention was to starve her.

The door creaked slowly open. The head that peeked inside the room was not Chatham's or the wretched butler's, however. No. It was . . . Fatima's, Chatham's mistress.

Tru did not relax her grip on the candlestick. For all she knew this woman wished her ill. So far everyone else she had encountered in this house did. Her face still hurt from Baxter, the pugilist butler. She knew she needed to remain guarded, but she could not help recalling that her husband's mistress had been rather kind to her the day they met.

Fatima's warm amber gaze halted on Tru. She jerked her head, indicating she should join her out in the hall. "Come. Make haste. He's not awake yet."

Tru shook her head in bewilderment. "What are you—"

"Come!" She waved her hand rapidly. "You must make your escape whilst Chatham sleeps. Now is your chance."

"Oh!" Prickles of relief washed over her. "Thank you! Thank you!" She rushed forward.

Fatima seized her hand, and together they raced down the corridor.

Tru was grateful to be led. She did not know this house beyond the entry hall and drawing room. The woman guided her down one set of stairs and then another. Doors whipped past her in a blur, and she could not help wondering which one might hold a sleeping Chatham.

When they reached the first floor she could have wept with relief. They tore past a footman who gawked at them, sputtering as he nearly lost hold of the tray he was carrying.

Heart racing, air crashing from her lips, they rounded a corner and collided into a veritable wall that happened to be—of course—the wretched butler.

Baxter's eyes rounded at the sight of Tru. "Gor!" One of his beefy paws snatched hold of Tru's arm. He gave her a hard shake, rattling her teeth as he growled, "What are you doing out—"

Fatima cut off the rest of his words with a swift knee to his groin that freed Tru. The man dropped to the floor with a howl.

Tru looked to the woman in awe. "Nicely done," she breathed.

Fatima took hold of her hand again. "If Chatham was not awake before, I am sure he is now at that racket." She nodded her head toward the writhing and now sobbing man on the floor.

They took flight again, racing past the drawing room doors and toward the promise of freedom—the front door. Her pulse pounded in her ears in rhythm with their footsteps.

Tru paused to gasp, "Come with me!"

She could not imagine leaving this woman in this house after she had risked herself to free Tru and had just brought the butler low. Chatham would not be pleased. He would likely turn her out.

Fatima nodded her head slightly in the direction of the door. "Let us get you out of here first, my lady. I'll be fine. I always am. Don't worry about me."

The sound of her dreaded nickname suddenly ripped through the bowels of the house in a roar. "Gertie!"

She sent a horrified glance toward Fatima. "He's awake!"

Footsteps pounded down the stairs like the thunder of artillery.

Tru glanced over her shoulder to spot him reaching the bottom floor, looking angrier than she had ever seen anyone look in her life. His shocked gaze arrested on his mistress. "Fatima!"

With his red, puffing face, he looked fit to collapse—or explode. Perhaps he would die right then of apoplexy.

He wore only his trousers. His florid face was a stark contrast to a pasty white torso that had likely never seen sunlight. His pale eyes narrowed on Tru sharply, flickering to Fatima once more before then settling back on Tru. The venom reflected there was palpable. *He's going to kill me.*

He pointed a damning finger at Tru. "You'll learn your place!"

Fatima's hand tightened around Tru's fingers, pulling her along. They stretched their strides, closing the last bit of distance to the front door.

He moved faster than she would ever have thought possible. She could *feel* him behind her, his presence much too close. She could *hear* him; the hard pants like that of a raging bull.

Fatima reached the door the precise moment Chatham's hands caught hold of Tru's hair. His fingers tangled in the strands and gave a brutal yank. She shrieked, reaching for her trapped hair, closing her hand over his in an attempt to ease the stinging pain assaulting her scalp.

He gave a tug and she tumbled against him. With one hand still clenched in her hair, he wrapped his other arm around her waist, hauling her back. Her heels slid along the marble floor helplessly as he dragged her away from the door.

"Where do you think you are going, my whoring wife?" he panted in her ear. "Do you think to leave me? Do you think you can be with *him*?"

Fatima wrenched open the door and sunlight and fresh air poured through the opening. The happy, busy sounds of Gresham Square greeted them. The clip-clop of hooves. The rolling of carriage wheels. The lyrical cry of a hawker selling flowers. All highly incongruous to her current plight. All. So. Close.

Freedom. So very near. She almost made it. Almost reached it.

Tru stretched out an arm as though she could still reach it, touch it, claim it for herself.

"Fatima, close the bloody door at once! I will deal with you later! No one is leaving this house."

A choked sob spilled from Tru's lips as she strained and struggled against her husband.

Fatima turned, framed in the light of the doorway, her bright, liquid-dark eyes flitting between Chatham and Tru, clearly debating her options. "Please, Chatham." A grimace passed over her beautiful features. "You cannot keep her locked away—"

"This is none of your affair, Fatima. I don't keep you to hear your opinions on what I do with my wife. As long as I provide for you, you belong to me. Just as she does."

His clenched fist twisted in Tru's hair as though to emphasize his point. Tears sprang to her eyes at the sharp pain.

No. No! He would not do this to her. She would not allow it.

With a shout of indignation, she released all the pent-up fury at what she had endured as this man's wife. With a balled-up fist, she twisted around and swung hard, catching him up the side of his head, cuffing him solidly in the ear, hard enough to sting her knuckles.

He cried out, his hold on her instantly releasing.

She bolted.

Fatima stepped to the side, clearing the way, shouting encouragement.

Tru didn't look behind her. She simply ran. Lifting her skirts, she vaulted down the front steps of Chatham's house as though the devil himself were after her . . . and in truth, he was.

She could hear him. His shouts. His curses singeing her ears as she burst into the morning light. She knew if he reached her, it would be over. She turned down the sidewalk and pumped her legs until they burned, dodging around pedestrians strolling at a sedate pace.

Fatima shouted a warning.

Tru shot a quick glance over her shoulder and her heart seized in her chest. Chatham was coming. He was after her and his expression was murderous.

Suddenly another shout penetrated her awareness. It was her name again, but this time the sound of it did not make her chest hurt.

This time the sound of her name rang beautifully in her ears.

She scanned the busy block, her gaze landing on Jasper across the street. He hurried along the walk, his tall figure anxiously weaving through a small flock of children being led by their governess.

She did not wait. She did not hesitate. She simply turned and launched herself across the street, narrowly missing a fruit cart before reaching Jasper and flinging herself against him. He caught her, his arms enveloping her in a warm embrace. His hand came up to caress her hair, cupping her head tenderly.

"My love," he breathed, and everything in her softened, sagging against him, so grateful to be free. She was in his arms. Nothing else mattered.

It did not matter that she was married to a cruel madman fast on her heels and that she had no right to this. No right to the warmth and security she found in Jasper's arms. She buried her face in his chest, reveling in his hands stroking her back, holding her, comforting her. Wrong or right, she did not care. She would somehow, some way, be with this man she loved.

Lifting her head, she looked over her shoulder. Tensing, she watched with dread as Chatham tracked her, his eyes flashing wild with fury. His chest heaved where he tottered on the edge of the sidewalk, appraising her with Jasper. His lips peeled back from his teeth with a sneer, and he darted forward, launching himself across the street—directly into the path of a swiftly moving milk carriage.

The sickening crack and smack of horses and carriage against his body was deafening.

Her mouth opened wide on a silent scream.

Jasper's arms tightened around her, his own deep gasp reverberating against her.

She was not certain if the shrill scream belonged to the rearing horses or gaping witnesses or Chatham himself.

She watched in horror as Chatham's body disappeared beneath the horses and wheels. The carriage rolled over him and limped along down the street with a rickety rattle until it managed to stop.

She froze, still locked in Jasper's arms, appreciating the comfort of his embrace now more than ever.

A gentleman jumped out in the street and examined the earl's broken body up close. It did not take long before he lifted his head. Removing his hat, he called out grimly, "He's gone."

A murmur passed through the gathering onlookers.

"Gone," she echoed, the single word barely a whisper.

Closing her eyes in a hard blink, she forced her gaze away from the horrible sight of his body crumpled in the middle of the road. Someone approached to drape a jacket over him.

She looked up into Jasper's face, losing herself in his soft gaze, the one pure and beautiful thing about this day. He was the only thing she wanted to see. Her refuge. Her shelter from the storm.

He reached for her cheek, gently stroking her bruised skin with the sweep of his fingers. "Did he hurt you? Are you—"

"I'm fine." She nodded, swallowing back a lump in her throat. "Numb, rather . . . but fine."

"Of course you are." He nodded slowly and hugged her again, his lips feathering her hair with a tender kiss.

It was the truth. She would be fine. They both would. The storm was over.

She was free.

Epilogue

The past matters only so far as it influences today.
—Gertrude, the Dowager Countess of Chatham

Eleven months later . . .
River Thames
London, England

It was the Dowager Duchess of Dedham's birthday and they would be celebrating it in high fashion.

"Are you certain this is a good idea?" Maeve asked, as always concerned with propriety. "It has not yet been a full year and one day."

Tru, Maeve, and Ros had arrived at the yacht early to make certain everything was in order for the arrival of Valencia and the other guests.

"It's been eleven months." Tru stepped aside for the grooms

as they grunted their way across the deck with their burden. She motioned where they should arrange the twin ice sculptures upon the linen-draped table. They were the last items to arrive, for obvious reasons. Dusk was setting, purpling the already pink and orange skyline over the Thames. "And it's not as though Valencia hasn't been in mourning far longer." Ever since her husband was first thrown from his horse all those years ago. That was when she truly lost him.

"Tru hasn't been locked away in mourning," Rosalind pointed out from where she settled herself upon one of the brocade chaises decorating the deck of the yacht.

"That is true," Maeve agreed slowly. "I suppose I forgot about that."

Maeve forgot about that because Tru only committed the bare minimum of her time to mourning Chatham. Oh, she wore darker colors. Just not strictly black. And she eschewed balls and parties and soirées because she preferred to not attend. Otherwise, she did what she wanted.

It just happened that what she wanted to do was spend time at home with Jasper and her children and darling Bettina. They took occasional rides in the park. Enjoyed a rare evening at the theater or opera. Society didn't know the extent of their devotion to each other—or of the nights they spent in each other's beds. Only Tru's closest friends knew about that . . . and that Tru and Jasper intended to marry in the next year, when a suitable amount of time had passed.

She was happy. Deliriously so.

As though she had conjured him, a carriage arrived from which Jasper emerged. She smiled and waved down wildly and without decorum at him from the deck of the yacht. He grinned up at her and blew a kiss. As arranged, Fatima accompanied him. Tru had become one of the opera singer's most loyal patrons. Of course Tima would be performing tonight for Valencia's birthday.

The celebration would be one for the ages.

It was time Valencia cast off her widow's weeds and solitude. She'd hidden herself away in her Mayfair mansion, waiting on the appearance of the new Duke of Dedham, some distant relative from God knew where, who would likely send her packing to her dowager's cottage in the country upon his arrival, which was rumored to be any day now.

Jasper joined Tru on the deck. After quickly assessing that their audience was only Ros, Maeve, Tima, and a handful of staff, he bestowed a kiss onto her upturned lips.

"Good evening, my love," he murmured. "Ready for this party?"

She smiled languorously. "It will be splendid."

"You sure about that?" Ros queried dryly, nodding toward the dock.

They all turned to watch as Hazel arrived on the arm of her doddering husband the precise moment Valencia descended from her carriage in a masterpiece of a red dress adorned with thousands of sparkling gold beads.

The two women stared at each other frostily across the short distance.

"Perhaps we should not have invited Hazel?" Tru voiced worriedly.

"Nonsense." Maeve waved a hand. "They're family. You could not have left Valencia's father off the guest list. So that means his wife is included, too."

Except the night was supposed to be about celebrating Valencia and she could not abide her stepmother.

Tru forced a smile and motioned for the champagne. "Come, let us greet Valencia."

They all moved to the top of the ramp to welcome the guest of honor . . . and Hazel.

Jasper caught Tru's elbow, stalling her for a moment. "Have I told you that you look beautiful tonight?" She glanced down at her daring gown. It was pink silk trimmed with white feathers. The plunging neckline was unique for her. A departure from her usual more modest dresses and darker colors of late. Except he wasn't looking at her gown or her neckline. His gaze was fixed on her face, on her eyes—on *her*. Always on her.

He plucked two champagne glasses off a passing tray and handed one to her. He clinked their glasses. "To you," he toasted as he leaned down to give her a kiss.

"No," she corrected, standing on her tiptoes to press another kiss to his lips. "To us."

An exciting sneak peek at

THE Scandalous LADIES OF LONDON

The Duchess

Available everywhere in early 2024

Chapter 1

The happiest two days of my life were my wedding day . . . and my husband's funeral.
—Valencia, the Dowager Duchess of Dedham

11 April 1822
River Thames
London, England

The Duchess of Dedham's husband was dead.

The wretch had expired nearly a year ago, found with a broken neck at the bottom of a flight of stairs. No one was surprised, given how poorly his health and how dependent he was upon whiskey and laudanum to get through each day. Perhaps the only surprise was that he had survived as long as he had before plummeting to his death in the midst of a country house party.

Now, as the *Dowager* Duchess of Dedham, Valencia was free and ready for revelry. Truth be told, she had been ready upon the discovery that she was a widow, but there were rules. So *many* rules. Rules that she had followed all her life. Rules that had changed now that she was a widow. At long last.

She was done with mourning. Done with her widow's weeds. Done with hiding away in her Mayfair house. Today was her birthday and her husband was gone from her life forever. That was perhaps the greatest present of all.

She did not have to suffer his glowering, controlling presence anymore. No more hugging the shadows. No more making herself as small as possible. She was celebrating life—the rest of *her* life—and she had long years of marital misery to make up for.

Over a dozen revelers, all her closest friends (and foes), occupied the less-than-steady vessel as it departed the docks and glided slowly down the dark waters of the Thames to the South Bank. Destination: Vauxhall. Objective: a carousing good time.

And who knew? Perhaps she would find a handsome gentleman to take her down one of the infamous dark walks. She would like that very much indeed. It had been far too long since a handsome gentleman made her heart race. Since she had been held. Kissed. Oh, she liked kissing. She had been good at it.

The yacht had perhaps exceeded its weight limit, but that did not concern her guests. They laughed. They drank. They applauded the opera singer who performed for them on a small dais. They hooted to neighboring boats—calling to people they knew across the water . . . and people they would like to know.

Ladies in gowns of every color lounged among the cushions, laughing and sipping champagne distributed by liveried servants managing the deck with acrobatic dexterity. Torches blazed along the perimeter of the conveyance, doing wondrous things for the glittering silks, satins, and brocades. Not to mention the jewels. Extraordinary gems winked from deep décolletages and coiffed hair.

The marchioness's improbable red wig flashed like flame in the night air as she laughed gaily. Valencia narrowed her gaze on her stepmother. *Tart.* If the woman was not married to Valencia's papa, she would not have invited her. Societal expectations and all that rubbish. Valencia rolled her eyes and sighed before sipping her champagne.

"Do not let the sight of her ruin your night," Tru advised, very correctly guessing at the reason for Valencia's sigh.

"I cannot believe I must tolerate her. Especially tonight." It was a celebration, after all, in *her* honor, and yet she must endure her father's *ridiculous* wife.

She eyed Papa with reproach. His gnarled, paper-thin-skinned hands clutched the gold-knobbed and gem-studded cane as the conveyance rocked its way toward the entrance of Vauxhall. His equilibrium was poor, and yet somehow, with great assistance, he had managed to climb up the ramp of the yacht. She had not thought he would brave a party to Vauxhall.

A nearby barge of gentlemen noticed their yacht. It was hard to miss. They waved and hooted across the waters at them. One handsome young man stepped dangerously close to the edge and pressed both hands over his heart as he called to them, "Beautiful ladies, please accept my escort throughout the Gardens!"

Valencia gripped the railing and waved gaily back at them with a laugh. She glanced again to Tru. "Look at all those randy young bucks. Could Hazel not have chosen one of them? Why did she pick my father?"

Maeve shrugged, ever rational. "Why not your father? He's wealthy and titled and dotes on her."

Valencia shook her head. "All these years later, and I still can't believe Papa married her." *His mistress.* He had married his mistress.

"Of course you can," Maeve returned. "Like so many men, your father is a vain man, and it feeds his ego to have a young and beautiful wife. He's not extraordinary in that respect."

"Could he not have chosen someone who was *not* a paramour to half the gentlemen in our set?" she grumbled.

"Oh, you exaggerate," Tru chided.

"Exaggerate she does not," Lady Ashbourne inserted, sliding into their conversation and nodding in the direction of the marchioness, lifting her glass in mocking salute. "I know my dear Ashbourne dipped his quill in *that* inkpot." The lady deliberately lifted her voice, making certain to attract Hazel's notice with these words.

Hazel frowned and inched closer toward them. "Are you speaking of me, Lady Ashbourne?"

The lady looked Hazel up and down with a flare of her nostrils. "In truth, I was speaking of your, er . . . inkpot."

Hot color splashed Hazel's cheeks.

Valencia could not deny it. She was enjoying watching her stepmother's discomfort. Until Hazel suddenly reacted. The marchioness lifted her hands and shoved Lady Ashbourne hard, pushing her squarely in the chest. The action sent the lady colliding into Valencia, the force of which propelled her directly over the railing of the yacht.

Valencia plunged into the dark waters of the Thames with a scream. Brackish water rushed into her mouth. The weight of her beautiful gown pulled her down.

She fought, clawing water, kicking at the tangle of skirts, fighting to rise to the surface. It was impossible. Suddenly she was no longer certain which way was up or down. The fight seeped out of her. Her lungs burned like fire, and her limbs turned to lead, helpless to save herself.

She was drowning, dying . . . dead.

On her birthday, no less.

Bloody hell.

Without warning a hard band looped around her waist and she was yanked, soaring, breaking free through the surface. She gasped and coughed, sucking in sweet air.

That band around her waist was an arm that belonged to a man. A man who was rescuing her, pulling her aboard a boat.

Grateful for the solid surface beneath her, she rolled onto her side, coughing and spitting up ghastly river water. A large shadow fell over her, blotting out the torchlight. She came up on an elbow and glanced wildly around. This was not her yacht.

She was on a barge. *The barge full of randy young men.*

Her gaze shot to the soaking wet man crouched over her, his impossibly broad chest rising and falling from his exertions. *From jumping in and saving her.*

His mouth lifted in a crooked, much-too-handsome grin. The kind of grin that said he knew just how handsome he was. "You didn't need to jump in the river if you wanted to get my attention, sweetheart."

ABOUT THE AUTHOR

SOPHIE JORDAN grew up in the Texas Hill Country, where she wove fantasies of dragons, warriors, and princesses. A former high school English teacher, she's the *New York Times*, *USA Today*, and internationally bestselling author of more than fifty novels. She now lives in Houston with her family. When she's not writing, she spends her time overloading on caffeine (lattes preferred), talking plotlines with anyone who will listen (including her kids), and cramming her DVR with anything that has a happily ever after.